Lauren,
I hope you
enjoy the ride!

Blood Lily

Jenny Allen

First Edition

Fulton Books, Inc.
Meadville, PA

Published by Fulton Books 2021

ISBN 978-1-63710-580-1 (paperback)
ISBN 978-1-63710-581-8 (digital)

Printed in the United States of America

To Jason Ratcliff, who always pushes me to stand up for myself and is the best pseudo-brother a girl could ever have.

Emily Kirk, my first proofreader, my sounding board, and dear friend. Chris Howard, who creates all my beautiful covers.

Eric Deardorff, my soul mate and endless inspiration for flirty banter. Amanda Clark, Robin Sullivan, and Travis Tramble, my test bunnies.

And to all the people that influenced my life, which culminated in this book.

Thank you.

Lilith Adams Series

Blood Lily

Rose of Jericho

The Lotus Tree

Ghost Orchid

Chapter 1

It takes a tremendous amount of force for a wooden stake to break through the sternum and penetrate the heart. Lilith snapped on purple nitrile gloves as her mind wandered to the movies and TV shows littering pop culture. It always appeared so easy, she thought.

After a light thrust from an ordinary human, usually a cheerleader, *bam*, no more vampire. The weapon could be anything wooden. A pencil, the broken end of a guitar, a random twig off a tree, and they turn to dust or explode in flames, leaving no trace of the demonic monster. If cleanup were that easy, her job would be obsolete. She could trade in her forensics case for a dustpan and a little brush that sponsored breast cancer awareness.

She stared across the large studio at the man, or, rather, the corpse, lying on the hardwood floor. A rough wooden stake protruded from his chest as if imitating a gruesome scene from a Hollywood movie. However, this crime scene was real. There were no geeks with vials of dyed corn syrup waiting in the wings, no groupies giggling in the corner.

The air was thick with the coppery scent of blood warring with the ever-pleasant odor of early decomp. She paused, placing the back of her gloved hand against her nose, taking a moment to adjust to the overpowering scents.

Even from the doorway, the body's pallor was alarming. Rice powder makeup obscuring a vitamin D deficiency made the most sense. The inadequate levels would also cause bone softening. Although it would make the killer's work less arduous, it would still take more than a light jab from a ninety-five-pound girl.

The fact that his black shirt lay open with the glints of missing buttons scattered around the room showed a certain intimacy. The scene told a story. Either the assailant had a personal connection to the victim or a peculiar ritual-style of killing. Since this was the first staking she had seen in a couple of years, she was betting that whoever hammered a chunk of wood into his chest knew him.

The body was far too thin and malnourished, devoid of any real musculature. The smooth sunken chest indicated the victim might be underage, perhaps a runaway from an abusive home. Of course, severe-enough nutritional deficiencies would stunt his growth.

His long hair lay across his face in a shaggy mess, complete with a harsh black-dye job. Mascara and thick eyeliner ran down his prominent cheeks in watery globs. His pants were vacuum tight and predictably black. Goths were pathologically allergic to color, especially pastels. Red was the only acceptable exception, well, that and purple or hot pink for girls, but only in trace amounts. Silver chains draped all over his pants and glistened in the large pool of blood. Yeah, no doubt, Hollywood pegged this guy for a vamp. He was probably brooding and sorrowful too.

A beep from her Bluetooth interrupted her train of thought. She slipped little fabric booties over her simple flats before reaching up and pressing the call button. She meticulously picked her way into the room, keeping a straight line toward the body.

"Lilith?" The tinny voice of Detective Alvarez sounded bored.

"Expecting someone else to answer?"

His soft chuckle crackled in her ear. She needed a better Bluetooth. "Hey, you never know, might catch you with *company* one day. Perhaps male company." His voice lost the bored edge, sounding almost energized with liberal hints of a Spanish accent.

"Cute. Take you all night to think that one up?" She smiled as she studied the room. Nothing seemed out of place, not that she could tell. The sloppily painted black walls displayed makeshift murals of pentacles and fangs that an asshole in Manhattan might call art.

The once-grand hardwood floors hid behind layers of paint splatters, scuff marks, gouges, water damage, even candle wax. It was beyond any hope of repair. Candles and fishnet clothes littered every surface, including milk crates and mismatched furniture that he either picked up off the street or bought at Goodwill. Runaway seemed an accurate assumption based on everything she saw so far.

Empty pizza boxes warred with takeout containers in one corner amid a garbage pile. Guess the self-loathing didn't extend to fasting. As Lilith walked past the takeout pile, a few dozen bugs scrambled around the garbage, and she swore she heard the squeak of a mouse. The scent of refuse now overpowered the blood and decomp, and she covered her nose for a moment again, trying to readjust. How could someone live that way? The thought made her skin crawl, and she had the overwhelming urge to scrub herself in a hot shower.

Her nose wrinkled as he laughed again. "Always a pleasure. So, I'm assuming you've reached the scene? Any thoughts?"

"Oh, plenty of them. My money is on the landlord. The guy trashed this place beyond repair." He chuckled warmly but waited for her to get the goods. "I haven't examined the body yet, but first impressions? A Goth kid took his masquerade too far. Seriously, Alvarez, this is about as stereotypical as it gets." She stepped past a few Anne Rice novels spread across the floor and crouched down next to the body, carefully avoiding the cooling puddle of blood seeping into the hardwood.

"Well, you are the expert of weird. I'm sure few forensic investigators get to spend every night examining possible vampiric activity with police support. Especially not support as alluring as my fantastic self." Alvarez appeared to be in his midforties, with a wife, three kids, and the growing belly and receding hairline to match. He liked to think of himself as a Casanova, but he was only a mild, average family man. Well, average for a vampire. He was all bark.

She was more than aware of how devoted he was to his wife, Gloria. They immigrated to the States together from Spain right before the Prohibition era. They were one of those annoyingly adorable couples who tried to set certain single people up with family friends. Even though Alvarez didn't exactly share that habit, he knew better than to tell his wife no. Of course, Lilith wasn't successful at turning her down either. She grinned and endured the awkward, nauseating dinners, praying for her phone to ring.

"Well, Detective Alluring. Are you going to chatter in my ear all night or let me do my job?" Her voice sounded annoyed and impatient, but she smiled as she popped open the metal case next to her. She took out a small thin metal probe and pushed up his bluing lips. Looking wasn't necessary, but she was curious. Sure enough, a bad dental cap job elongated the canines. The dark red skin at the gumline screamed late-stage gingivitis. Of course, he was dead now, so the possibility of losing teeth didn't matter.

"And here I thought you loved the sound of my voice. I'm wounded. I would hang up out of sheer principle, but I need the test result first. Rules are rules."

"Getting to that now… So, how's Gloria? She still freaked out about Erica delving into the dating world?" Her keen eyes studied the wound, the puffed red skin around the stake, the drying blood. He was alive when someone impaled him. She glanced at his hands, his arms, no signs of defensive wounds or restraints. The only contusions she saw were around the cause of death. She carefully reached into her kit and pulled out a pipette, a glass slide, and a tiny vial filled with pink liquid.

Alvarez was more than happy to rant about the family that he adored while she worked. "Gloria wants to handcuff the girl to her bed! I don't think she remembers being sixteen, or maybe she does, come to think of it!" His throaty chuckle crackled in her ear as she deftly secured a tiny sample of blood from the wound and dropped it on the slide. Then she pulled a drop of pink liquid to dab on top. No reaction.

"Human. The victim, though I think your wife might have the right idea," she stated plainly and stowed the materials back in her case. "I seriously doubt this had anything to do with us. I see a metal mallet, and the stake's top is splintered and flattened all to hell. This took a while, and the perp didn't have an overwhelming amount of upper-body strength. Let homicide deal with it."

She glanced up near his shoulder. Something torn was half hidden by his shirt. With care, she moved the silky fabric enough to see a photo torn in half. On one side was the victim's gaunt face pulled into a sullen scowl that was all for show.

The other half revealed the woman he had his arm around. She was older than him, perhaps early thirties, with silvery blonde hair cut into a sharp bob. Her emerald green eyes were bloodshot and unfocused, with black eyeliner smeared sloppily around them. Her cupid face pulled into an almost hysterical smile that shouted intoxication. Maybe she was trying to reclaim her youth with a younger guy and a bit of kink. Perhaps playing vampire hadn't been the fantasy she thought it would be.

"Hey, Alvarez, you may want to include that the victim most likely knew his attacker. It might be an ex-girlfriend. The perp probably drugged him or knocked him unconscious. I didn't check for any head wounds, but he didn't struggle, and he was alive when someone decided to pound a stake through his heart."

She tugged off her gloves and stowed everything neatly into the aluminum kit. She grabbed the case and headed out of the room, careful to stay in the same straight path as Alvarez chirped in her ear again. "Done, sent the info over to them. These vampiric cases keep popping up lately, kids staking each other or getting dental implants and biting each other. All because of this stupid media hype. My kids are fighting over team vampire or team werewolf! If I have to sit through another of those stupid movies again with that damn Jarrod's Jewelry action figure, I swear—"

"Alvarez." She had to cut him off, or his pop culture rant would never end. "Preaching to the choir, man. That Jarrod's Jewelry line was damn awesome, though. I'm going to use that. Anyway, I gotta head out. Take care and tell Gloria she owes me some cookies for Thursday night."

"Oh, come on. Bill wasn't that bad. He owns the accounting firm." A defensive inflection seeped into his voice, but she knew it was more about defending his wife than Bill, the accountant.

"He wouldn't be that bad if I liked balding, awkward creepers. I thought you were supposed to screen Gloria's setups."

"I am powerless against her wiles." He heaved an overdramatic sigh, and she could hear the smile in his voice.

"She still owes me cookies, and none of that sugarless, gluten-free crap. I like the curves I have. Thank you very much," Lilith said flatly, trying to hide the amused smile.

Alvarez cackled. "Gloria has nothing against your curves, bonita. You know her. She gets a bee in her bonnet about the newest fad and makes us all her test bunnies. Don't worry. I'll tell her to bake those oatmeal chocolate chip cookies dripping with unhealthiness you love so much. You be careful. Night, doll."

Sometimes she wished her race reflected the ones depicted in movies. They were amped-up superhero versions of the real thing. Yes, vampires were more robust, faster, had better senses, but not Superman's level, only slightly enhanced. Immortality? Well, that was debatable.

Some purebloods lived long lives, perhaps thousands of years, some merely a few lifetimes, and half-breeds only a couple of decades longer than your average human. It all depended on the strength of the racial blood in their veins. Lilith had a strong lineage, but she was still young, only twenty-seven years old, a blink of an eye to her father. She had no clue how old Gregor was.

Bitten vampires were only a hypothesis. Theoretically, 99.5 percent would die during the process. At least that was the number her Uncle Duncan quoted. The human body can evolve to remarkable things, but evolution forced into such a small time frame was next to impossible. The fever alone would kill them. So many changes in the basic chemistry create a tremendous amount of heat. It would disrupt the homeostasis that keeps humans alive and would cause extensive, permanent brain damage. Still, she'd always wondered if it would be different somehow. Now, *that* would be something to study.

Her thoughts turned back to the case with a sense of deflated futility, another in a lengthy line of false alarms. Only a dozen or so documented vampire families lived in New York City, and half as many undocumented. The percentages of vampire violence versus human crimes were heavily skewed toward humans since they outnumbered them about a million to one.

It was a rare occasion when she honestly had to use her kit. Of course, that should be a good thing. Somehow, she couldn't put her heart completely into that thought. She wanted something to chase, a mystery to figure out, a reason for her to stare at dead bodies every night. It felt odd to wish for a vampire killer or victim, but there it was. She wanted a purpose.

She slipped into the hall and closed the door behind her. Hopefully, she could make it to the apartment, get a hot shower, and freshen up.

Lilith got halfway up the stairs to her second-floor Manhattan apartment when her Bluetooth beeped again. She pressed the button and stubbornly continued up the stairs. Nothing would keep her from that shower, especially not when she was so close. The dead bodies could wait. They weren't going anywhere. "Lilith Adams."

"Lily, darling, are you at a scene?" Her father's voice was comforting like a worn-in blanket on a wintry night. A smile tugged at her lips as she reached the door and dug out her keys.

"Nope. Just wrapped up, and I'm unlocking my door. If you want to meet for dinner, I need about an hour. I desperately need a shower."

The living room was all clean, modern lines, modest, with few embellishments. The gray couch sat low with dark wood end tables and a matching coffee table, clean and simplistic. She dropped her keys in a dish by the door and set her aluminum case on the counter before continuing back toward the bedroom.

"I'm not sure I have time for dinner, but I do wish to speak to you about something, and perhaps you could bring that kit of yours along with you?" She stopped with her hand on the doorknob to her bedroom. Her heart pounded, yes, it still did that, and she froze. "Gregor?" Her voice was cautious. "What's wrong?"

The usual velvety tone of his voice dropped away. "You know me too well." He sighed softly and then continued. "I have a little something I'd like you to look into for me."

"Dad, I'm a forensic investigator, not a plumber who can fix your leaky toilet. I investigate crime scenes. So, again, what's wrong?" Her fingers turned white as her grip on the door handle tightened. Suddenly, she was taking back all the earlier hopes for a real crime scene to investigate. Damn. Careful what you wish for.

"Lilith." He used her full name, a startling rarity. "I don't want to discuss it over the phone. Freshen up and meet me after. I'll text you the address." He hung up as soon as the last word crackled through the Bluetooth, leaving all her questions dead in her throat.

As her mind reeled through endless possibilities, she twisted the knob and opened it to her bedroom. It was a stark contrast to the living room. Vibrant red walls rose to meet gold-treated crown molding. Swaths of luxurious fabrics in reds, golds, and purples covered the room. Teakwood embellishments from India accented the walls and squat tables.

This room was her sanctuary, the one part of the apartment that was absolutely her. Of course, no one ever saw it. Like the most important parts of her, it stayed hidden away, secret. Dates weren't allowed here. She didn't want anything to taint her small version of Eden. She kicked off her shoes and crossed the plush carpets, reveling in the sumptuous texture on her bare feet.

After a quick shower, she pinned her wet auburn curls back, threw on makeup, and slipped into the closet. After a longing sigh, she passed up the comfy jeans and grabbed a pair of sleek dark purple dress pants and a lavender button-up blouse.

She shimmied into her clothes, grabbed a dark green coat to keep out the fall chill, and crossed the room. A little red light flashing on her phone announced a new text message. The address Gregor sent wasn't one she was familiar with, someplace near Central Park. Not a neighborhood for strolling around at night, so after calling a cab, she jogged down to the lobby with her aluminum kit.

It wasn't an opulent apartment building, but modest with a security officer cost a small fortune in New York City. Tasteful neutral tile covered the lobby, with a small counter set to the side flanked by fake plants. An aging man in a crisply starched gray shirt smiled up from the desk. Lines crinkled around his eyes as he tipped his hat.

"Ms. Adams, lovely to see you."

After returning his smile, she set her case down by the desk. "Hey, Charlie. How's your night?"

Charlie had been working at the security desk of this building for over forty years. He knew every single tenant by name and thought of them as his family. Littering the wall behind the counter were pictures of tenants, their kids and grandkids, birthday cards, and even wedding announcements. The complete lack of Charlie in any of the photographs led her to believe the building was his only family, which only made him more endearing.

The man shrugged his thin shoulders and glanced down at the security screens. "All's quiet, Ms. Adams. Are you leaving on foot, or would you like me to call you a taxi?"

She flashed a soft smile at Charlie. "I already called a cab, and it should be here in a few minutes, but thank you."

A bright gaze lit his smile-wrinkled face, and he pulled open a drawer. "I nearly forgot, miss." He slid a cream envelope across the counter. "Someone dropped this off for you."

She frowned at her name, scrolled on the front in vaguely familiar calligraphy. It tugged at her, but she couldn't quite place it. She flipped the envelope over, but it was blank.

"Who dropped this off?" Inside was a small slip of parchment paper with a faint rubbing of an arrow. She opened the envelope wide, but nothing else was inside. A strange uneasiness settled over her shoulders.

He shared her confusion. "Well, I don't know."

She glanced up sharply from the odd scrap of paper as the uneasiness tingled up her spine. "How is that possible?" She tried to keep the edge out of her voice. Charlie was old and charming, but no matter how lovable he was, she paid handsomely for the safety of a building with a security guard and video surveillance.

"Well, I left the desk for a moment, had to use the men's room. Anyway, when I got back, this was sitting here. I didn't see anyone." Charlie appeared a little nervous because he took his job seriously. "I...uh...tried to watch the tape, but that new guy, Gary, he didn't switch the tapes out this afternoon." He shook his head with a stern frown. "I understand if you want to file a formal complaint with the apartment association." Charlie straightened up like a man preparing to take his punishment.

The anger leaked out of her as she stuffed the slip of parchment back into the envelope and plunged it into her coat pocket. Blowing up at Charlie would accomplish nothing. She couldn't file a complaint because the poor man had to take a leak. It wouldn't reveal the author of the mystery note. It would only achieve scaring an old man that loved his job and already felt incredibly guilty.

A car honked outside and brought her back to her senses. "Everything is all right. That's my ride. Have a good night." She flashed a smile and grabbed her aluminum case. She pushed through the lobby doors and into the chilly night, her dark green heels clicking against the pavement.

Lilith stared out the cab window, then dug out her phone and double-checked the address. This death trap couldn't be the place. She looked back out at the decaying building.

Plywood boards covered the vast windows, artfully decorated with numerous layers of graffiti. The canopy consisted of fading shredded material that only slightly resembled the classic colors of green, red, and white. Whatever the name had been, it was impossible to tell. The fluorescent sign was unrecognizable, smashed to pieces, glass littering the ground below. Most of the streetlights were either burned out or broken, leaving the place shrouded in unsettling darkness.

A small cough from the front seat shook her out of her trance. She checked one last time. Yep. Fading numbers on the side of the building confirmed it. Her father wanted to meet in the decaying corpse of an Italian restaurant.

With a sigh, she handed over the cab fare and slipped out of the car with her case. The air was colder here, and she pulled the green coat tighter around her. It didn't seem to help. Somehow, she doubted that the crisp fall air had anything to do with the chill traveling up her spine as the cab sped away.

The boarded front door left her looking for another way inside. There had to be a back door or sidewalk access to a basement. She didn't see anything up front, but a faint glow from the side alley drew her attention. A lone bare light bulb over a faded green doorway shone weakly in the grave inky blackness. It had to be the delivery door to the restaurant. She frowned for a second and leaned against the wall. Why in the hell did Gregor want to meet here?

She swallowed the nervous lump in her throat. It was just an alley, an ordinary alley like ones she'd seen a hundred times. The clink of a bottle falling against concrete echoed from the dark recesses. It was only a creepy-ass alley in the middle of a run-down block in a bad neighborhood in New York City. So much for the inner pep talk.

Not for the first time, Lilith wished she had more in common with Hollywood vampires. Wouldn't it be nice to throw on a black latex suit and be an instant badass? Hey, it worked for that chick in *Underworld*.

With a deep breath that wasn't anywhere near as comforting as she thought it should be, Lilith edged into the mouth of the alley. Rusting dumpsters loomed at the light's edge with empty boxes and garbage haphazardly littering the wet pavement—plenty of places for a psycho to hide.

A genuine fear crept up her spine, deep down in her bones. Something was wrong here. She could feel it, smell it in the air. It couldn't merely be her hyperactive imagination. Her olive eyes fixed on the impenetrable darkness cloaking the depths of the alley as she held her breath, straining to hear something. Nothing.

She quickly fished out the pepper spray from her case and kept her finger poised over the trigger. With a resolute sigh, she strode past the dumpsters, every nerve tensed in alarm. There were a few sounds of scuttling feet too tiny to be anything more substantial than a cat, but nothing else.

The tip of her dark green heels hit the faint cone of light from the bulb, and at once, she felt better. Funny how it felt like light would scare away the bad men. Of course, technically, it only made someone easier to see. Yet, it was still a universal comfort against evil thanks to the early Renaissance cathedral architects. Oh yeah, her inner monologue was rambling nervously.

The terrifying screech of grating metal sounded behind her, and she jumped, whirling around. Her heart leaped right into her throat and pounded in her ears. She panted for a shaking breath as she stared down the darkness. The air smelled cloyingly sour like death and decay. True, the dumpsters might have been the source, but deep down, she didn't believe that. The metal scream sounded again, running across her nerves like razor wire.

She whipped back to the door and pounded her fists against it with all her might. She bounced impatiently and kept looking around as the metal screech tore through the air, followed by a faint wet gargling sound. "Come on. Come on. Come on," she whispered under her breath as her terrified heart tripped in her chest.

She tried as hard as she could to banish the thoughts of a million different horror villains as her whole body trembled with the instinctual desire to run. Her pulse quickened with every passing second, and her lungs became painfully tight as the gargling sound grew louder.

As she was about to run for the street in sheer panic, the door swung open enough to let her into the bright kitchen. She scrambled inside so fast that she bumped right into a six-foot-three wall of lean muscle. Even in her heels, she had to look up as Chance closed the door and flipped the locks.

His laugh was warm, deeper than Alvarez's, as he caught her by the arms to steady her. "Whoa, beautiful. Someone chasing you?" His hazel eyes showed flecks of green, and they glinted with his magnetic smile. One that typically made any woman melt, and he knew it.

The smile faltered as soon as he took a good look at her. "You're pale as a ghost. Are you okay?" There was a strong undercurrent of concern in his voice. When she didn't answer, he carefully examined her, his eyes finally narrowing in on her face. "Lily?"

She pushed away from him with a frustrated frown. "Uh…yes." Yeah, it didn't sound convincing to her either. Now that the impending sense of doom was wearing off, it left her agitated and defensive. "Could you guys have picked a worse place? I think someone is sharpening their machete at the end of that alley. Perhaps using it on some poor animal."

His smile brightened for a minute and then eased into a frown. He leaned back against a counter with all the agile grace of a jungle cat.

Unlike most men his height, Chance was neither overly built nor lanky. He was all lean muscle with a casual air of being comfortable in his skin.

"Hello, Chance. Nice to see you? How have you been? Thank you for saving me from the machete-wielding madman. You're my hero." A sarcastic smile spread across his lips, which only earned him a scathing scowl.

"Everyone's in a cute mood tonight, it seems. What the hell is—"

He held up a hand to stop her. "I don't know why Gregor wanted to meet here, and I have no idea why he wants to talk to you. When I asked, he said he needed privacy." That warm, magnetic smile returned as he quirked a curious eyebrow. "And for the record, did you call me…cute, *cherie*?" There was a faint Cajun accent inflecting his voice. It was a subtle undercurrent that most people never noticed until he used a word like *cherie*. His head tilted to one side, and she almost gave him a genuine smile despite herself. Almost.

She playfully glowered for half a second and then pulled on her sickly sweet smile. "Yeah, cute. Like one of those puppies at the pound, all scraggly and mangy, but you can't help feeling sorry for the cute little guy."

She winked and patted him on the shoulder as he faltered with a comeback. She ignored his stunned pout and crossed the vacant kitchen to place her case on the countertop.

"Harsh, Lily. I'm a dog now?" His voice almost sounded wounded. She turned with a smile, enjoying the hurt tone.

"I call them as I see them. So, how's Sonja?"

He let out a tired chuckle and raked his fingers nervously through his hair, the bright light of the kitchen exposing glints of auburn. The casual style he perfected could have looked sloppy on anyone else.

"Last week's news. That girl was all kinds of insane. After a couple of dates, she wanted to stitch our names on pillows and exchange keys." His bravado faltered as his eyes fell to the floor momentarily. When he looked up and pushed himself away from the counter, he was all business. "Well, if you've calmed down from your brush with death, I can point you in Gregor's direction. I don't want to keep you distracted all night."

"If you intend to list all the insane people you've dated, we'd be here all night. Like I said, dog." They both laughed this time, a warmly familiar feeling.

Lilith first met Chance thirteen years ago when her father found him in a children's hospital in Louisiana. He was a seventeen-year-old half-blood orphan that had fallen through the cracks, which sadly happened a lot.

Vampires weren't born needing blood. It didn't hit until puberty, and half-bloods only required supplements once a month or so. Most human doctors couldn't figure out their subtly unusual physiology. The differences were too slight to notice, resulting in physicians misdiagnosing it as anemia or an iron deficiency. The second one led to a lot of deadly toxicities.

Some of the more thorough doctors labeled their condition as thalassemia. Chance would be what they call a severe case. His blood had insufficient levels of hemoglobin, and he required infusions of blood monthly. The doctors would be at a complete loss with a full-blood like her who needed daily replenishment.

Most of the documented cases of thalassemia were in the Mediterranean, India, Thailand, which makes a certain sense since that area was the cradle of civilization. The families stretched back a long time there without much dilution of the bloodlines.

Gregor found Chance in the underfunded city hospital he'd spent seven years in and took him under his wing. He trained in a dojo and took courses in criminal justice at the community college, working his way through school by running errands for her father. Contrary to widespread belief, they didn't come standard with badass fighting 101. Those that cared to train did so like everyone else.

Eventually, Gregor brought him on board as his bodyguard and head of security. Lilith spent a fair amount of time around him over the years, but nothing beyond a little friendly banter between acquaintances. Her father never talked about him much. He was a part of the scenery, not an active participant when it came to dinners and meetings—impressive, but still scenery.

"Well, as much as I enjoy swapping dating horror stories with you, I should see what Gregor wants." She pushed off the counter and grabbed her kit again.

"Oh, come on, kitten. Swapping implies you have any stories to share." He winked and strolled past her through a double swinging door. Sadly, staring daggers at his back wasn't remarkably effective.

Chapter 2

The large dining room held a sad collection of urban decay. Dirty linens clung desperately to abandoned tables. Dead flowers drooped from glass vases with brown petals and leaves scattered chaotically. Chairs either littered the floor haphazardly or formed jumbled piles. Cracking holes filled the plate glass windows. Some were the size of rocks, while others suspiciously resembled bullet holes.

The person that thought a fancy restaurant would go over in this neighborhood discovered how wrong they were in a hurry. Of course, none of them lasted long. At least five restaurants opened each week as four or five of them closed. It was the social cycle of New York City, which extended equally to nightclubs.

Chance led her to the stairs in the back of the room and started jogging upward as Lilith trailed behind him. The wooden boards creaked dangerously as her pointed heels clicked against the surface. She peeked up to see him leaning against a wall at the top with his arms crossed and a mischievous grin on his smug face.

"The price you women pay for those things…" He nodded at her shoes and laughed as she flipped him off and stepped onto the landing. Some people argued that a five-foot-nine woman didn't need high heels, as if their sole purpose was to make a woman taller. She shouldered past him with a glare and opened the only door, closing it firmly behind her.

"Lily." The affectionate richness of Gregor's voice wrapped around her with glowing comfort. She was a daddy's girl, but she made no apologies for it either. There was nothing wrong with having a good relationship with her father. Of course, it was about as rare as a movie vampire in a polo and khakis.

She turned to see her father leaning against an old desk and took a second to glance around, taking in the layers of dust everywhere except the office desk and the chair in front of it. A huge glass window covered in spiderwebs looked over the floor below. It allowed the diffused light from downstairs to give Gregor an uncharacteristically angelic silhouette.

Typically, he was the moderately attractive man blending right into the background. She was always amazed by how unassuming he could appear. With his average face of lightly patterned smile lines and soft skin, it made his age ambiguous. Even the light sprinkles of gray in his dark hair and carefully trimmed beard weren't much to go on. He was forgettable, which was the whole point.

Memorable people caught interest from all the wrong places, especially reporters. It was hard enough to stay out of the public eye, being a successful investor in New York City. The last thing he needed was some reporter prodding him on his antiaging secrets. It was getting more challenging to hide in the electronic interconnected age of Homeland Security.

"You two arguing again?" Sharp humor infiltrated his voice. He was very conscious of the friendly banter between them. Still, a speck of anxiety always accompanied the pleasant wit, and she never understood why.

"Come on. You'd be worried if Chance and I weren't fighting." She dropped her case by the chair and walked up to hug her father. "We haven't gone out in a couple of weeks." She soaked in the solace before pulling back with a fixed stare. "So, what is up with the clandestine meeting? I thought I was going to be hacked to pieces before the door opened."

The smile faltered on his face for a split second, and he shifted slightly, sitting farther back on the desk. "Have a seat, Lily. I'm glad you made it safe. I was a little worried about asking you to meet me here, but if I sent Chance, it would broadcast who you were meeting. It wouldn't be unreasonable for one to assume you were processing a crime scene here."

A familiar hint of disapproval edged into his voice. He made no secret of disliking her career choice, but now wasn't the time to discuss his overprotective urges.

"I may be processing one in the alley tonight." She meant it as a joke, but it came out as a flat statement. She slowly lowered herself into the chair with an anticipatory look and waited for him to continue. When he didn't say anything, she figured he needed a little help. "So, what is this delicate situation?"

Gregor stared down at his hands, pausing like he couldn't figure out where to begin. "I received word from Spencer today."

The words caught her attention. Lilith hadn't heard from her cousin in over a decade. Her uncle, Duncan, and his family lived down South somewhere. Alabama, Georgia, Tennessee, one of those states. With advancements in technology, a mass of vampires in one city would draw far too much attention. As a result, they were all pretty spread out. Gregor kept in regular touch, but nothing about his body language suggested a conversation anywhere in the realm of normal. A subtle knot of worry began building at the bottom of her stomach. "Is he okay?"

"Oh yes, he's fine." He waved off her concern as he continued to try and find his words.

"Okay…then what is wrong?"

Gregor exhaled and reluctantly lifted his sky gray eyes to meet hers. "Duncan is missing." He hurried through the words like he was ripping off a Band-Aid. "He's been spending more and more time at his winter home south of Knoxville. Spencer and Miriah were supposed to have dinner with him the night before last, but he wasn't home. They figured Duncan forgot, so they stayed in the guest rooms. He never showed up, and Duncan wouldn't stay out past dawn. He's too old to survive that." Gregor's voice was heavy with concern as he stared back down at his hands. The expression aged him instantly.

"Could he have gone back to the city?" She knew as soon as the question left her mouth that it was an idiotically obvious one. Spencer wouldn't have called without checking something so simple.

Gregor shook his head. "He checked. With the current talks among the elders about going public, Duncan's disappearance creates a very delicate situation. The only people aware outside of the elders themselves are you, Miriah, Spencer, and Aaron's son, Michael. Something may have leaked out. If someone abducted Duncan, it could be retaliation." He was deep in thought, running through things in his head as if she didn't exist. Suddenly, he appeared drained.

"Surely, people aren't opposed to that degree. I understand people don't like change, but with technology advancing and national securities tightening down, it's getting harder and harder on us. If our private labs didn't develop treatments and we didn't secure small blood banks, we'd be in a world of hurt. However, it only takes one determined reporter to bring it all out in black-and-white. Exposure is only a matter of time."

He nodded with a faint trace of pride in his smile. "Not all of us old stuffy bastards are comfortable leaving the shadows. They fear the knee-jerk reaction due to popular culture's portrayal of our kind. We also must consider the possibility of them dissecting and studying us. None of these are unreasonable concerns. But this? Turning on our own kind?" He let out another tired sigh. "I want to say it's impossible, but…"

A tense silence vibrated in the air as he sat buried in his thoughts. She glanced down at the shiny aluminum kit next to her. "So, a little off-topic, but why did you ask me to bring my kit?"

An actual smile tugged at the corner of his mouth. "Oh, that. Yes, well, I thought carrying it would be appropriate in case someone followed you. Can't process a scene without a kit, right?" A familiar glint lit his eyes for a second. He enjoyed the cloak-and-dagger intrigue, which was almost hypocritical. He didn't like her working crime scenes, but making some secret superspy meetings in a dangerous part of town was cool?

She narrowed one eye and watched him. Something else was hiding behind the humorous twinkle in his eyes, something he clearly wasn't saying. "Why would anyone follow me?"

"If Duncan's disappearance has anything to do with our plans, it is entirely conceivable. I only wanted to be cautious." He shifted his weight a bit. He was lying. He'd never lied to her before, but the signs were unmistakable. The slight pause in his voice, the quickness in his eyes, the small flex of the muscles around his mouth, the slightly elevated pulse. It felt like a slap in the face, but the steely undercurrent in his tone was enough to tell her not to push the issue. At least not now.

She swallowed the lump in her throat and tried to focus on something else. "What about other motives? Duncan did a lot of research in the Goditha lab down south somewhere. I mean, he was instrumental in developing cloned blood to keep us farther under the radar. Did he have enemies? Perhaps he had another breakthrough, something someone wanted or wanted to stop?"

"It is not beyond the realm of possibilities, though his work in the lab has been minimal as of late. He's been devoting more and more time to his research projects at home. He hasn't felt it necessary to share the details with Spencer or me."

"What about Miriah? Would she have any idea what he's been doing? He's always been closer to her than Spencer anyway."

"Not that I'm aware of." The uneasy constraint surrounding her father rubbed her the wrong way. He was holding things back from her, but why? If he wanted to find his brother, why not lay all the cards on the table?

Being able to read faces was sometimes a curse, especially with close relationships. She lost a few boyfriends that way. White lies compound, and she started to notice every little one until she couldn't trust anything about them. She didn't want that kind of relationship with her father.

"Okay, listen." She leaned forward, resting her elbows on her knees with a grimace of firm determination. "You're not telling me everything, and you better have a good reason. So, let's move on to the part where you tell me how I can help."

Lines of worry and nervousness flickered across Gregor's tired face. The honesty may have caught him by surprise, but he recovered quickly. "I need you to fly down to Knoxville and examine this for me. You're exceptionally skilled in your field of investigation, and you're the only one that knows all the possible facts."

Her eyebrow arched at that last bit, which was not missed by her father. "I can see how that makes sense. Even without knowing *all* of the pertinent facts…" Gregor had the excellent taste to at least appear apologetic.

"I'll make a call to Alvarez. Talk to him about covering things for a few days." He was about to protest when she barreled ahead. "Don't worry. I won't tell him the reason. I'll say a conference popped up, pack a few things, and arrange for a flight out tomorrow." Her mind started running through mental checklists. She always found it oddly relaxing.

"Lily." Mild amusement warmed his voice. "Hold on. Make the call to Alvarez, but I do have this for you." He handed her an envelope and dug his phone out of his pocket, pressing a few buttons.

After peeking inside, she glanced up at him with confusion. "Two tickets?"

Suddenly, the door swung open, and Chance leaned inside with his casual grace. "You rang? Need me to escort Lily home? You sure did pick a seedy neighborhood."

"Not quite. I'm sending you with Lilith to Tennessee." Chance blinked in complete shock. Guess he wasn't lying when he said he didn't know why Gregor wanted to meet.

"But, sir…" Her father held up a hand and fixed him with a firm stare that said his decision was final.

"I've already talked to Timothy. He'll take over your usual duties. We have a situation down south that I need Lilith to investigate, and I don't want to send her alone. I can trust you implicitly, and that's not something I can say about many people. I made promises to her mother before she died, and I won't neglect them, so I need you to protect her. You, of *all* people, will do whatever it takes to keep her safe." A weirdly significant stare passed between them before her father turned to face her. "She can brief you as she sees fit." He held her gaze, which contained an unspoken novel of emotions.

Chance dutifully nodded, and she couldn't refuse the escort because her father used his ultimate trump card. Her mother, Rosaline, passed away eleven years ago. Someone attacked her in Central Park, a robbery gone wrong. She might have recovered from losing a tremendous amount of blood, but by the time someone found her, it was too late. They tried blood transfusions and experimental medications, but in the end, she was too old to deal with the trauma.

The lore of ancient all-powerful vampires never made sense to her. How is it consistent that bullets couldn't penetrate vampire skin, but a nudge from a stake was like a hot knife through butter unless the vamp happened to be ancient? Years eventually weighed heavily on a vampire, and they couldn't cope with injuries as well as they could in their youth, much like humans.

Age doesn't only affect the body but the mind as well. Yes, they had decades or centuries of experience. Still, they had to adapt to changes in technology, social structure, and the world in general. The past two centuries alone held earth-shattering advances for someone who grew up with swords and chamber pots.

It sounded like Duncan might be struggling with that very problem. He was drawing away from usual activities, isolating himself, fixating on the past. They were all classic signs.

However, it was pointless to draw conclusions yet. She shook off the mingled thoughts and slipped the envelope into her case. "So, I'm guessing we don't have time for dinner then?" She succeeded in sounding light and humorous, which almost surprised her.

Gregor slid off the desk and held out a hand with his warm, casual smile. "I'm sorry, Lily." She took his hand and stood up as he pulled her into a hug. "Be careful. Be sure to call me, I'll worry. I don't like sending you, but I have no one else. If anything happens to you..."

He released her and stepped back, turning toward Chance as his smile faded, and that cold, commanding facade took its place. As tranquil and mild mannered as her father seemed, he was quite capable of intimidation.

"I'm trusting you with a lot, Chance. Do not disappoint me." His voice was severe, but something unspoken lurked behind his words. It hung in the air, filling the small room with a tension she didn't understand, and then, like that, it was gone.

Chance cracked his easygoing smile and shook Gregor's hand in agreement. "Yeah, I'll be careful, too." His sarcastic tone would have been a dangerous move with any other employer. Her father merely raised an eyebrow and shook his head.

"The flight leaves in a couple of hours. You two should pack. I'll have a car pick you both up at Lilith's apartment. I included some cash in the envelope for expenses, hotel rooms, and whatnot." Gregor started toward the door and then turned quickly with a snap. "I almost forgot. I put in a request. The car will have a cooler of supplies. With your medical license, Lilith, and the paperwork in that envelope, you shouldn't have any trouble transporting the *samples*. I don't trust the supply in Knoxville to be uncompromised or accessible. Call me when you arrive and settle in." He leaned in the door and pressed a kiss against Lilith's cheek.

Once he was gone, Chance and Lilith exchanged helpless smiles that felt incredibly awkward. "Well, travel buddy. Should I meet you at your place in a bit?" His smile was friendly but held a definite undercurrent of fear that she couldn't comprehend. His job was far from cushy. Gregor was too old to go out during the day, so he conducted all his business at night in New York City. She knew of at least a dozen times he'd protected him from muggers over the last few years. Maybe he was scared of flying.

"Why don't we share a taxi? Stop at your place and then head to mine. Safety in numbers and whatnot."

He forced a laugh and fell into another strained silent pause. "Well, since I am your newly appointed bodyguard, I suppose that would only be fair. I'd be in a world of shit if something happened to you before we left town."

"Yeah, well. Here's hoping I survive your apartment." She paused and tapped a finger against her lips. "Maybe I should wait in the car. It might be safer. You could have one of those stalker chicks scoping out your place, waiting to pounce on anyone that gets between the two of you."

Chance appeared offended as she walked past him down the stairs. "Ha. Funny." His sarcasm was a little flat and dull. After a brief pause, she heard him jogging to catch up with her.

Lilith stared out the window at the aging warehouse in complete shock. She figured Chance didn't live in an uptown apartment complex, but this? Broken dusty windows, brick crumbling at the worn corners, and layer after layer of spray paint from local gangs covering the walls. "Holy crap! I was kidding when I said the car might be safer! Please tell me you do *not* live here!"

He frowned at her and reached for the door handle. "Suck it up, *cher*. I'm not leaving you in the car."

Hesitantly, she followed him to the darkened entrance. There was no light inside, only inky blackness that didn't feel any better than the alley outside the restaurant. "You do get paid, don't you? I mean, seriously, Chance. I've seen homeless shelters that are more inviting. You aren't squatting, are you?"

"I like my space. Besides, it's the safest place in the city. Who the hell would rob a place like this? And I'm not squatting. I own it." There was a strange mixture of pride and embarrassment in his voice as he talked about the place. His muscled shoulders slumped down as he disappeared into the dark.

She stared after him, biting nervously at her lip. She didn't know if it was better to follow him or wait. A second later, the entire building lit up, golden light pouring from every window. Somehow that simple thing changed the atmosphere of the whole structure. Funny how that happened. It was still creepy, but at least it didn't feel as deadly.

Chance appeared in the doorway, looking impatient. "You gonna stand out there all night? Because seeing as I'm responsible for you, it'll be tough to pack and watch you out here at the same time."

She rolled her eyes, cautiously stepping into the open doorway. The bottom floor matched the outside. Abandoned junk, empty bottles, and rusty hardware littered the dirty, dusty interior. Her heels clicked against the concrete, which echoed eerily through the cavernous space. Chance rummaged in his pockets and pulled out a small key ring. He was standing in front of a freight elevator, complete with an old wooden gate. He crouched, fiddling with a lock before holding up the gate and making a gallant gesture for her to enter.

"After you, m'lady." A cheeky smile pulled at his lips, but there was an edge of something in his face. Nervousness maybe? Odd.

"Am I gonna need a tetanus shot after this?" She glared at him, hesitating as she inspected the rusting monstrosity. He flashed a sharp scowl, and she begrudgingly pushed past him.

"Keep it up, and I'll leave you locked in here. Hmm." He turned around to consider her for a moment with pure amusement. "You know, that's not a bad idea."

"Stuff it." She crossed her arms in a huff. The ancient machine lurched into motion, making her hands fly out to grip the rail tight with a small yelp. There was no missing the smug grin he attempted to hide. The elevator droned and rumbled as it crept upward. After a few torturous moments, the metal beast lurched to a stop, and he bent down to pull the gate up, holding it open for her again. She started to shoulder past him with an irritated glare and stopped utterly still as her eyes took in the view.

Gorgeous hand-scraped hardwood floors in a slight gray wash stretched the vast open space. The artfully designed lighting was a living entity of the room, drawing your attention to the black-and-white photographs along the steel blue walls. The pictures included haunting shots of lone trees in the fog, austere buildings with magnificent architecture, the back of a woman standing in a field, the wind blowing her hair. They all had a common theme: isolation.

She gaped back at Chance, who squirmed a bit under her gaze. He moved anxiously around her and dropped his keys in a little bowl on a marble-topped table. "Well, make yourself at home. I better grab my stuff." He hurried to a flight of curving stairs that led to a loft.

After setting down her case, she slipped off the high heels. Her bare feet were warm on the wood floors as she stalked past a clean and efficient kitchen in blue hues and stainless steel. "So, this is your woman-snaring pad?" Her voice echoed loudly, and after a couple of minutes, he peeked over the wood railing.

"You are kidding, right?" He quirked an eyebrow and stared down at her. The weight in his eyes felt somehow noteworthy. "It was a fight to get you in here, and you've known me for thirteen years. If

I brought a stranger to this building, they'd think I was some serial killer." After flashing a sarcastic smile, he disappeared again to the sound of her amused laughter.

She ran her fingers over a soft sage green blanket laid over the back of a low gray couch. She curled up in its comfort and glanced over the books scattered across the marble coffee table. There were a few cookbooks and a couple about prominent photographers. Then there were the ones that didn't surprise her, including a few magazines on home improvement and an owner's manual for a Honda motorcycle.

As she flipped through one of the photography books, Chance jogged down the stairs with a medium black suitcase. He stopped at the bottom of the steps and stared at her.

"You never told me you liked photography." Lilith slid the book back onto the table with a casual smile.

"Yeah, well, you never asked," he grumbled as he traversed the room and grabbed his keys from the table by the elevator. She watched him from the couch until he turned around, a six-foot-three mass of seething tension. "Are you finished? We should get to your place."

She was surprised by the strong hints of defensive anger. Her mouth opened to say something, but she couldn't think of anything and settled for a nod. The monstrous contraption was just as terrifying on the way down, and the silent hostility made it even worse. She still had no idea what to say when the cab pulled up. She didn't have the faintest clue why he was upset.

Finally, Chance let out a soft sigh and stared at her over the taxi. "Lily. Look, I'm sorry. I didn't mean to snap at you. I'm not used to having people in my place."

She forced a smile and shrugged. "A territorial thing. I get it." Just like her bedroom sanctuary. She slipped into the cab before he could say anything else. The ride to her apartment was quiet but comfortable.

They were in and out of her place in a matter of minutes. She managed to keep him out of her bedroom while she packed. He settled for browsing her book collection and hollering out questions about them every few minutes. Somehow, she thought that was more about keeping contact than wanting to know about the specifics of ballistics or entomology.

Charlie waved to her over the blue curly hair of one of the elderly tenants. She didn't know her neighbors. Her busiest times were at night, and most of her apartment building consisted of people that turned in after *Jeopardy*. Occasionally she'd get invitations to building parties or birthdays. However, the truth was she didn't want to get to know her neighbors. She only wanted peace and solitude when she was home.

She walked up to the desk, apologized to the older woman, and turned to Charlie. "I'm heading out of town for a few days. Could you be my hero and hold my mail until I get back?"

"Of course, dear. I'll let Gary know first thing in the morning." His smile made his entire face crinkle into deep lines. "Have a"—his eyes traveled to something behind her, and there was a sudden happy light in his eyes—"wonderful time, miss."

Her eyes followed Charlie's line of sight to Chance leaning against the door. She couldn't help but laugh. "Oh, no. Not that sort of trip. Business only."

Charlie winked at her.

The sleek black town car was waiting out front for them, idling at the curb. While Chance grabbed the bags, the driver jogged up to open the door for her.

"We should be at the airport in about forty-five to fifty minutes, miss." She nodded and climbed into the smooth, black leather seat. It was a far cry from the conventional cabs that smelled like day-old Indian food and cheap air fresheners. The anonymous driver closed the door, and seconds later, Chance joined her in the back.

The town car pulled away from the curb and into the surprisingly light traffic of the early morning. In a few hours, it would be rush hour gridlock from hell. Driving in New York only had one rule. If it was bigger than you, get the hell over. Stoplights, road signs, cops, none of it mattered. Only the golden rule kept you alive.

That was the main reason she didn't bother buying a car. Not only was it pointless, but she'd wind up killing the first asshole that dented it. By her observations, that would happen in no more than twenty-four hours, so she left the driving to the veteran taxis.

"So..." Chance turned to her, and all the tension and defensive posturing from earlier was long gone. He sat there with his familiar nonchalant attitude. "Since we have some private time, would you like to brief me?" A sly smile curved his lips while she grinned and rolled her eyes.

"Phrasing, you pervert," she muttered with a smile. Lilith took a moment to collect her thoughts, remembering her father's heavy look. "Gregor's brother, Duncan, is missing. Spencer and Miriah are freaking out, so we're going down to check into things."

He appeared suspicious and doubtful. "You need a bodyguard to chase down an old vamp that probably shacked up somewhere for the night? I'm Gregor's head of security, not some brain-dead meathead." He seemed vaguely insulted as he slumped into his seat.

She sighed softly, trying to figure out what to say without bringing up the whole supersecret talks about going public. Without that angle, sending a seasoned bodyguard didn't make a lot of sense. "He's family, Chance. Gregor doesn't have much of that left. There's no sign of him at his place in Knoxville or his winter home. I think he's assigning you to me as a precaution. He's kinda nervous about things these days."

"Sorry. I guess that came out wrong. I didn't mean to imply—"

"I know," she interrupted him as his cheeks blushed pink with embarrassment. It was almost cute on him.

"I'm just as concerned about him wanting you to go. I think there may be more to the story that he's not sharing." He didn't seem overwhelmingly surprised by that statement, but she didn't notice, too lost in her thoughts. "Why you? Why not send Timothy?" She wasn't asking him, more like talking out loud. However, she soon realized that Chance was frowning at the rude line of questioning, and Lilith scrambled to recover. "Not that I don't enjoy your company."

Chance leaped at the opportunity to leave the in-depth talk behind and return to the casual banter. "Aww. Are you going to crochet my name on a pillow or maybe buy us matching shirts?" His eyes glinted with confident humor, but somehow it seemed like a hollow facade this time.

"Is that a new fetish? Wait. Nope. Don't want to know." Chance's laugh wrapped around her like a warm blanket, which, of course, pulled a smile out of her.

"You are such an ass," she chuckled the words as Chance bumped his shoulder against hers.

"Oh, come on, Lily. You wouldn't have me any other way." He winked, and she settled for flipping him off.

They arrived at the airport an hour later and, thanks to their tickets, rushed through most of the security until it came to the biohazard cooler. The officer was a squat Middle Eastern man in his late fifties that nervous fliers kept eyeballing. He scrutinized her license and paperwork for what seemed like an eternity. After opening the container and looking over the half dozen bags of medical-labeled blood and a package of red gelcaps, his bulbous nose scrunched in distaste. "What's it for?" he grunted with a heavy accent.

"It's there in the paperwork. We're transferring research materials to a lab in Knoxville." She pointed impatiently at the document in his hand. He turned his pockmarked face up at her, and the frown of disgust didn't leave. "The pills." He barked it with the kind of disdain reserved for people that peered down their nose at him.

"An experimental treatment for thalassemia. I can't go into any more detail. Companies and their bureaucratic secrecy. Always a pain in my ass," she huffed and crossed her arms, hoping she'd spark a mutual hatred for upper management that would get her through this faster. The bait paid off.

The thick man's face brightened, and he closed the container, handing her back the paperwork.

"The damn need for secrecy is what makes my job harder. Not your fault. Everything looks okay." She flashed him an enigmatic smile that brought a ragged toothy grin out of the man. Chance faked a cough and nudged her forward as she grabbed her stuff.

"Thank you, Officer. Enjoy the rest of your day." She beamed an apologetic smile as Chance herded into the terminal.

They ran to their gate and finally boarded the plane. Chance leaned over her shoulder and whispered, "I left Spencer a voice mail with the flight info while you were busy with the undercover terrorist. Speaking of which, I never knew you were such a charmer, Lily. Probably made that guard's year, you know?"

He bumped her shoulder again with a chuckle, and she playfully nudged her elbow at his stomach. "Don't stereotype. He's an honest man earning honest pay. I feel like I'm traveling with a sixteen-year-old. Why does Gregor keep you around again?"

"Because of my infinite charm, my rugged good looks, and my crazy skills." He wiggled his eyebrows, and she shook her head.

"I am *not* going to ask why Gregor would keep you around because of your good looks. That says volumes about you and my father that I never, ever want to know."

"Wow. I didn't see that backfire coming. I must be losing my touch."

"Assuming you had it to begin with, of course." The sugar-sweet smile she flashed over her shoulder earned her a playful scowl that made it all worth it.

Chapter 3

"So, Spencer should be down at baggage claim." Chance contorted his tall frame to pull down their bags from the overhead bins while people pushed and nudged their way past him. Lilith sat calmly, content to wait for the tide of people to pass. While straining to grab the last bag, his faded black T-shirt pulled up enough to show a glimpse of color to the right of his navel.

"What's the tattoo?" she asked casually from her comfy seat.

He tossed the bag on top of the others and glanced down at her, startled. After quickly tugging at his shirt, he looked around, tight-lipped. "Nothing. Does the line of people ever end?" Another passenger elbowed past him, making him lurch forward over the seats. The growl was almost feral as his hand gripped the armrest so tight, his knuckles turned white. "This is goddamn ridiculous." His typically smooth voice became rough and gravelly.

"Sit down and wait for them to pass. Does testosterone poisoning always make you take the path of most resistance?"

With a rebellious scowl, he stood straight up in the middle of the aisle. A middle-aged woman with a clueless smile bounced right off his back, making the people behind her stagger like dominoes. While cracking a satisfied grin, he grabbed the bags off the seat and gestured forward. "After you, *cherie*." The faint Cajun accent was thicker than usual, his anger bringing it out.

Lilith shook her head and hurried out of the seats, flashing an apologetic smile to the line of disgruntled passengers. Without another glance backward, she rushed off the plane. This was going to be a *long* trip.

Chance caught up to her at the gate, but she kept walking. "Well, thanks for waiting, especially after I held back the masses for you." The quiver in his voice was not because he was out of shape. The silence continued as she steered them toward the baggage claim. "No glib little comment?" When she still didn't answer, he jogged in front of her and stopped.

When she moved to the right, he mirrored the motion. She responded by glaring daggers at him and moved to the left, which he mirrored again.

"Enough macho crap. If you want to be a stubborn ass, fine, but don't expect me to be all happy fluffy. No one likes planes, especially getting off them. Deal with things like an adult. Hell, you almost knocked that poor lady on her ass."

He dropped the bags and held up his hands in surrender. "I officially apologize for being a *stubborn* ass and succumbing to my testosterone-based alter ego. Truce?"

It was a struggle to keep the scowl on her face. "Fine, fine. Let's go. Spencer is waiting."

He didn't move out of her way, though the playful abandon left his face, and his tone deepened. "In all seriousness, Lily. I apologize. Those planes are so damn small and confining. The claustrophobia makes me itch to get the hell out as fast as possible."

She smiled softly up at him and patted his stubbled cheek. "Aww. Poor guy. Keep your attitude in check. We don't need undue attention. Speaking of which, we really should get to baggage claim. Someone is going to mistake us for a bickering married couple or something."

"You should be so lucky." The sudden grin was contagious. It wasn't his usual playful facade but a genuine smile that made his cheeks dimple a bit.

"Well, I'd take a number, but I'm not sure you have any left."

"Where in the hell is he?" Nearly an hour passed with no sign of Spencer, and Chance was getting restless. "Try his cell again."

"I tried three minutes ago. His phone is going straight to voice mail." Calling again was pointless. "He either turned the thing off, or the battery is dead. Either way, he's not going to answer."

"Well, we have the address to the Madisonville house. Perhaps we should rent a car."

"You're right. We can't sit here all day. Plus, I don't want to depend on Spencer to run us around."

"You don't like him much, do you?"

"What?" The question caught her off guard.

"Spencer."

Lilith took a second to figure out what to say. "I don't dislike him, but we have conflicting personalities. He's an urban-style art appraiser, and I'm a CSI, not much in common."

"Hey, you could always argue about the value of graffiti in New York City." He chuckled and pushed the luggage trolley toward the car rental lot.

The fall air was warmer here, with sweet floral scents on the light breeze. The sun was climbing up the pale blue sky through hazy patches of clouds. She took a moment to soak in the beautiful morning before following him.

"Why don't you wait with the bags. I'll be right back." With an agreeable nod from her, he jogged up the steps into the office.

She scanned over the bland mixture of economical cars. They were all the same, boxes with wheels in varying shades of bland. Why did people bother buying them? Perhaps for the same reason that people bought identical houses and trending clothes. The overwhelming urge to fit in, blend with the crowd.

A sharp chirp from her pocket interrupted the internal rant with a jolt. She fished her phone out and answered without looking at the caller ID, expecting it to be Spencer or Gregor. "Yeah?"

"Well, that is no way to answer your phone. What if Bill was calling?" Gloria's sweet Spanish-inflected voice made her smile.

"Bill was a nightmare. I thought you had a higher opinion of me. He looked like the kinda guy that lingers at eighteen-and-under clubs."

Gloria's light chuckle rumbled through the phone and pulled another smile to Lilith's lips. "Sweetheart, I'm running out of people to fix you up with."

"Well, that's the best news I've heard all day."

"Aww. Don't crush an old woman's dreams. So, how's Florida? Felipe said you had a last-minute convention?"

"Yeah. These damn re-certifications. Florida is Florida. Humid, crowded, and smells like rotten fish." She suffered a pang of guilt for lying to her best friend, but Gregor was implicitly clear on the rules of what she could and couldn't say.

Chance came strolling out of the office, jingling keys with a grin. The loose jeans hung low on his hips, and the faded black T-shirt clung to him as he moved. The sun accented the specks of auburn in his short tousled hair. She saw why the ladies made such a fuss but never entertained any delusions.

To him, she was only Gregor's daughter and nothing more. He didn't ask questions or show any real interest in her. Their interactions were all charming anonymous small talk. Fun but insubstantial, unlike his lengthy history in the dating world. To each their own.

However, the thought occurred to her that she'd never seen him in the sunlight. In thirteen years, she'd only seen him under fluorescent bulbs or in the moonlight. It seemed like an odd thing to witness for the first time, and the distraction made her entirely miss what Gloria said.

"Uh… I have to go. The hotel shuttle just arrived."

"All right. I'll expect a full report of your social activities when you return, *bonita*."

He stopped in front of her with a smile and flashed a curious glance at her phone.

"Of course, Gloria. You always have dibs on my social life, even if it is on life support." She nodded at him and returned a nervous smile of her own.

"Well, liven up, so I can live vicariously through you. Be safe, and call me later."

After tucking the phone back in her pocket, she busied herself with picking up a few bags. "Sorry. Gloria was checking in to see if I found Mr. Right on the plane."

He ignored the opportunity to poke fun of her, which seemed uncharacteristic, and bowed in a grand gesture. "Well, in the meantime, your chariot awaits."

She followed him through the rows of cars until he stopped in front of a petite blue Yaris. "Please tell me you're joking. Could you have gotten something a little smaller?"

"Hey, don't knock it. Toyotas have great gas mileage."

She arched an eyebrow and skeptically stared at him over the low roof. "It's a clown car."

"Do you see a lot of other options here?" He sighed and climbed into the front seat. She slipped into the passenger side and busted out laughing. Her knees were touching the dash, but poor Chance had to fold himself in half. His tousled hair brushed the roof, and his face pinched in pain.

"Oh, yeah. This is going to be fun. Speaking of which, do you need me to drive? Oh, wait, we could remove the front seat, and you could drive from the back like High Tower in *Police Academy*." She bit back another laugh as he glared over at her. "Hey, don't knock it." She grinned sarcastically.

"Shove it, princess." He pulled the seat back as far as possible, still not anywhere near enough to be comfortable, and put the car in drive. "Put the address into the GPS and be useful, for a change."

She flipped him off before focusing on the enormous touch screen, which took up a third of the dash. Seconds later, the robotic voice led them south, out of Knoxville's crowded streets and into the middle of nowhere.

They traded work stories for the first half of the trip. He talked about his awkward meathead students at the dojo, and she shared her *stupidest criminal* award winners.

The first-prize story involved a little person dying from two punctures to the neck. Of course, her liaison with the police, Felipe Alvarez, called her in, thinking it might be a vampire attack. The assailant turned out to be a *World of Warcraft*—obsessed geek who was best friends with the guy.

Apparently, they both read somewhere that blood drawn directly from the jugular of a dwarf mixed with an energy drink would guarantee success with the ladies. The geek missed the vein on the first attempt, hit on the second, but couldn't stop the bleeding. Where the hell did people come up with these ideas? Chance was laughing so hard, he nearly choked.

When they ran out of stories, he flipped on the radio and tuned in to a classic rock station. She stared out the window at minuscule strip malls, aging gas stations, and rolling hills. The leaves were golds, browns, and reds, a cornucopia of colors dotted in among vast flat expanses of cow pastures and cornfields. Little mom-and-pop stores were fading on the side of the road along with vegetable stands, hand-painted signs, and crumbling barns. These seemed like all the signatures of fall in the South, not that she'd know.

The sprawling countryside was a whole other planet from Manhattan. However, she understood why Duncan liked coming out here. It was quiet and quaint. He was always a fan of simple pleasures. The one time she remembered her uncle visiting, he'd called New York the *concrete jungle*. His tone hadn't rung with the shiny wide-eyed enthusiasm that most visitors had when using that phrase. For Duncan, the lack of greenery was a drawback, and he was not particularly impressed with Central Park. He called it a "pathetic attempt to *honor* the nature they abolished."

They turned off the four-lane highway, and Chance weaved around tight corners and up hills with boyish glee. It was like some crazy roller coaster. They barely missed tractors and pickups around every bend, which played hell on her nerves. She gripped the door handle tightly and forced herself to focus on the tall trees that lined the road. The view opened to expansive pastures with black-and-white cows watching them pass by.

Five miles in, they rolled to a stop outside a tan house with a double garage, and Lilith breathed a sigh of relief that they survived. The property sloped down steeply from the front of the house, looking like it was seconds from falling off the face of the earth. The front yard was bare and lifeless, with only a few young trees newly planted near the split rail fence. A large shed stood closer to the road bearing the same rusty star she'd seen on dozens of barns along the way.

Disbelief rang in his voice as he stared out the window at the unassuming buildings. "His place looks so...normal. I was expecting a plantation-style mansion or the Addams family house or something. We sure this is the right place?"

She double-checked the address with the numbers on the cow mailbox. "This is the place. Guess he didn't want to stand out any more than he already would. People in small towns are nosy. I'm sure things are bad enough for humans who don't go to church in this town, much less a guy living alone that only comes out at night."

"Well, what's the plan? No car in the driveway, Spencer is MIA, and we don't have a key. I somehow doubt that they left the place unlocked."

"Well, they might have parked in there…" The white doors of a two-car garage dominated the front of the house.

Chance shrugged and pulled himself out of the car with a great deal of effort. He groaned in relief and took a moment to stretch before walking up to the massive doors at a casual pace. He peeked in the half circle windows before jogging over to the passenger side of the car.

"Nothing. So, what now?"

She glanced around, calculating their exposure. A neighboring single-story house sat across the street, only partially hidden by some large shrubs. On the left was another home less than a quarter mile down the road. A thick line of trees ran behind the property, but she spotted one or two neighbors on the hill beyond that still had a view of the house.

"I think you should go knock on the door."

A confused frown pulled at his lips. "What? No one is here. What good would that do?"

She pointed out the neighboring houses discreetly. "You can bet at least one of them is watching. All we've done is peek in the garage. If we drive off, I can almost guarantee one of them will call the cops. Knock on the door, wait a few minutes, and then walk back to the car. After that, we'll find a hotel room, take a nap, and eat some food. Our best option is to come back tonight when we're less likely to have an audience."

He stared at her for a minute, not bothering to hide his surprise while she glared at him in annoyance. "Yes, I'm aware that I have a brain and am pretty damn good at my job. Go!"

"Does your job require you to be a criminal-minded sneak?" The words sounded critical, but an unmistakable excitement filled his voice.

She raised her eyebrows in surprise. "Are you serious?" When he still appeared lost, she continued. "You do know what I do for a living, right?"

"You work with the cops on crime scenes." The words started as a statement but ended up sounding more like a question.

"More accurately, I show up at very particular crime scenes ahead of the CSI team. I decide which investigations I need to manage in-house and which we kick to homicide. Few cops know what I do. I access crime scenes without any trace that might contaminate the evidence or make the other officers ask questions. That means being an exceptionally gifted sneak."

A grin crossed his lips. "Well, well. I never knew you were so diabolical. I always assumed that you were a squeaky-clean, by-the-book type since you work with law enforcement."

"If I do my job right, I don't have to collaborate with any cops besides Alvarez and Boyd from Homicide. Can we please stop playing career day? And speaking of law enforcement, you need to go knock on the door before we get to play with Tennessee's finest?"

He pushed off the car with a conspiratorial grin and strolled back to the double garage, disappearing around the corner. A couple of minutes later, he reappeared, shrugging his shoulders. "Guess he's not home yet." His voice projected loudly enough for any neighbors with open windows to hear him. Subtle. Before attempting to squeeze back into the car, he death-glared the tiny seat.

"Okay, mission accomplished. That should identify us as disappointed visitors. So, oh mighty navigator, do you want to find us a hotel with that thing?" He nodded over at the GPS on the dashboard.

"Well…looks like Town and Country out on Highway 411 or the Motor Lodge."

"Town and Country! Punch it in, navigator." His enthusiasm was almost contagious.

"Are you always this chipper? 'Cause if this is normal-Chance mode, I think I need more coffee."

"Hey. So far, this is the first vacation I've ever had." This time his smile was infectious, tiny dimples and all. She couldn't help but grin as the GPS began barking electronic directions. In the back of her mind, she hoped he still considered it a vacation once they figured out what was going on. So far, it didn't appear likely.

They pulled into the *Town and Country*, which turned out to be a dingy, run-down motel. The single-story L-shaped monstrosity sported cement block painted white with a faded blue tin roof. A rusting beast of a dumpster sat in front of the parking lot next to a questionably tilted telephone pole. A vending machine, sun bleached into oblivion with an *Out of Order* sign, sat next to the office. They both stayed in the car, contemplating their options as they stared over the cracked paint on each of the ten red doors.

He shifted as much as the cramped car allowed, which wasn't much and stared at her. "Okay, we've been shoved into an airplane and then squeezed into this small ass car. We have to go back to Duncan's tonight, so driving any farther would be pointless. I say we take a room here and go back out to check Duncan's place. If we don't hear from Spencer or Miriah by then, we drive to Knoxville and find someplace less likely to kill us while we're asleep."

She chuckled despite herself, "First off, weren't you the one that said this car would be fine?" He flipped her off as she continued. "Secondly, I think you mean *rooms*, plural," she amended.

All the humor fell from his face, and he shook his head. "Oh, hell no. This place is one step from the Bates Motel. No room for prim and proper, *cherie*. We'll get a room with twin beds or something, but only *one* room."

She opened her mouth to protest, but the thought of staying in this place by herself sent chills up her spine. Having another person, any person, in the room would make her feel better. They were only staying long enough to nap anyway. She nodded and dug out her wallet to hand him some cash. "All right. We'll share a room, this once." She emphasized the last bit, which only made him smile and wink at her.

"You say that now." He grabbed the bills, painfully extracted himself from the car, and jogged up to the office. While he was busy getting their room, she stared across the gloomy parking lot and rubbed goose bumps from her arms. She spent most of her time around dead bodies and crime scenes. Still, ever since that alley, she'd had a nagging sense that something was horribly wrong. First, Duncan goes missing. Then, Spencer is incommunicado. What the hell was going on?

While sitting in the car, she called Gregor's cell, hoping to leave a message. The standard robot voice answered, reciting the phone number and nothing else. "Spencer didn't show at the airport, so we swung by the house. We'll try again tonight. Until then, we are going to rest at a hotel. I'll call with more later." She didn't want to leave anything too specific. Her father took extreme precautions to brief her on the situation. The least she could do was indulge his paranoia and leave a vague voice mail.

As soon as she hung up, Chance emerged from the office. He stopped and turned back to lean in the door as if answering a question. A moment later, he rested an arm across the roof on her side of the car to whisper. His vigilant eyes never left the parking lot, displaying a palpable gravity to the seriousness of his scowl. If she expected some earth-shattering insight, he left her disappointed.

"I swear to God. I don't know what the hell that man said to me. I think it was something about guns and a raccoon." She choked back a startled laugh.

"Are you sure he said raccoon?" Lilith didn't consider herself a racist person, and she didn't like to make assumptions, but this was the South and well off the beaten path.

"He may have said he makes a mean chicken Florentine for all I know." She coughed over her chuckle, and Chance's scowl lifted to a casual smirk.

"You're from the South. Can't you interpret the lingo?"

He tore his eyes away from the parking lot with an insolent glare. "I'm from Cajun country, *cher*, not whatever the hell country this is." After the laughter subsided, his voice dropped down to business mode. "We have the first room." He nodded at the faded door behind him. "I want to give it a once-over quick. Stay in the car, fiddle with your phone, and I'll come out and grab the bags."

He pushed away from the car and cautiously stalked over to the room. Although he appeared carefree as he unlocked the door, she knew he was absorbing all his surroundings because of an undercurrent of tension pulling at every muscle. Once he disappeared inside, she held up her phone, pretending to push buttons, and stared intensely at the door.

The minutes passed at a torturously slow pace. How big could the room be? She had her fingers curled around the door handle when he finally came out. A slight nod as he strolled by, heading for the trunk, told her all was clear. After exaggerating the motion of putting her phone away, she stepped out of the car. Her rumpled dress pants, wrinkled blouse, and high heels wouldn't cut it. Tonight's mission required something dark and comfortable.

A few minutes later, she was staring down a queen-size bed after unloading the car. "I thought you were getting two twins?"

Chance popped his head out of the bathroom. "I tried. All the rooms are single queens." With a nonchalant shrug, he stepped back out of sight.

She released a frustrated sigh, feeling exhausted as she scanned the tiny room with increasing despair. The yellowing wallpaper was still intact, with a few exceptions. A sixties-style dresser with plastic wood molding dominated the wall on the right. A petite round table stuffed into the corner by the window left no room for chairs. An ancient TV with actual push buttons stood on the far edge of the dresser. If nothing else, it'd make a hefty self-defense weapon.

A horrendous comforter with swirl designs in salmon pink and melon green covered the queen-size bed. Just looking at the thing made her skin itch. Hanging above was a beach scene painted with the same hues—yay for color coordination.

She dropped her aluminum case on the dresser and cracked it open. When Chance walked into the room, all the lights were off, and Lilith leaned over the bed. She held a purple flashlight, meticulously running it over the sheets while sporting stylish orange glasses.

"What the hell are you doing?"

She glanced over with a frown. "It's a UV light. I'm checking the bed."

He strolled up, curiously peering over her shoulder. "Checking for what?"

"Blood, urine, saliva, semen…" She continued to move the light over the sheets in methodical sweeping lines.

"Why would you even check for that?" His disgust bordered on offended as he backed away.

She huffed and glanced up at him. "Maybe you don't care, but I don't want to sleep in a redneck sperm bank, okay?"

Chance leaned back against the wall, laughing. "Holy hell, Lily. You sure do have a way with words. So, what's the verdict? Are we cuddling in the tub?" She glanced up in time to catch him wink suggestively.

"You wish." She flicked off the UV and turned on the overhead light. "Surprisingly, clean. Either no one ever stays here, or these sheets are new."

"I'm betting on option one. You aren't the *ignorance is bliss* sort, are you?"

"Nope. I always pack a set of flat sheets to sleep on, just in case."

"How practical." He flopped down on the bed, stretching out with a groan before folding his arms behind his head. The bare bit of skin between his shirt and his jeans revealed a tiny glimpse of color again. Overcome with burning curiosity, she sat on the bed and made another attempt to wrestle the truth from him.

"Come on. What's the tattoo? I won't laugh, scout's honor."

She didn't miss the slight frown on his face. "I told you it's nothing. Just let it go, Lily."

"Oh, come on. Let me guess." She thought for a minute, ignoring the irritating glare from the other side of the bed. "Hmm…some bad tribal? No, a band tattoo… Led Zeppelin? Wait…" Her lips curled into a sly grin. "The name of a crazy ex-girlfriend? Maybe the one that turned you off normal relationships?"

He released an agitated sigh and stared at her, but she could see the shock he was hiding. That last guess had to be right. "Knock it off and let it go. Damn, I don't remember you ever being this stubborn with your dad."

She held up her hands in surrender. "Fine, don't share. And I've always been this stubborn. You've just never paid attention."

He lifted an eyebrow and let out a snort of disbelief. "The car today was the first time we've had a real conversation that wasn't meaningless jokes or discussions about Gregor. Communication is a two-way street."

It was her turn to be surprised, not because he was right, but because he'd noticed. "I suppose so." She tried for a relaxed tone but failed.

The lull in conversation stretched into an awkward silence that left her searching for a way out while he was content to lay there with his eyes closed. In a hasty attempt to escape, she grabbed her suitcase, fished out some clothes, and sauntered off to the bathroom.

From the time Gregor asked for her help, Chance started exhibiting odd mood swings. Friendly and genuine one minute, snappy and defensive the next. Maybe the uneasiness was simply the process of getting to know someone that you've *known* for thirteen years. Whatever it was, she was hoping they both found an equilibrium and fast.

"But first…a shower," she mumbled to herself and silently prayed she wouldn't find a crime scene on the other side of the curtain.

The shower was cramped but surprisingly clean. The hot water rained down and washed away the thoughts milling around. Water always had a calming effect on her. If she had any faith in astrology, she'd chalk it up to being a Scorpio. Too bad she'd met plenty of people that didn't fit the star charts. There was no astrological sign that said, *One day, you'll be a serial rapist that enjoys seeing the light die in people's eyes. Success will find you today.*

After throwing on a comfy pair of sleep shorts and tugging on a navy blue tank top, she stepped out of the steam-filled bathroom. She peeked around the corner and saw Chance passed out, fully dressed, and twisted up in the sheets. The smooth lines of his face were peaceful and instantly younger. She pulled her wet hair into a loose bun and tiptoed to her side of the bed.

Lilith curled around a pillow and let the magic of the shower lull her to sleep. For once, she had no dreams, no nightmares, only blissful, mind-numbing nothingness.

A loud, obnoxious ringing startled Lilith out of her deep sleep. She blindly reached for a lamp that wasn't there. Suddenly, she realized this wasn't her room. A drowsy moment of disorientation nearly blossomed into fear before she remembered the motel. It was pitch-black, so she fumbled her hand along the wall to find a light switch while she answered the phone.

"Lilith?"

"Felipe. Is something wrong? Are Gloria and the kids okay?"

"We're fine. Gloria insisted I call and make sure you're still surviving Florida. She would have called herself, but she's forcing Erica to bake cookies for the cheerleader's fundraiser. Guess baking is better than handcuffing her at this point. How's the conference going?" Somehow his tone didn't sound genuine, but she was way too tired to point it out.

"Doesn't start till Friday. I'm just getting some rest before the meet and greet tomorrow." She rubbed the sleep out of her eyes and heard a groan next to her. "How's the caseload? Anything interesting?"

Chance blinked at the bright light, groaned again, and rolled off the bed, stumbling toward the bathroom.

"I have one case of interest that popped up early this morning." She half listened while she grabbed for the biohazard cooler. Of course, the room didn't come with a microwave, so the blood packs were out for now. The stuff was repulsive when cold.

She grunted something in agreement and dug out four of the gel caplets. They would hold her over until she found a microwave. Alvarez was still droning on about the case, and she was still half listening, downing the pills in one dry gulp. The rattling of the ancient pipes announced the shower was starting up.

"So, the place is going to be gutted. About time, I say. That damn pit is a hazard, a haven for squatters and gang members. So, when is this conference over? I'm not used to doing the legwork."

A deep yawn interrupted her. "Sorry, Alvarez. The trip wore me out. I'm hoping to be back by Sunday. You can't tell how these things will go. I'll keep you posted, and please tell Gloria to stop worrying about me. She has her hands full with Erica anyway. Oh, and if you want me to look at that case, email me the report and crime scene photos."

"You're my girl. Take care, Lily." Alvarez hung up before she could say anything else. She flipped through her messages on her phone, still rubbing the sleep from her eyes. Eleven o'clock at night, and all she wanted to do was sleep. The shower stopped while she dug through her suitcase.

When the bathroom door opened, releasing a cloud of steam, Chance strolled out with a towel wrapped high around his waist. All his lean muscles glinted with water, and his skin flushed pink beneath the even tan. Lilith quickly glanced down at the comfortable flats in her hand as if *they* were the most fascinating thing on the planet, not the half-naked man in the room.

"So, who the hell calls you at eleven o'clock at night?" he growled and shook a second towel through his auburn-flecked hair. "Boyfriend checking up on you?"

She swallowed the lump in her throat and forced her sleepy muscles to move. "Alvarez. He wanted advice on a case." She snatched a long-sleeved black T-shirt, a pair of dark jeans, and black shoes before closing her suitcase. "I do typically work nights, so calls aren't that unusual."

"Oh?" A curious tone filled his voice as he threw the luggage on the bed. "So, what's the case?"

She stood with an armful of clothes and started for the bathroom, trying to avoid looking in his general direction. "I can't discuss open cases. Protocol."

He huffed and rooted around in his bag. "Oh, come on. We're in Tennessee. Besides, what am I going to do? Run screaming to the reporters for a tell-all?"

"Good point. I still can't tell you. I was half asleep and didn't pay attention to a word Alvarez said. I'll peek at the files when he gets around to emailing them."

He let out a howl of laughter that followed her. "And here I thought you were some perfect computer, *cher*. Wow… I'm so disillusioned right now."

"Hey, before we play mission impossible at Duncan's place, we should rustle up some food."

She peeked out of the cracked door to see Chance's muscled back leaning over his luggage. The casual T-shirts didn't do him justice. "Um, yeah. Good idea. Maybe we can find an all-night diner or something." Hesitantly, she pulled herself away from the door and finished wiggling into her jeans.

After packing the car, they grabbed a greasy breakfast with coffee strong enough to burn through linoleum. An hour later, they were back in the clown car, weaving through the dark country roads toward Duncan's house. Chance cut the lights as soon as they turned onto the last street. The car slowed to a crawl, and Lilith scanned the neighboring houses. They were all dark. The night was quiet except for the faint echoes of dogs barking and cows mooing in the distance. They parked the car behind the shed, shielding it from view as much as possible.

"Okay. I'll go in, check the house, and if it's clear, I'll signal you. Then you can do your thing." He reached for the door handle, but she stopped him with a hand on his arm.

"I need to go in first."

He turned to stare at her in disbelief. "Oh, hell no."

She sighed and grabbed a hair tie from her pocket. As she pulled up her wild auburn curls into a bun, she fixed him with a stern stare. "Look. I get that you have a job to do. However, you would compromise the scene, and I don't exactly have time to teach you the basics of forensics."

His hand left the door, and his face became all hard lines. "First of all, you don't know this is a scene. Second, I'm sure Spencer and Miriah have already done plenty of damage. I promise I'll be careful, but I can't let you in first."

"Stop right there." Her voice was iron strong, and her mouth was set in a stern frown. The surprise on his face displayed his unfamiliarity with anyone but Gregor ordering him around. However, she never let anything compromise her work. "I know Gregor sent you to keep me safe, but this is me drawing the line." She held up a hand to cut off his protest. "I investigate crime scenes every single day *without* macho backup. My father sent me to do a job, too, and I can't do that with you underfoot. I'm going in. You can stand at the door."

He glared out the windshield sightlessly. Every muscle in his face flexed and strained. His internal battle waged on as he gripped the steering wheel so tight, she thought he might rip it right out of the car.

Finally, he glanced at her, displaying an entire novel of emotions on his face, mostly centered around the *pissed off* theme. His voice came out thin and forced. "Fine, but you maintain voice contact at all times, so I know you're okay. You clear a room. Then I move in. You will stay within one room of me at all times. Understood?"

She nodded, but he still looked like a powder keg. With a profound sigh, the anger leaked out of his muscles, and he slumped back against the seat. When he spoke again, he sounded tired. "You're even more stubborn than your father." When he eventually met her eyes, he forced a smile.

Chance was all calm business when he hauled himself out of the tiny car. He bent down and pulled something from under the seat. The light from the half-moon high in the cloudless sky glinted off the gun in his hand. His eyes scanned the surroundings with calculating scrutiny, a look that screamed security. She waited for his nod of approval and crept out of the car with her aluminum kit.

Unlike the macho cops in the movies, he didn't aim the gun to do a sweep around the house. Instead, he held it casually down by his side as he methodically made his way to the front door. Every muscle in his body drew tight, waiting to pounce. She dug in her case, grabbing the lockpick before following him.

Mere seconds passed before the front door popped open. She paused long enough to pull on a pair of gloves and slip the booties over her shoes. He gazed down at her feet with an amused smile and shook his head. The land around the house was dry red clay dirt, which was fine as sand. It was unlikely that any dirt tracked in would hold a helpful pattern. Still, this was part of her process, her ritual.

She was about to step over the threshold when he held out an arm to stop her. He leaned in close and whispered while he stared into the dark hall. "Remember, one room at a time, and keep talking to me. Okay?" She glanced up at him, and his eyes caught hers for a second with a severe warning in them. Somehow, that look finally made her realize she was entering a possibly hostile scene. Until that very moment, she hadn't been scared, but now she swallowed the sudden lump in her throat before nodding.

Reluctantly, he let her go and pulled the gun up, training it just over her shoulder. Now things felt like a movie. With her stylish orange glasses in place and her UV light clicked on, she stepped into the dark.

Her olive eyes scanned over every surface of the entryway. A high table sat to the right of the door with a gilded painting on the wall of a generic country scene. Dried flowers lay in a squat basket next to a set of keys someone tossed carelessly on the corner. They probably belonged to Duncan, so she tucked them in a ziplock bag.

"Entryway is clear. I'm stepping into the room on the left. Try not to touch anything. In case I need to go back through and dust for prints." She took her search around the corner into a pale blue room. A cheap faux wood desk with a computer monitor dominated the area. Family photos hung from the walls, cluttered the counter, and covered the short shelves on the opposite wall. The Indian-style rug in odd light blue and cream hues was spotless. The whole room had the air of planned chaos, like a staged photo shoot trying too hard to appear used.

"Any startling revelations yet?" He leaned into the doorway, but he was still watching the dark living room in front of him.

"I don't think he ever used this room. The computer monitor isn't plugged in, and the cabinet is empty. There's nothing here but a ton of family photos."

"Maybe someone stole the computer."

She scanned the computer desk with a calculating stare. "No. I see a fragile layer of dust indicating they haven't opened the computer cabinet in a while. This is all for show. Besides, Duncan hates computers, doesn't trust them." She was standing back up when her eye caught a splash of color. A large family portrait hung on the wall near the door. She remembered the photo. Ten years ago, the entire family got together in St. Louis for a reunion.

It was a year after her mother died and a few months before her seventeenth birthday. Duncan, Gregor, and Aaron stood in the center, the three brothers, surrounded by the rest of the family. She'd only met Aaron's son, Michael, that one time, and he wasn't much of a conversationalist. Spencer left the next summer for Scotland to study at the Glasgow School of Art. Miriah and her husband, Malachi, were married the summer before.

Reminiscing wasn't going to solve the case. She needed to keep moving. Her uncle's smiling face gnawed at her mind as she grabbed the case and slipped past Chance, who still lingered in the doorway.

"You gotta give me a little room here."

He sidestepped out of the way in response. "Can I close the door to this room since it's clear?"

She appreciated the question and nodded. "Sure. Use these." She tossed him a pair of gloves before making her way into the living room.

She swept her UV light over an ample open space with a cluster of couches and chairs closing in around a big-screen TV. A river stone chimney in the corner framed in pale lacquered wood was the inescapable focal point. The wood trim extended across the ceiling to the front door. Rustic.

There was nothing noteworthy in the living room, which took her an hour to determine. Chance spoke up every minute or two from the hallway, breaking her concentration. He had eyes on her, so she didn't know why he needed to talk about nothing continually. Her skin tingled with irritation by the time she finished.

All she could figure out was that this room saw more activity than the first one. The couches and chairs appeared worn with use but clean. Considering Duncan's reluctance to move into the age of modern technology, Miriah and Spencer probably used the big-screen TV more than Duncan. She couldn't precisely picture her uncle sitting in a recliner watching *American Idol.* However, the thought was funny enough to calm her fraying nerves for a moment.

She moved on, checking two bedrooms that Duncan never used. Sheer curtains were the only defense against the sun, and Duncan needed a light-tight room. Not all vampires developed an allergy to sunlight in their old age. Still, with the archaic ones, like Duncan, it was almost a guarantee and often deadly.

At a quarter till four, she'd found nothing but Duncan's keys. The kitchen and dining room were less than helpful, as well as the two bathrooms. She wasn't going to waste her time dusting for prints, not until she found something that stood out.

Lilith stared down a flight of stairs leading to the basement as Chance came up behind her. Before he could say anything, she turned around and held up her hand. "Stay here. I'll keep talking. We've been here a while. If someone wanted to attack us, I think they would have made their move by now. Don't you?" Her tone left no room for objections.

He frowned but stayed silent at the top while she slowly felt her way down the stairs. Logically, she knew turning on the lights would only advertise their presence to Duncan's neighbors. Unfortunately, logic wouldn't banish the looming sense of dread quickly seeping into her bones and making her limbs feel heavy. With determination, she continued without the irrational comfort of light.

As she reached the bottom of the stairs, a chill crept along her spine. The air was colder down here, but it wasn't the source of her unease. The air felt unnaturally still, like the entire basement was holding its breath before swallowing her whole. Stray bits of moonlight trailed into the area, not enough to see anything, but enough to be creepy. The tint of her stylish orange glasses only made it worse.

She clicked on her UV light to peek into a bathroom on the left before moving into an ample space with a bay window. The front half of the house was a basement, but the property's steep incline made the backside ground level.

They frequently used the exterior door near the bay window according to the red dirt caked into the mat, but it wasn't the only one. Another door leading outside sat at the end of the basement with faint moonlight seeping through its curtained window. There were also two interior doors on the right, most likely bedrooms. She swung her UV light in even lines over the floors and walls, carefully making her way.

"Lilith?" Chance's voice sounded tentative at the top of the stairs.

"I'm fine. Still checking the main room. Stay put."

"If the stairs are clear, I can wait at the bottom. I don't like this, Lily." Professional pride dominated his voice, which made a certain sense. Not letting a client out of sight was bodyguard rule number one.

"Give me a minute," she replied absently as her flashlight caught sight of something. She switched to her standard flashlight and found a couple of dark drops on top of the well-worn doormat. Blood. More specifically, vampire blood. She followed the faint trail until it disappeared under the door to the first room. Until now, she'd been more concerned about Gregor's hidden agenda than Duncan's safety. The scales were tipping fast.

Her heart began to thud in her chest as she examined the trail, following it back to the doormat. The drops were small and spaced out, something from a minor injury. She had no way to tell how recent it was. Still, someone should have seen it, noticed it.

Perhaps that explained why Spencer freaked out when he called Gregor. Admittedly, he would mention this to him, so why wouldn't her father pass it on to her? Is that why he sent Chance with her? She was becoming uncomfortable with this secretive side of her father. She'd always trusted him implicitly and never had a reason not to.

Lilith forced herself to focus on the evidence in front of her. Worrying about her dad's motives wouldn't help her process the scene. She needed to know if there was more blood and what the trail meant, even if she had limited tools.

Unfortunately, the usual method of luminol and hydrogen peroxide proved useless in her specific line of work. The concoction reacted with the iron in hemoglobin to produce a blue glow. However, vampires had a significantly deficient hemoglobin level, which was the entire reason they needed blood to survive. Exceptions existed, of course. A sample from either a pureblood right after feeding, or from a half-blood, like Chance, would react. Still, neither would be as bright as a sample from a human.

She crouched down by the outside door and dug some fingerprint dust from her kit. It was a cheery salmon color that sadly reminded her of the comforter in the motel. Still, it was the best choice when working with a low amount of light.

As she dusted the powder over the door handle, she suddenly realized it was unlocked. She stepped back with her blood pounding in her ears. The fingerprint powder tipped over, and the brush clattered to the floor. Panic rose in her chest, knowing something was very, very wrong. That feeling surged over her, leaving her shaking.

"Chance…the door," the strangled whisper barely escaped her lips as something moved at the end of the room. Her head whipped around, straining to pinpoint the sound of footsteps on the concrete floor. With a shaking hand, she moved her UV light down the long room. Every single muscle in her body screamed, but words only died in her throat.

A pale face flashed inches away from her, but before she made sense of it, the side of her head exploded in white-hot pain. Her flashlight flew forward as the world spun on its axis and her with it. The smell of burning skin and a high-pitch screech rattled angrily through her head. She vaguely heard the glass door shatter as footsteps thundered down the stairs, and her head hit the floor with a sickening crack. Darkness consumed her as someone screamed her name, and then there was nothing.

Chapter 4

A phone rang somewhere in the distance, and each note seared like a bullet through Lilith's brain. When the deafening noise finally stopped, Chance's muffled voice rumbled through the air, but she couldn't make out the words. Trying to open her eyes was a mistake. The soft light of a lamp cut like a white-hot dagger into her right eye. The right side of her head throbbed with an unbearable ferocity, forcing her to clench them shut.

After a few steadying breaths, she slowly inched her way up against the headboard. Waves of nauseating pain crashed down with each movement. Only once she was upright did she try opening her eyes again, prudently avoiding the direct glare.

Confusion clouded her mind as she scanned the unfamiliar room. No windows, undecorated walls, and a closet across from the bed. One of the basement rooms? That made sense, at least. Not that her intellect was fully functional at the moment. Two empty blood bags sat on the nightstand, sending her mind spinning. What the hell happened that required two units?

Chance's voice suddenly boomed into clarity from behind the door. "I don't fucking care, Spencer! Get here now! You better have a damn good explanation!"

The shouting rattled through her brain like ricocheting shrapnel, but she was determined not to pass out. Squeezing her eyes shut, she gritted her teeth as a dizzy spell nearly dragged her into unconsciousness. The door squeaked open, making her wince even with her eyes sealed against the flood of sunlight.

"Sorry." His voice was so tender, she couldn't be sure it was Chance until she cracked one eye open. The agony lessened a bit when he shut the door, enough for her to watch him sit on the edge of the bed. Carefully, he tilted her chin toward him, examining the right side of her head. Sympathy mixed with disgust pinched his face, which didn't lift her spirits.

"How are you feeling?"

She winced again as his fingers brushed over the fringes of a colossal knot. "Did someone hit me with a Mack truck? What happened?"

Fingertips traveled lightly over her cheek before his hand fell to the bed. "God, Lily. You scared the crap out of me. Something hit you in the head damn hard and smashed its way through the door. By the time I got downstairs, you were out cold on the floor, bleeding like crazy." He released a heavy sigh, and his eyes fell, guilt weighing heavily on his shoulders. Out of pure instinct, she reached out and took his hand.

"I'm okay… I think. This was my fault, not yours." A sudden stab of pain made her slump back against the headboard with her eyes closed. "So, two bags… That bad, huh?"

"Blood was everywhere." The haunting timbre of his voice sent a chill down her spine. "After the first bag, you still didn't wake up. Hell, I didn't find a definitive pulse until the second bag." A moment of silence stretched out as she tried to wrap her mind around those words.

"For a while, I thought I was unemployed." His failed attempt at some much-needed levity was her life raft. A perfect excuse to avoid thinking about how close she came to dying.

She started to laugh, but it hurt too much, so she settled for a smile. "Dad totally would have fired your ass." He chuckled half-heartedly as the vicious throbbing in her head made the world spin behind her eyelids. "Do you think Duncan has any Tylenol, morphine, horse tranquilizers, anything?"

She peeked with her left eye when he didn't respond. A heart-rending vulnerability filled his eyes as they stared down at her hand, still resting on his. Then, just like that, the impersonal facade clicked back in place. "Yeah, I'll go check." He rose from the bed and opened the door with an absent stare.

"Chance." He stopped in the doorway and peeked back at her. "Are you okay?" The question surprised him for some reason. Sure, she was the one with the extensive head injury, but she never saw him so defeated in all these years. Anger, rage, fury, those she expected, but this?

"I'll find something for the migraine." The empty, emotionless words were unexpected as he ignored her question entirely. "Oh, and Spencer is on his way here."

"Spencer?" The pounding in her head made it difficult to organize her thoughts. A subject change so abrupt was like mental whiplash. "Where was he?"

"Last night, Miriah called and asked him to chase down a lead. He's on his way back now but hasn't heard from her since."

Something else nagged at her, but she couldn't force her brain to work. The sharp torment was like a chain saw trying to split her skull open. "The phone..." After several deep breaths, she tried to form the words. "Why didn't he answer?"

"He forgot his charger, and the phone died while he was investigating. He didn't realize Miriah was MIA until he picked up a new one and listened to our voice mails. He's somewhere in east Tennessee, so we have a few hours."

She swung her legs off the bed and tried to stand, but a dizzy spell hit her like a gigantic wave. Her knees buckled, sending her toward the floor like a pile of bricks. Thankfully, he was there in a split second, strong arms wrapping around her waist, keeping her upright. "What the hell are you doing, Lily?"

Before opening her eyes, she sucked in a few steadying breaths. Exasperation flooded his voice, but his face was full of worry. "I should investigate the last room. Has to be something here, something someone was looking for that's possibly still here."

She was *not* eloquent with a head wound, and standing only made things worse. In a desperate attempt to make her mind function, she squeezed her eyes shut. When she opened them again, all she saw were his hazel brown eyes flecked with green.

"Lilith..." He kept his voice slow and calm as if talking to a suicide jumper. "You can't even stand. We can search the room later.

Please, please, Lily. Relax for now. Okay?" The low rumble of his voice flowed over her skin like warm velvet as he pleaded with her. It must be the head injury.

Carefully and a little reluctantly, he lowered her to the bed. Without another word, he disappeared through the door, leaving her to sink into the pillows. Lying down made all the difference. The pain settled to a moderate roar that pulled her into a drowsy state. He was right. She should rest for a bit. A few minutes to close her eyes, and then she could get back to work. Only a few minutes…

When she woke again, her head was a million times better. A dull throbbing ache still pulsed behind her right eye, but the world wasn't spinning anymore. She slowly sat up, moving her legs off the edge of the bed. Pulling herself to her feet, she stood still for a moment to be sure she wouldn't fall over. This time she kept her balance, which was a blessing since her bodyguard wasn't there to catch her.

Lilith pulled the door open to the sunlit basement, a complete transformation from last night's house of horrors.

"Lily, you're up."

She yelped in surprise and stumbled backward into the doorframe as Chance sprang to his feet beside her.

"Holy crap!" She bent over with her palms on her knees, gulping in air. Still shaking like a ninety-year-old with Parkinson's, she stood and leaned against the wall. "You trying to give me a heart attack?"

"No, I just—"

"Got tired of standing in *front* of the door?" she chuckled while trying to catch her breath.

As he sighed heavily, a stern expression pulled his lips tight. "I'm trying to do my job." A mass of seething fury lit his eyes that she was confident had only one target: himself. "You need something to eat." He awkwardly declared the words and stormed off toward the stairs, leaving no room for refusal.

"Not hungry, but thanks," she muttered to the empty air. What she really needed was water and a mirror—time to assess the damage.

The immense pool of drying blood stopped her dead in her tracks, unable to take her eyes off the brownish-red stain. It was a pint of blood, maybe more. If Chance hadn't reached her as fast as he did...

Shaking off the thought, she resolutely marched into the bathroom. Once she faced the enormous mirror, her mouth fell open in absolute astonishment. The right side of her face was a mass of purples, greens, and sickly yellows. Four butterfly Band-Aids caked in blood held together the edges of a nasty gash on her temple. Did Babe Ruth clock her with his bat while swinging for a home run? She couldn't even imagine how bad it was before two units of blood and hours to recuperate.

With tentative fingers, she palpated the colorful splotches and grimaced at the sharp, searing pain. Too bad they didn't heal instantly like movie vamps. Walking around in public would be problematic for a few days. Her father wouldn't be too happy if some hick cop threw his head of security in jail for domestic abuse.

A startling thud resonated through the basement, and she cautiously peeked out to see Chance cradling his right hand. He stood in front of the broken door, jaw clenched painfully tight as he stared daggers at a fist-size dent. Before she could move, he reared back, slamming his fist into the door again while muttering under his breath. Quickly, she marched right up to him.

"Whoa! Chance, stop!"

A piercing glower made her pause for a moment. His whole face screamed, *Stay away*, but she had to put a stop to this.

"Better?" Her voice was surprisingly less judgmental than she thought it would be. With a sympathetic half smile, she stepped forward and reached for his hand.

"Leave me alone." He jerked his arm away from her with a scowl, his voice rumbling like distant thunder.

"Let me see." When he made no move to comply, she lifted her chin and held out a hand expectantly. His eyes shifted from hers to her outstretched palm and back again. "Now is not the time to be stubborn."

Standing still as stone, he stared mutely at the right side of her face.

"So, you think breaking your hand will make us even? What happens if someone attacks us again, and you can't do anything because you had some guilt-fueled moment of self-mutilation? Hand! Now!"

Once he begrudgingly gave in, she began assessing the bones and joints for fractures. "I don't think anything's broken." He cringed and drew in a sharp breath as her fingers pressed against the base of his third metacarpal. "First aid kit?"

"Bathroom," he answered in a gruff whisper, not daring to meet her eyes.

A few minutes later, they sat on the bed while Lilith dabbed hydrogen peroxide to the cuts across his knuckles. Chance was still sullen with his eyes focused intensely on some random spot of dark green carpet.

"Thirty-seven," he whispered as she reached for the antibacterial ointment. After the lengthy quiet game, his voice almost startled her.

"I'm sorry?" Her head tilted as she peered at him in confusion.

Staring down at his hand, he continued. "Thirty-seven. I've saved Gregor's life thirty-seven times in the last six years." When he paused, she stayed silent, knowing he needed to vent. She allowed him all the time he required while focusing her energy on smoothing ointment over the cuts and abrasions.

"I'm with you for twenty-four hours and can't even protect you once! Fuck, you almost died last night. Keeping people safe is my only job!" The wrath seeped back into his voice, growing more forceful with each sentence.

She dropped the Band-Aid and grabbed his chin firmly, pulling his face up to stare him in the eye. "Listen to me. I gave you orders. I almost got myself killed—"

"No!" His wounded hand clenched, the scabs cracking open. "My job is to determine the safety of the situation. I should never have let you come down here by yourself."

"Come on. You didn't fail. You saved my life." His temper and crippled sense of dutiful pride made her uncomfortable. What else was she supposed to say?

His eyes narrowed like an intense laser locking in on her. She wanted to crawl to the other side of the bed and hide, but she refused to squirm out of pure stubbornness. "If you fail at your job, more people die. What if you missed some pivotal clue that caused innocent people to suffer?" Well, that certainly hit home. He perfectly summed up every investigator's worst fear. "I fucked up last night."

As much as she wanted to disagree with him, she would react the same way if the roles were reversed. Still, that didn't fix the immediate problem. He needed to snap out of his remorse-driven funk and focus.

"You think you're responsible, but you need to stop hogging all the blame. I see this going one of two ways. Either you guilt yourself into a coma, which will get me killed, or you'll become so overprotective that I'll have to kill you myself. Enough! You had your moment. Now, snap out of it. This"—she gestured at the right side of her face—"this will heal. So, let's do something constructive and figure out what the hell is going on. Okay?"

He stared at her slack-jawed. Tough love had its place. Finally, he blinked a few times and nodded. "You're right. When did you become so brilliant?" One by one, every emotion left his face until only his businesslike attitude remained. She went back to bandaging his hand, ignoring the rhetorical question. She was worried about him coming unhinged, but saying anything more would only make things worse.

"And for the record…" She peered up at the sound of his voice and saw a glint in his eyes. "I would kick your ass if you tried to kill me."

"Is that so?" Arching an eyebrow, she pressed the Band-Aid down on his hand with a little extra enthusiasm. A stifled yelp escaped as he jumped and yanked his hand back.

"God, you're evil." His attempt to appear pissed off failed, and he only succeeded in grinning like a bobcat.

After flipping him off, she slammed the first aid kit closed. "Now that you punished the door and your fist, I want to check out Duncan's office. Call me paranoid, but I'd rather you be in the room."

"So, you don't think I'll compromise the scene? It sounds like you're humoring me."

"I haven't seen much in the way of forensic evidence anyway. The blood trail isn't much, and now it's contaminated with…" She hesitated, letting it sink in. "With my blood." Rushing through the words was not only for her benefit but for his as well. "We need to find out what Duncan's been working on, and I could use some help."

"Speaking of help, we should board up that door. I brought down some plywood I found in the shed. Wouldn't want the place overrun with opossums."

"Or a raccoon. I hear people go after them with shotguns around here." The reference from their nightmare hotel finally coaxed a laugh out of him.

After patching up the door, they stared wide-eyed at Duncan's office. The room was below average size, but he utilized every square inch with tall oak furniture. Antiquated sketches, old maps, and medieval rubbings covered any wall space left. Hundreds of books centering on the dark ages sat haphazardly on the shelves. Surrounding them were novels on history, alchemy, and even some on superstitions and legends.

On the desk sat a newer collection on quantum physics, string theory, and herbal medicines with random papers strewn everywhere. Organized chaos. At least she hoped the mess held some mysterious structure. Of course, her mystery assailant probably ransacked the place or started to before she so rudely interrupted.

Once she slipped on her nitrile gloves, she flipped through the stack of papers on his desk. "Well, he sure had diverse research habits."

Chance shrugged and leaned against the doorframe, allowing him to watch her and keep an eye on the outer room. "Perhaps he just liked to read nonfiction."

One of the bigger drawers in the desk contained a dozen or so notebooks. She pulled them out and scanned a few of the handwritten pages. "No, he was researching something. These are full of notes." She stacked up the journals and gazed over at her aluminum case on the floor. "Hey, can you grab a large bag out of my kit? They're in the bottom center."

"This?" Frowning in confusion, he held up a folded brown paper bag. She quickly peeked up and nodded.

He stepped into the room far enough to slip the bag on the table before hastily retreating to his guard post. "Let me guess. You don't have enough funding, so you pick up supplies at Apple Tree Supermarkets?" The smug grin on his face typically made her flip him off. However, this was a hell of an improvement from his earlier attitude, and she was grateful for the return of conventional Chance, so she indulged him.

"Cute. To answer your question, no. The department issues these for most evidence collection. We only use plastic for air-sensitive things, like bloody clothes or anything with a liquid sample. Plastic contaminates evidence, and the restricted air movement can be damaging as well."

She didn't bother glancing up to gauge his reaction. Instead, she grabbed the brown paper bag and stuffed the notebooks inside. She knew this wasn't the mother lode her attacker was trying to find, but she was curious about her uncle's research.

"Hmm. Interesting." Kudo points for genuinely sounding intrigued. Typically, when she *nerded out* about work, people gave a deer-in-headlights look and quickly changed the subject. "So, real life isn't like CSI with everything in cool plastic bags sealed by fluorescent orange tape. Wow. I'm so disillusioned."

She glanced up and chuckled at the bewilderment on his face. "Aww. Did I shatter your sense of reality? If you think that blows your mind, I'll have to tell you about the famous *shocking a flat line* myth sometime."

"Wait. What?" The authentic surprise in his voice made her grin.

"Well..." She uncovered an old tape recorder and about a dozen cassette tapes amid the chaos on the desk. After shoving them into the bag with the notebooks, she continued. "When someone has no pulse and no heart rhythm, simply a flat line on the screen...what's the first thing they do besides CPR? And hand me the jar of white powder and the fluffy brush, please?"

After quickly rummaging around, he crossed the room to hand over the supplies. "They use the paddles and shock them. So..." She let him sit and ponder for a few seconds while dusting a light coat of powder over the deep oak.

"The screen shows the path of electricity in the heart. The *paddles*, which are now stickers, disrupt a bad electrical rhythm, hoping the heart will default back to a normal one. It cannot create electrical pathways. A flat line, asystole, is the complete absence of electricity in the heart muscle, a physical failure..."

"Holy crap. Those lying Hollywood bastards! You can't shock a rhythm that doesn't exist. You can't *jump-start* a heart. Is that what you're telling me?"

"Yep!" Lilith grinned at his quick uptake as well as his expression of absolute, world-bending astonishment. "The only option is to do CPR and give epinephrine while trying to reverse the cause of physical failure."

"Man... I'm questioning everything now." Deep in thought, he collapsed against the doorframe as she compared the few prints she found. All the same. Not surprising, but also not helpful.

Frustration began to nag at her, making the right side of her head hurt. There had to be something here. Assuming her attacker was also Duncan's, he had to be here for a reason. She needed to find it. "If I was a secret bit of ultra-incriminating evidence, where would I hide?" she mumbled to herself.

More than an hour passed as she went through every nook and cranny of the expansive desk that dominated the room. In her gut, she knew something vital had to be here. Her uncle spent most of his time in this one room. That much was clear. So, if a clue existed, this was where she'd find it.

When she opened the last drawer, things didn't appear quite right though she didn't understand why. In a desperate frenzy, she began pulling everything out, tossing it carelessly to the floor. Once empty, she inspected every inch, trying to work through the puzzle in her mind. What was bothering her? Then, her eye caught a dark smudge on the interior, right below the screws for the handle. She tilted forward to get a better look, and a jolt ran right through her bones. Faintly burned into the wood was a crude arrow. She saw the design before.

"Throw me the pocketknife."

Chance crossed the room to hand it to her. "I can't believe you told me to throw a knife at you."

After snatching the knife with a snort, she flipped it open and pried at the base along the corners. There had to be a false bottom, not only because the depth on the outside didn't match the interior but also because she needed to find something. Besides, the crude arrow couldn't be a coincidence. The same one mysteriously showed up at her apartment. Someone wanted her to find this, someone who got an envelope to her in New York without using the post office.

Finally, she caught the edge with the tips of her gloved fingers. A thrill of excitement ran through her as she popped it up with a small splintering sound. She stopped pulling and slid her slender gloved hand between the layers, feeling her way around until her fingers brushed over a thin container. Bull's-eye. "Give me a hand."

He rushed over and stared down inquisitively. "What do you need?"

Brimming with excitement, she motioned toward her hand. "I need you to pull back on the piece of wood. Give me enough room to get this out." Telling him to pull on gloves was pointless. There was no way her assailant would take the time to put everything back in place with meticulous care, which meant they hadn't found it.

"I could pull the whole thing out for you." He started forward, grabbing for the edge.

"No. Don't break it. I want to leave everything intact. And… phrasing." A Cheshire-cat grin curled her lips as he choked on a laugh. The thrill of finding a clue was a little intoxicating.

"Besides, if whatever's under here is as important as I think it is, I don't want anyone to know we have it. Maybe no one else would ever think to search under here. But I guarantee if anything is broken, people will realize something is missing. Until we understand what's going on, I don't want to make myself a bigger target."

He nodded and deftly pulled back on the panel with careful fingers. Thankfully the thin prefab sheet bent and didn't snap. As she pulled the box out, her glove rolled down, and the back of her hand scrapped sharply against the rough edge. She drew in a hissing breath and bit her lip as the treasure came free. Slowly, he lowered the piece back in place and tapped around the edges.

Pressing the hem of her t-shirt against her hand stopped the bleeding quickly. Thankfully, the abrasions were superficial. When she inspected the drawer, it appeared almost perfect. A few little dings along the side where she used the pocketknife were the only blemishes, but they wouldn't stand out. "Can you throw all that stuff back in for me?"

He stared at her hand while grabbing an armful of baubles off the floor. "You okay?"

"Just a few scratches."

With a satisfied nod, he began tossing the eclectic objects back where they belonged. Crystal vials, antique buttons, old Coca Cola tins, a china doll stained beyond recognition, a leather pouch of dice, four pairs of scissors, a few rusty hand tools, and the ever-popular ziplock bag of random batteries. "What the hell is with all this crap? This is like a mini edition of *Hoarders*."

"To conceal this." The six-inch square container was a faded motley of colors so chipped and scratched that she couldn't make out the design. "When looking for something important, you check places people will remember. No one recalls what they threw in the junk drawer. Plus, the clatter from all the bottles and whatnot would cover the sound."

"What do you mean by *cover the sound*?" His frown deepened while throwing the last few things inside.

"This was in a space much larger than needed with nothing to keep it from sliding around when someone opened or closed the drawer. If you opened something filled with papers and heard a metallic clink, you'd know something was up, right?"

He smiled and leaned against the desk, folding his arms over his chest. His body posture alone said volumes, impressed but defensive. He was holding on to something, a secret of some sort. She noticed it several times before, but she didn't have time to dig. In fact, she wasn't entirely sure she wanted to. "So, what's in the thing?" He lifted his chin toward the box in her hand.

"Only one way to find out." She flashed him a smile and pried at the tin box's rim. When the lid finally popped open, a musty smell filled the air. A myriad of small items lay inside, including tiny portrait paintings and several things wrapped in linen. Underneath those, she found a handful of parchment, some blank and some covered in ancient scrolling letters. She reached for the first covered item with delicate fingers, concentrating hard on being careful. The sudden thunder of a screaming voice made her jump in the chair, and she almost dropped the box.

"Lilith! Chance! Where are you?" Spencer's voice echoed down the stairs as she scrambled to keep all the contents inside.

"Office," Chance yelled back.

Leaping to her feet, she grabbed his shoulder with a stern resolve. "I want to keep this to ourselves until we know more, okay?" The gravity of her tone weighed down on him until he met her stare in a moment of genuine understanding. "I don't want to show our hand yet." She trusted Spencer, he was blood, but she didn't know what this thing was or why Duncan went to such extremes to hide it. Perhaps it had nothing to do with his disappearance. What if he were simply hiding stuff from his kids, things he'd rather they not see?

A smile stretched across his lips as he nodded in agreement. "Let me guess. Texas hold 'em?"

She tucked the thin box into the waist of her jeans and tugged down her bloodstained T-shirt. The dried blood sticking to her skin made the task far more difficult. "Do you study a smart-ass textbook or something?" With a laugh, she shoved at his shoulder. "I prefer spades anyway."

"Can't handle a real game of poker?"

She quirked one eyebrow at him with a playfully indignant snort. "Phrasing… So if money isn't involved, it's not real? You're on for a game. Now, I need a shower and a change of clothes before this shirt permanently adheres to my skin."

"Do you want me to grab your suitcase?" His grin melted into a smile that was soft and genuine.

"Thank you, but I can manage. I need to stow my case anyway. You might be able to find something out. I spent a lot of time with Miriah over the summers, but I was never close with Spencer."

"Well, now, that hurts my feelings." Spencer's Southern drawl was unmistakable. His voice would have been something girls dreamed about if it were a couple of octaves lower.

She blinked, astounded. If passing him on the street, she wouldn't recognize him with his disheveled sandy brown hair, rumpled clothing, and bloodshot eyes. Tremors coursed through him, and a frenzied panic pulled at the corners of his mouth. He was a lot thinner than she remembered, tall and lean, his clothes hanging off him. The painfully forced smile on his face made goose bumps fly over her flesh. He looked like a meth head on the verge of a breakdown.

Chapter 5

"Holy crap, Spencer. You look like hell." The words came flying out before she could stop herself. Chance stared at her wide-eyed and stayed the silently tactful one. Spencer's eyes narrowed, clearly saying, *How dare you judge me?* "Sorry. I… I know things are crazy." The tightening muscles in his face betrayed the barely chained anger waiting to burst out. "Are you okay?"

"No," he snapped the word through clenched teeth. Then he paused, releasing a slow breath. All the anger leaked away, leaving him exhausted. Before he could say anything else, a violent coughing fit doubled him over. After a few ragged breaths, he recovered enough to continue.

"Like you're one to talk. Your bodyguard said someone attacked you. I guess that explains the nasty gash, blood, and boarded-up door." After realizing his sarcastic tone might not be constructive, his gaze fell to the floor with a heavy sigh. "Sorry. I'm glad you're okay. Everything is so fucked." His red-rimmed eyes glistened with apologetic fear, but it was his trembling hands that caught her attention. His raw, bruised knuckles flexed as he rubbed at his temples, grimacing in pain.

Tension strummed through every fiber of her body with a sudden realization. He displayed all the classic signs. "Spencer…" She spoke as if trying to talk a jumper off a ledge, which wasn't much of a stretch. "Have you *eaten*?" She wasn't talking about a burger and fries at a rest stop, and most vampires understood the subtext.

Without looking at her, he shook his head. "Not in a few days."

Her eyes snapped up to see a worried expression dawning on Chance's face. Slowly, he stepped in front of her, guiding her behind him.

Going too long without feeding was a dangerous thing for a vampire. They had deficient hemoglobin levels, a protein that formed bonds to oxygen molecules and carried them through the body. When they didn't feed, the brain suffered from oxygen deprivation. This condition critically affected the ability to think, and caused massive headaches, coughing fits, and drastic mood swings, impairing control. In that state, they reverted to baser instincts and attacked.

"Hey. Why don't we heat some blood for you? I have a few units in the kitchen." Despite the concern in his eyes, Chance kept his voice casual.

Spencer nodded and wandered out of the room toward the stairs. She released the breath trapped in her lungs and dropped her forehead against Chance's back.

"Thank you, but you know if he snapped, I wouldn't be the one he came after." Taking her blood wouldn't solve Spencer's problem, but Chance, being a half-blood, naturally carried more of the protein in his bloodstream.

He didn't turn around, but she could hear the smile in his voice. "I can handle myself. My job is to keep you safe, remember? I'll take care of things and throw him in the general direction of a shower. All I ask is that you let me take him upstairs first. He's unstable, which isn't only due to his bad eating habits. If you think he won't attack you, you're wrong. He will lash out at anything he can create a reason to attack. You saw his hands, Lily."

A tear welled in her eye as she nodded. That wasn't the Spencer she watched grow up. Where was the quiet squirrely kid who always found someplace to hide away and draw? Today was the first time she witnessed him utter a single cuss word. This situation was wearing him down and fast.

Once Chance had her cousin sitting at the kitchen table with a warm mug, she crept out the front door and made her way to the car. While pulling out a fresh pair of jeans and a lavender T-shirt, the aluminum tin dug into her side. They didn't have the time or privacy to examine the contents, and until they did, she wanted to keep things under wraps. Spencer could be a target, and he didn't need a bigger bull's-eye on his back.

She needed someplace safe, someplace no one would search. That ruled out the bags, so she tugged them out of the trunk. A circular inspection of her surroundings helped her ensure no one was watching and gave her time to think. Nothing set off alarm bells. The only thing that stood out was the neighbor's flat tire on their orange SUV. That was it! In a moment of inspiration, she pulled open the hatch to the spare, unscrewed the lug, and slid the little box under the tire.

After meticulously putting everything back in place, she scooped up her clothes and jogged back into the house. The boys continued talking in the dining room, and to her surprise, they both sounded friendly. She stole a peek around the corner to see her cousin staring down into his mug. The slight nod of Chance's head as he spotted her indicated Spencer was doing much better. A weight lifted from her shoulders, and she breathed a sigh of relief as she crept back down the stairs.

Peeling off her blood-caked shirt proved difficult since the thing clung to her skin like tape. The divine bliss of the shower eased her stress right up until she stuck her head under the hot water. As soon as the powerful spray pelted against her bruised head, she flinched back so fast, she almost fell over. By the time she finished carefully washing her blood-crusted hair, the water was cold.

Lilith pulled on her clothes, and bravely faced the mirror with a small bottle of foundation. They would have to venture into the public eventually, and she couldn't walk around looking like the poster girl for domestic violence. The colors changed, the deeper purples receding into sickly yellows, greens, and browns. The gash in her forehead was practically closed but still tender as she removed the butterfly Band-Aids.

With slow, delicate fingers, she worked with the foundation, making the glaring bruise a mere shadow. She teased her copper curls down to cover most of the cut. After a final glance, she tossed her dirty clothes in the garbage and jogged up the stairs to join Chance and Spencer.

She breezed into the dining room and slipped into a chair between the two of them. Chance grinned, his eyes taking in her vastly improved appearance. "Well, well. You can hardly tell someone knocked you in the head." The slight undercurrent of guilt still tugged at the muscles around his mouth, but his tone stayed relaxed and cheerful.

She flashed him an appreciative smile and turned to her cousin. He still appeared homeless, but his skin had more color. A sullen calm replaced the menacing attitude from earlier without any of the tremors or coughing fits. Physically, he was better but emotionally still a wreck. He clung to the dark blue mug like it was a lifeline, preventing him from falling off the world.

"Have you slept at all?" She kept her voice soft and comforting, filled with a deep well of sympathy. First, someone abducts his father, leaving only an ominous blood trail. Now, he couldn't get a hold of Miriah. In his situation, the last thing she'd do is sleep. However, Spencer's ability to function was critical since they had little else to go on.

He glanced up, his eyes still bloodshot and full of misery. Tremendous guilt pulled at every muscle in his body. "How am I supposed to sleep? I should never have… You saw the blood. This is my family." His voice broke with the raw emotion shredding him from the inside. His wounded hands flexed, cracking the scabs as blood welled around them. Lilith reached out and patted his arm in genuine empathy.

"What happened to your hands?"

Spencer gazed down like he didn't recognize them. He flexed his hands again and stared at the seeping scabs while guilt and shame washed over his face. "I… I tend to punch things when I'm angry."

Concern tainted her smile as she nodded. The last thing she needed was both Chance and Spencer losing control. Still, she understood the impulse. "I'll do everything I can. Can you tell me what's been going on with you, Miriah, and your dad?"

Anger flashed across his face in an instant, eyebrows drawing together, lips narrowing. They gave a split-second warning that allowed her just enough time to duck as he threw the coffee mug across the room. He surged out of his chair, which clattered to the ground. The coffee cup shattered, leaving bloody remnants dripping down the wall.

"What the fuck is that supposed to mean?" He spat the venomous words as she jumped back. Chance moved with no hesitation. In one smooth motion, he yanked Lilith behind him and held his hands up in surrender.

"Whoa! Calm down. We are not the enemy, Spencer. She is trying to figure out what happened and why anyone would want to hurt the family. That's all."

She tried to move past Chance, but he dropped his hands and held her still. Trying to peek around his shoulder was easier said than done since her five-foot-nine was no match for his six-foot-three.

Tight-lipped, Spencer pulled his chair off the floor, slumped down into it, and leaned forward on his arms. "Christ. I'm sorry." His breaths came in quick huffs, but this time it wasn't due to low oxygen. Stress, coupled with a lack of sleep, had him on edge, exhausted. He rubbed his hands over his face and released a heavy sigh.

"Dammit. I haven't slept in three days, and I've done nothing but drive and make phone calls to find dead ends."

This time, she shoved Chance's hand away when he tried to stop her. "I'm sorry if that came out wrong. You should try to sleep. Chance and I found some research in the office. We can go through it while you rest."

Spencer opened his mouth to protest but then nodded. "You're right. I'm not doing anyone any good in this condition. I'll get some sleep. Then we can grab dinner and share what we've got." A forced smile stretched his thin lips, but at least he tried.

Spencer scanned Chance with a calculating stare in a typical testosterone-based fashion. "You move pretty fast for a half-blood." His eyes darted from Chance to her and back so fast that she almost thought she imagined it. "If you're as protective with Gregor, I can see why he keeps you around."

Chance nodded mutely, upholding the unspoken man etiquette to acknowledge compliments, even backhanded ones. That was the reason she didn't spend much time with Spencer growing up. As a kid, the few times he left the safety of his hermit hut, he came off as snobby and elitist. In a way, he began preparing for his job as an art dealer at an early age.

Spencer moved sluggishly from the chair without another word and stumbled through the kitchen to the small bedroom. Once the door closed, Chance whispered, "He's a real charmer."

"Spencer is exhausted and still recovering from withdrawal."

He turned and frowned down at her. "I hope so. If he's a raving lunatic going over the edge, he'll be more harm than help. Believe me. If that's the case, I'll lock him in the trunk."

"He's always been standoffish. Once he rests, I'm sure he can help."

Chance shrugged before clapping his hands together and rubbing them to announce the subject change. "Well…what about that box? Should we do some proper sleuthing?"

After careful consideration, she shook her head. "He could walk out of that room at any time. The tin must be significant since Duncan went to such extremes to keep it hidden. Somehow, I don't think Spencer knows it exists. Yes, Duncan may have lost his grip on reality, but if he didn't mention anything to Spencer, he had a reason. Besides, if the maniac that attacked me wants it, I don't need to put Spencer in any more danger than he already is."

Nodding thoughtfully, he ran a hand through his chestnut hair. Unmistakable frustration burned away his playful attitude, leaving a conflicted mass of anxiety. "Are your cases always like this? No evidence, no clues, nowhere to start looking?"

"Life is not a TV show drama that has one hour to wrap things up. Suspects don't appear with nifty red bows. However, I usually turn up more than this, but then I always start with a body. In this situation, we have no real forensics, no body, and no good intel. Since Duncan wasn't in close contact with New York, only three people may know what's going on. One is too tired and distraught to be any help right now, and the other two are missing."

"What about Miriah's husband, Malachi?"

"Okay, three are missing."

"So, what can we do while waiting to see if Spencer's cracked?" The need to do something productive itched under his skin. After all, he was a man of action. Of course, her plan wouldn't help much.

She glanced up from the table with a weak smile, fully conscious of what his response would be. "There's the massive number of journals and tapes I found in the office. Our mystery man left them, so I doubt they're crucial. They may not solve the case, but they might point us in a direction if we can figure out what Duncan's been doing." She shrugged at his disgusted frown. "Hey, we might get lucky. What if he hid something in plain sight? Finding a motive would be helpful."

"So, your answer is reading a bunch of old scribbled journals?" The left side of his nose creased, and she smiled, despite herself.

Resolutely, she pushed her chair back and tapped him on the shoulder as she passed by. "Come on. You can listen to the tapes if the big bad books scare you, tough guy."

Chance huffed and reluctantly followed her. "Yay, research." Definite sarcasm. "This is why I'm a bodyguard and not a cop."

"Well, lucky for you, you get the best of both worlds today."

Four hours later, Chance listened to the last tape while Lilith poured over the second notebook. The recordings hadn't revealed anything useful. They were Duncan's verbal notes on books he needed to buy, philosophies on medical treatments, and other scientifically interesting but otherwise useless information.

However, she found Duncan's written notes fascinating. Before this, the extent of her knowledge about her uncle consisted solely of him spearheading their medical initiatives. These pages held a gold mine of history and theory. The first one centered around his ideas on the rapid evolution of their species. He deduced that fangs were dwindling in size with the farther generations because of environmental adaptations. If correct, it meant their species was evolving thousands of times faster than any other.

Vampire fangs were composed of rigid cartilage that folded back to conform to the roof of the mouth. Much like a snake's, they stayed hidden until their jaw fully opened. The small puncture wounds they produced allowed them to acquire what they needed without being lethal. Nature wasn't in the business of mercy, but killing off the food supply was wasteful and illogical.

Far removed half-bloods, like Chance, barely had nubs, a useless nod to their heritage. Duncan believed this had more to do with the invention of tools than the purity of bloodlines. He cited confirming measurements from his first generation of children versus Miriah. Remarkably, a half-inch difference existed between them.

The second book began as a dry account of some historical families in medieval Scotland. Muddling her way through, she found a few references to an encoded text that kept his accumulated knowledge safe from prying eyes. He later removed several pages, the ones too dangerous despite the cipher, and put them in a safe place. Centuries ago, someone stole the book, which circulated through various hands, and then wound up in a museum. As much as he wanted it back, he couldn't walk in and say, "Hey, that's mine. Yeah, I wrote it about six hundred years ago."

Toward the end, she found several pages about Gregor and his family in fifteenth-century Scotland which made him much older than she thought. He never discussed his past, but she relished the opportunity to understand the life he'd lived till now. Unfortunately, the cryptic entries only consisted of Duncan's thoughts on events he never explained.

> *I still feel such pity for poor little Mary, the light of Gregor's eye. What happened to her was pure tragedy. I didn't believe Gregor would ever recover. Something changed in him that day. The day poor Mary passed on, followed shortly by the loss of his wife and other children. A man can only lose so much.*
>
> *All the years since, Gregor never took another family, not until he met Rosaline. Thank the maker*

> *for Rosaline and Lilith. They resurrected the man. The day Lilith came into this world was the happiest I have seen Gregor in centuries, and the man deserves some peace and brightness. I worry how much Lilith resembles Mary, but she is a centuries-old wound, and I worry too much for an old man.*

Duncan must have written this before her mother's death. Memories of Rosaline were bittersweet. A million times, she wished to take back all the hurtful things she'd said to her mother that fateful night. People assumed their parents would be around forever, that there would always be another day to make things right. Too many times, that was not the case.

Chance threw down his headphones, and Lilith jumped, startled out of her thoughts. "Dammit. None of this is useful. He keeps droning on and on and on about alchemical theories." He rubbed at his face and tapped his head against the wall while releasing an exasperated grunt. "Please tell me you're having better luck."

One side of her mouth lifted in a half smile. "They are fascinating, riveting, but not particularly useful."

"How many do you have left?"

She waved at the towering stack behind her. "Enough to keep me busy for the rest of the week." She flipped the next page, and there lay a small piece of torn parchment bearing the familiar arrow. With a thrill of excitement, she flipped it over to see faint markings appearing around her finger. Her eyes shot up to Chance, with sudden thoughts racing through her mind. "The tapes, most of them talked about alchemy?"

Chance pulled his head away from the wall and gazed at her, confused. "Uh, yeah. He was big into the stuff, I guess. Why?"

She stared down at the small piece of parchment, the marks disappearing as her finger pulled away. "Heat!" She grinned at him deliriously. "Do you have a lighter?"

He arched an eyebrow with a puzzled expression that bordered on disgust. "I don't smoke. What the hell are you talking about?"

She leaped to her feet and searched around desperately. "I need a lighter, a match, anything that'll make a flame." She rummaged violently through the drawers, slamming one closed and tearing open the next.

"Whoa. Hurricane Lilith, you want to clue me in?"

She growled in frustration and glanced up. "Alchemists are exceptionally secretive about their work…"

"Could have fooled me by the dozen tapes he recorded," Chance growled sarcastically.

She pinned him with an aggravated stare. "Not helpful. As I was saying, the thought of anyone stealing their secrets terrified Alchemists. So, they used codes, ciphers, and other ways of concealing their work. One effective way is a special ink that reacts to heat and acid. Heat alone will make the letters briefly appear, but smooth a little lemon juice over it first, and they won't disappear when the paper cools."

"Come on. You're kidding me. It's not more Hollywood bullshit?" A guarded frown pinched his face as he slowly stood up.

"It's real, but you won't find anything on the back of the Declaration of Independence, if that's what you mean. Go upstairs. Check the fridge for lemons. They have the highest acid content. Also, I need my green coat from the car and a lighter."

He smiled over at her, sharing a moment of pure excitement. This could give them a direction, a lead to chase. He disappeared through the door as she flipped the scrap over, smiling at the arrow. A couple of days ago, it felt as friendly as the reapers calling card, and now this was a symbol of hope. Strange how context changed everything.

By the time she had the desk cleared off except for a few swabs and the UV light, Chance rushed into the room.

"Why did you need your coat?" He handed it to her before setting the lemons and lighter on the desk.

She dug through the pockets and came up with the envelope. "This is why." She held it up next to the torn slip she'd found in the book. "Same arrow."

He frowned and stepped back against the wall. "Where did you get that?"

"While leaving my apartment to meet you and Gregor, the guard stopped me. Someone dropped this off at the security desk during the day. I forgot about it until we found the arrow inside the drawer."

"You got a cryptic envelope and forgot? Does that happen often? A typical Tuesday night in the life of Lilith?" Chance crossed his arms over his chest and watched her ambivalently.

Ignoring his icy stare, she laid each piece out delicately. Then she focused on cutting the lemons, soaking the swabs, and dragging them over the paper. When Chance cleared his throat, insisting on an answer, it interrupted her methodical work.

"Seriously? I shoved it in my pocket on the way out. In case you forgot, a lot has happened since then, my nasty head injury, for instance."

"Like I could forget." The pause stretched into a brooding awkwardness that he finally broke by returning to casual-Chance mode. "So, what's the verdict?"

She fanned the flame over the New York parchment, the heat slowly pulling letters to the surface. There was no mistaking Duncan's handwriting.

Lilith,

If you are reading this, then you are as brilliant as I always thought. Things are dire. I'm sending word to Gregor, but I'm unsure if my ruse will be successful. As hidden as this letter may be, I cannot take the chance it might be intercepted. So, I will only say that the past has come back for us.

Search for my mark, and it will lead you to what you need. My dear niece, I will pray for you. I know that Gregor will send you, and only you, to my rescue if anything happens to me. I wish I could prevent that because, by then, I will be beyond help and will only drag you down with me. Gregor will lose everything again, and I shall join him in that fate. Perhaps we deserve it.

—Duncan

Lilith swallowed the lump in her throat. She felt as if all the blood drained from her body as she stared hopelessly at the letter. Duncan knew what was coming and tried to warn her against traveling to Tennessee. "This is not good." Her voice sounded haunted. She showed Chance the letter and watched him pale.

Her mind whirled through the cryptic words. The letter held an ominous, desperate plea but was devoid of any information except hints about the past and Gregor. *Perhaps we deserve it* kept repeating eerily in her head. How could they deserve to lose everything? None of it made sense. Could this be the ravings of a man losing his tenuous grip on reality?

"Let's hope the other piece is more specific. So far, I'm not feeling better about any of this." The disturbed tone of his voice echoed the chill creeping into her bones. She gave the same careful attention to the torn paper, praying he was right.

I have tracked down a series of properties here in Tennessee. I am not sure what he is up to, but it cannot be good. Somehow, he purchased the Phipps Bend property from Surgoinsville County. What could he want with this place?

I have consulted Miriah since she is now invaluable to me. I've devoted more and more time to my research, leaving her to take over my responsibilities within the family. I must send word to Gregor, but I need to know more first.

It is harder and harder for me to keep my focus. These notes are dangerous, but I need them. I believe I may be losing my grip on the present.

Perhaps my obsession with the past has disconnected me. I only hope that Miriah and M—

The torn parchment abruptly ended Duncan's thoughts of the future. Gregor mentioned her uncle becoming more reclusive, but she doubted he understood the extent of his brother's despair. Her poor uncle. With a heavy heart, she handed the page off to Chance. "He sounds so sad, like his entire life is coming to an end."

The slight upturn of his chin as he read through the journal entry said volumes. He picked up on the sorrow in the note as well, and something deep down echoed those feelings.

"I should leave Gregor a message," she whispered as she dug the phone out of her pocket. The message light flashed a brilliant blue. A few clicks later, she was glancing over the report from Alvarez on a homicide. She forgot his request to consult on the case, which was violent, judging by the transcript. An unknown assailant tortured the victim for several hours with no ID found on the scene and no forensic updates. A compelling case, but she had more important things to deal with right now.

Just as she was about to close the email, something caught her eye, and she stopped breathing. She recognized the address. The Italian restaurant where she'd met Gregor. Someone discovered the body at the end of its terrifying alley. She frantically searched for the time of death, and when she found it, her heart pounded in her chest. Time of death was always tricky to determine, but the window of opportunity fit. Quite possibly, she'd heard the victim's torture while arriving at the old restaurant. A sudden wave of nausea left her cold and clammy.

She flipped over to the crime scene photos and squinted at them. Blood splattered every surface, and dark pools soaked into the cracked concrete. Hundreds of cuts and bruises covered the body, and the right arm bent at an impossible angle. Lifeless eyes stared out at her from the next photo, and her heart froze. She dropped the phone and recoiled as if death might infect her on contact.

Chance surged forward, looking her over carefully before bending down to grab the phone. "What's wrong? Do you know him?"

Tears stung her eyes as a million thoughts raced through her mind. "Oh my god. This is fucked, completely fucked. I have to call Alvarez."

Chance frowned and peered closer at the photo. "Lily, who is this?"

Ignoring him, she grabbed her phone and dialed her partner. He didn't pick up until the fourth ring.

"It's Lilith. Yeah, that case you sent… I have an ID for you." Her eyes found Chance, knowing she couldn't hide her sadness and despair. "Malachi Sanders… Yes, Miriah's husband. Do me a favor. Go over to Gregor's and tell him in person."

His mouth hung open in horrified shock as she tucked her phone away. "Holy shit." He fell back against the desk as if someone hit him. Things weren't getting better, which was a definite understatement.

Chapter 6

"Why the hell is Malachi in New York City?" Chance stalked the room back and forth like a caged lion, a barely restrained powder keg of tension writhing through every muscle.

Lilith slumped in the chair, trying to make sense of things but failing miserably. "I don't know…but someone tortured him less than fifty feet from where I stood, Chance." Her haunting words hung ominously in the air as she stared sightlessly across the room. The same two things kept repeating through her mind: Malachi's lifeless eyes and the flesh-rending sounds from the alley. The vicious cycle of swirling thoughts made her stomach churn violently.

"Alvarez is going to send the autopsy report as soon as possible, but that won't be for another day or two. If Miriah was with him…" She couldn't finish that sentence. Leaning forward, she buried her face in her hands, trying to force her brain to work.

"No. Spencer sent her to pick us up at the airport. She couldn't be in New York. Perhaps Duncan sent him? That might explain how the cryptic letter arrived. But why didn't Malachi stay there and wait for me? Why drop the note and run?"

A warm hand touched her shoulder as her shaking breaths threatened to release a flood of tears. For a moment, she didn't move. Instead, she focused on keeping the sorrow at bay. It wasn't only Malachi's horrific death. The way he died reminded her too much of her mother's brutal attack. Everything cascaded down like an avalanche overwhelming her.

"Lily." The tenderness of his voice was so inviting. She wanted to wrap it around her and escape the world. She looked up to see him kneeling in front of her. Both his hands caressed her arms, his eyes full of worry. "I know you think the world is falling apart, and perhaps you're right, but I need you to keep it together." She wanted to be angry, scream at him for being selfish, but she only stared.

Fingers brushed a stray hair from her face, making her heart pound like a drum. "You are amazingly brilliant, and you are the best chance to find Duncan and Miriah alive." Despite her best efforts to keep from breaking down, her lip trembled as tears filled her eyes. She sprung forward and wrapped her arms around him so fast that he released a surprised grunt. His stiff arms slowly folded around her, and for one selfish moment, the warmth melted everything away.

When she finally pulled back, her focus began to return. Distantly, she recognized the sound of Chance moving away as she wiped her face and took in several deep breaths. Once her nerves settled, she glanced up to find him leaning against the doorframe, staring out into the basement. Frowning at his back, she suddenly realized that hugging her bodyguard might be unprofessional.

"I'm sorry if I crossed a line." Having to apologize to his back made her feel a little wounded. Things had been so comfortable and casual, and now a stagnant vacuum encompassed the room. When he refused to respond, a sudden surge of unreasonable anger clenched her fists.

"Fine. Never hug your bodyguard. Now I know the rule." She snapped the words and began clearing off the desk as her mind bounced all over the place, out of balance.

She heard Chance cross the room but pointedly ignored him as she threw things haphazardly in her case. "Lily." He sounded more tired than upset, which only inflamed her rage. The target of that temper was uncertain. Was she mad at him, herself, or the world that slaughtered Malachi?

"Lilith." Still refusing to acknowledge his existence, he grabbed her arm and tugged her away from the desk.

"Dammit, Lily." Every micro-expression of pain haunted his soft chiseled face and red-rimmed eyes. "I am here to do a job. I can't let my feelings get in the way of that. I need to keep you safe. That is my sworn duty. Gregor trusts me, and I won't let him down or you. He sent me, specifically, because of that reason."

She tugged her arm away from him and stepped back as her mind stuttered. Why the hell was she so furious? She felt disconnected from the emotions controlling her body, watching everything happen but powerless to stop it.

"I understand. You work for my dad. Nothing personal." The words rang with malice, and she instantly regretted every one of them as he hung his head. The illogical wrath inside her cut him deep and now appeared sated, slinking away, and leaving her back in control.

"Chance…" Her voice came out like an unsteady whisper. "I am so sorry… I didn't mean…"

The sound of laughter startled her. When his head rose to meet her stare, his bloodshot eyes still glistened. "Nothing personal?" The laughter increased to a fevered pitch as he shook his head. His hand ran through his hair as he turned away, walking toward the door. Abruptly, he stopped, turned back with a determined scowl, and walked right up to her.

"Did you listen to a word I said? Gregor sent *me* with you, not Timothy or Ray, for a reason."

"You're his head of security, and he trusts you?" The words began as a firm statement but ended as an uncertain question.

"No. It is *entirely* personal, Lily. That's why I can't do this."

"Do what?" Her head tilted as she frowned at him, trying to figure out what the hell he was saying.

He released an exasperated huff. "You remember that tattoo you kept harassing me about?" Anger surged in his voice, but she didn't understand the connection. "I got it as soon as I turned eighteen. Any idea what it is?"

She shook her head without saying a word.

"I planned to make it a surprise, but when I talked to Gregor, he went ballistic. So, I buried everything, kept it all to myself."

Lilith frowned and took another step back. Confusion and fear clouded her mind as she tried to find her voice. "What is the tattoo?"

Chance clenched his jaw and stared down at the desk for a moment. When his eyes snapped back to her, they held a mixture of pain and anger. "A lily."

The words left her flabbergasted, knocking all the air out of her lungs. Before she could compose herself, Chance stalked through the door. "I'll wait for you upstairs. We should get some work done." His flat voice echoed, and seconds later, she heard him stomping up the steps.

Lilith dropped into the chair, reeling, and disconnected. Rubbing her temples, she tried to organize recent events. Someone abducted Duncan and possibly Miriah. Malachi died at the hands of a madman in New York City. Spencer might be insane. She came close to dying of a massive head wound. Now Chance revealed he got a tattoo for her over a decade ago as some grand gesture. She burst out laughing. "Holy hell. All this sounds like a damn soap opera." Still a little shaky, she pushed out of the chair.

Ultimately, Chance was right. With so much riding on the line, the last thing they had time for was personal crap. Still, a warmth glowed in the pit of her stomach. Certain moments on the trip stood out, but she immediately dismissed them. Chance never dated women longer than a week. He never played head games and clearly stated his lack of interest in anything serious. The thought never occurred to her that he might have a reason why.

She needed to get her head back into the game, not reevaluate her love life. So, what was the next step? What leads did they have left? Miriah's apartment in Knoxville might turn up something since Duncan entrusted her with a lot. The property mentioned in his note was another possibility. She could research the place online or head to the county records office, perhaps get lucky and find a name.

When she made her way upstairs, she found Chance staring out the dining room window with his arm against the frame. Standing there, he embodied the isolation she'd noticed in his home and the artwork hanging on its walls. No one knew him. He made sure of that.

Clearing her throat, she watched his spine stiffen as his head dropped to one side. The movements indicated a willingness to listen but not to turn around.

"You're right. There is work to do." She fought against the nervousness rising in her stomach. "Thank you for snapping me out of it. I had no right to be so cruel to you, but I couldn't stop myself. You did nothing wrong, Chance."

Inch by inch, he relaxed and finally turned toward her. As soon as she saw his face, she continued. "However..." His eyes widened as he froze with a deep-down fear. "Do not think for one damn second we aren't having a long discussion about this tattoo thing later. I understand why you need to clear the air, but this is not the most convenient time." She flashed a soft smile at him that instantly eased the terror in his face. Over a decade was a long time to keep a secret buried, which explained the mood swings and defensive behavior.

While contemplating whether to drop the subject, she slipped on her coat, pulling her auburn curls out of the collar. She glanced up at him with an amused grin. "Seriously, though, a lily?"

He laughed, but she saw the vibrant blush on his cheeks. "Yeah, well, you know what they say about best-laid plans."

"Second-guessing that right about now, aren't you?" She chuckled and reached for the forensics kit, thankful that they could still laugh.

"Actually..." He smirked and grabbed the heavy bag of journals. His green-flecked eyes caught hers, sending a shiver up her arms. "Not for a second." A soft genuine smile lit his face, full of everything but promising nothing.

Before her brain could analyze his words, Chance shifted the conversation. "So, boss lady, what's the plan?"

"Well, I don't want to wake Spencer, considering how unstable he is. I found the address to Malachi and Miriah's place in the office. We could head up to Knoxville and poke around. The drive should take about forty-five minutes, I think."

He peeked down at his watch and nodded. "If we leave now, we can miss rush hour traffic. Let's hit the road."

They managed to limit the conversation to theories on the case and avoided any mention of tattoos, thankfully. With so much to process, throwing that into the mix would overwhelm her. The mere thought of someone holding a decade-long torch for her was terrifying.

"Miriah's an accountant, and Malachi's a real estate agent?" Chance frowned in distaste at the four-story condos masquerading as British cottages.

Lilith nodded. "Yeah, they own their businesses, which, according to Gregor, are moderately successful." They kept using the present tense, talking about Malachi as if he were still alive. Her subconscious refused to acknowledge his death because he suffered more than anyone should endure.

Chance's voice shook her from the morbid thoughts. "Why not buy a house? I mean, this is a gorgeous place and all, but if money isn't a problem, why live here?"

She shrugged and started up the front walkway. "They hate yard work? They like having neighbors?"

He shook his head, baffled by the idea someone would choose to live in a boxy condo if they had other options. The thought never occurred to her. She lived her whole life in apartments, except for that regrettable six months in college.

"Oh, come on now. Your place is a loft apartment hidden inside a warehouse. I didn't see a yard unless you count the black mold as foliage."

His eyes narrowed at her smug grin. "My nonexistent love of landscaping isn't what makes a home more appealing. It's the absence of loud, nosy neighbors."

"Well, you went to the extreme on that one. Go big or go home? Your only neighbors are the drunk vagrants that you shoo away from the bottom floor."

This time his frown deepened beyond the realm of playful. "I like my space, and I take precautions. There aren't homeless people living on my property. Thank you very much."

Lilith chuckled and bumped his shoulder with hers. "Touchy."

Reluctantly, he returned the shoulder bump as his wounded pride took a back seat to a smart-ass smile. "Keep it up, princess, and I'll make you brave the whole bottom floor…at night…with a bottle of booze as bait."

"You wouldn't." She feigned a dramatic gasp.

He turned to her with a sly grin, holding a twinkle of mischief. "Oh, don't tempt me." The playful wink sent tiny shivers over her skin. "Now, why don't we check out that apartment?"

"Only one problem." She peered through the glass door leading to the inside stairs. "We don't have a key." She scowled as if that would scare the door into magically opening. Using her lockpick gun could prove problematic. If anyone walked by, they would be in big trouble. Ending up in jail for breaking and entering was the last thing they needed.

"Leave this to me, Lily." He stepped up to the bank of buzzers and pressed the button for the apartment across from Miriah's.

Seconds later, an older woman's voice crackled through the speaker. "Hello?"

While holding down the button, he smiled brightly at Lilith. "Hello, ma'am. My name is Allen, and I'm with Miriah's cousin. We drove down from New York City to visit her and Malachi, but they aren't answering. They gave us a key to the apartment, but they forgot to give us one to the outside door."

"Oh, but of course! How lovely of you. I'll buzz you right in." She sounded ninety years old, although the crackling speaker distorted the voice too much to be sure. He turned, flashing a brilliant grin, and tipped his invisible hat. The buzz sounded, and he swung the door open for her. "After you, m'lady."

"Why, thank you, *Allen*." With a soft laugh, she breezed through the door and started up the stairs. When they reached the third-floor landing, a woman stepped out of the apartment on the left. Plump wrinkles creased around her eyes and mouth as she smiled, revealing a long history of happy days. Lilith placed her age somewhere between seventy and ninety, not far off from her earlier estimation. The woman shuffled closer, wearing a white housecoat covered in tiny blue roses that matched the slippers on her feet and her thinning hair.

Chance stepped forward and beamed at her. "I'm Allen. So wonderful to meet such a helpful neighbor."

"My pleasure, dear." She patted his cheek with a gnarled hand and then glanced over at Lilith.

"Forgive my manners." Not missing a beat, he pulled Lilith over to him, his arm possessively hugging her waist. "This is my fiancée, Lily, Miriah's cousin."

The sweet old woman brightened and turned her smile on Lilith, who quickly shook off her startled expression. "What a beautiful name." Her tired eyes drifted back to Chance. "My name is Ida McCleary. Miriah and Malachi have been my neighbors for quite some time. You certainly seem like a sweet couple. I'm glad they have some *good* family."

The emphasis on her last statement made Lilith stop. "How do you mean?"

Ida peered up, surprised and a little embarrassed. "Oh, I don't mean any offense, dear. I'm an old-fashioned woman. I don't think a man should fight so much with his sister."

"You mean Spencer?"

The woman nodded. "I believe sibling squabbles should stay out of the hall." This time her nod was more of an exclamation point. "Family business should stay in the family. Ah, but listen to me, going on and on. I'm sure you two are tired. If you need anything else, please don't hesitate." With that well-worn smile stretching the wrinkles in her face, she turned and shuffled back into her apartment.

When safely inside the Sanderses' apartment, Lilith leaned against the door and chuckled, "Okay, bizarre doesn't cover it. Allen?"

He peeked back at her for a moment. "That's my middle name, so technically not a lie." He began scanning the apartment for security threats.

"Chance *Allen* Deveraux? I pictured something more exotic like Xavier or Gambit or something."

"What am I, part of the X-Men? It's after my dad." The sharp tone resonating in his last words made it clear that discussing family was off-limits.

"And fiancée? I mean…a bit fast, don't you think?"

A sly grin curled his lips. "Well, why else would a girl bring a guy over to her cousin's place? Could you imagine Ida's face if I told her the truth? I figured we should play a more traditional role for the locals. To be safe." He disappeared into the living room before she could respond.

Black-and-white pictures from various countries in simple black frames covered the hallway. As she walked past them, she recognized a few from Japan, Germany, and Italy before the hall opened into a surprisingly spacious living room.

She quickly realized Miriah shared her father's hatred of bare walls as the myriad of frames continued. Most displayed images of her and Malachi, including their wedding photos, vacation pictures, and random candid shots. An eerie sadness settled over her shoulders as she browsed the smiling pictures, knowing Malachi was lying on a slab, and Miriah was missing. No matter what happened now, they would never take another happy photo together.

Low simplistic furniture gave the room an Asian feel, which blended with the miniature kimonos and bamboo paintings over the couch. A curio of Japanese dolls sat on the mantle above a slate rock fireplace with a gas insert. Miriah never talked about Japan or the Orient, so this had to be Malachi's influence on decorating.

Chance wandered off down a narrow hall as she opened the first door, which led to the master bedroom. An artful blend of mahogany and delicate blue made the room sophisticated but not overly masculine or feminine. She pulled open a drawer in an espresso-colored nightstand and frowned at the odd contents. A mottled mixture of pills, hotel shampoos, razors, and small personal items littered the inside as if someone carelessly dumped them in the drawer. Of course, her job didn't include judging the organizational skills of others.

The nightstand on the opposite side of the bed held various things Lilith wished she could unsee. It appeared Miriah strongly believed in the electronic age, something she did *not* need to know about her cousin's private life.

After flipping a light switch, she opened the door to an OCD dream. There was a walk-in closet with no clothes on the ground, no junk on the top shelf, and no boxes littering the corners. A small suitcase sat to the left of the door with a beautiful collection of shoes laid perfectly straight along the right wall. She glanced along the twin rows of crisply ironed clothes, all organized by color, and noticed a few items crumpled with deep wrinkles. Odd.

"Chance?" She peeked out into the empty hall and opened the next door, which revealed a clean and spacious bathroom. Moving on to the last room, she found Chance standing over a desk, shuffling through papers. "You find anything interesting?"

"A bunch of accounting paperwork. Miriah's been dealing with all the family finances, plus her normal work."

She grabbed a few pages and peered over the Excel spreadsheets, whistling as her eyes scanned the page. "Wow. A whole lot of accounts. Everything from real estate to medical research."

"What about you? Find anything?" He left her to deal with the paperwork and walked over to the shelves filled with a random collection of books and knickknacks.

"No." The clothes still nagged at her. "Except… It's probably nothing, but a few outfits are wrinkled all to hell, hanging in their insanely clean and organized closet."

He opened his mouth to say something when his cell phone rang. Shrugging at the number, he answered and walked toward the door. "How are you feeling, Spence?"

She took a seat at the desk and went through the drawers while listening to Chance's side of the conversation.

"Good. I'm glad to hear it… Nah, we are up at Miriah's place, poking around… Don't apologize, Spence. We didn't want to wake you… I don't think Miriah's neighbor likes you very much." He laughed wholeheartedly at some witty response, which was a relief. He sounded stable, and hopefully, he could stay that way. "Well, sure. Of course. Okay. See you then."

After hanging up, he turned to Lilith with a half smile. “Man, he hates the *old bat* living across from Miriah, which I assume is Ida. Anyway, he’s meeting us here in about an hour. I figured we should tell him about Malachi in person.”

“You’re right, and perhaps he can shed some light on all this. If Miriah kept anything here for Duncan, he might at least know where to look. All I know so far are three things.” She ticked each item off on her fingers as she spoke. “One, Malachi loves Asian culture. Two, they are meticulous about cleaning but not about what they dump in nightstand drawers. And three, Miriah must stockpile batteries somewhere.”

Chance glanced up at that last bit. “Do I want to know?”

Lilith flashed a quick awkward smile. “I doubt it.”

Silence settled in while they both continued the search until Chance changed the subject. “You know what I don’t get? Why do you think he only mentioned Miriah in the letter and not Spencer?” As Chance thought out loud, he leafed through a book with glossy pictures of some ancient text.

“Miriah has always been the more responsible one. Accountant versus art appraiser. The duties he passed on to Miriah required her mathematical skills. I suppose he didn’t have much for an art appraiser to do.”

“Hmm, makes sense, I suppose.” He didn’t sound 100 percent convinced but didn’t elaborate on his doubts, content to continue thumbing through the book in his hands.

“What are you reading?” While squinting at the cover, she closed the overly organized drawer of office supplies and reached for the next one.

“A pictorial of a famous book, known as the Voyruich Manuscript. It’s one of the oldest texts in known history but a total enigma. I saw an exhibit at Yale’s Beinecke Rare Book and Manuscript Library a few years back. Fascinating piece.”

Lilith arched an eyebrow and stared at him like he’d grown a second head. He glanced up in time to catch her expression and scowled. After flipping his middle finger in her general direction, he returned his attention to the hardcover.

"Just because I'm a bodyguard doesn't mean I'm mindless. I happen to appreciate history." When she still said nothing, he sighed heavily and continued. "Plus, Gregor took a tour of the Yale Museum a few years ago. He loves puzzles, especially the one in this manuscript."

She chuckled while combing through some more papers in a file drawer. "Ah. The truth finally comes out. Interest by proximity."

Deciding her retort wasn't worth responding to, they continued the investigation in silence. Chance kept himself entertained with various books detailing the Voyruich Manuscript. Meanwhile, she found nothing but reports on personal finances and investments. A gold mine if she wanted to conduct an audit, but otherwise, useless.

"You guys still here?" Spencer's voice came from the front hall.

"Yeah, back here in the office." After shelving the book in his hands, he gracefully hopped up from the floor.

When Spencer peeked into the room, he glanced up at Chance, who towered over him by a good nine inches. He still appeared vaguely homeless, but his eyes were clear and sharp.

"You guys find anything here?" He stared at them both anxiously. The hopeful expectation on his face made telling the truth about Malachi more unbearable.

"Why don't we go out to the dining room and talk? I'd like to hear things from your view. The most insignificant, mundane things can end up being important. Plus, there is news from New York we need to tell you." She busied herself with placing items on the desk in their proper places, keeping her eyes down and rushing through the last sentence.

"Sure." He sounded uncertain, which she could understand. His mind already dreaded the worst, and her cryptic words didn't help his anxiety level.

Lilith and Chance took one side of the table, and Spencer sat across from them. Neither of them wanted to rush into things, so they waited for him to start. While he stared around the room, she noticed his blue eyes sat closer to his thin nose than his sister's, pushing him from handsome to beady-eyed.

He pulled a photograph off the wall and stared down at the image of Duncan, the unlucky couple, and himself. His mouth tightened in a guarded line with darker things lingering below the surface, not surprising given his situation.

"I haven't been close to Dad in a long time." His voice came out flat as he ran his long fingers over the glass. "Dad's been so damn preoccupied with his pet projects. He dumped the business on Miriah and Malachi and humors me with dinner now and then."

"When did he hand the business over?" She started small to avoid triggering the defensive aggression he displayed earlier.

Rubbing his stubbly chin, he frowned in thought. "A few years back, right before he became obsessed with true crime stories. He freaked out over some reporter's death, but I can't remember his name. After that, he dove into research, spending a little more time at the Madisonville house. At first, a few days every couple of months, then every month, then weekends." He sighed heavily, placing the frame on the table and finally meeting their eyes. "This is the first time he's left that damn house in six months."

"So, you don't know what he was working on?"

Meeting her steady gaze, he huffed out a short chuckle. "I evaluate art, which is the limit of my usefulness to him. If Dad had a question about paintings, he came to me, which never happened. If he had questions about anything else, he went to Miriah."

The subtle contempt that pulled at his lips almost surprised her, but then what family didn't have inner struggle?

"Gregor said you and Miriah went to the Madisonville house for dinner that night?"

He slumped back farther into the chair and draped one arm over the back. "Miriah's idea. She wanted to keep the whole family vibe going. She thought that would help Dad. He forgot things, important things. If he were human, I'd say he had Alzheimer's."

"Was Malachi with Miriah?"

His eyes snapped up in confusion before drifting back to the photo on the table. "No, he left on some trip. I didn't ask where. Malachi and I weren't exactly friends. When Miriah and I showed up, Dad wasn't home, so we waited for him. We ended up crashing in the guest room upstairs. In the morning, he still hadn't returned, and we knew something must be wrong. Miriah found some drops of blood down by the office and freaked."

"Yeah, I saw those." She thought back to the bedroom, which appeared untouched. But then, considering Miriah's precise personality, she probably made sure the room was picture-perfect before leaving. Frequently, cleaning and organizing masqueraded as coping mechanisms to deal with extreme stress.

Ignoring her words, he continued as various emotions flickered across his face. "Miriah drove back to her office while I checked out Dad's place in Knoxville. I called Gregor when I didn't find anything. Then the other day, early in the morning, Miriah asked me to check into a warehouse outside of Nashville. Something she started checking into for Dad, I guess. When I told her about you coming down, she volunteered to meet you guys at the airport and drive you to Madisonville. That's the last I heard from her."

"What did you find at the warehouse?" Lilith glanced over to see Chance studying him, ready to latch on to the first whisper of a lead they'd come across.

After running both hands through his hair, Spencer rubbed at the back of his neck. "Dead end. Only a dank building abandoned for years. I was furious with Miriah until I realized she never showed up at the airport. If I stayed… If I didn't leave her… This is all my damn fault." The frustration still lingered on his face, blurred by a pang of regret.

"Any idea why Malachi would be in New York City?"

With no pretense of surprise, Spencer slowly turned his stare on her. After a few seconds, it melted into an indifferent frown as he shrugged. "Is that where he is? Probably some real estate thing. He's always running off somewhere, leaving Miriah alone." Spencer never made his dislike of Malachi a secret, not even at their wedding.

"He's dead, Spence," Chance spoke up with a pointed glance at Lilith. Guess he didn't want her to drag things out.

Spencer's face crumpled and went blank, staring sightlessly past Chance and Lilith. At some point, people lost the ability to be surprised, conditioned by the torrent of awful events. She couldn't read anything at all in his face, but perhaps there was too much to decipher. "How?"

"Someone tortured him as a warning or a message, I think. The one thing I am sure of is that it's connected to whatever is going on down here. The timing makes mere coincidence impossible." Lilith kept her voice neutral, scared of Spencer turning on her. Except for a briefly clenched jaw, he remained perfectly still.

Spencer shook his head and grunted, leaning back in his chair. "This is insane. Malachi… Lord knows I didn't like the man, but…" His eyes drifted to the ceiling, and he ran his hand through his hair again, trying to work through his frustration. Then he fell into silence, closing his eyes and taking deep, purposeful breaths.

"Have you found *anything* since arriving?" Animosity seeped back into his voice. As Chance stiffened beside her, she realized she wasn't the only one who noticed.

"Honestly, not much more than vague references. One note I found said Miriah started helping him with research. I didn't find anything here. Any chance she kept stuff at her office? Or Malachi's?"

He scratched at his shoulder and let out an aggravated sigh. "I wouldn't know. I haven't set foot in either one. Hell, it's been a few weeks since I've been here at the apartment. Miriah and I… We disagreed a lot. The usual family stuff. She kept wanting me to do more and then got mad whenever I tried to help out." The nervous energy itched under his skin as his eyes drifted back to the family photo in front of him. She could understand that. He wanted to find his dad and sister, even if they didn't always get along.

"Why don't we split up and search the offices? Perhaps we can find something useful?" Her voice was too high and sweet as if talking down a kid verging on a tantrum.

Spencer didn't miss the condescending tone. He cocked his head to one side and stared at her for a moment. His already thin lips stretched into a forced smile that made her skin crawl. "Sure thing. Do we get walkie-talkies and secret spy names too? What about matching trench coats and decoder rings? I'm not some five-year-old you need to coddle. If you want to talk to me, do it like an adult." His lip curled in a sneer full of old wounds. "You want to help so bad? Find my damn family instead of trying to play therapist. Otherwise, you're wasting my fucking time."

Before she could wipe the startled look off her face, Chance hopped off the chair, his hands gripping the table aggressively. "You are an ungrateful prick. Look, I know you're going through a lot, but stop the attitude. We are here to help. So, if all you want to share are snide remarks, keep your mouth shut."

Spencer's eyes widened in surprise but quickly hardened into an icy stare. An amused glint lit his face while he stared down Chance as if past the point of caring. "What are you going to do, half-blood?" With nothing to lose, why not pick a fight with the biggest guy in the room?

In a split second, Chance sped to the other side of the table, grabbing the front of Spencer's shirt and hauling him closer. "You want to find your dad and sister? Stop being a dick and let us help." With a disgusted look, he shoved Spencer in the chair and stalked back to his seat.

The men locked eyes with equal contempt for an intense moment, and then Spencer finally dropped his head, conceding. He stared down at the table, his disheveled hair hiding his face.

"You're right." His voice trembled as he pulled in a shaking breath that rattled his shoulders. "I'm so tired of chasing dead ends. I've been fighting with Dad and Miriah, and because of that, I'm not any help. I shouldn't be taking my anger out on you."

He slammed his fists down on the table, making Lilith jump in her chair. "I'm tired, so damn tired of being useless!"

Making a conscious effort to be more careful this time, she spoke in a calm and casual tone. "Then help us."

"Sorry. I know you guys are trying to help, and I can't blame you because we don't have any leads." Spencer's mouth quirked into an awkward smile like someone trying it for the first time.

"All right. Do you know where your sister kept the keys? Using one would be easier and less suspicious than picking the lock."

"Yeah. I'll take Malachi's office. I know more about real estate than accounting. I'll grab the keys." He slid out of the chair, staring at the floor like a kicked puppy. A few minutes later, he returned with two key rings, one of which he tossed to Chance. "Meet back here in two hours?"

Chance and Lilith shared a look and then nodded at Spencer. "Sure, buddy. Sorry about the tough love, but you need to stay in control and stop blaming people. Especially the ones that are trying to help you."

One side of Spencer's mouth came up in an unattractive smile that appeared almost smug. However, she couldn't be sure with the mangled mess of visible emotions on his face. "You gotta do what you gotta do. You guys head out. I'm going to grab a quick shower and borrow some of Malachi's clothes. I'm sure he won't mind if..." Spencer abruptly stopped as he thought back over his words. Slumping his shoulders, he waved them to the hallway. "Anyway, happy hunting."

Chapter 7

Chance and Lilith squeezed into the tiny rental car and started toward Miriah's accounting office. The tail end of evening rush hour left the traffic heading downtown sparse. The handful of shops and bars didn't illustrate much of a thriving nightlife. However, people here obeyed general traffic laws like red meant stop, unlike the city she called home.

"Spencer harbors a lot of resentment." Chance stared out the windshield, dodging slower cars as he sped down the road.

Lilith shrugged into her seat. "Families are complicated. He may feel left out, but I can tell he wants to find them."

"Trust me. I'm all too aware of how complicated families can be, but Duncan is a good man, a good father." A flicker of emotion crossed his face briefly, displaying his intimate knowledge of how bad a father could be. "I still don't like his attitude. If he doesn't stop lashing out, I'll put him through a wall. Not slapping the smug look off his face took all my restraint."

"I'm impressed. If you ever decided to leave security, you'd make an excellent interrogator."

His eyebrows flew up in surprise, and he glanced at her before returning his eyes to the road. "I'll try to take that as a compliment. Thanks for thinking I'm scary enough to beat a confession out of someone."

A bubble of laughter popped out, and she clasped her hands over her mouth at a death glare from Chance. "Not some inquisition interrogator. A real detective questions witnesses and suspects, which takes a lot of psychology. I'm only saying, with your instincts, you'd do well." The pale glow from the instrument panel revealed a blush creeping over his cheeks.

He ran a hand through his hair, his nervous tic. "Uh…thanks." He peeked over at the warm smile on her face and couldn't help but smile himself. "I appreciate the compliment, but I couldn't deal with those situations every day. Besides, Gregor's my boss, and I love my job."

The slight pull of his lips and tightness in his jaw contradicted his late sentence, which surprised her. "You don't." She blurted the words before thinking.

He glanced over at her in confusion. "I don't what?"

She contemplated dismissing the issue, but she wanted to know. "You don't love your job, not completely." She sank as far back in her seat as possible, waiting for the screaming to start.

Instead, Chance gazed at her for a second while sitting at a red light. "I love Gregor like family. I don't need a paycheck to protect him, but no, I don't *completely* love my job. Gregor is a wonderful man, but he knows the power he has over people and uses it. My life would be different if I didn't work for him." His eyes caught hers for a significant instant and then turned back to the road as the light changed.

Her arms folded over her chest, and she frowned across the car. An instinctual need to defend her father burned inside. "Gregor isn't a tyrant. Come on, Chance. He doesn't play people like pawns. He's always open and honest. So, the man flipped out when an eighteen-year-old kid got a tattoo for his sixteen-year-old daughter. What father wouldn't go ballistic? Don't make him out to be some super villain that controls your life. The concept is juvenile."

The car jerked to the side of the road, and Chance slammed on the brakes. She clutched the dash, holding on for dear life as the tiny car rocked to a stop. "Are you insane?" She tried desperately to catch her breath and control the trembles running through her arms.

Chance twisted in his seat, leaning over the center console, and tilted her chin toward him. His hazel brown eyes flecked with green bored into her from inches away.

"Knowing one thing doesn't mean you know the whole story. You take one or two facts and think it entitles you to fill in everything else. I'm not a crime scene, and you see your father through some huge rose-colored glasses. He's a survivalist. He needs to be. I understand, but don't sit there and tell me he doesn't manipulate things to his advantage. You only see one side of him. I have been with him almost every waking moment of his life for the past six years."

"I..." The intensity startled her beyond the ability to form a sentence. She couldn't make sense of his animosity toward Gregor. Squashing a teenage crush wasn't the work of an evil mastermind. She swallowed the lump in her throat, attempting to form words when he cut her off.

"Yes, Gregor went ballistic over the tattoo, saying sixteen was too young. So, I waited. I worked hard to be the best at my job, tried to show how well I handled responsibility. On your eighteenth birthday, he sat me down and told me the truth. He calmly told me, in crystal clear terms, that this"—he motioned between the two of them—"would never happen."

She stumbled through her thoughts, trying to reconcile the conflicting views of her father. "What? He threatened to fire you?"

"No, Lilith." His jaw clenched tight, and he stared into her eyes, willing her to understand. "You don't get it, do you? He threatened to ship me off to the ends of the earth. No medical supplies, no support, nothing. A death sentence."

Her eyes widened as her entire world turned upside down. "Why?" The word came out as a weak, breathy whisper. Her father rarely raised his voice, much less threatened people's lives, and Chance was like a son to him.

"You're a pureblood, Lily. You've got centuries to live." His eyes fell, and the intimate sadness in their depths made her tear up. "I've got one century if I'm lucky. Assuming I don't die in the line of duty, which is entirely possible. Then there's the dilution of the bloodlines. Gregor explained everything to me, and although I disagree with his methods, he's not wrong. You need to realize your father is ruthless when protecting his family."

The tightness in her chest felt like her lungs might explode. She wanted to take away all the hurt and sadness lingering in his face, but none of his words made sense. She tried to get her brain working, which took a tremendous amount of effort. "But you are family, Chance! Gregor took you in, raised you like a son."

"No. I'm a fixture, a tool. I realize in some way Gregor cares about me, but it's not like family. He assigns a deeper meaning to that word. You, Duncan, Miriah, Malachi, Spencer, Aaron, and Michael are his family. I'm only the hired help."

"Why are you telling me all this? Why now?"

His green-flecked eyes met hers again. "Because you deserve the truth, and I can't keep all these secrets when we're working so close together. I need you to understand why things are the way they are and why they have to stay that way." His words sounded resolute, but something uncertain in his eyes longed for things to be different, no matter what he said.

Her heart pounded in her chest, drowning out everything else. A tension thick enough to cut with a knife filled the car, pulling her in a million directions. Without thinking, she whispered, "Shut up." Her lips brushed against his in a torturously tender kiss, causing every little hair to stand on end.

At first, Chance sat there, paralyzed, and blind panic began to rise in the pit of her stomach. Preparing to be beyond embarrassed, she started to pull back when his thin control snapped. His arms slid around her, holding her close as his lips pushed against hers in a fiery kiss. He tasted like sunlight, warm and electrifying. Fingers drifted softly against her ribs, making her gasp. Chance pulled back abruptly, resting his forehead against hers. He drew in a ragged, shaking breath. "God, you cannot do that, *cherie*."

Her back stiffened, and she pulled away from his arms. Righteous fury flooded through her as she rubbed at her flushed cheeks. "I am a grown woman, Chance. My father doesn't make my decisions for me."

A lazy smile stretched his lips. "*That* is not what I meant. Believe me. I noticed you're a full-grown woman."

Relief rushed over her so fast, she felt dizzy. Her cheeks burned as the blush crept down her neck. "What *did* you mean then?"

His eyes glazed as he rubbed a hand over his chestnut hair. "Gasping. I wanted to kiss you from the moment I saw you thirteen years ago. I'm mostly human, after all." His smile held subtle undercurrents of pain, and then the doubt trickled in. She saw the truth of his earlier declaration eating away the edges of a perfect moment.

Scared of it slipping away, she ran her palm over his cheek, the stubble tickling her soft skin. Chance closed his eyes and leaned into her touch as the doubt eased from his face.

Then, the full weight of the truth hit her. His whole life depended on being the strong one, the tough one. Now, he sat here, vulnerable, finding solace in something as simple as her touch. The thought shook her right down to the core.

His eyes drifted open, and seeing the edges of fear on her face, he tugged her close, his lips caressing hers. Sparks followed the path of his hand as it slipped over her cheek and sank into her auburn curls.

A sharp tap on the glass burst the little bubble, and the real world came to a very crisp focus. Traffic flew past on a busy freeway while red and blue flashes filled the car. "Perfect," she murmured, glancing through Chance's window to see a sour-faced cop with his flashlight.

The policeman shined his bright light into the car, and she shied away, blinking. Chance rolled down the window and took the brunt of the blinding brightness.

"Y'all okay?" The cop's thick Southern accent didn't hold a single trace of concern, more like semi-polite suspicion. He shined the light again at Lilith, who winced against the glare, and then settled it back on Chance.

"Yes, Officer. I pulled to the side of the road when my girl and I tried to figure out directions. I don't like to drive distracted."

Officer Humphrey, as his name tag stated, watched Chance silently for a few minutes. She opened her mouth to break the awkward quiet, but the officer spoke first. "Seems y'all made up. The shoulder is for emergencies, boy. Take it elsewhere."

Chance nodded. "Of course. Sorry, sir." Officer Humphrey didn't move. Instead, he studied them, his flashlight bouncing all over the car until it stopped on Chance's bandaged knuckles.

"I noticed this is a rental car. Where are y'all visitin' from?" His question wasn't born of casual curiosity but shrewd interest.

"New York City. We flew down to visit family." Never in her life had she heard Chance so polite. At best, he played the role of silent muscle while Gregor played the suave face man. Guess he picked up a few tricks while working for her father all those years.

The light fell on Lilith again, and she blinked, trying to control her rising irritation. "Don't your woman speak?" The tone of contempt in his sentence didn't help, and she clenched her jaw to keep from saying something she'd regret. "You have a license on you, miss?"

After digging into her aluminum kit, she pulled out the trifold, which held her driver's license, forensics badge, and consultant ID. She leaned over Chance and handed it to the cop. "Here you go, Officer." She smiled sweetly, managing to keep the annoyance out of her voice. The muscles under Humphrey's eyes tightened before he grabbed the wallet and flipped it open.

His expression changed instantly, contempt melting into something a bit friendlier. "New York City Forensics Team, eh?" He inspected her license and badge in silence for what felt like an eternity. Seemingly satisfied, he turned his calculated stare on her. "I reckon you're smart enough to know when someone's no good." Her mouth dropped open in surprise as she struggled to find something to say.

Before she came up with a response, the cop handed her wallet to Chance and fixed him with a hostile glare. He leaned in the window and pointed a finger in his face. "You better wise up, boy. If I had any right to bring you in, I would. You might think that kind of thing is all right down here in the South, but I take it quite seriously. Watch your step, boy, and get this young woman home safe." The officer stormed away from the car and back to his cruiser.

Lilith sank back against the seat with her heart racing. "What the hell?"

When the cop car peeled off the side of the road with a roar of power, Chance burst out laughing. He tossed the trifold wallet into her lap and leaned against the steering wheel, trying to breathe through the laughter.

She stared at him, openmouthed. "What the hell is so damn funny?"

Chance tapped the right side of his head and kept laughing.

Her eyes widened, and she yanked down the mirror above the sun visor. The pale light from the cosmetic mirror lit up the myriad of colors along the right side of her face. The makeup she applied earlier was gone, leaving a pattern of sickly yellows and faint purples along her temple. "Shit." She hissed and twisted over her seat, reaching for the front pocket of her bag.

He continued to laugh as she flopped back down in the seat, smoothing the concealer over the bruises. "Oh, come on, *cherie.* That's funny as hell. Between my knuckles and your bruises…"

She glared at him and continued blending her makeup. "You wouldn't be laughing if he hauled your ass to jail or worse."

Those words stopped his chuckles in a hurry, and Chance blinked with a sobering look. "True." Then his face cracked into a crooked grin. "I reckon you're smart enough to know when someone's no good." His impression of Humphrey's thick Southern accent pulled a reluctant smile from her.

"Well, at least he got one thing right." She tucked the bottle into her jeans pocket and snapped her seat belt back into place. "Let's get to Miriah's office before another cop comes by and accuses you of being a woman beater."

She stared out the window, watching the lights pass by as the quiet drive continued. Her thoughts wandered over the kiss and fell on the subject of her father. The accusations Chance leveled against him sat like an uneasy weight on her heart.

Although she never thought of her father as controlling, it made sense when she considered Duncan's notes. They hinted about him tragically losing a daughter, which made his protective urges understandable. Still, this new image of her father made her stomach churn. She thought about Spencer and wondered. Was it better to know her father and resent him or be blissfully ignorant about who he was?

The chirping tone of her phone startled her out of her thoughts. She stared down at the caller ID for a moment with the irrational belief that Gregor could somehow read her mind. She clicked the answer button hesitantly. "Dad?" Chance glanced at her before returning his attention to the SUV in front of them.

"Alvarez came to see me."

Malachi's smiling face in all the photos littering the apartment flashed across her mind. "I'm glad he told you in person."

"I made arrangements to take care of Malachi. Is Miriah aware of his trip to New York City?"

She cursed under her breath. She should have called Gregor and updated him after they heard from Spencer. "Miriah…is missing as well. A lot happened, and I'm following every lead I can, which isn't much, to be honest."

The line went silent, and for a moment, she thought the call dropped. "Lilith. Are you okay?" Playing the rare full-name card made Gregor's voice more commanding than usual.

She hesitated, which was enough to give him an answer. Best to bite the bullet. "An attack occurred last night while investigating the Madisonville house. I'm fine, thanks to Chance." The smile in her voice was unavoidable. "There's no need to worry."

When they pulled up to a red light, Chance peered over with panic on his face. "I'm glad I sent him with you, then. As for the attack, my nephew-in-law's body is lying on a slab, so I think we are well beyond worrying. What leads do you have?" She rarely encountered the straightforward business side of her father, and it rubbed her the wrong way.

"Duncan had a lot of notes, I'm still going through them, but I found a few encrypted ones mentioning Mary and vague references to medieval Scotland. Miriah helped Duncan with research, but I didn't find anything at her apartment, so I'm heading to her office with Chance."

Another long silence stretched across the phone line before Gregor spoke again. "What did he say about Mary?" His voice changed from impersonal authority to quiet vulnerability.

"Only that she was your daughter, and something horrible happened to her. He didn't give any specifics. Is there something I should know?"

"Nothing relevant. However, I think you two should come home." He sounded casual, but the undercurrent in his voice was adamant.

"I can't, Dad." Her jaw set into a firm line, and her whole body stiffened in the seat. "You are acting protective because Malachi is dead, but that's all the more reason for me to keep digging. Miriah, Duncan, and possibly Spencer are still in danger."

"Lilith Marie Adams, you and Chance are to board the next plane out of Knoxville, or I will send someone to get you. I am not negotiating. This is a direct order." The calm, commanding tone reminded her of smoldering coals, daring her to supply the fuel.

Whether caused by revelations about her father, the illicit kiss, or the reasons to stay, a righteous rebellion roared inside.

"No." Surprisingly, her voice didn't shake once. "I am not leaving Tennessee when Miriah and Duncan might be out there alive, and I'm not leaving Spencer to go raving mad. I have a job to do, so tell me how any of this pertains to Mary?"

Without a single pause, Gregor's forceful voice rattled through the phone. "This has *nothing* to do with Mary. Duncan is losing his mind, and Malachi is dead. I want you home." He paused a moment, and when he spoke again, a pleading tone edged into his voice. "I can't protect you from here." Her fearless father was scared for the first time in her memory. That alone made her hesitate, but only for a second.

"No. I'm finishing what I came here to do." She hung up the phone before her nerve gave out. Chance stared at her like she just stuck her hand in a crocodile's gaping mouth. The phone rang again, and she turned it off. A car behind them honked, and Chance snapped forward, speeding through the intersection.

"I can't believe I did that." She whispered the words, thinking out loud. Her hands shook as she sucked in a steadying breath. Once her confidence returned, outrage followed suit. "I'm right, and he is wrong. He sent me here to do a job, and I'm doing it. End of story."

Chance sighed and glanced over at her. "Is this about the job or the kiss?"

She scowled at him, and he quickly turned to stare forward. "Not everything is about you, but he was wrong to make threats." She let out an aggravated growl and slumped back in her seat. "He's wrong about this case too."

Chance pulled the car into the center parking space in front of a quaint little strip mall. He sat still in his seat, obviously torn between saying something and saying nothing. "Don't pick a fight with Gregor because of me. He is still my boss. He saved my life by finding me in that state hospital and taking me in. But, if he decides to cut me off, my odds of survival are pretty damn small."

His soft brown eyes, with their green flecks, displayed a deep well of sadness. "I carry a torch for you, Lily, and I always will. The kiss…" His voice trailed off as the corners of his mouth lifted into a grin. "The kiss is irreplaceably special, but it can't happen again. Right or wrong, Gregor is in charge. Perhaps we should head home."

She frowned at him while grabbing for the door handle but stopped when he touched her hand and turned back to face him. "No, I'm not going to be ordered around like a mindless debutante by you or Gregor. This isn't about you. Ordering me to leave when his brother and niece are still out there is dead wrong. He's acting out of fear…and, perhaps, so are you."

She wrenched her hand away from him. The wounded irritation in his face almost made her want to take everything back. Almost. "Do you *really* believe Gregor would banish you and leave you to die? When you were a kid, sure, but now? Perhaps hiding behind his threats and a line of women felt safer than opening up. If that's the life you want, then keep your damn torch." She swung the car door open before Chance had an opportunity to respond and slammed it on the sound of his voice.

She closed her eyes, took a steadying breath, and attempted to purge everything from her mind, but nothing helped. Chance didn't want to do anything about the floodgate he opened. He dumped his feelings on her doorstep with an apology and no regard for her thoughts on the subject.

Still, how could she be mad at him? In his mind, he took a considerable risk telling her all this. Did she have any right to ask him to change his life, risk everything on one kiss? More importantly, did she want him to?

Chance dragged himself out of the tiny car, and she turned away, staring across the parking lot. *Get a grip, Lilith*, she thought. She needed to shake all this emotional turmoil and focus on the case.

A few agonizing minutes later, she heard him walk toward the office and turned to follow. He came to an abrupt halt at the door, and the drama in her head vanished like vapor. He reached under the back of his shirt in one fluid motion and pulled his gun from the holster.

As she moved to the side, the entire world seemed to tilt, bringing her back to reality with a harsh change of perspective. The door hung open ominously, with the frame splintered all to hell. He put his hand on the door, and she caught his eyes, mouthing, "Don't touch anything." He shot a harsh glare, cutting her right to the bone. Oh yeah. Enraged was an understatement. Having a six-foot-three Cajun pissed off at her was terrifying, but not as much as what might be waiting for them inside.

Keeping the gun trained on the door, his foot slowly pushed it open. As his hard eyes scanned the interior, he motioned for her to stay put, then slipped into the room. She started to peek around the edge, and her eyes widened in shock. The place reeked of blood. Nervously, she studied the parking lot, her skin itching as if a million eyes watched her from the dark recesses.

She couldn't stay out in the open. Something was dead inside that office, and their rental car parked out front was incriminating enough. She needed to grab her case and get out of sight as fast as possible.

After running back to the car, she grabbed her kit from the back seat and slid into the office. She stood still with her back against the wall as her eyes frantically searched through the dark space. At last, they focused intensely on the only other door as if she could magically make Chance appear. Every muscle in her body burned with tension, making her hands shake. She wrapped her arms around the aluminum case, giving her something substantial to hold.

Unlike her usual crime scenes' inherent anonymity, the body here was most likely a family member. Beyond that, the probable assailant knew her and almost killed her once already. What if he was still here?

To avoid spinning out into blind panic, she ran through the crime scene checklist. They both needed to wear gloves. Inevitable police involvement made it imperative that they leave no trace behind. The dry weather meant footprints shouldn't be an issue. The empty parking lot and lack of lights in the surrounding buildings indicated they might be lucky and avoid having an eyewitness place them at the scene. Any lingering doubts of foul play disappeared with the complex scents of urine, sweat, feces, and blood. Whatever happened wasn't quick.

Abruptly, Chance stepped out of the back room, put his gun in the holster, and dragged a hand through his hair. "It's all clear. You're going to need the kit." His eyes stared hauntingly at the aluminum case. "I'm sorry, Lily. I think it might be Miriah."

Chapter 8

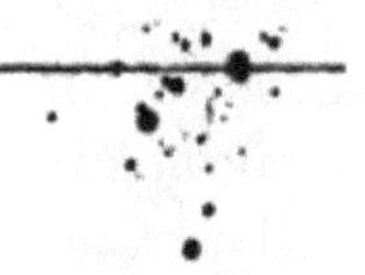

A sickly pallor crept over Chance's skin as he collapsed against the wall. The office door stood open, dark and ominous, like the gateway to hell from Dante's *Inferno*. Her mind replayed what he said. *It* might *be Miriah*. Although he didn't spend his life around dead bodies, she knew horrifying things awaited her. Still, she investigated crime scenes for a living. She could do this. She *had* to do this. If he was right, Duncan still needed her help.

With a brave grimace, she stepped up to the doorway and glanced at him. "Can you stay out here? I feel safer with someone watching the door." His face flooded with relief as he nodded a silent thanks. "And put these on." She passed him a pair of purple gloves. "We can't leave *any* trace."

Without a single wisecrack about the color, he pulled them on. Then, the tension in his throat made her stop. She grabbed his arm, supplying an anchor as he fought to keep his food in his stomach.

"Chance." She waited until she held his wavering gaze. "If you need to puke, find a trash can small enough to take with us. They can extract DNA from saliva and bile. We don't need yours all over the floor, okay?" Seeing the way he bristled, she cut him short. "No macho pretenses. You can't protect me if the cops arrest you for murder with your DNA found on-site." He nodded but still appeared vaguely offended.

With him in check, she entered the room and immediately doubled over from the pungent odor. She dropped her case by the door and dug out a little jar of Vicks VapoRub, her secret weapon for situations like these. Dabbing a bit under her nose blocked most smells. Although the forensics community utilized it regularly, the trick rarely appeared on TV crime dramas because it didn't look sexy. As if the dead bodies weren't enough of a turnoff.

She grabbed a dull probe, a thermometer, and a few other supplies, tucked them in her pockets, and closed her case. She straightened to face her fears and strode forward while pulling on gloves. At first, her eyes couldn't make sense of it, refusing to see the mangled mess as a person in a useless attempt to protect her.

Golden blonde hair flowed over the desk's edge, which seemed untouched compared to the rest of the body. *The body.* Suddenly, her mind clicked into painful clarity, and the mayhem began to resemble its original shape. Her world spun, making her so dizzy, she nearly collapsed. After squeezing her eyes closed, she focused on Gregor, Duncan, Chance, Spencer, all the people depending on her to solve this thing.

"This is just another job, another nameless corpse." The pep talk helped as she set up the voice recorder on her phone and placed it on the fax machine cart. Even though this wasn't an official case, the process kept her calm and made her think aloud.

"Female body found at 10:14 p.m. in the accounting office of Miriah Sanders. The victim is laid out on the desk in a supine position, a particular arrangement of the limbs, implying an act of display."

True to her routine, she plunged the thermometer through the skin. "Liver temperature is 89.6 degrees, 9 degrees lower than normal..." Lifting one stiff shoulder revealed dark purple staining in a consistent pattern. "Lividity and rigor mortis are set, which together with temp puts the time of death about six to eight hours ago."

The mangled legs dangled off the desk with purple marks along the underside, peeking through patches of fabric. That, coupled with a lack of staining on the soles of the feet, told her something important. "The victim laid flat for a long time after death, allowing the blood to pool evenly within the body. Then someone moved it here, most likely in the last hour or so." She moved back to the top of the desk with the dull pointer in hand. "Victim's hair is approximately two and a half feet in length, blonde." To be thorough, she pushed her probe into the bright golden strands. "The hair is damp underneath." Scenarios raced through her mind until she landed on the most likely one. "Someone washed it postmortem, which explains the lack of blood or debris. Perhaps, a signature?"

She took a deep breath, preparing for what came next. Until that point, her eyes avoided the face, but she couldn't put it off forever. Staring down at the mangled flesh, she tried to find someplace to start.

"The assailant removed the eyelids, both upper and lower, from inner to outer canthus, with clean cuts following the curve of the ocular cavities. This displays a desire for the victim to see something. They also removed the nose with surgical precision. Destroying the centerpiece of the face shows intense hatred, but they maintained enough restraint to be precise.

"Swelling and bruises, most likely resulting from multiple fractures, makes facial identification impossible. Judging by the coloring of the bruises, these injuries occurred a day or more before death. Several visible fractures to the nasal and vomer bones occurred around the same time." She glanced back at the eyes, resting loosely in their sockets. The thick and cloudy aqueous fluid caused a glaze, masking the pale blue irises. Miriah had blue eyes. She took a step back as Miriah's smiling face from the myriad of pictures in the apartment flashed through her mind.

No. She needed to stay impartial to get through this. "Possible fractures to the zygomatic and frontal bones around the ocular cavities." She crouched to one side, flicking on a penlight, and studied the hairline. "More possible fractures around the temples. The head took a vicious beating that doesn't display any of the restraint evident in the incisions. Whoever pounded the victim's face had no control over their rage."

Lilith pushed the probe at the bluish lips, but it slipped right back through to the surface. She frowned and leaned in closer with the penlight. "The assailant sliced the lips multiple times, most likely with a scalpel." Senseless evil for evil's sake. After swallowing the breath caught in her throat, she tried again to pry the mouth open.

The penlight revealed nine missing and three cracked teeth, consistent with the beating. She opened the mouth wider, checking the roof to find two gaping holes behind the front teeth. "Fangs were removed…" She felt queasy as her tongue unconsciously ran over her own fangs, tucked away.

"No, not removed. The attacker ripped them out before the victim died. The amount of congealed blood places it around the same time as the precision work. The killer possessed knowledge of our species."

She squatted down, gathering her thoughts and fighting to breathe. The odds that she was inspecting Miriah's body were sky-high. Beyond that, this was the worst corpse she'd ever seen, leaving her flushed, hot, and nauseous. The wounds and scents told the story of hours and hours of painful torture. How could anyone do this? Once she swallowed the bile rising in her throat, a driven determination forced her to keep going.

"Thousands of superficial lacerations cover the body, inflicted by a sharp blade slicing through the dermis and into the skeletal muscle. A razor or scalpel is the most likely weapon. Blood patterns indicate the cuts are all antemortem and that the victim was standing during the process. Rope burns coupled with massive contusions at the neck, bottom of the rib cage, wrists, and ankles are indicative of being bound."

Lilith turned the arms over and paused, squinting at a tiny mark. "Venipunctures in the antecubital space of the left arm…and the right. One explanation is the assailant supplying her with blood or medications to prolong the torment. None of the incisions cut deep enough through the skeletal muscle to reach the bone, probably to prevent the victim from going into shock."

She took a step back, contemplating the patterns, and trying to see their function. "This is far too systematic to be simple fun. The perpetrator acted with a singular purpose. Perhaps, they wanted information from her…or someone who cared about her. Oh, god…"

If Duncan was there… If the killer forced him to watch… The hot stabbing headache came back with a vengeance, making her stomach churn. Turning away from the corpse, she put the back of her hand against her mouth, struggling to keep the bile down and block the stench of unimaginably cruel torture.

"Stop. This is the one thing only you can do. Bodies tell a story, and you need to know this one, as horrible as it might be." With a determined push, she made her way back to the desk and forced her eyes to focus.

She worked her way back down the body, verbally cataloging every wound as she went. Closer inspection revealed a patchwork of burns, exposed muscle, and chunks of missing flesh, all performed with the same surgical precision. The sadist even sliced her ears into ribbons. God. She fought back another wave of nausea and wondered who the hell would think to shred a person's ears like julienne fries?

When she got to the wrists, she came to a halt again. The purple masses of flesh barely resembled the shape of a hand. Moving her deft fingers along them, what she found made her blood run cold.

All twenty-seven bones were broken, from the tiny carpals of the wrist to the phalanges of the fingertips. The coloring in the bruises varied a great deal, some darker, some lighter. That coupled with numerous dimples in the skin suggested the killer used a tool to fracture each one individually. This monster had no soul, only a sickening amount of patience and an absolute obsession.

She forced herself to keep going, despite her roaring headache getting worse and worse. The feet were intact, probably so she could support her weight as much as possible. Dammit. Examiners used neutral terms like *victim* and *assailant* instead of *him* and *her* to stay impartial, keep their sanity, and retain their focus.

She had to stop thinking of the corpse as a person, stop picturing her attacker from the basement. Her emotional grip slipped with every passing second, considering how close she came to lying on this desk instead of Miriah.

Another deep breath brought her back to the body with a steely resolve. Distinguishing shreds of clothing from the brutalized flesh proved difficult. Exchanging the probe for tweezers, she pulled at a button glistening in the center of the chest. The fabric attached to it was stiff and sticky with blood, and the flesh below revealed more incisions.

The more she saw, the more confident she was that two separate people murdered Malachi and Miriah. The difference between the two bodies was day and night, like comparing a Monet to a fingerpainting. However, the patterns were similar enough to show a connection. Perhaps the killer in New York was imitating this one.

Despite her better instincts, her eyes glanced up to the mangled face, knowing it belonged to her cousin. Nothing else made sense with the fang sockets, hair and eye color, location, and circumstances. Squeezing her eyes shut, she tried to block the image from her mind. *Damn it.* How many pep talks did she need to give herself?

"Snap out of it. You do this every day. Finish, and you can get out of here." With an angry huff, she focused every fiber of her being and found the victim's waistband or what remained of it. The burns and cuts covering the hips and thighs made it impossible to tell where cloth stopped and flesh began. The distinct stench of urine and feces penetrated the menthol coating. She covered her mouth with the back of one gloved hand and choked on the ammonia fumes burning her nose.

When the coughing finally stopped, she homed in on the pants, trying to identify every scrap she could find. Her tweezers caught the curving line of a pocket, and she used them to lift the material, peering inside with her penlight. A slip of stiff paper, soaked in blood, lay wedged into a small fold in the fabric. A ray of hope penetrated the desperation seeping into her bones.

She carefully extracted the delicate paper with a hand so steady it would make the bomb squad proud. She took her time, prying the fabric away, and finally pulled it free intact after numerous attempts. The thing was an unrecognizable mass of red to the naked eye, but she could analyze the ink with different light spectrums in a lab. For now, it remained a mystery, so she gently placed it in a plastic evidence bag and sealed it.

Now she only had one thing left to do. "The cause of death could be septic shock, exsanguination..." Her eyes stopped at the bruising rope burn on the neck. From her point of view, down at the victim's waist, something looked odd...different.

Moving along the desk, she peered closer at the rope burns and saw a thin flap. She prodded along it with her tweezers and realized the razor-thin slice ran through the windpipe and jugular, from ear to ear. "The assailant sliced the neck, a quick death once playtime was over."

She jammed the stop button on her phone with a bloodless finger. That was everything she could do with limited time and poor conditions. Now that her responsibilities were over, she couldn't stay in the room a minute longer.

Her whole body trembled as she backed away from the desk, clutching the plastic bag holding the blood-soaked paper. Tears stung her eyes, and exhaustion burned as the strength flooded out of her. The logical side shut down, and reality crashed over her with a bone-crushing force. All that remained of Miriah was a mutilated corpse on a table, with lifeless lidless eyes staring at the ceiling.

Panic rose in her chest as she backed out of the room, unable to take her eyes off the damn desk. Arms grabbed her from behind. She screamed, but before she could fight back, Chance sank to the floor with her, whispering in her ear. "Hush, hush. You're safe. You're okay." She turned in his arms and buried her face against his chest. Everything she held back came roaring over her. Barely contained nausea hit her in hot waves as her head throbbed. Huge heaving sobs wracked her body, hands clutching his shirt.

His arms wrapped around her, providing a cocoon of warm safety, and she drank in every drop as her tears soaked his shirt. He rested his chin on the top of her head while whispering. Her mind couldn't make sense of his words anymore, but the soft, deep sound comforted her anyway. Her legs drew in close to her body, still shaking after the crying stopped.

When she found her voice, it came out weak and broken. "What they did to her…" Her heart pounded furiously again, and he smoothed a hand over her back.

"Shhh. Lily. You don't need to tell me. I heard everything." Tears lingered in his voice when he continued. "God, I am so sorry. I… I should never have let you… You didn't need to see that." Gently, he continued to rock them back and forth.

Closing her eyes, she focused on his beating heart, letting the steady rhythm chase everything away. They stayed on the floor for half an hour or more before Lilith opened her eyes again. She craned her head back to stare up at him as he wiped the tears from her cheeks. After pushing a stray auburn strand back, he pressed a soft kiss against her forehead, filling her with warmth. When he pulled back, his eyes still on her, she saw so much more than he would ever admit.

She swallowed the sudden lump in her throat, her eyes welling up, and forced her brain back to the present. "We need to leave. The body isn't a danger. Human facilities won't pick up on the anomalies, and the killer removed the fangs. We need to get out of here now." When he didn't say anything, she continued.

"This is still a case for violent crimes, extreme enough to warrant the FBI. They're going to ask questions, and people have seen us around her apartment, perhaps here as well. Running won't look good."

Pulling his arms tighter around her, she stared at a random spot and rattled her thoughts together. "Moving the body is too much of a risk. We have no way of doing that without leaving evidence, and we don't have the equipment to remove every trace of blood in that room. Plus, someone will report her missing. At least one other person works here, so there will be an investigation no matter what we do. The police will question us, and if they find any evidence on us or our car, you can guarantee we won't receive a fair trial. We need to leave her here."

"Guess the nameless phantom is forcing our hand." He exhaled and pressed his cheek against the top of her head.

Lilith frowned at the blood specks on his arms, left by her gloves. She pulled them off and tucked them in the bag with the bloody scrap of paper.

"He is a very purposeful man. Every single wound on her body…" Her voice broke, and she swallowed hard again before continuing.

"He inflicted every wound with a reason, one originating from hatred but executed with cold, logical precision. Only time, lots of time can make that possible. The body isn't here to scare us, and the placement is not random. This is a message, but I don't know what the killer is trying to say."

"Perhaps he wants the complication of police involvement. What if we head things off and call them now?"

She mulled the thought over for a moment before finally shaking her head. "No. We can't say we found her and then stopped to examine the body." She let out a heavy sigh. "If we leave now, there is a possibility no one saw us. If that's not the case, I can say we came to meet with Miriah, waited, and when she didn't show, we left. Calling the cops now limits our options. If someone spotted the car, the police would want to know why we sat inside with her body for over two hours before calling."

"Okay, but that's a simplistic excuse. Why wouldn't we try the door?"

"The parking lot is empty. We would have no reason to leave the car."

"Should I be worried about how easily you fabricate lies?" The gentle humor brought a smile to her lips.

"I've heard all kinds of excuses, and I know which lies sound like crap. Two out-of-towners waiting on a family member to meet them someplace convenient isn't an odd thing at all. Besides, Ida can attest we showed up at Miriah's place looking for her. Simplistic is best. The fancier the story, the easier you are to trip up."

He nodded, opening his arms as she peeked nervously over her shoulder. "Thank you."

He smiled weakly and avoided eye contact by gazing at the economy carpet.

"I need to grab my kit and tools from…" Her voice trailed away as her eyes fixed on the door leading to the room of horrors.

After sanitizing her tools, they scoured the rooms, packing anything incriminating into ziplock bags. Then they piled into the tiny rental and sped toward the apartment, praying there wasn't an eyewitness to tie them to the scene. Once they left downtown, she called. Considering Spencer's erratic behavior, she figured calling was safer than telling him in person this time.

"We found her." She tried to keep things discreet. She never trusted the privacy of cell phones.

"You found her? How the hell?" The utter shock in his voice blared loud enough for Chance to hear across the car. "Sorry, I mean, is she okay? Where was she?"

"No, she's not okay. I'm sorry…"

"Impossible." The word emerged as a confused whisper. Denial was the typical response in her experience. The silence stretched, and she waited patiently for a while, checking the phone to be sure he didn't hang up. Finally, she got tired of waiting. "Spence? Are you still at Malachi's office?"

"Yeah."

"Can you see if he has any records on the Phipps Bend Property?"

"The old nuclear place? How do you know about that rubble pile?"

"Duncan referenced the place in some notes. Since Malachi worked in real estate, perhaps he helped Duncan with his research on the property."

"Sure. I'll meet you back at the apartment when I finish up here. It might be a while, though. You can give me the full report then."

Spencer hung up before she could say anything else. She stared at the phone in confusion for a minute until Chance spoke up. "Since he'll be late to the party, it should give us enough time to rifle through the tin you found."

"Sounds like a plan." She flashed a smile, letting go of the random half-formed thoughts about Spencer.

When they arrived at the apartment building, Lilith began pulling suitcases out of the trunk like a Tasmanian devil. Chance stood back with his arms crossed, staring at her in bewilderment. "What are you doing?"

She grunted while pulling open the spare tire hatch. "I'm getting the box. Why don't you see if Ida is still awake? Hopefully, she can buzz us in."

"I think one of these keys might work." He grabbed their suitcases and jogged up to the front door.

As she reached under the tire, her fingers grazed the tin, resulting in a frustrated growl. "Come on." She pushed her arm deeper, fingers dancing around the prize, when her phone rang. The sudden sound made her jump, smacking her head on the trunk while simultaneously scratching her arm on the tire well.

She cursed and stubbornly shoved her hand in, fingers closing around the elusive box. While pulling it out, she clicked the answer button on her phone before checking the number.

"Yeah?" she grumbled while twisting her arm to inspect the rough scratch. Damn it. Couldn't she go at least one day without losing blood?

"I *cannot* believe you hung up on me and turned off your phone." Gregor's voice went beyond mere anger to pure fury.

"Dad, I can't deal with this now. I'm not leaving. I just examined Miriah's body, and *your* brother is still out there. So, don't waste your breath telling me to come home. *You* sent me here." As soon as the verbal flood left her mouth, she silently cursed herself. So much for discretion.

"Miriah?" The patronizing tone vanished at once. "Tell me about the body?"

"I don't think I should tell you over the phone, and I don't have the time now." After repacking and locking the car, she jogged up the front steps, trying to summon the tenacity to hang up again.

"Make the time." The iron firm voice left no room for refusal.

Lilith sighed as she knocked on the exterior door. "Fine. Someone used her face for a punching bag a day or two before she died. A second assailant tortured her with cold, systematic methods. He removed the eyelids and nose surgically and shredded the lips and ears with a scalpel. Thousands of burns, cuts, and incisions covered the entire body. I believe they fed her blood to keep her alive and were considerate enough to wash her hair." A shiver ran up her spine as she recited her findings.

"Did you say they washed her hair?"

Flashbacks threatened to crawl out of the recess of her mind as Chance jogged down the stairs to push the door open. After mouthing Gregor's name, he silently fell into step beside her.

"Yeah. Postmortem. She died six to eight hours ago, but the hair was still damp."

"Dear god. He must be alive." Gregor breathed the words so softly that she couldn't be sure he said anything at all. "Listen to me. This situation is a million times more dangerous than I thought when—"

"You think?" She cut him off, all the suppressed frustration and betrayal erupting to the surface. "You sent me here to find your brother, not examine my cousin's brutalized body. You know something about what's going on. You knew *before* I left, but I was too blind to believe it. I'm giving you the benefit of the doubt that you didn't know the severity, but do *not* lie to me again!"

"You're right. I suspected Duncan uncovered something from our past, but I swear to you, I didn't think this man was alive for one second. You and Chance need to leave *right* now. I cannot stress this enough. If he has Duncan, you cannot save him." His words eerily echoed her uncle's letter as pure terror made his voice tremble. Her father, the once-great pillar of strength in her life, sounded petrified.

She stopped outside Miriah's apartment, frozen to the spot as the world spun around her. "Who?"

"His name won't matter. He's a ghost and a vicious man who's been inflicting horrors upon my family for over six hundred years. Please, Lilith, *please* get on a plane, any plane!" Blood pounded in her ears so loud, she couldn't hear the rest of his plea. Every inch of her screamed to obey Gregor's request. However, there was a massive problem with running home.

"Malachi wasn't safe in New York. Leaving won't solve anything. We need to end this." If only she felt as brave as she sounded. Finding Miriah was terrifying enough, and this revelation only made things worse. She hung up the phone and stared at it, misty-eyed.

Chance moved in front to open the door and stopped dead in his tracks when he saw her face. His hands lightly gripped her shoulders as he studied her expression. "Lily, what's wrong?"

She raised her eyes, wishing they could disappear. "Gregor begged me to fly out of here."

"Maybe he's right." When she opened her mouth to protest, he cut her off. "Just listen. Whoever is behind this got to you our first night and almost killed you. He had no problem getting to Miriah. We have muscle in New York. I can keep you safe there." His hands tightened on her shoulders, his voice sounding as desperate as Gregor's.

She sucked in a deep breath and shook her head. "Running is not the answer. It sure as hell didn't save Malachi."

"Lily, you said yourself the wounds on Miriah and Malachi didn't match. We don't have any proof that their deaths are connected."

"Someone butchered him in the alley of the building we met Gregor in, possibly while we were there. A meeting that sent us here where we find a body with a strikingly similar MO?" She arched an eyebrow, and the frown on his face clearly said he didn't think it was a coincidence either. "Perhaps he's collaborating with other people, but they are connected. The patterns are too alike."

"Okay, point, but no one knew Malachi was in New York. He was on his own, and we wouldn't be. With Alvarez, Boyd, Ray, Timothy, Gregor, and the handful of bodyguards on his payroll, we'd have protection."

"What if we play right into his hand by running? Whoever is behind this knew enough to leave Malachi's body in that exact location. They can find us in New York, and it would endanger every person you named and more. No. Gregor thinks this is a phantom from his past that's been attacking the family for centuries. If he's right, then we need to end it here and now because someone like that doesn't give up."

His shoulders fell forward, and he pressed his forehead against hers. The trepidation flooding her body lessened as his breath tickled across her lips. "I'm only one man, Lily." The tender whisper made her heartache. "If anything happens to you..."

Cradling his face between her hands, she pulled him back enough to search his eyes. "If anything happens, it won't be through any fault of yours."

A slow smile crept across his lips. "You are your father's daughter, diplomatic, fearless, and inspirational." The shine in his sad eyes made her ashamed. She didn't deserve that kind of adoration. She was a hot mess trying to pull the fraying ends together, not a legendary icon of strength and bravery.

After snorting a nervous laugh, she pushed past him into the apartment, too frazzled to look him in the eye. The decision to stay could be a death sentence. Suddenly, she realized he would never leave her, which meant it could be a death sentence for him, too, and it would be her fault.

"What's so funny?"

"Are you serious? I'm terrified all the time. I'm jumping at shadows constantly. People say acting in the face of fear is courage. I typically believe acting despite fear, which is there for a damn good reason, is stupid. But I need to do something!"

Chance closed the apartment door and pulled her around to face him. His expression held a rugged determination, which somehow surprised her. "You are stronger than you give yourself credit." His eyes bored into hers, willing her to believe.

"Okay. Message received. Can we look at the magic box holding all the answers now?" A few chestnut strands hung out of place, and without thinking, she slipped her fingers through his silky hair, straightening it. A smile pulled at his lips, and his head moved subtly toward her hand.

She stepped back a little too quickly on shaky legs, worn out emotionally, physically, and psychologically. "We need to get this done before I fall asleep." With a stifled yawn, she made her way to the dining room table and fell into a chair.

"You know, once Miriah is found, this is the first place they'll come." His voice remained flat and emotionless as he spoke, back to business as usual.

Lilith absently nodded as she rubbed her temples.

"We have a cooler of blood in the car. Not to mention everything from Miriah's office."

Her head snapped up. "Damn it. We can't bring the cooler in here, and despite the paperwork, it won't look good if they search the car." She heaved a heavy sigh and sank deeper into the chair.

Chance sat across from her, resting his elbows on the table. "Neither of us has the energy to drive back to Madisonville tonight. We can't help anyone if we die in a car accident."

"Not to mention, Duncan's house is still connected to Miriah. They might include his place in the investigation, especially if they find out he's missing. My blood all over the floor is damaging enough." Lilith popped open the tin while airing her thoughts. She tipped a small satchel, and a glass vial of blood rolled into her hand. Odd. When held up to the light, the blood showed no coagulation, which meant someone preserved the specimen.

Blood separated over time unless someone introduced an additive. The only time she saw it utilized outside of hospitals was in cold cases, keeping the DNA viable for later testing. Then, an idea came to her.

"The Lab!" Chance looked up at her with a frown. "Duncan owns a private medical laboratory here in Knoxville. They shuffled the deed and corporate records through a dozen different dummy corporations. The police won't find it, especially not with Miriah as a starting point. We can drop everything there for safe storage and ask them to analyze this." Duncan understood blood inside and out. If he kept this sample carefully hidden, there was a reason, a purpose.

"Do you think the place is still open?" He glanced at his watch and winced.

She glared at the phone for not magically making time go in reverse and rubbed her face. "Wow. It's a quarter after midnight, and all I want to do is sleep."

"Me, too, but I'll feel better when we don't have incriminating evidence in the car." His tone was too flat for his usual humorous remarks. "There's no way the lab will be open." He looked and sounded exhausted.

Closing her eyes, she forced her chaotic thoughts to fall in line. "Okay, let's think. Duncan did most of the research, and he can't deal with sunlight. So, the facility is more likely to be open now than at noon."

"Brilliant." Unable to deal with the warm admiration, she shied away, preferring to gaze at the tabletop. "We should see if anything in the box can tell us about the vial. Knowing what tests to run and what to look for might be helpful, I'm guessing?"

She stared at the vial in her hand, knowing, somehow, the answer to a million questions lay inside. "You really would make a good detective. And yes, you're right." She set the vial gingerly on the little cloth bag. Then she returned her attention to the other contents, which consisted of several miniature portraits, a dozen pages of old parchment, and a few newer scraps of paper. She started with the oldest ones, but when she flipped them over, they were blank.

"Blank. Like the others you found?"

"Perhaps. Of course, if we don't have any citric acid, we won't be able to read them."

Chance hopped out of his chair and jogged to the kitchen while she glanced over the next several pages. They contained more diary-style entries, a living history. "No luck." He sank back down into the chair with a weary sigh. "So, what do you have there?"

"More journal pages, but much older, ancient, in fact. I'm not fluent in Old English, but I recognize a few words from college history classes. They mention something about athelings, noblemen, and unfrith, which I think is a break of peace. Gregor's name is here as well as Duncan's and one I don't know, Ashcroft Orrick. To understand this, I need an expert in Old English."

"What about these portraits?" Chance picked one up, flipped it over, and stared at it intently.

Lilith studied the rest of them. "Well, I think this one is Gregor, and these two might be his sons. I don't recognize the brunette woman or these men." She glanced up and noticed Chance still staring at the one in his hand.

"Didn't Duncan's journal say you resembled one of Gregor's daughters from back then?"

"Yeah," she tentatively replied, waiting for him to get to the point.

"Well. This is a blonde version of you." He turned the miniature painting, and she glanced up to see a mirror image of herself from fifteen years ago, minus the flaming red hair. The girl in the picture smiled with an innocence that felt alien to her now. It was enough to make her skin crawl.

Logically, she was aware Gregor must have had other children at some point, but her parents raised her as an only child. Staring at the tiny oil painting made her wonder if she was nothing more than a replacement for the daughter he lost. A brooding melancholy fell across her shoulders, weighing her down. With a slow breath, she closed her eyes, trying to find her balance. The world she'd been so sure of was changing around her, leaving her behind.

Sensing her inner turmoil, Chance stayed blissfully silent. When she opened her eyes again, they refocused on the rest of the contents. As lost as she felt, she had no time for personal baggage. Lives hung in the balance.

She flipped over the sneering portrait of a middle-aged man and discovered lettering on the back, *Ashcroft*. Hmm. A possible suspect. The remaining linen wraps held little pewter trinkets shaped like crude figurines.

At the very bottom, a deposit box key rattled around. Unfortunately, Duncan filed off all the unique markings. Yet another dead end.

She snatched the Old English pages and stared at them in pure frustration. Mary's tragic story was right there in front of her, and she couldn't read it. "Dammit!" She slammed her hands down on the table and rocked back in the chair. "Let's go to the lab. I'm sick of feeling useless, but I'm too tired to think anymore."

"What about all this?" Chance motioned to the contents strewn across the table.

After running a hand through her hair, she scratched at the back of her head, aggravated. "Let's take it. This stuff may not be useful to most people, but the killer is from Gregor's time. If he's correct, the bad guy could read these, and I don't think he'd like what they have to say. What if he was looking for this box at Duncan's house the night we showed up? If so, we might have an advantage."

Once he replaced the pieces and closed the box, he handed it to her. "You should put this somewhere safe, and I think it's best if I don't know where that is."

She frowned down at the unassuming container. "Why?"

"Call me paranoid, but it's best to keep crucial information to the smallest number of people." His casual shrug held traces of genuine concern beneath the surface.

Usually, she'd dig into his clouded motivations, but she was too tired. "Fine. The sooner we leave, the sooner we sleep." She tugged her green coat on and spotted blood on the sleeve. "Crap."

Chance stopped with a *What now?* expression. "My coat has Miriah's blood on it." She released a bone-weary sigh. "I need to change." She scanned his clothes from across the room but didn't see anything. Still. "You should take off those clothes"—Chance flashed a devilish grin before she could continue, his eyebrow arching suggestively—"*and* immediately find something else to wear." Her voice sounded annoyed, but the faint pink blossoming across her cheeks told another story. "They might have blood on them." She dug a plastic bag out of her coat and handed it to him. "Change in the shower. That way, I can bleach it to ensure we don't leave any traces."

"I will eventually get these back, right?"

She chuckled while looking over his casual jeans and faded black T-shirt. "You're worried about them?"

Chance frowned defensively and smoothed a hand down his shirt. "This happens to be my favorite T-shirt."

Lilith rolled her eyes and laughed. "Yes, yes. You'll get it back. I'll leave the clothes at the lab until I have an opportunity to clean them properly."

"Thanks. Why don't you go ahead and change first, though?"

"How gallant." With a suspicious smirk, she headed for the bathroom and changed clothes in record time. All she could think about was the blissful nothingness of sleep. After dealing with the crime scene, her overstimulated brain was on the verge of a migraine.

Once she surrendered the room to Chance, she began rambling off a to-do list, pacing the floor. She was so deep in thought that she jumped when he lightly gripped her shoulders.

"Hey, we will take care of everything. Relax and breathe. Oxygen is your friend. Promise." With a tired smile tugging at the corners of her lips, she leaned her forehead against his chest. "Come on, Lily.

Let's go." She reluctantly stepped back as he shoved the bag of clothes into her hands.

"Make sure I get those back." He winked at her, which widened her smile.

Chapter 9

At a quarter till one in the morning, they pulled up to an unassuming squat building. The single-level cinder block rectangle appeared abandoned, but a small sign by the door read *Goditha Laboratories*. Calling the barren red dirt with islands of brown grass a lawn would be a stretch. The weeds cracking through the sidewalks represented the only *living* foliage. Once upon a time, the peeling paint might have been khaki, but now it was a stained, faded mess. Nothing about this place said high-tech laboratory, which was the point.

What concerned her was the lack of vehicles. One lone security truck sat in the parking lot under a solitary light. A moment of panic made her want to hit something. No. She had to be right. Shuttling staff made sense in a smaller city, diverting unwanted attention.

They made their way to the front of the building and found a buzzer panel at the door labeled with Sections 1 through 9. After pushing the first button, a deep rumbling voice crackled from the speaker with bored authority. "Goditha clinic is closed. Please return tomorrow during business hours if you'd like to speak to someone."

"Well, that didn't sound rehearsed at all." He started to turn away, but she snatched his arm and pressed the button again.

"This is Lilith Adams. Security code A09178." The door popped open with a buzz, and she held it open for him. "Are you coming?" He stared at her for a moment.

"You have universal access?"

"Gregor insisted since there are only a handful of crime scene investigators in our ranks."

"Hmm." He strolled past her, careful eyes taking in the surroundings. The barren walls glowed under the fluorescent lights with the same bland green covering every hospital. White linoleum floors made her black flats squeak with its fresh coat of wax. The only thing visible was a sprawling desk at the end of the hall with a full bank of monitors.

A large man, with skin the color of burnt coffee, sat hunched over the screens. The shadow of hair on his head blended into a razor-thin line tracing his square jaw. Her best guess put him in his midthirties, but then physical appearance didn't necessarily mean anything. After all, she spent her life dealing with vampires. The truth was she couldn't tell if a person was a vampire without testing their blood, so it was highly probable she'd dealt with vamps, not knowing what they were.

As they approached, the guard's eyes lifted from the screens, and he sat up tall, *very* tall. The man, whose name badge read Coffee, was colossal at over seven feet and broad like a giant linebacker.

"Ms. Adams. I'll need identification." His voice resembled the sound of a huge bass drum, so deep, it vibrated in her bones. A pleasant smile lit his face when he studied her but vanished as his eyes moved to her companion. They narrowed in intimidation, and his mouth became a thin, firm line. "Name?"

While digging out her trifold, she smiled sweetly and introduced her escort. "Chance Deveraux. He's my bodyguard assigned by Gregor Adams. You can verify that with him if need be." She handed over the ID, and the enormous man scanned over the information. Then he examined her and went back to studying her ID before holding the trifold out to her.

"I will have to call unless Mr. Deveraux has a code?" His eyes stayed on Chance as his voice rumbled.

"Nope, sorry. I'm not part of the club. Gregor can vouch for me, though."

Coffee picked up the phone and dialed, from memory, something that rarely happened anymore. Since the age of cell phones, people didn't memorize numbers anymore.

As he dialed, Coffee's daunting stare never left Chance, who was usually on the other side of the situation. He tried to appear unbothered by the intense attention, but she saw the anxiety pulling his muscles.

A moment later, he hung up the phone and swung his gaze to Lilith. "No answer. I'm afraid I can't allow Mr. Deveraux any further without clearance."

The fact that Gregor didn't answer a call from this *particular* facility troubled her. "Thank you, Mr. Coffee, is it?" She flashed a sweet yet professional smile as she tucked her ID away.

He nodded proficiently as if storing energy for later instead of wasting it on pleasantries. "Richard Coffee, head of Goditha security, ma'am." His dark lips curled into a boyish smile, which made him seem ten years younger.

She extended her arm for a handshake. The dark mahogany skin made hers appear drastically pale as his giant hand engulfed hers. "A pleasure to meet you. I'm sure Mr. Deveraux doesn't mind staying here. I only need to drop off a few things, submit a sample for testing, and grab a few supplies. Is anyone else working tonight? We didn't see any cars."

Richard's eyes darted to Chance again but quickly returned to her this time. "Yes, ma'am. We use a shuttle service. Do you know which division you need?" Avoiding specifics on personnel in front of an unauthorized individual was a good indication of quality security.

Despite resembling a mindless wrestler that dominated a WWF ring, Richard Coffee was articulate and knew his job. "Blood Analysis, Cold Storage, and somewhere I can restock my crime scene kit."

When Richard nodded again, it seemed a bit warmer. "You'll find Blood Analysis in Section 2, down the left hall, first door on the right. Our storage refrigerator is in Section 3, which is the second door on the right. Supplies you can find in any of the labs." The rumbling tones were like smooth velvet, a definite asset to someone with his job title. Arguing with someone who sounded like the late Michael Clarke Duncan reading a bedtime story was impossible.

A sudden thought occurred to her, and she flashed a quick smile. "Do you have anyone in local law enforcement?"

Mild surprise pulled at his brow. "We have one man in forensics who catches any trace evidence. We don't have enough incidents in this area to warrant anything else. Why do you ask?" His voice sank to an unnatural octave.

"A situation is about to come to light, and we'd appreciate your man's help." After jotting down the address, she continued. "We examined the scene, but I like knowing someone has our back."

His enormous head nodded with professional appreciation. "I'll call my man and forward this to him." He paused, eyeballing the person without clearance, and frowned. "His name is McClung if you need to contact him." "Thank you." She turned to Chance, grabbing everything before smiling up at him. Nervousness filled his eyes, and she realized the tension in his body wasn't only a response to authority. He was worried.

"This is a secure facility, and I won't take long, I promise. Ten minutes, tops." Hidden from view, she lightly squeezed his hand and winked, which coaxed a grin from him.

"Don't leave me here too long." The whispered words clearly said, *Don t stay out of my sight for too long.* After what happened in Duncan's basement, she didn't blame him for the gut reaction.

Taking several steps backward, he put his shoulder against the wall. She loved the casual lean he'd perfected, but his smile felt hollow, a show for her benefit.

"Be right back."

The first stop was Blood Analysis, where she met several scientists who happily put aside their routine work. Not surprising since they all resembled hermits with no social skills, and she was a curvy redhead. They eagerly agreed to run DNA analysis and compare the blood vial with Law Enforcement and private databases. They promised preliminary results by tomorrow night, which was impressively fast, despite what inaccurate TV shows claimed.

The techs scattered as she sterilized her tools again and refilled her kit before moving on to Cold Storage. The room was thankfully quiet. Either the crew working there was gone for the *day* or hadn't come in yet. She labeled the cooler and bags of clothes, adding "D.N.D." (Do Not Disturb) stickers to be safe.

Then she laid out what remained, the baggie with the bloody paper and the chipped metal box. She stared at them with tired eyes and tried to think of anything she may have missed. She could analyze them with the equipment here, but she'd probably pass out over a microscope and lose an eye. Besides, she couldn't leave Chance standing out there all night.

After a weary sigh, she tucked the tin and evidence bag into the cooler. This facility was the safest place in the entire state of Tennessee to hide them until she had more time and energy.

"Did I miss anything?" Running through her crime scene checklist made her calm and organized. No. That was everything. The police couldn't tie them to Miriah, at least not with physical evidence. Now perhaps they could get some rest.

Lilith turned the corner, and her visions of sleep came to a halt. Chance leaned against the wall with the casual grace of a poster boy for men's cologne, but with clothes on. How could she not appreciate six feet, three inches of lean muscle, calm and relaxed but capable of springing into action at a second's notice? He sure was easy on the eyes. Focus, Lilith, focus.

Richard Coffee swung his stare away from her bodyguard as she walked toward them. He pushed his chair back, standing, and she amended her original estimation of his height to well over seven feet.

She paused and exchanged a startled look with Chance, who moved off the wall. She strode forward, with a slight tremor in her knees. Mr. Coffee was beyond intimidating and scary. Lilith was quite sure his snarl would make the boogeyman quake with fear.

"Find everything you need, ma'am?" His baritone voice boomed through the air.

"Yes. Thank you, Mr. Coffee." She came up to Chance's side and smiled up at Richard. Way up. "I trust my friend didn't give you any trouble?"

The smile stretching his dark lips was a genuine one full of things she didn't want to know. Scary things. "Wisely enough, no." From the corner of her eye, she glimpsed a half smirk from Chance. "I should escort the two of you out."

She nodded nervously, and the giant named Richard moved around the suddenly tiny desk. They trailed behind him in silence, staring at his impossibly wide back. He carried weight around his waist as most linebackers do, but no one would dare call the man lazy. Hell, his fist was the size of her entire head.

When they reached the outside door, Richard shook her hand again, making her feel like she was about three years old, and held the door open for them. Chance started after her, but Mr. Coffee's heavy hand dropped on his shoulder. His booming voice took on an earnest tone. "You take care of her."

Chance glanced over his shoulder at Richard's broad face and nodded solemnly. "I would take a bullet even if it wasn't my job." On the surface, the response appeared light and casual, but the undercurrent was complete sincerity. He wouldn't hesitate to sacrifice his life for her, and that was terrifying. Every decision she made now affected them both. She held his life in her hands.

Coffee responded with a grin full of professional respect and then shut the door on them.

Chance didn't say anything else until they squeezed into the tiny rental car again. "Holy crap! Was he Andre the Giant's big brother from Africa?" He blinked a few times and slunk into the seat as much as the cramped confinements allowed. "He wasn't some hallucination from sleep deprivation, was he? Damn, he had to be over seven feet, maybe eight."

"Kinda makes you feel tiny, doesn't it?" she chuckled and rubbed at her tired eyes. "Duncan sure knows how to hire the right people. He could dissolve a normal person into a puddle of fear by simply growling at them."

"Yeah, no kidding. Okay. I need some fast food, and then I need some fucking sleep." The dark circles under his eyes were more pronounced in the glow from the instrument panel.

Now that she thought about it, he hadn't slept since their short nap in the dingy hotel. After her attack, while she was unconscious, he guarded the doors and tracked down Spencer. She felt terrible for saying a single word about being tired. Of course, the life-threatening head injury was the only reason she got more sleep than he did, so she guessed that made them even.

After sucking down some much-needed greasy burgers, they crawled up the stairs to Miriah's apartment on the verge of a food coma. Ida didn't make an appearance, not that she expected her to. It was two in the morning, way past a typical senior citizen's bedtime. Lilith kicked her shoes off just inside the apartment door, exhausted after an emotionally taxing day.

Chance rubbed at his bloodshot eyes and stalked over to the Japanese-style couch. "You can take the bed." He flopped down on his back and sprawled his long body out with one arm curved behind his head. Lilith caught herself staring, then stumbled toward the bedroom and the queen-size world of comfort that awaited her.

She had just enough energy to shimmy out of her jeans before she collapsed on the bed. As soon as she curled up under the covers, the right side of her head began to throb, a pointed reminder of her injuries. With an irritated moan, she flipped to her left, hugged a pillow, and surrendered to blissful darkness.

She crawled through a narrow passage in the rough and jagged ground. Stones, pebbles, roots, all bit into her hands and knees painfully, but an orange glow ahead lured her forward. Muffled cries and shouts echoed through the air, a terrifying sound raising every hair on her body. The stench of wet earth was so pervasive, she choked on her deeper breaths, forcing her to keep them short and shallow.

The tunnel opened into a large cavern with stalactites and stalagmites closing in on the space like jagged teeth. Liquid dripped down the wickedly sharp points, and at first, Lilith thought it was water. Then, she noticed the thicker viscosity. When the realization hit her, all the overwhelming scents in the cave unfolded into the poignant smells of blood, death, and decay.

The rocks were weeping blood, which collected in the pools hollowed out of the stone floor. This had to be a dream, but everything looked, felt, and smelled impossibly real.

The glow that lured her from the tunnel originated behind a massive stalagmite about ten feet wide. The light flickered and wavered like a living flame as the torturous cries continued, weighing heavy in the air. *It's a dream. It's a dream.* No matter how many times she repeated the mantra, she couldn't wake up.

Pulling herself out of the tunnel with a heave, she tumbled to the rough ground, which was like ice on her naked skin. She glanced down in confusion at her bare feet, her bare legs, her bare everything. She wrapped her arms around herself, trying to block the chill from her vulnerable skin. She crouched down, not wanting to move, but the haunting cries urged her forward, pulling her as if by strings.

Her careful foot skidded forward, feeling for anything sharp before putting weight on it. Each echoing sound made her body tremble, terrified someone or something would hear her. Tedious step after tedious step, she made her way to the dominant stalagmite in the center. When she reached it, her foot caught the edge of a sharp pebble that made her swallow a yelp. More sharp stones followed until the soles of her feet burned with bloody cuts, but she forced herself to keep inching around the monumental rock.

She leaned out, searching for the light source, and spotted Gregor strapped to a chair. Blood dripped from thousands of oozing cuts all along his battered body. Defeat filled his eyes, resigned to his fate, and that sight chilled her more than any of the wounds.

Clear tubing ran out of each arm, one to a hanging bag of blood, the other to a bucket on the floor. His blood overflowed and spilled across the stone, adding to the pools around the room. She bit back a scream, her fingernails gripping the rough surface so tight, one of her nails snapped. The blinding pain burned up her arm like napalm, bringing back her focus.

Someone stood at the edge of her vision, holding an old-world lantern high over Gregor's head. A sudden peal of laughter made her entire body shiver in disgust as she cringed. She had to help her father, but how could she fight off anyone naked and unarmed?

She watched helplessly as the mystery man smashed the lantern at her father's feet, the flames climbing up his legs. Gregor's agonizing screams almost blocked the sound of blood thundering in her ears. Panting from her hiding spot with tears stinging her eyes, she scanned the dark floors for something, anything to help. Meanwhile, her father's screams echoed so loud, they shook the rock formations in the ceiling.

Nothing. There was nothing she could use, nothing she could do. The madman might as well have bound her to a chair next to Gregor. She clasped her hands over her ears, rocking, trying to wake up. The excruciating shrieks only became louder. She couldn't cower there, powerless, while Gregor burned. If she couldn't wake up, she had to do something.

With a determined grimace, she ran for him. However, as soon as she emerged, a face flashed in front of her lightning fast. Dark hair clipped short, a long pointy nose, a slim mustache above thin cruel lips, eyes dark as night sunken deep into his skull. She recognized him, but the tiny painting didn't show the network of scars that crossed his face, ran down his neck, and disappeared beneath his collar like a map of misery.

The man cackled and snatched her, his talon-like nails piercing her arms to the bone. The sudden agony stole all the strength from her legs as she screeched. The horrifying face loomed closer, moving along her neck, drinking in her scent as his eyes closed in rapture. "Mary." The words slithered past his thin lips like a lover's whisper, and her stomach lurched. Slowly the black pits of his eyes opened, and a sickening smile stretched his mouth, revealing rows of jagged, stained teeth.

He pulled one hand away, bringing a single blood-drenched finger to his lips. His beady eyes bored into her as his mouth closed sensuously around his finger. The sucking sound made her want to curl into a ball under a rock and never come out again. She tried to pull away, but his talons buried in her left arm made it impossible. Every movement dragged her closer to the brink of unconsciousness.

With a fierce, guttural growl, Ashcroft snatched her right arm again, nails scratching sickeningly against the bone. The wave of pain tore bloodcurdling screams from her throat and nearly pushed her over the edge. Her vision fluttered as his hungry eyes drank in her misery with maniacal glee.

Her shrieks mixed with Gregor's in a hideous cacophony that caused pure panic to cloud her mind, all logic leaving her to suffer.

We're all going to die, she thought, weeping uncontrollably as her body gave out. Struggling pushed his nails further into the bone, making the pain unbearable. She couldn't fight anymore. If this wasn't a dream, it was the end of everything.

Without warning, the monster's nails ripped from her arms in sudden blinding terror, and she collapsed to the ground. Sluggishly, she pulled herself up, every slight movement making her wounds burn and screech.

Blood poured over her pale skin, making her hands slick on the floor. When she raised her eyes, she saw Ashcroft hit the massive stalagmite with a sickening crack, and he crumpled to the floor.

Her arms gave out before she could spot her savior, and she collapsed against the cold stone. As the blood oozed from her wounds, it took all her strength with it. Then, she caught sight of Chance fighting the flames engulfing her father.

He managed to put them out, but by the thick scent of burnt flesh, she knew it wasn't soon enough. Her chest heaved with heartbroken sobs as she vainly tried to crawl closer. *"No!"* She meant to scream the word, but it came out as a weak, hopeless whimper of despair. Her nails scratched uselessly against the stone floor as her muscles refused to cooperate.

Chance ran to her and slid down, pulling her into his lap. He was warm and secure, tugging her close and crying against her hair. She weakly struggled to get past him to her father's body, but his arms were like steel. The blood loss made her dizzy and lightheaded, so she stopped fighting, collapsed against him, and stared up at his face.

A golden light shone beneath his skin, making him resemble an avenging angel. His eyes blazed green, and his hair glinted with fire and bronze. His ethereal visage stopped her breath, and she reached to brush her fingers across his cheek in captivated awe. Before her hand reached his face, all her strength dissipated, and it fell limp to the floor.

A metallic glint flashed in the corner of her eye mere seconds before a bony hand snatched Chance by his unearthly hair. In a split second, too fast for a vampire, a knife slid across his neck. Chance didn't have time to scream. Wet gargling gasps left his gaping mouth as she stared at the panicked terror in his eyes. Endless shrieks made her throat raw, and she backed up, unable to look away from the blood cascading down his shirt. *God, no.*

The celestial glow beneath his skin began leaking away, and his hair lost all its blazing shine. His eyes stayed fixed on hers, those beautiful hazel eyes flecked with green. The light dimmed and vanished, shattering her heart into cruel pieces, tearing her apart from the inside. Her screams turned to raspy croaks before giving way to uncontrollable weeping that racked her body.

Ashcroft moved laggardly toward her, his knife dripping with Chance's blood, but she didn't care. She stared at the lifeless bodies of Gregor and Chance, knowing every piece of her died with them. She couldn't breathe past the gut-wrenching sobs as her world collapsed into nothingness.

Ashcroft stood over her, his knife directed at the dead cavity where her heart once thrived. Still, she kept her eyes on Chance. The only thing his blade could do at this point was to bring her a merciful end.

The vicious blade plunged into her chest, stealing any breath she had left. For a moment, everything went black. Then, Miriah's lidless eyes and noseless face circled her, contorted with manic laughter. The bloody ribbons of her ears slapped against her bruised cheeks, and the sickening wet sounds made the bile rise. "You let them die. You let us all die." Miriah's voice gargled as blood spilled from the incisions of her shredded lips.

Lilith shot bolt upright in bed with a bloodcurdling scream. A sheen of sweat covered her clammy skin. She sobbed through the pain, fighting for each panicked breath. Then, the sound of pounding fists on the door registered past the blood booming in her ears.

"Lilith?" Chance kicked the bedroom door open and ran into the room. Without any hesitation, he pulled her out of bed, his arms folding around her. "God. Are you okay?"

He was the only thing keeping her upright as she pressed her face against his chest and continued to sob. She couldn't stop. The images of her father burning, Chance dying, Miriah's mutilated face laughing played over and over in her mind, tormenting her.

He pulled her in close to keep her from falling and stepped forward. After sitting her on the bed with tender care, he dropped to one knee. His hands shoved back her matted hair to cup her face, but once the weeping stopped, she stared sightlessly past him.

"Please, Lily." He frantically searched her shell-shocked eyes. "What happened?"

"So awful…" The words emerged from her raw throat, rough and breathy. "You… Gregor…" She couldn't finish before tears doubled her over, making her gasp for air.

While smoothing his fingers through her damp hair, he made the same comforting sounds he had earlier at Miriah's office. "I'm sorry, *cherie*. I tried to get in, but you had the door locked." When she didn't stop crying, he released a little moan of despair and pulled her off the bed, curling her up in his lap. He held her so tight, she couldn't move if she wanted to, which she didn't.

A spot of blood caught his attention, and he gingerly inspected her right hand, finding the middle nail broken past the quick. "Lily." Heartache drenched the whispered word, causing her chest to tighten.

When the tears stopped, she lay against him, listening to his heartbeat as reality began to sink in. It was only a horrible dream. Gregor was safe in New York, and Chance was here, alive, warm, and real. Miriah… Miriah was dead, and all Lilith could do for her was to ensure her death stood for something.

"I'm right here, Lily." His breath tickled against her skin as he plucked the words from her frantic thoughts. "I'm not going anywhere. I won't let anyone hurt you. You're okay." The terror began to leak from her body, replaced by a detached calm.

It took clearing her throat several times before she managed to speak again, coming out as a hoarse croak. "Ashcroft tortured Gregor and set him on fire." She paused to draw in a deep breath, which rattled in her chest. "He attacked me, and…you tried to save me." She swallowed the lump rising her throat before continuing. "He… god…he killed you while we sat exactly like this."

He saw the blind panic welling in her eyes and squeezed tighter, his lips placing a tender kiss against her clammy skin. "No one is here but us. You're safe."

"When he killed Gregor and then you…" Her red-rimmed eyes drifted up to his, and she knew he saw everything. All the terror and heartache lay naked in her face. She shook her head, squeezing her eyes closed, and drew in another shaky breath. "I wanted him to kill me. To end it."

Lilith felt his hand glide over her cheek and opened her misty eyes to meet his. A stunning bolt of electricity shot straight down her spine as his lips crushed against hers, salty with tears.

When his hand swept through her damp hair to cradle her neck, she melted into him, lost in the fiery kiss burning everything else away. All the trauma dissipated like vapor as she wrapped her arms around his neck, fingers twining into his silky hair. A deep primal moan brought her body to life, awakening every inch in breathless passion. Catching his bottom lip between her teeth, she flicked her tongue against it in a languid motion, making his heart race.

Instinctually, she turned, draping one leg on either side to face him. His strong hands massaged up her back, pulling her closer. Her palms caressed his cheeks, enjoying the tickle of his soft stubble on her fingers.

As the kiss deepened, her head spun, lost in sensations, drunk on power, breathing in his rich scent. He was so bright and delicious that the darkness of her nightmares didn't stand a chance against him. The control she felt, the way she could easily illicit a response, overcame the powerlessness she felt in the dream. She wanted more, needed more, to drive away all the evil things tormenting her.

Without warning, he pulled back, gasping, his body trembling with every pant. "I can't," he whispered in a paralyzing moment of confusion before continuing. "I want to." Raw need filled his words, and when his eyes opened, she saw it echoed there. Fingers trailed feather-soft up her neck to cradle her cheek, and she leaned into his touch. A spark lit her body as his breath came out in a rush, warming her lips. "Not like this." He swallowed hard. "This isn't right."

Chance sighed again like he couldn't believe he was saying all this. "I've wanted this for so long, but I won't be used to make the bad things go away." His cheeks burned red as his eyes stared past her, unable to hold her questioning gaze. "I would do almost anything for you, but this is not real, and it's not fair."

Reluctantly, he pulled away, and all the warmth disappeared with him. She stayed frozen on the floor, feeling lost and uncertain, torn between anger, frustration, and embarrassment. He thought she was using him to make herself feel better, but she would never be so selfish.

In a surge of anger, her fingers curled into fists, and pain flared up her arm from the broken nail, making her yelp. However, the sting brought clarity. He was right, and it made her chest tighten in shame. No matter how much she cared about him, her real purpose at the moment was chasing away the demons in her head. She drew her knees in, wrapping her arms around them as tears of humiliation rolled down her cheeks.

Chance found his feet before leaning down to scoop her up in his arms. After gently placing her in the bed, he brushed her hair back with a longing stare. She reached out in sudden desperation, catching his hand, and sliding her fingers between his.

"Please, don't leave." The tightness in her chest stole her breath as she swallowed the nervous lump in her throat. "You're right, and I'm sorry. I didn't mean…but please. I don't want to be alone." The pleading tone of her voice brought tears to his eyes.

Without another word, he slipped into the bed and wrapped his arms around her. As he shielded her from the night, she listened to his heart rate slowing. Within minutes, the tension leaked from her body, lulling her into a dreamless sleep.

Chapter 10

Lilith blinked her heavy eyelids as dust particles glinted in the streams of light filtering through the blinds. A sudden deep breath made her realize someone else was in the bed. Chills ran down her spine until she spotted the hand draped over her hip, and her brain clicked things into place. A smile curled her lips as she soaked in the warmth of Chance's body against her back. His breath ebbed out slow and steady, tickling along her neck. For one greedy moment, she lay still and let his presence keep reality at bay.

Slow and meticulous, she inched out of Chance's embrace. When only his hand on her hip remained, she twisted to peek at his face. The handsome line of his mouth quirked up in a smile, and his eyes raced behind his lids. She didn't want to wake him, particularly from a beautiful dream, which she knew firsthand was rare. Last night may have been the worst night terror, but not her first.

Most people assumed nightmares came with the job, but hers started long before she landed her forensics position, back in her college days at UCLA. The thought flickered through her mind, picturing the horrible night for the millionth time. No. Today required her to focus on more pressing matters.

She slid her hand under his and gradually lowered it to the bed. With one last lingering look at his chiseled face, she slid out of bed and tiptoed to the bathroom.

When she glanced in the mirror, a deep blush rushed over her cheeks. The T-shirt and lavender boy-cut panties didn't leave much to the imagination. For some reason, her lack of clothing was more embarrassing than Chance breaking down the door to save her from a bad dream.

At least the bruise over her right temple lightened to pale shadows of yellow and tan. She needed a shower to deal with her matted, frizzy mess of flaming curls. Hopefully, it would help with the dark circles under her eyes and frightfully pale skin, which made her resemble a raccoon.

Once she closed the bathroom door, she stripped off her clothes and stumbled into the shower. Exhaustion, both physical and emotional, left her feeling used up. She cried more in the last seventy-two hours than she had since her mother died. Scrubbing as fast as she could, the melancholy emotions seeped out with the grime swirling around the drain. When she stepped out of the steaming, hot shower, her spirit felt a million times lighter.

After a bit of makeup and Miriah's hair dryer, she resembled her old self again. Nibbling her lip, she cracked the bathroom door to see Chance passed out with the sheets twisted around him. She lingered in the doorway, holding her towel tight around her, and grinned.

Her entire world changed in a matter of days, most of it for the worse. Chance embodied a bright spot, as confusing and complicated as he may be. If only she took the time to get to know him sooner. What if Chance told her back then? Back when Gregor brought down the hammer? No. Even if her father didn't keep his word about shipping him off to Siberia, a teenage romance wouldn't last. Perhaps Gregor's interference was commendable, but it didn't justify his deplorable methods.

In the end, none of it mattered, and dwelling on the past wouldn't help her now. She quietly picked up her small suitcase and tiptoed into the living room. After rummaging for a few moments, she pulled on a pair of curve-hugging jeans, a dark green fitted blouse, and tan strappy heels.

Searching the kitchen for food proved a pointless endeavor. Either Miriah and Malachi never ate at home, or they survived solely on takeout. All the world's creativity wouldn't make canned olives, mayonnaise, a stick of butter, and a can of tomato paste into anything appetizing. Then, she remembered the little coffee shop on the corner across from the apartment building. After jotting down a quick note for Chance, she grabbed her wallet along with Miriah's keys and strolled out of the building.

Carloads of people bustled toward downtown under the brilliant blue sky as a hum of anxious energy filled the crisp fall air. The line at Honeybee Coffee & Bakery extended outside to the corner. So much for grabbing a quick breakfast. Hopefully, Chance wouldn't wake up while she battled her way through the masses of caffeine-deprived commuters.

Thirty minutes later, Lilith emerged victorious with a bag of buttery croissants and two piping hot coffees. While crossing the street, she spotted Ida shuffling toward the front door with an armload of groceries. Lilith hurried down the sidewalk and up the steps, unlocking the door before the elderly woman made it to the top.

Ida peered up in surprise, her weathered face curving into a friendly welcome. "Oh, thank you, sweetie." She shuffled through the door, and together, they started up the stairs. "Lily, right? Allen's fiancée?"

Lilith nodded as she considered the likelihood of the police questioning the neighbors. "Actually, his name is Chance. Allen is his middle name. He always thought his first name sounded too… hippie."

Ida let out a polite laugh, the kind that made Lilith wonder if she said something funny or something stupid. "Are you two staying with Miriah and Malachi?"

"For a couple of days. Miriah sent us the key, but they haven't been home. We're a little concerned."

"Oh, dear." Ida's face darkened as they started up the second-floor steps. "The last time I saw them was"—she stopped to think—"four nights ago, on my way out to meet my granddaughter at the theater, Monday night. They were in quite a hurry with a suitcase, so we didn't chat."

Monday. The night before her flight from New York to Knoxville. She wondered when and how Malachi wound up in New York. The timeline still didn't make sense.

"Do you have enough space for proper sleeping arrangements?" When Lilith appeared confused, Ida clarified. "Spencer? Well, I saw him…late Wednesday morning with luggage, so I assumed he was staying there as well."

Lilith forced a smile. "He's checking into some things for Malachi. Are you sure it was *this* Wednesday?" If Ida was correct, he stopped here before meeting them at the Madisonville house, but why?

Ida paused at her door. "Oh, I'm quite sure. I spotted him while leaving for my Wednesday afternoon class at the senior center." Her lips curled, and the edge of her nose scrunched, a subtle but unmistakable show of contempt. Then, her face brightened in a crinkling smile, like flipping a switch. "Well, thank you, sweetie, for walking an old woman to her door. I do hope you hear from Miriah and Malachi." Lilith nodded and started toward the apartment door. "They are such lovely people and have been through so much lately." The comment stopped her in her tracks.

"I'm sorry?"

Ida's eyebrows soared. "You don't know? Oh…well, I suppose they might have been too embarrassed to say anything to their family."

Lilith stepped closer, the little hairs on her neck standing on end. "Embarrassed by what?"

"Well, the tests. About a year or two ago, Miriah discovered that she could not have children, bless her heart. The poor darling was devastated. Then, last week, they found out Malachi was sick. She didn't specify, but I got the impression it was severe."

"You're sure? Malachi is a pretty healthy guy." An overly robust immune system was one of the few pop culture myths that rang true. Infertility and illness were impossibilities, considering the strength of their bloodlines. Malachi came from a family in Greece as pure as Miriah's. He wouldn't be susceptible to disease. Perhaps Alvarez could secure a blood sample from Malachi's body and send it to Solasta, their lab in New York.

Ida tried to balance her groceries and unlock the door with little success as she responded. "I'm quite sure. Miriah was distraught, and I think it resulted from some sort of attack. When she spoke to me about it, the focused anger in her eyes said she held someone accountable."

None of Ida's revelations appeared connected with their immediate problems, but they represented a considerable threat if she was right. "Well, I won't tell Miriah you told me. Here let me take those." Lilith smiled sweetly at the old woman, switched the coffees and croissants to one hand, and held a bag of groceries so Ida could unlock her door. "If Miriah confides in me, I'll act surprised."

The elderly woman graciously accepted the help and shoved her door open. "You are a dear, sweet woman. That boy is a lucky man, indeed."

She stood in humorous shock as Ida shuffled inside and closed her door. With an amused little smirk that pushed her gloom to the back burner, she crossed the hall. As soon as she had the door open, she kicked off her heels and tiptoed toward the bedroom.

Chance still lay wrapped in the sheets, dreaming, judging by the smile on his face. She made her way around the bed and sat on the edge. When he didn't move, she placed the breakfast goodies on the nightstand and leaned over to brush a stray strand from his forehead.

Chance snatched her wrist with lightning-quick speed, scaring a yelp out of her. His drowsy eyes blinked open and eventually registered her face. Then he realized he had an iron grip on her wrist. "Shit, sorry." He gently tugged her hand to his lips with a lazy smile and pressed a kiss against her skin. "I'm not used to people waking me up."

She crooked an eyebrow and chuckled, "Don't let them stay the night, huh?" Her smile faltered a bit, and she pulled her arm back. "On second thought, don't answer the question. TMI."

A wide yawn cut off any response and left him blinking. "Did you sleep at all?"

"Yes, and thankfully, dreamless." She twisted behind her to grab the coffees and the bag of croissants. "And I got breakfast." She flashed a bright smile and took a long sip of her overly sweet cappuccino.

He stared at the cup of coffee in his hand and then turned his steely stare on her. "I hope they delivered." She took another deep sip, stalling with a rising panic swelling in her chest. He closed his eyes and breathed a heavy sigh. "Do *not* tell me you left the apartment by yourself."

Defensive pride caused her to sit a little straighter, her jaw clenching a touch. "Fine. I won't tell you." She pointedly dug into the bag and wrestled out a giant flaky croissant.

"Don't be a smart-ass, Lily." He kept glaring at her while she took a huge bite.

After she swallowed the delicious morsel, she mirrored his disapproving scowl. "The place is literally across the street. I had my pepper spray, and I walked with Ida most of the way. I think I can manage to grab food without an armed escort."

"Yeah, I bet Miriah felt the same way." As soon as he said it, regret flashed across his face, plain as day.

"You're welcome." She rose from the bed, coffee and half-eaten flaky delight in hand, and sauntered toward the living room. "When you're done being an ass and feeling bad about it, perhaps we can talk." She didn't turn around or glance over her shoulder. She just walked calmly through the door.

Lilith borrowed a notebook and a few pens from Miriah's office before taking a seat at the dining room table. The timeline had so many factors, she couldn't keep it all straight in her head. Halfway through mapping everything out, Chance appeared with his cup of coffee. She watched him out of the corner of her eye while jotting down a few more notes.

He walked right up to her, grabbed the pen from her hand, and flung it on the table. She frowned at the discarded pen and reached for it, but he gripped her wrist first and tugged her up from the chair. He held her hand against his chest and stared down at her with such warmth, her cheeks burned.

"Thank you for breakfast." A smile crossed his lips, tugging one out of her even though she'd rather slap him. *Damn him.* How the hell could she stay mad at him? The cheating bastard. "First, green is an amazing color on you." Her cheeks blushed bright red. He was *definitely* cheating. "The croissants and coffee are delicious, and the sentiment means a lot to me. I've never had a woman bring me breakfast in bed."

"Oh, so that's usually the men, huh?" The deflective humor lacked her normal confident tone. When in doubt, revert to what's familiar, and for her, that was sarcastic wit.

Chance released a surprised chuckle. "Yeah. And somehow, *I'm* the smart-ass." His hand slid sensuously up her neck to cradle her cheek with tingles following in its wake. "Please." His lips hovered over hers, only a breath away, causing her heart to race in her chest. "I don't want anything to happen to you. So please, promise me you won't go anywhere alone again."

The instinctual tension to fill the space between them pulled at every muscle, and it took her brain a moment to realize what he said. "This is extortion." Her breathy whisper didn't illicit a single twitch from him.

"Only if it works." He cracked a smile as his eyebrow arched in pure confidence. "Promise?"

"Yes, yes. I promise," she huffed the words between clenched teeth.

"Now that wasn't so hard, was it?" He pressed a tiny kiss to the tip of her nose, walked right past her, and took a seat at the table. With a casual, nonchalant air, he draped an arm across the back of the chair. At that moment, she had no idea if she wanted to kiss him or slap the smug grin off his face. "So…what are we discussing?" His eyelashes batted innocently, and her scowl almost cracked at the outrageously unmasculine expression.

"You are such an ass!" She stomped over to her chair and slumped down, trying to keep a straight face.

"Oh, don't get those lovely lavender panties in a twist, kitten. Business now, pleasure later." He winked as her face turned candy apple red. "I won't tell. Scout's honor." He held up two fingers in the Scout's salute, and she held up one, the middle one.

Lilith snatched her pen and forced her concentration on the paper in front of her, hands still quivering. "I'm trying to nail down this timeline. One benefit of my taboo excursion to the bakery was running into Ida. She had some interesting things to say."

"By all means, share with the class." Chance nestled comfortably into his seat, sipping coffee and devouring a large croissant.

"According to her, Miriah and Malachi rushed out of here on Monday night. Then sometime Tuesday, Spencer called Dad. We met Gregor around midnight that night, and the coroner estimated Malachi's time of death around the same time, between midnight and two in the morning." She took a breath, pushing away the thought of Malachi's torture taking place while she met with her father. "We left New York City about four AM and arrived in Knoxville at eight AM with no one here to pick us up."

"Did Ida mention Miriah and Malachi carrying suitcases?"

She shook her head, studying the paper. "One. Wait. Did Spencer ever say when Malachi left on his trip?"

After mulling it over while turning the coffee cup in his hands, he finally shrugged. "No, I don't think he ever said."

Lilith scowled at the paper. "If Malachi was still here on Monday night, he had to know Duncan didn't show up for dinner. Why would he pick up and leave his wife to fly to New York City when her father could be missing?"

"Now, *that* is an excellent question. What else did Ida say?"

"She said Spencer carried some luggage into the apartment Wednesday morning."

"But Spencer said he hadn't been here in weeks." Chance appeared confused as he took another bite of his croissant.

"Yeah, but we specifically asked about him spending time with Miriah and Malachi. Perhaps, he didn't count dropping something off as the same thing."

Lilith scrutinized her notes as she rubbed her temples. "Something else bothers me, though. I couldn't put my finger on what until now. Spencer claimed he was on the phone chasing down leads, but we kept calling from Wednesday to Thursday morning, and his phone always went straight to voice mail."

"Now that I think about it, when I first spoke to him, he said his phone died, and he had to buy a new charger. What are you saying, Lily?" Chance wrapped his hands around his coffee cup with a meaningful stare. She thought about her next words, running through everything she learned.

With a deflated sigh, she slumped forward over the table. "Dammit, Spencer is family, and I hate this, but nothing he says adds up." A thought popped into her head. "Wait. Luggage…the suitcase!"

Chance watched her, riveted, as she tore down the hall to the bedroom. She swung the closet door open and grinned triumphantly.

She dragged the squat black carry-on into the center of the room and opened every single zipper, a total of twelve, but found nothing. The excitement faded with a disappointed sigh, and she sunk to the floor. Something white on the handle flashed in her vision. She pulled at an airport tag. "Depart TYS." She couldn't make out the rest through all the scuff marks.

Chance appeared in the door. "Hey, care to share?"

"Whoever this belongs to flew out from Knoxville but didn't fly back. I can't read the date or the destination, but airlines remove old tags before putting on new ones, which cut down on lost luggage. So how the hell did it end up back in Tennessee, and what was Spencer doing with it?"

"I don't know…"

"I feel like I'm trying to put together a puzzle when someone's stolen half the pieces. Nothing fits." She rested her head against the bed, thinking through everything. "Did Spencer give you an address to the warehouse in Nashville Miriah asked him to check out?"

"Yeah, he wrote it down for me." She glanced up to see him studying her as if deciding how to ask something unpleasant. "Do you think Spencer might be involved?"

"He knows something, but he loves his family and hates what has happened, no matter how complicated their relationship. But involved?" She sighed again and gazed at a random spot of carpet. "Perhaps he did something unintentional which started all this and didn't want to admit his culpability. His reactions are genuine with real pain and shock. Nothing about his demeanor indicates intentional, direct involvement."

Chance nodded in relief. He didn't like asking tough questions, no matter how necessary. With a huff, she tore the tag off and stuffed it in her pocket. "It might raise some awkward questions with the police."

She stowed the enigmatic piece of luggage back in the closet and returned to her list, jotting down a note about the tag. "I think we should head back to Goditha. I want to run some tests on a few things, namely that piece of paper I found in Miriah's pocket."

"Sounds like a plan." Chance grabbed his shoes, a cross between sneakers and hiking boots, and perched on the arm of the couch to pull them on.

Midway through her mental list of equipment, she noticed him making a face as she slipped into her strappy tan heels. "What?"

"Don't you own some practical footwear?"

"Well, gee, I'm not planning on sprinting from evil today. We're only going to the lab."

His eyebrows lifted, and a smile crossed his lips. "You don't exactly sit down with evil and schedule an appointment. But hey"—he shrugged and finished lacing his shoe—"it's your feet, *cher*."

After rolling her eyes, she crossed the room and reached for the doorknob. Before she could turn it, someone knocked sharply from the other side. The ferocity ruled out Ida. She exchanged a worried expression with Chance and opened the door with more than a moderate amount of trepidation.

A man stood in the hall, about her height, stuffed in a cheap suit and tie, complete with coffee stains. He appeared to be about midforties with a thick graying mustache. Dark eyes hid behind a prominent furrowed brow, and his deep frown lines creased into a vaguely confused grimace. After checking something on a flip notebook, he peered back up at her.

"I'm looking for Malachi Sanders." The man's gruff Southern drawl, coupled with his unfriendly face, pegged him as the bad cop of a duo. So, where was his partner?

She hoped to have a little more time before the police showed up, but their involvement was inevitable. "Malachi is in New York." Not a lie. "I'm Miriah's cousin, Lilith Adams. Perhaps I can be of help?" She kept her face pleasantly neutral, but that didn't seem to help.

"Perhaps." A younger man jogged up the steps, taller, thinner, and wore a much more expensive suit. Warm brown eyes stood out against his sandy short-clipped hair as he stopped next to his partner, claiming his role as the good cop with a friendly smile.

"Sorry." The younger man panted and bent to catch his breath, although he didn't appear out of shape. All part of the act. "Ida can chat your ear clean off."

"You know her?" Lilith studied him with suspicion. "While I'm asking questions, who are you?"

Thick lashes and smooth facial lines made the younger one almost handsome. His only flaw was a weak chin, a classic trait in the South. He slapped his partner's arm, interrupting the gruff older man, and extended his hand to Lilith. The charming genuineness in his voice and actions made people trust him instinctually—a dangerous talent.

"Excuse my partner's manners. I'm Detective Cohen, and this is Detective Whitmore. And you are?" In her experience, the *good cops* were the most treacherous ones. Luckily, she could play the game too.

"Lilith Adams. I'm Miriah Sanders's cousin. Your partner was explaining why you gentlemen are looking for Malachi." She kept her voice polite and neutral.

"Yes, Miss Adams, or is it Missus? May we come in?" The charming smile may be a ploy to flirt with the prospective enemy, but she doubted his intentions were devoid of personal interest.

"It's Miss, and of course." She swung the door open and led them to the dining room table. She didn't see a single trace of Chance on their way, which seemed problematic. "I would offer you coffee, but for some reason, Miriah doesn't believe in keeping groceries in the house. Would you like some water?"

Detective Whitmore grunted, "No," and stood awkwardly near the table while his partner graciously accepted her offer and took a seat. A natural grace exuded with his movements, a stark contrast to his oafish counterpart. She placed a tall glass of ice water in front of the young detective and slid into a chair across from them.

Cohen opened his mouth to speak, but Chance chose that moment to stroll out of the bedroom, barefoot and shirtless. "Who was at the door, *cherie*?" He stopped to stretch with a massive yawn, fully displaying his six-foot-three stature as well as his muscled torso. Although he intended to intimidate the cops, the sight made her pulse quicken. He blinked and frowned at the two men glaring at him, neither of them with a friendly expression.

"Oh, sorry, I didn't realize we had company." Chance offered a polite smile to the men and glanced at her inquisitively.

"Detectives Cohen and Whitmore, this is Chance Deveraux..." After a significant stare, she reluctantly continued, "My fiancé." Chance turned his smug smile on the cops as she forced the words out. He started the charade with the neighbor, and now if they left the little tidbit out, it would appear suspicious. Cohen glanced from the half-naked man to her with a millisecond of disappointment on his face.

Chance stepped behind her, bent to press a kiss to her cheek, and whispered, "You love it." He settled his hands on her shoulders in a protective stance and focused on the officers. His gaze settled on Whitmore, who glared sourly at him. His big mustache twitched as his lips tightened under the towering stare. Leave it to Chance to single out the least friendly of the two and start a staring contest. She jabbed her elbow into his stomach with enough oomph to tell him she didn't appreciate his macho crap, but he recovered quickly.

"So, uh, what can we do for you, Detectives?"

Cohen flashed a brief half smile, trying to regain his composure. His fingers played with the condensation forming on his water glass before he homed in on Chance. "Well, we came to speak with Malachi Sanders, but your fiancée informed us he is in New York. Do you know when he left?"

"I believe Monday night or Tuesday morning." She decided to tell as much truth as possible. If they used enough harmlessly confirmable facts, the little white lies would fade into the background.

When Detective Whitmore spoke up, it became clear his gruff exterior wasn't an act. "You folks came to visit?" The sentence sounded more like a statement of disbelief than a question. Every line of his weight-padded body stood rigid and defensive as he crossed his arms, taking things beyond the simple role of *bad cop* into the realm of open hostility. Perfect.

"Yes, we arrived Wednesday morning." She pictured the whole logical line of questions in her mind, which hopefully meant she could head off any damaging ones.

"And where are y'all from?" Cohen cracked a bright smile as if chatting with new friends, eager to learn more. His talent for bypassing defenses worried her.

She smiled softly and turned away from Whitmore, leaving Chance to square off with him while she tackled the real threat. They could play *good cop, bad cop* too. Of course, they technically weren't cops, but a forensics investigator and a bodyguard were close enough. "We both work in Manhattan. Have you ever been?" Her smile overflowed with enigmatic charm.

A slight blush crept over the young detective's face, and he glanced down at his pad, making a few notes. "Uh, no. I hear it's an amazing place, though." He regained his composure and lifted his head with a curious smile. "What do you do for a living, Ms. Adams?" A spark of personal curiosity lit his tone again. If she could keep him interested, she could stay ahead of his suave routine.

"I'm an independent forensic examiner for Solasta Laboratories. I work closely with the New York City Major Crimes Division." She loved seeing the shocked expressions on both detectives. No matter how many times she saw that look on a macho man's face, she enjoyed it every time. "I'm assigned to most of the weird cases."

"Wow. Tough career path." Cohen sunk back in his chair, studying her as he reevaluated every assumption with a predictable look of appreciation and attraction. Despite the popular crime dramas, most people didn't expect a fit beautiful woman to work with dead bodies. Her role in the Major Crimes Division was even more surprising, which typically meant serial killers and mass murderers, not muggings and cardiac arrests.

"True. It takes a strong stomach sometimes, but pattern recognition and a keen sense of logic are more of a necessity. Most of my cases tend to be rather mild compared to their overall caseload." Being modest seemed smarter than informing them she could easily tolerate tortured bodies since Whitmore's shocked face bordered on the verge of disgust.

The sour-faced officer exchanged a long look with Cohen before he returned to staring holes through Chance. "And you?" The question was more of a grunt than actual words.

"I head a security team for Lilith's father, Gregor Adams. He's a reclusive investment banker in New York City." His answer resembled a threat, and Chance's tone held more than the usual amount of Cajun accent.

"Where are you originally from, boy? That's no city accent." Whitmore's chubby face pinched in a painfully menacing way.

"Breaux Bridge, Louisiana, mostly, the crawfish capital of the world. I moved to Manhattan when I turned seventeen." Chance casually stood beside her, but she recognized his tight tone from the plane. So far, this Q&A was routine, and not his first time giving a statement to the police. Still, something rubbed him the wrong way, and she needed to defuse the situation before the testosterone began to fly.

"I'm sorry, but what is all this about?"

Cohen, the eloquent one, took the lead, but he struggled. The signatures of stress, disgust, and cloying sympathy indicated he saw the body firsthand. After seeing something so horrific, so profoundly steeped in evil, it changed a person forever. "Someone broke into Miriah's office last night." Whitmore played the silent observer, gauging their reactions.

Lilith tilted her head in puzzled curiosity. "She's an accountant. Why would anyone break into her office?"

"Well..." His hands fidgeted nervously as he tried to figure out the best way to tell them. "We found a body at the scene." Then, he realized she would understand crime scene lingo, and his tension eased a bit. "We haven't identified the woman's body yet, but someone positioned her on Miriah's desk."

She shook her head and dropped her eyes to the table. Her acting abilities had limits, and the *big shock* was something detectives always gauged. The best she could do was give them nothing to judge. Whitmore barreled ahead before either of them could respond.

“Where were you two last night?” His voice dripped with venom, making it clear he didn’t like them. Of course, she didn’t take it personally. He probably didn’t like anyone.

Lilith kept her head bowed, and Chance patted her back, playing the concerned fiancé. “Well, we stayed in Madisonville the night before last, then drove up here and arrived at about seven? Does that sound right, *cher*?” Lilith nodded and wiped at her eyes. “Miriah’s brother, Spencer, came over for dinner about eight-ish. We planned to meet Miriah after, but she never showed up, so we drove around the city a bit and came back here to sleep.”

Another sharp knock interrupted Cohen’s next question. Chance patted her shoulders again before smiling at the detectives. “I’ll get the door since I’m up.”

He disappeared around the corner at a casual jog, but he wore a pained expression when he reappeared. A policeman in uniform trailed behind him, a familiar one. He marched over to Whitmore while throwing hostile looks at Chance. The name badge caught her eye, Humphrey. *Awesome.* This particular policeman already thought Chance was a vicious woman beater after lecturing them on the side of the road. Just when she thought she had everything under control. She bet Chance didn’t find the cop’s assumptions as funny as he did last night.

Chapter 11

Lilith's chest tightened as a slight bubble of panic grew. Maybe the officer wouldn't remember them? Humphrey's eyes glanced up at her and instantly scanned the right side of her face. No such luck. *Dammit.*

Humphrey fixed Chance, the *woman beater*, with a piercing glare before turning his attention to Lilith. "Ms. Adams."

She nodded and forced a smile as the uncomfortable silence settled in. Cohen picked up on the shift in mood. Of course, he'd have to be a brain-dead vegetable not to.

"If you'll excuse us a moment." Cohen and Whitmore stood at the same time and shuffled into the hall with Humphrey.

Chance crossed his arms over his bare chest, staring daggers at the hallway. "This is not good."

She shook her head, trying to stay optimistic. "Stay calm and give them as much truth as you can. Getting snappy or irritable gives them more fuel for the witch burning."

"What about your..." He gestured at the right side of her face.

"We can't tell them about Duncan." She thought for a few moments, trying to come up with something both plausible and not overused by abused housewives. "The bruising appears older than a couple of days, so we say someone attacked me on the job. Police declared the scene clear, but they were wrong. It's New York City. They'll believe it. You were upset that you weren't there to keep me safe"—the pointed glare from Chance said she hit a little close to home—"and punched the wall. We chose to take a vacation down here due to my accident. Alvarez is smart. He'll cover for me. If they ask for specifics, say I refused to talk about the incident because I was too shaken up."

He nodded grimly while staring at the table. "They're going to think I did this." His pale face contorted in disgust, and it broke her heart. She caressed his cheek and forced a brave smile to her lips. When his eyes met hers, volumes of emotions passed between them. As much as she wanted to ease his fears, she needed to prepare him for what was coming.

"I won't lie. Humphrey sharing his account of last night means they are going to take us downtown. They will put us in separate rooms and scrutinize every word looking for inconsistencies. Keep things simple and don't elaborate. They may think you're responsible, but they can't charge you without proof or a solid motive. We both know those things don't exist. You'll be okay." With a heavy heart, she pressed a soft kiss to his cheek.

Despite the pep talk, she was scared for Chance because the situation could go wrong in a million ways. If he lost his temper, things would only get worse. Knoxville was a small city, and their coroner probably wasn't equipped for cases like Miriah's.

Then, the officers breezed through the door, all three of them, and returned to the table. They didn't bother to sit down again. Cohen flashed a pleasant smile and tucked his notebook away.

"We'd like to give you a ride downtown to take your statements if it's not too inconvenient." The words sounded polite and indifferent, but she read between the lines. *We can't charge anyone, but we're going to hold you until we find something.* If they declined, they'd insist because Humphrey's addition bumped Chance from the witness list to the number one suspect with lightning speed.

The whole thing flashed before her eyes. Step one, separate the poor battered fiancée from her vicious man, hoping she'd feel safe enough to talk. Step two, push the woman beater into an anger-fueled confession. She needed to end the interrogation before they resorted to step three, lying to the monster and informing him that she'd agreed to testify. All their hopes rested on a confession because they had no evidence. She made sure of that. Unfortunately, they could hold him twenty-four hours on suspicion, and they'd use every second attempting to make him snap.

That also meant twenty-four hours without protection. The thought of falling into the hands of the monster responsible for butchering Miriah made her blood ice-cold. What if this was part of his plan, his reason for staging the body so elaborately? It didn't matter if this was some grand scheme. They had no choice but to play along and try to minimize the damage.

She pulled herself out of her thoughts and nodded politely at Cohen. A touch of sympathy contaminated his smile, and it set her teeth on edge. She never cared for sympathetic pity. She had her fill when her mother died.

Pity accomplished nothing. It was a useless emotion people hid behind instead of doing something to improve the situation.

"We'll grab our things."

Humphrey escorted Chance to his police cruiser when they were ready, while the detectives led Lilith to their unmarked town car. His eyes lingered on Chance as the officer tucked him in the back seat. The idea of being on her own suddenly scared her. They started this journey together, and it felt wrong to be apart.

Whitmore drove in absolute silence while Cohen lounged over his seat to chat about New York City. She calmly shared innocuous facts as they made their way. The young, almost handsome detective still exuded pity, and it took a concentrated effort to keep the casual smile on her face. No wonder battered women acted defensively. Of course, everyone meant well, so they should politely embrace the condescending puppy eyes.

When they arrived at the small station, they predictably ushered Lilith into a separate room without so much as a glimpse of Chance. Cohen removed his dark blue blazer, laid it on the back of a chair, and flashed an enigmatic smile. He didn't bother with his notebook because he didn't need to. Every interrogation room came equipped with microphones, cameras, or both.

Whitmore decided to leave her to Cohen while he intimidated the suspect. A predictable move. Still, she whispered a silent prayer for Chance.

"So, Ms. Adams, how long have you and Mr. Deveraux been engaged?" He made the question sound casual as he took the seat across from her. Although his question was straightforward, it was something they'd overlooked. Dammit.

"Not long. We've known each about thirteen years, though."

"How did you meet?" His eyes held hers with genuine intrigue. Cohen excelled at playing the part of a friend. On some level, the conversation felt more like two people talking over coffee than a detective questioning a suspect or victim.

"My father does charity work with hospitals all over the country." Not a lie, even if his motivations leaned more toward spotting half-bloods than aiding the institutions. "Chance was a seventeen-year-old orphan in Our Lady of Lourdes Children's hospital in Lafayette, Louisiana, misdiagnosed with anemia. Thalassemia, his true diagnosis, is a disease for which my father strongly supports research. He took him in, got him into treatments, gave him jobs to do, helped him through college, and, eventually, made him head of security for his investment firm."

"Your father must be an amazing person." His response sounded genuine, but he neglected the obvious question, *What is thalassemia?* Only three possibilities existed. One, he knew about the rare disease, which seemed unlikely. Two, he didn't care about the story, which was plausible. Or worst of all, three, he knew about her kind, which was only possible if he wasn't human.

His judging eyes stared at her expectantly, and she realized he was still waiting for an answer. With a slow sweet smile, she met his eyes as if reminiscing. "He truly is." She decided to cut the charade short and sat forward in her chair, resting her elbows on the metal table. "Detective Cohen, you're a pleasant man, so let me make this a little easier on you."

The faint traces of surprise on his face gave way to classic signs of satisfaction. "All right. I'm listening." He relaxed in the chair, crossing his arms loosely over his chest. His steel-gray shirt revealed that the young detective put lots of hours into the gym, almost enough to make up for his tiny chin.

"I deal with law enforcement daily, so I know what questions you're circling. Last night, Mr. Deveraux and I got a little lost while driving to meet Miriah. Chance pulled to the side of the road to double-check our directions, and Officer Humphrey stopped to investigate. The right side of my face was an ugly bruise, and the officer incorrectly assumed Chance was responsible."

Cohen simply nodded, taking everything in but revealing nothing. The standard cop poker face. "So, who was responsible?"

"A few days ago, I got called to a scene. The cops said it was clear, but they were wrong. I followed a blood trail to a closet when a meth-head asshole flew out. The maniac cracked me in the head with a damn baseball bat and jumped through a window. My liaison, Detective Alvarez, suggested I take some time off because my nerves are shot. I almost died on the spot." Real tears stung her olive eyes because everything she said was basically true.

Cohen's expression softened, and he twisted in his chair to retrieve a handkerchief from his jacket. He passed it over the table with the spark of a kindred spirit in his eyes. "The first time you've been hurt on the job?"

Lilith nodded as she wiped her face with the light blue linen square. "Yes. I'm a forensic investigator, not a cop. I fire my gun every other week to keep myself accurate for licensing, but I've never fired it at someone. I didn't have an opportunity to draw my weapon. It terrified me. When Chance found out, he took out his frustration on a wall, hence the bruised knuckles. He is my biggest supporter, holding me when I jump at shadows, comforting me when I wake up screaming from nightmares."

She held his gaze with the full power of truth behind her words. "He would never in a million years raise his hand to my family or me. He is not capable of what you saw, and he is not your suspect."

Cohen tried to look surprised, but she knew he faked it for her benefit. "Detective Whitmore is only taking his statement. We haven't charged him with anything."

"Which is cop speak for *We don't have enough evidence to charge him*." A half smile quirked her lips. "Out of professional courtesy, can we be straight with each other?"

Cohen bit his lip and leaned farther back in his chair, studying her with a calculated stare. A sharp intelligence hid behind his eyes, something she'd missed until now. He moved forward in a sudden motion, placing his palms on the table.

"All right, I'll be straight with you. This looks bad. Officer Humphrey was certain Mr. Deveraux caused your injury. The two of you happen to arrive in town right before one of the grisliest murders this department has ever seen. You are staying in the possible victim's apartment, and Mr. Sanders is conveniently out of town. On the plus side, Ida does corroborate your story."

"Do you really think it's Miriah?" Part of her hoped and prayed she was wrong.

"The fingers were severely damaged, but the coroner thinks he can obtain a useable print. It'll take a couple of days, but we hope to have a concrete ID soon. It is Miriah's office, and the victim is the right height, weight, and hair color." His shrewd eyes scrutinized her again. "Did you see Malachi in New York? There was enough time before you flew out."

"No. We must have missed each other. I didn't know Malachi was in New York until I talked to my father after landing here."

"So, your cousin's husband flies to New York, and he doesn't check on the traumatized member of the family? He doesn't call in advance and let you know he's coming to town?"

She frowned and consciously fought the urge to squirm in her chair. "I didn't tell my extended family about the attack. As for Malachi, I honestly don't know why he is in New York. He works in real estate all over the country, and he is not a social butterfly. He doesn't do much of anything without Miriah, except work."

The detective repositioned himself in the chair and kept watching her face with calculating eyes. "So, Miriah failed to mention her husband was in town when you spoke to her before flying down here?" Her preoccupation with the timeline in Tennessee distracted her from considering the details of arriving.

"Actually, my father arranged things with her brother, Spencer. I didn't speak to anyone." She needed to collect her thoughts and pull her confidence back on like a suit. Otherwise, Cohen would keep rattling her chain until she fell apart.

"And your father can corroborate your story?" There was no mistaking the cynical tone. The friendly facade vanished, and she found herself facing an impressively shrewd detective with a Southern drawl.

"Of course." She nervously thought back to Richard Coffee's failed attempt to call Gregor last night.

"When did you last see your cousin?"

"A few summers ago. Spencer gave us the keys to Miriah's place so we could spend time with her, but no one was home."

For several stressful moments, the two silently stared at each other. Cohen calculated his strategy to obtain information, while Lilith thought of ways to circumvent his ploys. Finally, Cohen broke thc tense silence hovering over them.

"I'll be honest. The crime scene was"—he paused, swallowing the bile in his throat—"the worst thing I've ever seen. I can tell you're trying to be truthful, but you're holding back. We are not all bigoted imbeciles down here." He rested his elbows on the table, and his eyes held a friendly glow again. "Work with me here. I genuinely believe we are on the same side."

Lilith's mind raced like a hummingbird's wings. Either Cohen was far too smart, or this was a last-ditch effort. She had two choices: disclose something or call him on his bluff. Unfortunately, she already took too much time to think while Cohen continued to stare at her. No choice. She had to give him something, but what? Something that wouldn't point to Duncan directly or the family in general.

"Miriah and Malachi were working on something that worried my father, which is part of the reason he wanted me to visit. They were following a money trail on a piece of property around here."

Cohen's eyebrow arched as she spoke, his face lighting up with excitement. "Do you know what property?"

"Someplace called Phipps Bend." Her clueless expression wasn't acting, which bolstered the validity of her confession.

"The old nuclear reactor site?" His brows knit together in a deep frown. "The county sold it?"

"I believe it was some sort of hush deal, but yes. I don't know any other reason someone might want to hurt Miriah." Okay, the last sentence *was* pure acting. However, if she said fuchsia elephants sang her to sleep, he wouldn't blink while mulling over an actual lead. This would kill two birds with one stone. It put her on the friendly side of the cops and, if she played her cards right, helped her find specifics on the property.

Detective Cohen pushed away from the table, struggling to keep his poker face. "I should consult with my partner. I'll be right back." He rushed out of the room, leaving her alone with her thoughts.

Her mind kept returning to Cohen's question about Malachi. Why did he drop the envelope and leave? Was he trying to reach Gregor? And how the hell did the killer find him? She buried her face in her hands. Too many questions needed answers.

With nervous energy bubbling over, she kept her hands clasped on the table and studied her surroundings. Every surface in the fluorescent-lit room held years of stains, from the dingy gray linoleum to the water-marked ceiling tiles, everything except the monstrous one-way mirror taking up the entire left side. Yeah, they were definitely recording her through the mirror, the *only* clean thing in the room.

The minutes seemed like hours, with only the whir of the air-conditioning to break the silence. Every minute in this damn place was a waste of time. She should be at the lab, getting answers, not stewing in some interrogation room, tap-dancing around questions that put her family in jeopardy. The monster butchering her relatives was dangerous enough without police involvement.

Then, a thought occurred to her. What if this mystery villain wanted police involvement to expose them? The discovery of Malachi's murder, in addition to Miriah's, would unleash all hell. A small police force wouldn't care about the glaring differences in the bodies. Besides, figuring this whole thing out, even stopping the man behind this, wouldn't solve their problems now. Everything unfolded in her mind, but what the hell could she do about it? She certainly couldn't tell the police the truth, and they wouldn't believe a lie.

Over an hour passed while she stewed in her thoughts, her mind running a million different scenarios. The door swung open, and Cohen breezed into the room. His sure-footed grace made her pulse quicken. Confident cops never boded well.

"Sorry to keep you waiting." He flashed a too-bright smile and settled into the chair across from her again. "I need contact numbers for your father and your partner, Detective Alvarez, to corroborate your story."

Thankfully, those were the only two numbers she bothered to memorize.

After jotting them down, Cohen laid his pencil on top of his notebook, clasped his hands, and slowly met her eyes. Classic cop body language for *You're not going to like this.* "We are holding your fiancé until we can confirm his statement."

They were letting her go. Logically, she'd seen it coming, but her face still fell at the prospect of leaving the station unprotected with a killer on the loose, targeting her, hunting her, toying with her.

Cohen reached out and patted the back of her hand with genuine concern. "We aren't charging him, Ms. Adams. I simply want to hold him until we clear this up. I promise if these men confirm your story, he will be free to go. You have my word."

"He's not your assailant. The man trains underprivileged kids in a dojo. He's worked security for my father's company for close to a decade, and he's saved my father's life thirty-seven times. He is a *good* man, Detective Cohen." The fear, her nightmare, flashbacks of almost dying rattled her right out of her calm, logical composure. She clasped his hand, staring into his eyes, willing him to understand.

"Chance is all I have. The *only* person I have to keep me safe from the vicious man butchering my family." Heart-wrenching fear stole her breath as her eyes welled with tears. "You can't hold him. I need him."

Cohen stared at her, shocked, blinking a few times as he struggled to think.

"Please!" She thought quickly, scrambling to come up with a solution. "We'll stay in the apartment. We won't leave until you confirm our stories, I promise. You can post police at the building, but please don't send me out there alone."

Cohen's brow furrowed into a suspicious frown. "What aren't you telling me, Ms. Adams?" Unlike his accusatory tone earlier, he now displayed genuine concern. "I can't help you if you don't talk to me."

Lilith's head fell forward, and she pulled in a shaky breath. "You wouldn't believe me if I told you." She took a considerable gamble by saying anything, but she was out of chips to play. By losing her composure, she'd tipped her hand, and now banking on Cohen's sincerity seemed the only solution.

Her words transformed his confused compassion into an unreadable mask. He pushed out of his chair, marched up to the one-way mirror, and made a slicing motion across his neck. What was going on? She studied Cohen's back as he stood in absolute silence. God. Did she make a giant mistake?

Blind panic kept her frozen in her seat as he stalked toward her and stooped down inches from her face. "I need you to come with me." His breathy whisper set off the alarms in her head. How much trouble did she just bring down on them?

Cohen grabbed her arm and gently pulled her out of the seat. She struggled to keep up with him in her stupid strappy heels as he led her to the door with a definite purpose. Perhaps Chance was right about her choice in shoes.

They exited into the hall, and Cohen dragged her into the next room on the right, the observation room behind the one-way mirror. Whoever he signaled turned off the video camera before leaving. He shut the door and glanced behind her into the second room. Following his gaze, she saw Chance hunched over in his chair, alone, looking utterly defeated.

"Mr. Deveraux is okay. He hasn't been thrown in a holding cell or mistreated in any way." When Lilith finally tore her eyes away from Chance, Cohen stood against the door with his hands in his pockets. "I'm not the bad guy, Ms. Adams, and I genuinely believe both you and Chance are not responsible for this crime. I also believe you are in real danger." His face displayed nothing but open honesty. He believed her, miraculously. So, what was the catch?

"I want to help you." He sighed again and tilted his head back against the door. "Hell, if the victim were anyone else, I'd ask for your help. We are not prepared for something this severe." When he lowered his head, a familiar frustration filled his eyes.

"We deal with country hicks moving into the city, thinking they're *in the hood*, so they join a gang." He rolled his eyes before continuing. "Or religious protesters who go too far at abortion clinics, or domestic abuse cases turning deadly. This…this is beyond evil." As he spoke, a subtle inflection told her he was downplaying his experience—an attempt to put her at ease or cover something personal. Either way, his demeanor didn't strike her as malicious.

"You make it sound awful." Remembering Miriah's body lying unrecognizable on the desk supplied all the inspiration she needed to appear shaken.

Cohen gazed at her with a soft edge of compassion. "I'm sorry. What your cousin endured, no one deserves that." His warm brown eyes filled with genuine emotion, which took her by surprise. Cops who cared too much saw one too many victimized children or mutilated corpses, and they broke down eventually. In this case, it would be a pity since reliable detectives didn't grow on trees.

Lilith turned and stared through the mirror to Chance's interrogation room. Like standing in the light that kept the darkness at bay, the sight of him made her feel better, safer, even if the idea was ridiculous. Her traumatized psyche clung to him like a lifeline, even though an entire building of cops would prevent him from coming to her rescue.

The shrewd detective missed none of the emotions in her face. "He truly is what you say, isn't he?" When she turned to him with a startled expression, he continued. "Whitmore likes him for this, but he's a lazy bigot who jumps at the first convenient suspect." He released a sigh of pure frustration, which almost became a growl. Those brown eyes rested on her again with a keen sharpness. "However, you two are not here to see family, are you?"

"That is *exactly* why we're here." If she wanted to see her uncle, she simply needed to find him first. Even if Cohen turned out to be trustworthy, he was still human. Revealing anything else would endanger her family and sign Cohen's death warrant.

"I can be your ally, Ms. Adams. I want to find your cousin's killer as much as you do." Lilith didn't want to find him as much as kill him, but semantics.

"I believe you." She rested against the glass, staring at the door behind him as her brain kept turning over the facts.

"Okay, let's go at this from a different angle. How long has Duncan been missing?" His question snapped her out of the spiraling thoughts. Spencer and Miriah would never go to the human cops, and Cohen wasn't a Madisonville sheriff. So, how could he know anything about her uncle?

"Who are you?" She moved away from the glass as a chill ran up her spine.

Cohen stepped forward with effortless grace. "I took you away from the cameras for a reason. I need to discuss a few things with you, ones not safe for *certain* ears."

The chill turned ice-cold, and the little hairs stood on the back of her neck. She took a step back as her heart began beating a touch faster. "I… I don't understand."

His rich, earthy laugh brushed against her skin in a way meant to soothe her fraying nerves. Instead, her alert mode kicked into high gear.

"I know all about Duncan and his sordid family history." The weight in his eyes held a grim significance that jolted her. He stopped at the sight of her startled face, realizing he'd crossed the line and spooked her. "I'm helping him with a few things. So, if you truly are his niece, you can speak openly with me."

Could one of the lead detectives on Miriah's murder case be on Duncan's payroll? No. Richard Coffee said his man on the force was in forensics. A homicide detective would be worth mentioning.

Her heart pounded faster now. She needed to get out of this room and fast. If he was bluffing, trying to startle a reaction out of her, he succeeded. If he wasn't bluffing, he either knew about or participated in his disappearance. Perhaps both. All the signs pointed to him being honest, but she couldn't take the risk.

The walls closed in, choking the breath from her as the panic swelled. She *needed* to get out of the room and away from Detective Cohen.

"Lilith, I didn't mean to startle you." He held out his hands in a sign of peace. "Take a deep breath before you pass out. Your heart's racing like a rabbit running from a fox." How the hell could he tell how fast her heart was beating? Even with her superhuman hearing, she couldn't make out a heart rate across the room. His face showed every marker of concern, begging her to believe him, trust him, but now it made her gut scream the opposite. Vampires tended to suffer from severe trust issues.

"Are we free to go?" She stood straight, clenching her jaw in determination.

"You are, I suppose." He appeared confused, and everything about him seemed harmless. It wasn't natural, like a perfectly formed facade to trick the enemy. She stared at a point on his chest to avoid looking at his almost handsome face and still monitor his movements. "As I said before, we are holding Mr. Deveraux until we can confirm your statements."

She struggled to keep anger from reaching the surface while wrestling the fear deep in the pit of her stomach. She nodded solemnly. Cohen wouldn't let Chance go until she talked to him about Duncan, which she had no intention of doing. So, Chance would sit in a holding cell for the next twenty-four hours, give or take.

Perhaps Alvarez could pull some strings, but she needed out of the tiny dark observation room for now. "Can *I* go?"

He stepped reluctantly to the side, giving her an open path to the door. As she walked past him, he held out his card. "If you change your mind and want an ally, call me. I apologize again if I frightened you. A killer is on the loose, and you *will* need my help."

She stuffed the card in her breast pocket as she reached for the doorknob. His last sentence hung in the air like a thick fog, chilling her right to the bone. She almost ran over Whitmore in her desperation to get away from Cohen.

His sun-worn face creased into a frown. "I wouldn't suggest leaving town," he growled in a gruff Southern drawl, his thick mustache wiggling as he spoke.

She nodded curtly and hurried past him, rushing for the doors like a diver fighting to reach the surface. When she emerged into the early fall sun, she took in several deep breaths, letting it burn away her chills. Then came sharp clarity as her spiraling fear came to a halt. Chance had the keys to the apartment. After Madisonville, she put her lockpick gun and her wallet back in her kit, which now sat in their rental car. Of course, he also had the car keys. All she had was a twenty-dollar bill and the change from breakfast stuffed in her pocket.

Lilith stared at the ominous building, torn. She had no desire to go back in there and face Cohen, but where could she go? She couldn't wait on the stairs until they released Chance, and she couldn't run all over the city, exposed and vulnerable.

Her brain buzzing like an epileptic bee trapped in her skull, she sank onto the nearest park bench to think. Every instinct screamed that Cohen's simple, young detective routine hid something immense and menacing. Who, or what, was he? Best-case scenario, Duncan confided too much to a human. Worst-case…the cascading thoughts chilled her to the marrow. Now she had no choice but to leave Chance with Cohen and a hostile bigot who considered him a grotesque murderer.

"Snap out of it," she firmly told herself. Step one, call Alvarez before they do. One touch showed five missed calls and one voice mail from an unknown Knoxville number when she pulled out her phone. She jabbed the voice mail symbol, and a nasally thin voice rattled through the speaker.

"Ms. Adams, this is Dr. Nichols at Goditha Labs. I need you to call or come by as soon as possible!" An unrestrained excitement made his voice annoyingly bright, the opposite of her current mood. However, the thought of a real lead lifted the weight from her shoulders, at least part of it.

The bizarrely fascinating message also gave her something to do in relative safety. Richard Coffee could pass as Andre the Giant's bodyguard, which made Goditha the safest place in the city. No one would bother her, not the cops or the mysterious threat looming in the dark.

With a clear, new purpose, she dialed the only cab company still operating in Knoxville. It was a dying industry in the Uber age, but Lilith preferred anonymity to GPS tracking and online profiles. She could call her partner on the way, and hopefully, whatever caused the doctor's elation would turn the tables.

Chapter 12

While waiting for her ride, Lilith sat, immersed in thoughts swirling too fast to focus on one. So, she gave up and turned her attention to her surroundings instead. The birds chirped, cars cruised by, and people laughed as they strolled with friends, family, and loved ones, enjoying the Indian summer. With October 31st fast approaching, storefronts featured an odd combination of Halloween and Christmas decorations.

She envied their blissful ignorance. What would her life be like without her ocean of secrets? No blood supplements, no overhearing private conversations accidentally, no fear of discovery... Instead of life-threatening situations, what if her responsibilities ended with finding a Halloween costume and completing a lengthy Christmas list?

To be honest, the complications in her life didn't end with her vampire heritage. She examined dead bodies every night and spent most of her time dealing with humanity's darkest emotions. That alone would negate the idea of being average.

A couple walked past the colorful trees sharing shy smiles. Every so often, he tugged her back to crash into him as she giggled and squealed with a shining smile. Their glowing happiness reflected her insides' negative image perfectly—isolated, terrified, cold, and desperate, especially with Chance in custody. Her only hope hinged on trusting Detective Cohen, whoever or whatever he was, to keep his word and release Chance once he spoke with Alvarez and her father.

The thought nagged at her again. Why didn't Gregor answer the phone when Richard Coffee called? Of course, plausible reasons existed, the same ones that prevented anyone from picking up, but the knot in her stomach refused to go away. Someone tortured and killed Malachi in New York City. What if he got to her father too? In a sudden moment of panic, she tried his cell, but it went straight to voice mail.

The cab pulled up as she dialed her precinct, hoping Alvarez was on duty since his home was the black hole of cellular reception. Not to mention that Gloria usually answered, and she wouldn't politely ignore the misery in Lilith's voice as her husband would.

She slid into the back seat and rattled off Goditha's address as the phone rang.

"Thirteenth Precinct. How can I direct your call?"

"Homicide, please."

A few clicks and some crackly elevator music later, Detective Boyd picked up, one of the few detectives that appreciated her work. "Lilith Adams." She heard the smile in his smooth voice. "I thought you were at a conference?"

"Oh, I am. I'm looking for Alvarez. Is he in?"

"No. Felipe turned in some personal days last night. Said he's having some trouble at home."

She didn't believe in coincidences for a damn good reason. Writing off the facts as happenstance quickly became a deadly habit. "Okay. If you hear from him, will you tell him I need his advice on something down here?"

"Helping some local cops, huh? I got a call from one not long ago in Knoxville, rooting around about you and asking all kinds of questions." He paused for dramatic effect. "I went along with your *attacked-at-a-crime-scene* story. I hope that's what you needed. You aren't in trouble, are you?"

"No, but a friend of mine might be." As her patience frayed, her voice became clipped and irritated. She usually loved chitchatting with Boyd, but today wasn't the day.

"Well, I hope things work out. I'll pass on the message." He sounded a little wounded.

"Sorry for snapping, and thanks, Boyd. I mean it." The curt apology was all the time she could spare for his bruised ego. She'd patch things up later, assuming she made it home.

Only one choice left, and her chest tightened with every number she dialed.

"Hello, *bonita*." Gloria's thick but beautiful Spanish accent felt like home, a bright spot within her emotional darkness.

"I'm trying to get a hold of your husband, and the precinct said he went home on leave?"

"No, I'm afraid not. HR forced him to take personal days since he was out of vacation time. Felipe went out of town."

A cold weight landed in the pit of her stomach. "Where did he go?"

"Well…to quote Felipe, he couldn't be specific for our safety." She pictured Gloria rolling her eyes. "I swear if he's after some *bonita punta…*"

She dissolved into Spanish, pulling a smile to Lilith's lips. She seemed too distracted by her husband's mystery trip to pick up on the haunting tones in Lilith's voice. "So, no, he didn't say. Sorry, Lily."

"Thank you for your help. I'll track him down and make sure he gets home safe and sound."

An infectious bubble of laughter crackled through the speaker.

"What about you? How is your vacation? Felipe mentioned that you took a travel partner with you. A tall, handsome one." The hopeful smile in Gloria's voice made Lilith want to tell her everything. However, she had no idea how to describe her tenuous relationship with Chance, and more pressing matters hovered over her head.

"He's quite charismatic, but he's worked for my father since I was a teenager. I'll fill you in later." After Lilith promised to eat some real food, she hung up as the car sped down the lane leading to the industrial park outside of town. The short chat with her best friend grounded her, connected her to home.

Constantly feeling cut off and alone was the worst part of her life. Getting too close to people proved dangerous. She could count on one hand the number of people she let close: her father, Alvarez, Gloria, and, now, Chance. None of them knew all of her, only facets. Living a guarded life made it hard to let down her walls to anyone. They grew familiar and safe, and she became accustomed to anonymity. If Gregor succeeded in bringing them out to the public, how would her life change?

At only twenty-seven years old, she had no clue who she was without choosing which side of her personality to display to different people. What if nothing cohesive existed behind the endless parade of masks?

She wrinkled her nose with a weary sigh. *Damn it.* Her inner monologue fast resembled the vampires in Hollywood, whining, "*Poor me. Nobody knows the real me.*" Soon, she'd be sparkling in the sunlight like some anorexic disco ball. As the car rolled to a stop, she realized her existential crisis would have to wait.

She handed the driver a twenty and scrambled out before the taxi burned rubber, leaving the parking lot. She shoved everything to the background and focused on the building in front of her. The voice mail indicated at least one doctor in the lab, so she jammed the button for Sector 2, Blood Analysis, when she reached the call box.

The same excited voice from the message droned out rehearsed lines across the crackly speaker. "Goditha Labs. We are closed to the public without an appointment."

"Dr. Nichols? This is Lilith Adams. Let me in."

Without a word, the high-pitched buzz of the door sounded. She snatched the handle and slipped inside as fast as possible. An immense sense of relief washed over her as she headed straight to Mr. Coffee's security desk. The massive mountain of a man cracked a broad smile that made her feel safer.

"Ms. Adams. A pleasure to see you again." His voice boomed like a roll of thunder while his dark eyes searched the hall behind her. "And Mr. Deveraux?" Either he had an excellent memory, or they didn't get many visitors. Most likely, the latter.

"Detained. We've come across a few complications." That sounded boring compared to *The dumbass cops threw him in jail because they think he punched me and butchered my cousin.* Summing things up made them resemble an extreme episode of *Jerry Springer*. Of course, they'd need to throw in some sex and incest to spice things up. Murder wasn't shocking enough on its own.

As Mr. Coffee pushed away from the desk, rising to his enormous height of nearly eight feet, the door to Section 2 burst open. A frazzled man came careening down the hall, looking a little worse for wear. His messy mop of light brown hair stood straight up in places as if he tried to pull it out over the last thirteen hours. The bloodshot eyes, complete with dark circles, didn't help either.

His rail-thin body came skidding to a halt at the security desk as he gulped in shaking breaths. Richard stood two feet taller and was four times wider, supplying a comical contrast when standing next to each other. Coffee seemed content to stare down at him as if he were a pet poodle doing something amusing. With an indignant huff, the man smoothed out his rumpled lab coat.

"Ms. Adams… I've been trying to reach you…for hours." He still panted for each breath. Obviously, he didn't follow the cardinal rule of cardio. In a zombie apocalypse, he'd be the first to go. Of course, if she spent all day in a lab protected by a giant linebacker on radioactive steroids, she wouldn't spare time for workouts either.

"You need to see this!" He snatched her hand and pulled her down the hall—social etiquette lost in the wake of his excitement. The frail man couldn't drag her anywhere she didn't want to go since he had the strength of a newborn puppy. However, she played along, eager to see what he'd uncovered.

They burst into the lab, and Dr. Nichols tugged her over to his workspace, complete with an enormous microscope. He flopped down onto a stool, gray eyes holding a manic shine of enthusiasm that bordered on terrifying. "Where did you get it?" His high-pitched squeal resembled a high school girl begging to know where she bought her shoes. "I *need* to know!"

Lilith frowned and collapsed onto a similar black padded stool. "Why? Did you find something?"

"Something?" The doctor's jaw hung open like a widemouthed bass. She shifted backward on her seat as his face began to resemble a mad scientist on the verge of snapping. Terrible things happened when brilliant minds cracked, the basis of every monster movie in the 1950s. "Two complete strands of DNA exist in that sample!" He surged to his feet, overemphasizing his statement.

"Well, that's not that uncommon if a vampire's recently fed." She crossed her arms over her chest, frowning at the madman. "Blood from the donor mixes in and takes time to acclimate to its new host."

The sound he made landed somewhere between a growl and a snort of contempt. "I am not some gibbering janitor playing doctor! I know how transfusions work! I was instrumental in their research, and I've worked in this lab longer than you've been alive." When she shrugged without the expected air of reverence, he snapped angrily. "Do I need to spell out everything? You're a forensic examiner. Surely you took biology classes." Her eyes narrowed at his infuriated face. "Of course, but rudimentary ones. I process crime scenes, and I know enough about DNA to do my job, which doesn't involve in-depth analysis."

With an overly dramatic sigh, Dr. Fredrick Nichols, as his badge stated, sunk his bony form into the chair. His back straightened, his long chin tilting toward the ceiling. After clearing his throat, he began his lecture. "As you *should* know…" She didn't miss the pretentious tone. "DNA's primary role is the long-term storage of information, a blueprint containing instructions needed to construct components of cells such as RNA molecules and proteins. How the DNA is packaged in chromosomes influences the expression of genes."

"The point? In English?" She leaned forward, rubbing her temple in annoyance.

His beady eyes tightened as he slapped the counter with booming authority making her jump, startled. "I *am* explaining in English. Pay attention." The odds of her avoiding the biology lecture seemed to be slim to none. With a nod and a permissive wave from her, he surged on.

"With regions that contain prominent levels of methylation of cytosine bases and low or no gene expression, modifications can be involved in the packaging." When her face went blank, he grunted. "For instance, cytosine methylation produces 5-methylcytosine, which is crucial for X-chromosome inactivation." Since he didn't see the dawning realization he wanted, he sighed gruffly and broke it down further. "What allows boys to be born by suppressing the second X chromosome?"

She nodded in irritation. "I still don't see the connection. I need answers about the specimen, not lectures."

The mad scientist ignored her protests. As he rambled, she wondered what kind of parents named their child Fredrick. Most likely, the kind that beat a kid for bringing home anything short of an A+. "When mutagens fit into the space between base pairs, intercalation, the bases separate, distorting the DNA strands by unwinding the double helix. This inhibits both transcription and replication, which causes toxicity and mutations. Now, this is similar to the vampire structure. The watered-down half-bloods appear to suffer from thalassemia, the structure mostly human with abnormalities shoved in the cracks. In purebloods, such as yourself, it is smoothly integrated into your DNA strands."

"Fredrick. What does this have to do with the blood sample? This is all fascinating, but not what I need."

"Patience! It's not my fault you don't understand *basic* biology. The specimen is unique because it contains two *complete* but *separate* DNA strands spliced together. The dominant strand fused itself to the other double helix by infiltrating the spaces between base pairs."

Her brow furrowed, and she looked up at him sharply. "Wait. How is that possible?"

A wild grin split his face. "It isn't! That's the point! This is impossible! It's exactly how our mutations attach to our DNA. However, in this case, the mutagen is an intact DNA strand of another person! This defies physics, defies everything! The possibilities of this sample are endless."

With a sigh of frustration, she pushed off the stool to pace the space between lab tables. "Well, the structure can't be impossible if it's sitting right in front of you."

Dr. Nichols scowled at her, harshly exaggerating every wrinkle. "This sample changes everything. I have no scientific explanation for its existence. You *have* to tell me where you discovered this!"

Unfortunately, the vial's hiding place wouldn't help anyone figure out how Duncan obtained it or why he had it. Perhaps there was a connection to this family secret of Gregor and Duncan's. Then again, maybe her uncle simply crammed a bunch of unrelated valuables in one box.

"I found the vial stashed someplace safe, but I don't have a clue where it came from." She collapsed against the table, her mind racing. "More questions and no damn answers." She glanced up at him, desperate for any sign of hope. "So, you don't have *any* theories?"

The doc bristled, sitting up straight, sharp chin lifting once again. This time his posture screamed defensive pride instead of aristocratic pomp. "I'm still working on the samples. Once the DNA sequencing is complete, I can identify the two different double helixes, which will give me a better idea."

"How long will that take?"

"A couple of hours."

She nodded, deep in thought, when something occurred to her. "Do they both contain vampire markers?"

"Well, that is another of the oddities. One strand shows robust vampire markers. The *other* holds several unknown gene expressions, and although it also contains the vampire markers, they are the strangest I've ever seen. They appear as impressions, like a mirror image of a mutagen and not the actual thing itself. An impossibility, of course, but that can be said for the entire sample."

She couldn't seem to wrap her brain around that one. "So, the one strand might be something else entirely? Not vampire?"

His thin face frowned with deep lines. "The blood is unique. That's the only way I can put it. I cannot exclude an entire species at this point."

She rubbed her face as a groan escaped her lips. "I'm heading to the cold storage laboratory. Let me know when the DNA workups are complete." He merely waved a dismissive hand and returned to his work.

She strolled down the sterile hallway, lost in thought, when her cell rang loud enough to wake the dead. Once her pulse dropped out of heart-attack range, she fished it out and answered.

"Lilith? You there?"

She jostled her cell between her cheek and her shoulder while opening the door. "Spencer? Where have you been? Are you okay? Why didn't you show up last night or at least call?"

"Yes, Mom." While his sarcastic tone held a touch of humor, it seemed forced and awkward. If Chance made the same comment, she'd laugh, but the words pissed her off coming from Spencer. "I went through all of Malachi's real estate records, and doing it discreetly took time."

"Silent mode and text messages do exist. So, did you find anything?"

"I'm sorry. I tried to help, but he had nothing on Phipps Bend. I want to drive out to the site, but I thought you two may have something. Any sign of Dad?"

"No, but the police came by the apartment this morning and took us downtown. Chance is in holding for twenty-four hours or until they can confirm our stories. I assume they want you to make a statement as well. If we play ball, perhaps we can avoid further complications."

"Well, fuck. So, you're all alone?" An audible tremble accented his words as they hung hauntingly in the air. "I mean, after the other day, I don't think you should be on your own."

"I'm not, not exactly. I'm at Goditha. One of the scientists is analyzing a vial of blood I found. In the meantime, I'll run tests on the slip of paper from Miriah's pocket. The thing is saturated, but I'm going to do my best." "Blood and a scrap of paper? That's all you have? At this rate, Dad will end up just like Miriah." Intense anger seared through the phone, but it seemed more like venting than blame. "What the hell are we going to do, Lil?"

"Well, I'm doing what I can. The paper is kinda thick, reminds me of a ticket or something." A thought occurred to her. "Hey, did Miriah take a trip recently?"

"I don't know. Why?"

"I found a suitcase inside the closet with a luggage tag from Knoxville on the handle. I couldn't read the date or the destination."

"Sis did lots of things for Dad. Maybe she did. I don't...*did* not talk to her and Malachi much." Rephrasing his sentence to past tense made her chest tighten. Someone murdered them both, and only lifeless husks remained. Remembering those facts proved difficult when all she wanted to do was forget.

"I'm sorry, Spence. You should head over to the station. We can always check out Phipps Bend later. The detectives in charge are Cohen and Whitmore, but be careful around Cohen. He knows about Duncan, maybe more."

"Wait. What do you mean *he knows about Duncan*?"

"I'm not sure. He claimed to know about his disappearance and said he was helping Duncan with things. Any idea why he would need assistance from a homicide detective?"

"No. Dad never confided in humans, much less human cops."

"Okay, well, be careful."

"Yeah, will do." He didn't waste time on pleasantries, hanging up without another word. She shoved the phone back in her pocket and scanned the room.

Four long black tables, similar to the ones in chemistry class, dominated the space, complete with oversize sinks. Utility shelves in the back of the room held a cornucopia of chemicals, and another set on the adjoining wall contained an array of equipment. Perfect.

After pulling everything out of the giant freezer, she laid out each piece, gathering her thoughts. What to do first? The growing headache began gnawing at her calm logic. Her eyes locked on the cooler of blood, realizing the two capsules she popped earlier couldn't compete with the stress of her day.

"When in doubt, take care of yourself first."

She filled one of the massive sinks and lowered a blood pack into the steaming water. The gradual temperature change didn't damage cells the way a microwave did.

While waiting, she went through their clothes. Chance's rich scent filled the air, bringing a smile to her lips, which dissipated quickly. She wondered if the cops told him they released her. Hopefully not. He would only drive himself nuts, nerves twisting up like a top, ready to spin out of control. She shoved the thought aside and placed the clothes in another sink to soak until the blood weakened. Then dunk them in a sanitizing solution, run them through a washing machine, and they'd be good as new.

Next up, the bloody scrap from Miriah's pocket. The dried blood made the paper stiff and uneven. The shape was a little bigger than a credit card, with rounded edges on one side and a perforated edge on the other.

As her brain rattled the possibilities around, she organized the instruments she needed. Without the ability to remove the blood, her only options beyond magnification were alternate light sources. UV and infrared would either make the ink visible or record its color spectrum, which would help narrow things down.

She trained a magnifying glass on the enigma before her. She couldn't quite make out the month and day, but it was from this year. Several other numbers appeared half legible, and a large 23A sat in the right-hand corner. A used plane ticket. It had to be. If she was right, the most important things on that paper were the date and destination.

With a thrill traveling through her bones, she flipped on the UV light, aiming it at her workspace. The entire piece blacked out, indicating the blood was mostly human, which made sense if Miriah's killer continuously supplied her with blood during her...torture. On to infrared.

With a flip of a switch, the ink jumped out at her, and she blinked, staring in shock. "What the hell?" Lilith shoved the infrared light and magnifying glass away as if they were poisonous.

The mystery paper was a plane ticket. More specifically, one for Miriah Sanders from Knoxville Airport to La Guardia on a red-eye flight Monday night. She flew up there with her husband, someone killed him, and then, somehow, Miriah wound up a mutilated corpse here in Tennessee.

She rubbed furious fingers against the growing ache in her skull. All her thoughts scattered before they formed anything cohesive. She snatched the warm bag of blood floating in the sink. Without the social niceties of a glass, she tore it open and drained every drop. The effect immediately warmed her stomach, which spread through her entire bloodstream. A sigh of relief flooded out of her as the headache receded, allowing her to think clearly.

Assuming Miriah went to New York City with Malachi, how did she end up here? Perhaps she escaped and ran home, but why would she? She had allies and protection there. Here, Duncan was missing, which only left Spencer on her side. Plus, she would never leave the love of her life to die. No. Then she recalled the older bruises covering Miriah's face, shattering her bones. Someone forced her to leave. It was the only timeline that made sense.

A flash of clarity almost knocked her from the stool. The suitcase in the closet, the wrinkled women's clothes, the haphazardly dumped toiletries in the nightstand… Someone other than her OCD cousin was responsible, someone with access to their home.

Spencer. Her eyes widened as a string of thoughts came crashing down on her like a physical weight. Spencer was out of contact and didn't show up at the airport because he was hours away. Ida witnessed him hauling a suitcase into the apartment while Lilith recovered from the Madisonville attack. Spencer killed Malachi. All that anger, resentment, rage, not focused on the enemy, but his own family. How could she be so blind? She saw every emotion but interpreted them as she expected, not how they existed.

Her soul sank into the numbing, cold darkness as terror vibrated through her bones. Spencer was working for their unnamed foe. She remembered how torn up his knuckles were and what he'd said. "I have a tendency to punch things when I get angry."

Chapter 13

No doubts lingered in Lilith's mind. Spencer beat his own sister's face to a bloody pulp, then tortured and killed her husband. But why? The haunting question twisted her guts in vicious knots as she tried to focus on the facts.

He must have driven Miriah back to Tennessee since loading her on a plane was an impossible task. That explained why he never showed up at the airport. Her death, however, illustrated someone else's work. The stark differences in precision and finesse made that clear. Did the mystery man order him to bring her back alive, or did he lose his nerve? Crap. She told him where to go, sent him straight to Chance. Her heart dropped like a lead weight in her chest.

She fished Cohen's card out of her pocket and stared at it. She had no choice. While the phone rang, she stuffed everything into the refrigeration unit. His silky voice didn't answer until she pushed her way through the doors at a running pace. "Homicide. You've reached Detective Cohen."

"This is Lilith Adams. I don't have time to explain, but Spencer MacEwen is on his way to you. Do *not* let him leave, and do *not* let him anywhere near Chance." She panted heavily by the time she reached the security desk. Dr. Nichols wasn't the only one that needed to work on their cardio.

"Your cousin? What is this about, Ms. Adams?" His deathly serious tone roiled with tension.

"I can't explain now. I'm on my way, and I promise I'll tell you as much as I can, but I need your word. Throw him in holding, arrest him, whatever it takes, but keep him there and *away* from Chance!"

"Yes…of course." As soon as he gave a bewildered answer, she hung up the phone and stared at Coffee. Even sitting, the man towered over her, which she found unnerving.

"I need a ride or a vehicle, something." His dark eyes widened in concern. "I don't have time to wait on a cab. It's urgent." Her voice trembled with desperation, but pulling herself together to save face in front of a stranger fell last on her priority list. Catching her cousin and saving Chance was all that mattered.

For what seemed like an eternity, Richard Coffee sat perfectly still. Dark eyes studied her, and she almost saw the cogs moving in his head. Finally, his booming voice rumbled out. "There's a security truck I can lend you. I can't leave the building unprotected, so you'll have to take yourself. Bring it back when you're done."

A key ring with a single key dropped on the counter, and she snatched it up. She turned to race off when a thought occurred to her. Spencer wanted her, and he knew she was here alone. With a frown, she glanced back. "Don't let Spencer in here, for any reason, with any authorization number."

She watched in fascination as his enormous brow furrowed into deep lines of confusion. "He never comes here."

"I realize that, but he may try today. I can't explain, but if he does contact you, don't give him any information and *definitely* do not let him inside."

Richard nodded in slow motion. "I hear Detective Cohen is on your case."

The menacing tone in his voice forced her to stop in mid stride. "Yeah? Do you know him?"

His massive jaw clenched into a firm line, not a good sign. "I've kept an eye on him, ma'am. He moved to the area a couple of months ago from some town in Alabama. Duncan harbored concerns about the man's interest in him and his research. Whatever he is, he's not human."

Her heart sank again, a common occurrence lately. "So, he's a vampire? But not with a recognized family?"

The skin around his eyes tightened, and the right corner of his lip crinkled a bit. "I don't think so, but research isn't my job. Be cautious around him."

Perfect. The last thing she needed was another player adding to the looming storm, which threatened to unleash its fury at any moment. She nodded and jogged for the door, a tricky task in her strappy heels. The black flats sounded like heaven right about now. She should have listened to Chance.

Minutes later, she scrambled into a white S-10 with "Goditha Security" slapped across both doors and the tailgate in simple black letters. The engine roared to life, and she threw it in gear, peeling out of the parking lot. Her focus narrowed on getting to the station as fast as possible. Chance was sitting in a viper's nest with no idea of what was coming. Her chest tightened with panic, blood thundering in her ears.

Her unswerving focus became a distraction, preventing her from seeing the car until it was too late. She glanced up at the rearview just as a red sedan smashed into the rear end of her truck. The whole thing lurched forward, and Lilith gripped the steering wheel as her head whipped forward. The seat belt kept her from flying through the windshield, but the jarring force knocked the air from her lungs.

As her panicked heart leaped into her throat, her foot slammed down on the gas, and she pulled away from the nineties-model Oldsmobile. The boring maroon rattrap looked nothing at all like the ominous black SUVs the bad guys drove in movies.

Her eyes nervously flickered from the rearview to the windshield and back again. The road ran straight for the next half mile, with cornfields and farms on either side. The city limits lay roughly fifteen miles away, with sparse pockets of civilization in between. A bright yellow sign revealed a sharp left turn ahead, and the red beater was gaining fast.

With her heart pounding from adrenaline, she gripped the wheel and floored it. Her eyes caught motion to the left as she turned. The Oldsmobile roared straight for her. The driver made no attempt at the curve, instead opting to T-bone her at the apex.

Her nerves rattled with panic as she slammed on the breaks and straightened the tires in a desperate attempt to minimize the impact. Off-road was inevitable, but hopefully, she could keep the truck from flipping. The world crawled to a halt as the red car careened toward her. Lilith swallowed the lump in her throat and held on for dear life as everything exploded.

The air filled with the deafening screech of metal grinding and glass shattering. The impact to the front quarter panel sent the light truck barreling onto the shoulder. Then, it scraped against a telephone pole with a sickening sound, which slowed her down, but not enough.

With a gut-wrenching groan of metal, the vehicle lurched downward violently, and the grill slammed into the side of a massive drainage ditch. Her head thrashed forward, bouncing off the steering wheel with a blinding pain that made her vision spin on the shattering windshield. White-hot agony flared up her arms.

The truck's light bed shot up from the momentum, leaving her dangling by the seat belt before it slammed back down, making the whole vehicle rock and groan. Her head flew into the headrest, and her vision swam out of focus again, with bright points and dark shadows. She didn't have time to blink before the darkness consumed her.

The sound of shattering glass pulled her from the murky depths of unconsciousness. Her entire body screamed for her to wake up, but her eyes struggled to open until hands dug into her hair and viciously yanked her head to the left. Pain seared across her scalp and down her battered body as she clawed blindly. The only thing keeping her attacker from dragging her through the window by her hair was the seat belt.

"Bitch!" The hands retreated fast after her nails raked hard enough to draw blood. "I told him calling Gregor was a mistake, but he wanted *you* here even though you're a meddlesome bitch!" Spencer's voice dripped with such anger, hatred, and resentment that she almost didn't recognize it.

She tried to make the world stop spinning, tried to focus, but a fist hit her cheek with a crushing blow, making her teeth rattle. The entire side of her face exploded in blinding pain as she fell over the center console. The plastic dug sharply into her bruised ribs, and her head began pounding ferociously. She needed it to stop. If she didn't focus right now, she'd die. With a flash of sudden clarity, she scrambled to unlatch the seat belt.

"He'll see. When I drag you back to him, he'll see I am right. I hope he lets me carve you since I had to play babysitter." He tugged at the handle, trying to open the warped door, so fixated on his rant that he was blind to anything else. "Doesn't matter. You'll all be together soon enough. Duncan, Chance, Gregor, you." His laugh exuded homicidal glee.

With her heart racing like a scared rabbit, she pushed herself over the console and into the passenger's seat. A glance at his cruel face, contorted in anger, told her no trace remained of the man she knew. She could only imagine Miriah's shock seeing the monster her brother became.

Her vision swam, and her stomach churned again, classic signs of a concussion. Miriah. He beat her face into a mangled mess. Through the noise and delirium in her head, she realized the same thing would happen to her if she didn't move. *Move!* The word echoed loudly through her mind as her shaky hands fumbled for the door handle. Once they found it, she pushed her shoulder against it, and a fresh pain shot up her arm, causing her to whimper.

That caught Spencer's attention, and his blue eyes glowed with pure hate. "What the fuck do you think you're doing?" He yanked at the driver's side door, but it didn't budge. Rage surged through him as he slammed his hands against the vehicle, making it rock. Panicked, she shoved harder at the passenger door, blinking back tears as the excruciating pain made her fingers go numb.

His arms shot through the shattered window and tried to snatch her legs. "No!" With fierce determination not to die, she gave one last giant shove at the door, finally pushing it open. As she fell, her heel kicked out, catching his jaw with a sickening crack. The impact rattled her bones, even with the thick grass to cushion her fall. If she lived through this, she'd be black and blue for months.

An extensive line of cuss words followed her as she scrambled up the hill, fingers clawing into the dirt, desperately climbing as her shoes slid on the wet grass.

The mystery man in charge wanted her alive so Spencer might not kill her yet. However, she knew precisely how that worked out for Miriah and refused to fall into the hands of the butcher, who made death a more appealing choice. If she couldn't escape…

"Damn it! You almost broke my fucking jaw!" She didn't dare stop to look for him. His location was irrelevant. She simply kept clawing, climbing, digging, desperate to put as much distance between them as possible.

When she finally reached the crest, she wildly scanned the area for somewhere to go—nothing but cornfields and cow pastures with no sign of help. Movement caught her attention just as he came running up the embankment, his red-rimmed eyes blazing with a fury that burned away any illusions of morality.

She tried to run, but he intercepted and slammed her to the ground. Terrified screams tore from her throat as she tried to push him away, but his iron-clad grip refused to budge. When she attempted to kick him, he swung a leg up and straddled her chest. The weight crashed down on her bruised and broken ribs, making her cry out in agony. After that, each breath she dragged in became smaller and smaller as her legs flailed uselessly.

"Where the hell do you think you're going…*cousin*?" He spat the last word at her like a dagger. The severe line of his mouth split into a demonic grin, making her skin crawl and her stomach lurch. The concussion combined with her inability to breathe became too much, sending her vision spinning in dizzy circles. Violent heaves racked her body, and she managed to thrust her head to the side enough to keep from choking on the vomit.

His hysterical laugh sounded like nails on a chalkboard as he jumped to his feet. As soon as the crippling weight left her chest, she sucked in a massive gulp of air that left her choking. However, his movement wasn't born out of mercy. With a sneering grin, he reared back and kicked her viciously in the ribs, sending her rolling onto her side as tears burned down her cheeks. Her lungs didn't contain enough air to scream.

"You might be smart, but you're not tough, are you, bitch?" His beady eyes watched her claw at the grass, struggling for each ragged breath.

"Why? Your own family?" The hoarse words sounded alien as they emerged from her raw throat.

"They didn't give a shit about me." His face contorted into an angry snarl as spittle flew from his mouth. He snatched her wrists again, squeezing so tight, her hands tingled and went numb. "*He* is the only one who wants me to succeed. You and your deceitful piece-of-shit father will scream, bleed, suffer, beg for mercy, and, eventually, die, but not until we get what's ours."

His sky blue eyes narrowed at her, and all she saw in her mind was his sister's lidless eyes of the same color. "I enjoyed every second of killing Malachi, the smug bastard." An insidious satisfaction slithered over his face as his tongue flicked across thin lips in a hungry smile. "You'd like it too. It's like nothing you've ever felt before."

His determination to find any kind of acknowledgment, good or bad, gave her an idea. He craved attention like a dying man craves salvation, so it had to work. With a nervous glance, she mumbled a few inaudible words.

"Oh, you have something else to say? Speak up!" His open hand struck her cheek like a lightning bolt.

Once she recovered, she mumbled again, keeping her voice quiet before choking on another harsh breath.

"I still can't hear you."

She peeked through her lashes to see him lean closer but not close enough. She tried again, choking and coughing in between hushed words.

Spencer bent right down to her mouth just as she knew he would. He craved validation, a pathetic addiction to negativity, brandishing it as a justification for his villainous deeds.

With grim satisfaction, she screamed the words *"Go to hell!"* and threw her head forward, cracking him right in the nose. Fresh waves of pain made spots dance before her eyes, but if it meant escaping, the trauma was worth it. She'd rather die of brain damage than let him take her anywhere, which was a distinct possibility at that point.

The monster jumped back, howling as he tried to contain the blood pouring down his face. She probably broke his nose, but she sure as hell wasn't sticking around to find out. She fought through the deafening roar in her brain and her wavering vision, clawing at the grass, pulling herself up on shaky legs.

The high heels kept sinking in the soft dirt, so she kicked them off and propelled herself forward. She ran with every ounce of energy she could muster, straight into the cornfields. Rocks, twigs, broken stalks, everything cut at her bare feet, but none of it mattered. She had to keep moving. Run or die.

The endless stretch of obscenities that followed her faded into a dull howl, but she held no delusions. He would chase after her. Her chest burned with each breath as the corn plants whipped at her, slashing her skin, drawing blood. Still, she ran full speed, even when every muscle screamed in agony.

Then someone shouted from the direction of the wreck. Spencer. "You and everyone you love will die slow, and I'll enjoy every minute. He'll slice you to ribbons while your precious daddy and your idiot bodyguard watch! Once their minds break, he'll do the same thing to them. Don't think I won't find you! You're gonna fucking pay!"

She heard leaves rustling far behind her, and a fresh wave of panic urged her on. She pushed past the burning in her muscles, forced each panted breath, and sprinted forward. When tears stung her eyes, she wiped them away defiantly. She couldn't fall apart now. They would all die if she did, and it wouldn't end with her. Her cousin's mad ramblings revealed that, somehow, for whatever reason, this all revolved around Gregor.

She burst out of the suffocating cornfield into a clearing and slowed down to weigh her options. A small house lay ahead, but there was no guarantee anyone was home with no cars parked outside. An old barn sat closer, covered in fifty years of faded, peeling paint. She saw no other buildings, no main roads, no people. So, she veered full speed toward the barn with every inch of her body crying out in pain. If she could hide long enough to call for help or grab a decent weapon, she could still avoid the grim fate that awaited her.

Skidding to a halt at the hay-covered floor, she began searching desperately for something, anything. Finally, she uncovered a pair of rusty hedge clippers before whipping around to the sound of movement in the sea of cornstalks. He was closing in. She grabbed the clippers and scrambled behind the tall bales of hay, barely squeezing her skinny body between them and the wall. When she wriggled into a space ample enough for her to crouch, she hit redial on her cell.

He picked up on the second ring. "Cohen."

She kept her ragged voice to a whisper. "It's Lilith. I need help. Use the GPS tracker on my phone, and send someone here now, please!"

Spencer shouted again, and this time he sounded a lot closer. Her heart tripped in her throat, making it hard to breathe, or perhaps that was the result of multiple rib fractures. "What's happening?"

"I can't talk. Find me, or you'll be putting me on a slab next to Miriah." She hung up and shoved the phone back into her jeans.

"Come out, come out wherever you are!" Spencer's shrill voice rose and fell in terrifying melodic tones.

She closed her eyes and concentrated on long, even breaths. He was too close for her to run now. She gripped the shears tight in her hand and prayed that he wouldn't smell the blood. Wishful thinking.

Her adrenaline, the one thing keeping her going, began to recede, slowly revealing her injuries. Her head throbbed with a violent pain that churned her stomach. The sharp aches burning over her face meant multiple hairline fractures. Every little breath seemed like a stab in her right side. She needed a hospital, but until then, she had to keep it together, stay conscious long enough to fall apart later.

Every silent second stretched into an eternity. The effort of clenching the rusty shears made her hands start to tremble. Then his voice boomed so close, she almost jumped, terror making her pulse race a million miles an hour.

"I know you're in here! Your blood reeks." His vicious sneering tones indicated his position, just outside the barn, dashing her hopes of a rescue. Her hiding spot, wedged behind the enormous hay bales, would only protect her for so long. Even the shears didn't supply much hope. More than likely, the moment she attempted to fight, her body would give out. In fact, the blood she gulped down at the lab was the only reason she made it this far.

Footsteps crunched across the hay, warped floorboards squeaking, getting closer, then continuing farther. She squeezed her eyes shut, focusing everything on the sound of his movements. Her nerves rattled, clenching her hands until the sharp tingling became too much. *Breathe.* With a slow exhale, she eased her grip on the weapon, letting the blood return to her fingers. The steps came closer again, terribly close, and then stopped.

"You investigated Miriah's body. You know what will happen." He moved past her again, casually pacing, toying with her. "Sis and her hubby...they begged to die, both of them, with every little slice of flesh. Leaving Miriah in her office was never part of the plan. You weren't supposed to see it coming, but he has his reasons. Anticipation makes the air sweeter, the fear more palpable. Soon, you and your precious loved ones will be fuel for *my* fire." Judging by his voice, he paused in front of her, a wall of hay the only thing separating hunter from prey.

Blood pounded in her ears, filling the deafening silence. Why was he waiting? Was he trying to taunt her out of hiding? Make his job easier? Well, to hell with that. She wasn't that damn stupid. If he wanted to waste his time talking, she wouldn't stop him.

"Your father will beg for his life, too, like the spineless coward he is. Guess it runs in the family. There will be no mercy for your muscleman, Chance, either." Her skin broke out in a cold sweat, and she almost dropped the shears as her nightmare flashed through her mind. Her father burning, Chance's lifeless eyes...

"I hope you haven't bled out back there. It would be best if you didn't die too soon. I have plenty of things I want to do to you, starting with that smart-ass mouth of yours."

A faint low crunch somewhere in the distance pulled her attention. She didn't recognize the sound, but the footsteps sprinted in the opposite direction, followed by the rustling of leaves. She sat there, dumbfounded at his quick exit. The approaching sound grew louder, but she still couldn't place it.

What would scare him away? Then it clicked. The sound of tires crunching on gravel. He didn't want anyone to see him. If someone saw him beating the crap out of her in the South, they were more likely to shoot him than call 911—saved by redneck justice. Hysterical tears of joy shone in her eyes as she let the shears clatter to the floor and slid out of her hiding place. It didn't matter who was driving. They embodied a chance of survival.

Once she left the support of the wall, she fell painfully to her hands and knees. Her muscles didn't want to work, and every inch screamed in pain. She choked back more bile as her head spun so fast, she nearly collapsed into unconsciousness. "No. No! Get up! Get to the truck!" Her cousin wasn't gone. He would linger in the corn, lying in wait, and if she missed this opportunity, he'd pounce.

Muscling every ounce of survivor grit, she crawled up a bale, pulling herself up onto shaky legs, and pushed forward again. She stumbled through the door and onto the crude driveway. As soon as her bare feet touched the gravel, she felt safer, like stepping out of the cold dark into the warm sunshine.

An old red pickup cruised up the long drive, and a surge of relief overcame her, negating the stinging bite of stones as she sank to her knees. The truck screeched to a halt a few yards out, and she drew in a painful breath, closing her eyes as tears streamed down her cheeks.

"Gracious meh, yuh aah-ite, ma'am?" Strong hands helped her up to her feet again. After several attempts, she managed to focus on the weatherworn face before her. Years of being in the sun made him appear alien. Despite the deep wrinkles and sun-dried skin covering his face, his eyes seemed far younger.

"Yuh look like yuh dun bin chewed up an' spit out." His thick accent made the words difficult to understand, but she got the gist.

Her legs gave out, and he hauled her up into his strong arms, carrying her to his vehicle. "Police station." Since her throat was raw from bile, the words emerged a hoarse jumble. The adrenaline leaked from her system and left her reeling from a tsunami of pain.

Her head spun like a merry-go-round on crack. Worse than a simple concussion.

"Girl, yuh got one oar in the water. Them cops caint fix yuh up. Ahma call 'em win we git yuh to thuh ER." The man settled her into the passenger's seat and pulled the seat belt across her. As soon as the weight touched her chest, she screamed out and pushed it away.

"Ahma jus' drive slow-like." He left the belt dangling and ran around the truck to hop in his side.

With a tremendous amount of effort, she managed to string together a coherent sentence. "Thank you for helping me, but I need to go to the police station first." She paused, trying to draw in a shaking breath through the sensation of daggers lining her ribs. "I need Detective Cohen. Please."

The old man never took his eyes off the road, but his head dipped a minuscule amount. "Yuh look like ten miles uh bad road, but aah-ite. Raah-ite to thuh hospital aftaw'rd, tho." He nodded firmly, emphasizing his point. With that settled, she relaxed against the seat, and everything gave out. Her eyes fluttered closed, and the soothing vibration of the truck cruising down the country roads lulled her into unconsciousness.

Chapter 14

A cacophony of muted sounds echoed in Lilith's throbbing head, her entire body flaring to life in blinding pain. Her head hurt ten times worse than in Duncan's basement. A groan escaped her lips as her eyes fluttered, the heavy lids struggling against the fluorescent light. Motion somewhere to her right sent her heart racing. Her eyes flew open, and she recoiled instinctually, her body screaming in protest.

"It's okay. You're safe." Although the silky voice was soothing, it didn't belong to Chance. For an instant, she focused on Detective Cohen's almost handsome face looming in front of her. Then, everything disintegrated into a blurry swirl of colors. "Don't move. You're pretty banged up." Steady hands reached out, repositioning an ice pack on her face as she begrudgingly relaxed into the soft leather of a sofa. The haunted shadow in his eyes indicated *banged up* was a sugarcoated version of the truth.

"Where am I?" The rough and husky sound coming from her raw throat surprised her, but nothing compared to the intense agony raging in her head. She fought down mounting waves of nausea, struggling to stay conscious.

"You're in my office. I followed the GPS signal on your phone with my lights blazing when a red pickup waved me over." She glanced up at his soft brown eyes. They reflected genuine worry and concern, which startled her. Between their odd conversation and Coffee's comments, she didn't expect compassion. "I think you frightened the old man half to death." His warm smile dazzled, almost making her forget his small chin.

"I guess he didn't expect a half-dead woman to stumble out of his barn." She attempted a smile but ended up wincing. Her face pounded, reminding her of all the abuse it took—hitting the steering wheel, Spencer's teeth-shattering punch, the hard slap, and the vicious headbutt allowing her to escape.

She moved tentative fingers along her cheeks, assessing the swollen, tender flesh. With a groan, her shaky hands fell back to the couch.

"Perfect," she mumbled, mostly to herself. "Now, I truly look like a domestic abuse victim."

Cohen bit off a snort of laughter and gently moved the ice pack. "How's your head?"

"It feels like I went fifty rounds with Mike Tyson." The initial sting of cold against her blazing skin melted into a soothing chill.

He shifted, moving off his chair. Her eyes opened to see him hovering, too close to ignore with his mouth drawn in harsh lines.

"What happened? I overheard a call about a security truck crashed in a ditch not far from the farmer's residence. That yours?"

She nodded, a huge mistake because sharp pain immediately flared through her head, making her vision swirl like a psychedelic acid trip. After overcoming the sudden urge to throw up, she leaned back. "Uh, yeah. I borrowed it." The deep breath she took to steady herself cut like hot blades thanks to the broken ribs, but she managed to meet his questioning stare. "Chance has the keys to the rental car."

"This isn't from just running off the road." His blue eyes burned with an unwavering determination. He had information about her family, and Richard inferred he knew about their race as well. Although she had no guaranteed way to tell if she could trust him, she had no choice. She needed help now, and no other options existed.

"Spencer, Duncan's son." Something passed over his face, but she couldn't figure out what. "If you want the whole story, tell me who you are. I know you aren't the wholesome human detective you're impersonating. You're investigating Duncan. Tell me why, because I need an ally, and I'm guessing you need information which doesn't apply to your…day job."

He sat back on his heels as a smile slowly spread across his thin lips that somehow transformed him. The expression belonged to the odd gracefulness he sometimes displayed, not the naive young cop. "You've done your homework." The thick Southern accent disappeared, leaving the twinge of something vaguely European.

The man considered her in silence, the pause stretching into uncomfortable territory. Then, he finally continued. "My family sent me here a few months ago in search of a key to break the encryption of an old book, which contains far too much information about them. After centuries of research, they tracked down the author, Duncan MacEwan. I planned on approaching him civilly to discuss the matter once I was certain about his identity. Now he's missing."

While he talked, she studied every line of his face, which showed flashes of mild resentment, even an air of rebellion. It seemed clear that he didn't share his family's sense of urgency concerning the damaging book. Of course, she wasn't as skilled at interpreting faces as she thought. She sure saw her cousin's reactions through rose-colored glasses.

"I'm not here to hurt anyone. I need Duncan alive, so it appears we are already on the same team."

"So, you are a vampire?" The grin that crossed his face sent chills down her spine, supplying the answer before he opened his mouth.

"No, and I'm not human. *There are more things in heaven and earth,* Lilith, *than are dreamt of in your philosophy.* What I am is not important, but my offer is. I help you, and in return, you help me."

He left her no choice. Her decision may come back to bite her in the ass, assuming she had one left at the end, but what other options did she have? With nauseating pain, she scooted up on the couch into a seated position. The small movement proved more excruciating than chewing a mouthful of glass.

"Get Chance out of holding, bring him here, and I'll tell you what I know." She released a hissing breath as she pressed the ice against the opposite side of her face.

Without any hesitation, he pulled himself up and stalked through the door. Again, she observed the strange grace to his walk but couldn't quite figure out why it seemed familiar.

Once he left, she glanced down at her clothes and groaned. The dark green button-up shirt, caked with mud and blood, clung to her skin in clumps of torn, frayed fabric. The jeans hadn't fared any better, and neither had her feet. Dirt covered the tops, and she didn't want to see the bottoms, judging by the searing pain.

When her fingers tried to dig through her auburn curls, they became instantly entangled. Wincing with each careful movement, she retrieved a hair band from her pocket and threw the bloody, snarling mess into a hasty bun. Then, she placed the ice back against her face with a resolute sigh. This was *not* her best day ever.

The intense throbbing pressure in her head grew louder and more excruciating with every passing second. Something was very wrong. She closed her eyes, leaning into the cold and taking shallow breaths.

A few minutes later, the door swung open. Lilith started to turn, but her muscles screeched in protest. Seconds later, Chance loomed into view, and the expression on his face said everything.

"Nice to see you, too," she croaked while moving the ice pack so it wouldn't obstruct her view.

He sank to the floor next to her in a boneless heap. "Oh god, Lily." The pained tone in his voice made her want to cry. His hand caressed hers, the only part of her body *not* in immense pain. "I should have been there."

"Why? So, you could almost die too? This is not your fault, Chance." Her voice wavered as tears welled in her eyes, tightening her already sore throat.

His expression hardened as the door closed, jaw firmly set as he stared down whoever stood at the door, most likely Cohen. "You're right." The hollow sound of his voice made alarm bells ring. "This is *his* fault." Chance surged to his feet, hands balling into fists.

Cohen strolled right past him without a care in the world and pulled two cheap office chairs over to the couch. He ignored the six-foot-three wall of rage and sat down, keeping his eyes on her.

"Your fiancé is here. Talk."

She watched the tension in Chance's shoulders, the tiny movement, and knew his intention. "Chance. Don't."

He snapped his head toward her, his chest rising and falling a little too fast. "Why? This asshole is responsible for throwing me in lockup while someone tried like hell to kill you. Why are we wasting our breath right now? He doesn't give a shit about what's going on!"

"We need his help, and the last thing you should do is punch a cop in a police station! Take a seat, please." Chance stood still, eyes burning a hole in Cohen's face.

Then a fresh wave of pain sent her reeling. When he heard her horrible moan, the fight drained out of him. After glancing at the chair next to Cohen, he sank onto the floor beside the couch, opting for maximum distance.

He focused on her, struggling to find some way to help. "He mentioned a car crash, but there's more to it, isn't there?"

"Yes. Spencer is working for the bad guy." His eyes widened while she sucked in a quick breath before continuing. "I was at the lab when he called me. I mentioned the paper I found in…" She stopped herself and glanced at Cohen. How much was she willing to tell him? Too late now. "At the scene. Then, I told him the police wanted a statement, and he said he'd head over right away. The paper turned out to be a plane ticket, Miriah's, for a flight from Knoxville to La Guardia on Monday night."

When Chance stared blankly at her, she explained. "She left with Malachi. Duncan must have sent them both, and Spencer followed them. They managed to drop the letter at my building, but they never made it to Gregor, their real goal. He killed Malachi, beat his sister's face in, and dragged her back here. He confirmed our nameless villain, the one that attacked me at Duncan's, killed her. It fits all the facts. He didn't tell Miriah to pick us up. By the time we landed, he was driving back to Tennessee with her as a prisoner."

"His *own* family? Why?" Behind the open disgust on the surface lingered something closer to empathy on Chance's face. Somehow, he knew how dark a family's secrets could be. "What did he…" His throat tightened, which choked off his words. He closed his eyes, trying to compose himself as his fingers twined through hers. The warmth gave her something to concentrate on besides her battered body.

"What did he do to you?" As soon as he spit out the question, his jaw clenched painfully tight, bracing himself for the answer.

Lilith adjusted the ice pack again as the noise in her head grew louder, verging on an ear-splitting roar. "He stockpiled a lifetime of resentment, like a rebellious teenager who shoots up a school because his sister got more attention."

She couldn't keep the revulsion out of her voice. "I imagine this enemy of Gregor's homed in on his dependent nature and cultivated it over the years. The way Spencer talked about him…he's a father figure, which is a million times worse than him just working for the guy. He's committed to the cause, heart and soul, seeking the approval and validation he never got from Duncan. He won't stop, he can't be reasoned with or turned, and he knows everything about Gregor and us." She released a soft sigh of futility. "He's also aware of the blood sample the lab is testing."

A sense of doom settled over her shoulders again, making her abused body shiver. All she wanted to do was curl up in a ball and sleep, but distantly, she knew the mounting pressure behind her eyes meant something worse than a concussion.

Chance squeezed her fingers, bringing her back to the conversation. "What did he do to you, Lily?" Answering would only send him flying into a rage, which was why she ignored him the first time he asked. The firm line of his jaw clearly said he refused to let her ignore him a second time.

"I borrowed a truck, and he rammed me off the road into a drainage ditch. I managed to climb out and made it up the embankment before he tackled me…" She paused as a flood of images and feelings tightened her chest again. "He nearly succeeded in killing me, but I broke his nose and hauled ass through a cornfield. Then I tried to hide in a barn, but he found me…" Her voice trembled as tears threatened to fall from her bloodshot eyes. "He tried to lure me out, saying awful things…but he ran off when the old man's truck came up the gravel. Now I'm here. End of story." The events sounded so mundane when sugarcoated and wrapped in a little pink bow. However, replaying the scene in her mind horrified her, haunted her.

"This may be a stupid question, but are you okay?" She caught the subtle undercurrent. Any traumatizing injuries, either physical or emotional?

"At least a few broken ribs and a hairline fracture in my jaw. The seat belt nearly sawed me in half, and I lost some blood. The worst is my head, though. I don't think it's just a concussion..." She moved the ice pack to the other side of her face again, sighing at the cold against her skin. The stabbing pain in her skull mixed with intense pressure and felt like a bomb ready to explode at any moment.

She purposefully avoided looking at Chance. A few days ago, she'd only seen two faces on him, casual humor and business. Now she was overly familiar with his pained expression of failure, and she couldn't handle seeing it again. When she finally gathered the strength to glance at him, he wore a blank mask of concentration as he checked out her wounds.

"There are a lot of scraps, some deeper cuts to your scalp, but I don't see anything major. Do you remember seeing a lot of blood?" The guarded tone in his voice cracked slightly, betraying his facade of calm detachment.

The question confused her at first. When she stopped to think about it, the blood she lost wasn't enough to cause her current symptoms. That only meant one thing—internal bleeding.

She'd almost forgotten Cohen was still in the room until he spoke up. "I seem to be a little lost, but before we go into the full story, I think I may be able to help." Although his smooth Southern drawl sounded casual, she now knew it was fake, like everything else about him.

"How?" Chance beat her to the punch. When she glanced up at him, his eyes fixed on Cohen, suspicion quirking the corner of his mouth.

The detective lounged in his chair with all the grace of a jungle cat. His usually warm brown eyes weighed on her, calculating each conceivable answer. He drew in a deep breath and let it out slowly. This time, he didn't bother with the fake accent. "What I'm about to tell you must never leave this room. My family would murder me for even thinking about this." The calm casualness ran out of his body, and he rubbed a hand through his hair.

"Look." He leaned forward, resting his arms on his knees and holding Lilith's gaze with a weight in his eyes. "With your injuries, even a vampire's regenerative powers won't get you on your feet for weeks, assuming you live through the next few hours, which, right now, looks doubtful. I need your help to find Duncan, so I have no choice."

"If you draw this out any longer, the suspense will kill me before the internal bleeding." No one else found it funny. Her chuckle turned to a cough, which racked her body in tormenting heaves. When the coughing stopped, she collapsed against the cushions in whimpers of mind-numbing anguish.

Cohen let the silence stretch into awkwardness. An inner battle waged behind his eyes, so she concentrated on staying conscious as Chance's fingers laced through hers, an anchor to the waking world.

Finally, the detective spoke up, having made his decision. "I can't tell you everything. Let's just say my blood will ensure your survival and get you back on your feet faster."

His statement was *not* what she expected. "Say what? How purple is flagging her?" She blurted the words out in total surprise, not realizing they only made sense to her. Cohen's eyes narrowed shrewdly, but Chance didn't seem to notice, too distracted by confronting the other man in the room.

He dropped her fingers, and his back straightened. She couldn't see his face, only his shaggy brown hair, which looked ragged from running his hands through it repeatedly. Weird how she noticed that. "What the hell are you talking about? Your blood? We don't even know who or *what* you are!" Cohen held up a hand, his almost handsome face set in hard lines. "I need your help, and right now, you need mine. This won't hurt her, exactly the opposite. There is a reason my kind is even more secretive than yours. Exposure would be hazardous. Humans would hunt and harvest us if this got out. If I do this, no one can *ever* know, or I'll ensure your silence permanently. Understood?"

"*If you do this?* How are we supposed to trust you?"

Lilith stared at Chance's hair, the voices seeming more distant with every word. The reddish streaks danced in the light, bringing a smile to her face until she realized his hair wasn't moving. It was her vision, wavering like some cheap intro to a flashback scene. The pounding in her head reached a full-on roar, making everything else sound hollow and tinny.

Cohen caught on first. He jumped out of the chair and grabbed a pair of scissors from the desk. "We are out of time. If she falls asleep now, she won't wake up. The internal bleeding is worse than I thought. She's dying."

"No!" Chance surged to his feet and blocked him as her eyes fluttered, losing focus with a groan that turned into a breathy giggle.

"Look at her, Deveraux! Do you want her to live or not? I certainly do. She may be the only one left that can help me. I will *not* let her die, even if it means killing you in the process. Step aside!"

"If anything happens to her..." The threat sounded like gibberish, but he moved aside, allowing Cohen to kneel next to her.

"Lilith." The voice echoed in her ears as if coming from a long dark tunnel. Someone grabbed her face. She tried to focus, but she was so tired, and her eyelids grew increasingly heavy. If she could just sleep for a while...

"Talk to her, Deveraux. Keep her awake until the blood is in her system."

A familiar scent filled the air, and she smiled deliriously. "Chance? You always smell like sunlight..." Her voice sounded curiously melodic, even to her.

"That's right. Hey...hey. Look at me, mon *cherie*."

Her eyes fluttered open, and she struggled as hard as she could to stay focused. She wanted to see his handsome face. Fingertips swept over her swollen cheeks, and her eyes stared right into his. She could gaze into those hypnotic hazel eyes with flecks of green forever.

"That's it, Lily. Stay with me. Cohen's going to give you something, and you need to drink it, okay?"

She loved the velvety sound of his voice, even if she didn't understand the words. Then, something warm and wet touched her lips, and she jerked back in surprise. Blinding stabs of pain shot up her neck and rattled around in her skull, releasing a moaning scream from her sore throat.

"Stay still. Drink, baby. Please, *mon cherie*." Tears stained his desperate words. "You can't quit on me, not now. *Mo lame toi.*"

The pain was so intense everywhere, and her mind tumbled in lost confusion, overwhelmed, disoriented. Then, he lovingly stroked her hair with a rush of comforting whispers, pulling her out of the chaotic spiral, calming her panicked nerves. When she licked her lips, the flavor exploded on her tongue like an atom bomb. She never cared for the taste of blood. It was like swallowing a mouthful of pennies, but this…

When the warm sticky thing returned to her lips, she grabbed it, ignoring the screaming pain in her arms. For the first time, her cartilaginous fangs clicked down and pierced her prey. She sucked hungrily as the sweet stuff burned down to her stomach and roared through every cell. The sensation escalated until her vision exploded in blinding white light, her body singing with vigor. Then, she fell into darkness again.

Distantly, Lilith felt her cheek resting on something firm and warm as the psychedelic show behind her eyelids continued. A familiar scent filled her nostrils, pulling her out of the brain-addled dreams until her eyes flickered open. She braced herself, expecting the light to stab at her sensitive eyes, but she merely blinked in the brightness. Odd. Then the violent memories flooded her mind, the car crash, the drainage ditch, Spencer, running until her feet bled. She waited for the insane torrent of pain to sweep over her, but it never came.

Her eyes traveled upward from the leg she rested on to see Chance staring off at some unknown point, deep in thought. Gently, she squeezed his fingers entwined with hers, and his eyes dropped instantly to her face. She sensed his heart stop for an instant as he gazed down at her with such tenderness it made her chest tighten.

The flood of relief washing over him vibrated through her as if it was her own emotion. Weird. Before she could diagnose the sensation, his free hand ran through her hair, and a smile tugged at his lips. “You look much better. How do you feel, Lily?”

She hadn’t stopped to think about it until he asked. The minor headache, tender areas, stiffness, and dull ache across her chest felt more like a hangover, a mere shadow of her earlier torment. How was that possible?

"I… Well, I'm fantastic in comparison." She kept trying to piece together the events in the office, but everything past Chance gearing up to deck Cohen in the face came in fuzzy glimpses, making no sense at all. "What happened?"

He wrapped his arms around her and buried his face in the curve of her neck. An unexpected surge of emotions, *his* emotions, overpowered her, and she clung to him like a rock in a raging river. Tears stung her eyes as she experienced how close to death she'd been through *his* grief. What was happening?

Then, lips brushed against her soft skin, making every nerve spring to life, instantly evaporating the fear gripping her heart. The sensation intensified, more substantial than anything she'd felt before, like the difference between a spark and licking a damn battery. Something wasn't right, wasn't normal.

"Wait. Wait." She swallowed the frightened lump in her throat and pulled back. "How long was I out?"

"Only a few hours."

For a moment, she thought she'd misheard him. Hours? Hell, even days, to go from death to this? Impossible! All the words caught in her throat, leaving her speechless.

"This is the second time I've almost lost you, Lily. You seriously need to stop doing this to me. No one likes a prematurely gray bodyguard." Although the words were playful, his tone screamed vulnerability, bringing her back from the edge of madness. She could psychoanalyze things later.

"Next time someone tries to attack me, I'll tell them I'm not allowed to play 'cause my bodyguard said so." She grinned at his shaky laugh, letting all her questions and uncertainty go for the moment.

He smoothed a hand over her pinned-up hair as his eyes searched hers. An eternity stretched out between them, and she wondered why she never saw it all before. The deep affection in his eyes made her breath catch and her heart race. She dreamed of seeing that look, the one from a million different movies, and now it belonged to her, all from the last person on earth she expected.

She caressed his cheek, the soft scruff tickling her palm. "When I left the lab, I only thought about getting to you before Spencer." Mentioning her cousin drew all the powerless feelings back into the light as the sense of doom settled back over her shoulders. "Things seemed bad before, but now…with him as an enemy…" She squeezed her eyes closed and fought back against the threatening tears. "He knows *everything*."

He pressed his forehead to hers lightly and smiled. "He doesn't know everything. You made sure of that."

While frowning in confusion, she leaned back to see his eyes. "What do you mean?"

"The tin. You never told Spencer, so he'll assume we didn't find anything. I doubt they'll kill Duncan until they have it. He's probably been at his father's tearing the place apart, and if he hasn't, he will."

A huge smile curled her lips, and she lunged forward, hugging him tightly, which left a giddy grin on his handsome face. "You're brilliant!" The elated surge came crashing to a halt as she remembered the most important thing inside the mystery box.

"The blood sample. Damn it. I told him the lab was testing it. I didn't tell him where I found it, but if his boss told him what he was searching for… We can only hope the blind trust isn't mutual. What time is it?" While squirming to dig out her phone, she nearly fell off his lap.

Strong arms caught her mid fall, and he chuckled in amusement. "Hold on, Tornado Lily. It's after nine. Why?"

"Crap! I hope the doctor is still there." She wiggled her phone free and dialed Goditha Labs.

"Richard… Yeah, about the truck, I'll replace it for you… No, no. I'll explain later. Is Dr. Nichols still there?… When did he say he'd be back?… Okay, thanks."

She leaned her head back against his shoulder with a frustrated sigh. "We have some time to kill. About four hours to be exact." Even through her agitation, she recognized how comfortable his arms felt, but what she needed most was a lead, a ray of hope in the dismal darkness.

Her cousin was only one piece of a much larger puzzle. "Maybe we should head to the lab. Dr. Nichols might have left some notes, a message, a file, or something." She started to slide off his lap with frantic energy, but he tugged her lightly back.

"Before we run off to play super cops…there's something I wanted to say."

When she turned and saw his vulnerable face, she stopped resisting and sat back down in concerned confusion. "What is it? Are you okay? Whitmore didn't hurt you, did he?"

His light chuckle erased all her worries. "I'm fine, Lily." His warm brown eyes dropped, staring at her fingers twined with his. "I…uh…well, I had a lot of time to think about things today, and… you were right"—he shook his head and finally met her eyes again—"about everything you said outside Miriah's office."

For a moment, she couldn't even remember what she said. Last night seemed like a lifetime ago. Then, it slowly came crawling back into her brain. Her father, Chance, the tattoo, the secret torch he carried. "I'm sorry. I should have kept my mouth shut. It's not my place…"

He pressed a single finger to her lips and smiled. "Let me say this, okay? I'm head of security, not a poet." When she grinned, he reluctantly dropped his finger.

Her whole body tingled, and for the first time since she left Manhattan, it wasn't from fear but anticipation. "I hid behind Gregor. Sure, at first, his threats terrified me, but then… I became accustomed to the idea of you as an impossibility. I thought he was right. I thought you were better off without me as a complication. I guess…a large part of me felt unworthy, and pining over you in secret felt easier than taking a risk. So, I buried my feelings in one-night stands and work."

"Chance, you don't have to explain anything to me." She pulled away, subtly, and rubbed a hand over her arm. Soul-baring talks weren't her specialty, one of the many reasons why failed romances littered her life. She kept breaking her own heart by losing herself in the endless facades a relationship required. So, a few years ago, she put an end to the masochistic cycle and dug into work, walling herself off from the world. Now, his words hit a little too close to home.

He slid his hands up to rest on her shoulders, pulling her attention away from the guilt-fueled thoughts eating away at her. "I'm done hiding, Lily. I care about you, and I always have. Even if I wanted to go back to the way things were, I couldn't." He paused, exhaling slowly as if terrified, capturing her undivided attention, and then continued.

"That first kiss destroyed the barrier, and now I'm drawn to you like a magnet. I could never stay away, not now. So, I guess what I'm saying is...when all this is over... I'd like..." He swallowed the lump in his throat and brushed a hand over her blood-caked cheek. "I'd like to take you on a real date."

After blinking in surprise, she bit back a laugh, but the damage was already done. He frowned, and she reached out, her palms cradling his face. "Oh, no, no. Don't be upset. Please." Then his frown turned to something worse, a wounded expression boiling over into anger and rejection.

"Don't be upset? After everything..."

"Stop. I'm sorry. For a second, I felt sixteen all over again. A *date* sounds so normal after the last few days." She pressed a petal-soft kiss to his lips and felt all the horrible emotions drain out of him. She pulled back to hold his gaze, wishing she could telepathically transmit the depth of her feelings. "I would love to go on a date with you, more than anything."

The bright smile that curved his lips made her entire body shiver. "I've waited to hear those words for thirteen years." His arms squeezed her tight, and he nuzzled into the curve of her neck again. "Spencer and his pal are dead meat. There's no way we aren't making it home now." When he pulled back, his teasing, casual grin felt wonderfully familiar, like seeing an old friend after spending years apart.

Before she could comment, the door swung open, and Cohen breezed in. His eyes ran over the chairs, and he finally saw them tangled up on the couch. An actual blush crept over his cheeks, and he hesitated with his hand on the doorknob. "Uh, sorry, but…well, someone is here to see you."

They both flinched with instant confusion. Who the hell would look for them here?

Alvarez's stocky form filled the doorway and stopped dead in his tracks. "Wow! Some seminar." Irritation melted into concern as he finally saw past the tangled body parts. "*Mierda santa!* You look like death."

"It looks worse than it is. I'm okay, promise." She quickly hurried off Chance's lap and into an office chair. "What the hell are you doing here, Felipe?"

Irritation hardened his expression. "Well, hello to you, too, partner. If you're done playing house, Gregor wants to see you both at his hotel. I wouldn't mention"—his deep-set eyes flickered between the two of them, and he waved his hands through the air—"whatever the hell this is. He isn't in the best mood." Although humor flecked his rolling Spanish accent, the undercurrent revealed his anger. The fact that she wasn't the sole target of his fury made her wonder if he knew about Chance's crush.

"Back up. Gregor's *here*?" Her nerves shook again. If her father was here, then they were playing right into the enemies' hands. "Shit. He shouldn't be here. We have to get him the hell out of here before—"

"Stop. If Gregor is in danger, you better tell me why. And before you start fabricating another cover story, I'm not an idiot. Who takes a red-eye flight on Tuesday night for a weekend conference? The worst cover I've ever heard. And who the hell is this guy?" He jabbed a thumb in Cohen's direction before running a rough hand over his receding hairline.

She felt a momentary stab of guilt for lying to her partner, even if she was simply following her dad's orders. "Felipe, I'm sorry—"

Cohen cut Lilith off, stepping right up to her with an unexpected menace pulling at his face. "We had a deal. You're not leaving this station without me." She felt Chance bristling behind her like a tangible tingle over her skin. Bizarre, but she had no time to analyze things with this much testosterone poisoning the air.

"Fine, then tag along." She waved a hand in frustration. "We don't have time to argue."

"No." Alvarez blocked the door with his stocky body, his dark eyes tired and impatient. "This is *family* business. We will not indulge the local police."

Cohen spun on his heel with open hostility, dropping all pretense of the country bumpkin. For the first time, he appeared threatening and dangerous. "I am no mere cop, and I do not need to explain myself to you. My arrangement is with Lilith…not you." The European tone overcame the fake Southern drawl once again. Tension swam around the room so thick, it pressed against her skin with a physical weight.

Chance pulled himself off the couch while Alvarez and Cohen stared each other down like rivals in a deathmatch. If she didn't intervene, the situation would go from bad to worse in seconds.

She quickly muscled her way between Cohen and her partner, pushing them apart. As soon as her palms touched them, she jerked back. They were blazing hot, like dipping her hands in a deep vat fryer. What the hell was going on?

"Damn it. Compare dick sizes later!" She concentrated her stern gaze on her partner. "Do you seriously want to push for a fight when Gregor is in danger?" His face crumpled, all the confrontation seeping away.

"And you!" Her gaze swung to Cohen. "If you want information, stop picking fights with my people and get us out of here."

Once they stopped puffing their chests and appeared suitably humble, she stepped back and stared down each one in turn. "We all done? Great. Gregor is a sitting duck, so we'll play catch-up all at once."

As she spoke, Chance stepped up behind her in a show of solidarity. A tingle of strength tickled over her skin, beyond simple emotional security. It wasn't her imagination. Something weird was happening.

"We all have a lot to talk about." Her eyes rested on Cohen with a significant weight. One not wasted on him as he nodded solemnly in reply.

Perhaps having most of the players in one place at one time would shine a light on this rat's nest of random crap. She needed answers from everyone, *especially* her father.

As they filed out of the office into the police station, Chance leaned over her shoulder and whispered, "Remind me never to piss you off." Something simmered under the humor in his voice, and it took her a moment to place it—raw desire.

"Still want that date?" Despite everything, a smile tugged at her lips.

"Are you planning on drugging me and selling my kidney on the black market?"

"Uh, no." She couldn't help but laugh.

"Then, yes. You are a badass, after all."

"Whoa. Calm down. I don't have any latex bodysuits in my closet." She bumped his shoulder without thinking and earned a twinge of pain. However, considering her arm was fractured a few hours ago, she felt terrific.

Chance whispered in a rumbling tone, "No one's perfect."

Chapter 15

The ragtag group filed out of the office, heading straight for the door with purposeful strides when Whitmore stepped in front of them. His wrinkled face scrunched into a sour look as his eyes roamed over every single one of them before resting on his partner.

"What the hell is going on? You aren't going anywhere, boy." He jabbed his thumb at Chance with righteous indignation. "I told you we need to call the FBI, Cohen. And now you're letting some…*cop* from New York City run off with our suspect?" The snarl he threw at Alvarez with the word "cop" betrayed his racist thoughts. How… unexpected.

The young detective moved forward, clapping a hand on Whitmore's shoulder. She realized he was a good foot shorter than Cohen's lanky height with the two of them facing off. Young, lean, and tall versus badly aging, overweight, and short. Even if Cohen were human, it wouldn't be a fair fight.

"Bob, we have a lead, a promising one. The informant is a little skittish, so I'm going to escort these folks to approach him on neutral ground in good faith." Cohen stooped, just a little, making sure his eyes met Whitmore's.

"If we call in the Feds, we'll be cut out of the investigation. Give me a chance. This kind of case is a career changer. I promise. If we don't find anything, I'll make the call myself." The sweet Southern drawl rolled off Cohen's tongue in hypnotic tones.

Bob wrung his hands nervously, a weird expression for him, considering his suspicious anger seconds ago. "I should go with you. We are partners, after all."

Cohen patted his shoulder affectionately. "You've been working this thing since last night. Go home. Spend time with Martha and get some rest. I'll call you when I find something. No sense in us both bein' too tired to think."

He responded without any hesitation, "Yeah, Martha's probably going nuts right now. You're right." Then, Whitmore turned on his heel and shuffled off. The irate man suddenly trotting off like a demure kitten was the weirdest thing she'd ever seen. Either Cohen knew every button to push, or she'd witnessed something inexplicable. The list of things to discuss with their new ally kept growing longer and longer.

Once Alvarez and Chance climbed into the unmarked cruiser, she glared over the car at Cohen. Now was as good a time as any.

"What the hell was that?"

He glanced up at her, startled. "What was what?"

Her eyes narrowed suspiciously. "Seriously? Whitmore abruptly changed his mind about throwing Chance in holding and calling the FBI to rush home to his wife like some meek househusband?"

"Martha's not his wife."

The odd detail derailed her train of thought. "What?"

"Martha. It's not his wife. He's not married." The smug casual air to his grin gave her the overwhelming urge to smack his almost handsome face.

"Girlfriend, boyfriend, whatever. Not the point."

He crossed his arms on the roof, lounging like he had all the time in the world. A sparkle lit his crisp gray eyes, revealing his enjoyment. She frowned for a minute. Gray? Weren't they—

He interrupted before she finished her thought. "Martha is his dog, a basset hound, to be precise. I merely reminded him she's been cooped up since last night."

Her face tightened in anger. "Get in. We'll talk about this later." She slid into the back seat without another word, slamming the door behind her. They didn't have time to play games, and from the time he blew his cover, that's all he wanted to do, apparently.

Alvarez gave Cohen the address, and they headed off toward the Tennessee River District. Gregor had straightforward rules for staying in hotels. He never chose the most expensive place because of the attention from the staff. Her father also never stayed at the cheapest dump because it appeared suspicious. Instead, he strove for mediocrity, which typically meant a Holiday Inn.

However, if her father wanted anonymity at a run-of-the-mill hotel, he failed. He seriously needed to view the pictures of the hotel *before* booking his room.

The Marriott gleamed brazenly in the night, perched on a hill-top overlooking the Tennessee River, a modern marvel of concrete and glass.

The massive structure resembled a slanted A. One side went straight up over ten stories while the other angled dramatically up to the apex, like half a pyramid. Huge windows mimicked the design, and a glass elevator tower rose from the center, sticking up higher than the rest of the building. It was the most bizarre hotel she'd seen outside Las Vegas. So much for subtle.

Cohen skipped the valet service and pulled into a parking space in the back nine of a packed lot. "All right, time to share all our toys. Let's go." He jumped out without waiting on anyone, keeping his purposeful stride as he headed for the lobby.

Alvarez glanced over at her as he scrambled out of the passen-ger's side. "What is up with that guy?" His dark eyes stared after the young Detective in complete confusion. "Is he…one of us?"

"No, but he's not human. I'm hoping we're about to find out who and what he is, though."

Chance climbed out last with his eyes fixed on the weirdly entrancing hotel. She caught a stern expression on Alvarez's face moments before he grabbed her wrist, holding her back as Chance followed Cohen.

"I hope you know what the hell you're doing." He whispered the words as anger rolled off him in unmistakable waves. "Gregor told you to give me some fluff cover story. Fine. I get that." The sting of betrayal pulled at his pockmarked face. "But you bring a stranger into our business and now this thing with Chance?"

A vibrant blush crept over her cheeks, making any attempt at denial a blatant lie. Plus, Alvarez already walked in on them curled up like lovebirds. "He's…he's kind of amazing." The flustered lack of words irritated her, shifting her embarrassment to anger. "Why should this concern you? We have work to do. We need to stop a vicious killer, which is slightly more important than who I'm making googly eyes at?" She snapped the words and pulled her wrist away.

He scratched at the side of his head as his jaw set in a firm line. "It concerns me because I'm your partner, and I care about what happens to you, *estúpida*. But, fine. Let's go. Your dad is going to lose his shit, though."

"Isn't that what dads do best when it comes to their daughters? Isn't Gloria doing the same thing?" She almost chuckled, thinking of his wife handcuffing their eldest daughter to keep her from sneaking out.

"Look, Felipe, I didn't mean to snap. I know you are only looking out for me, but I'm a grown woman. Gregor can be pissed if he wants, but this is not his decision to make."

He stopped and stared at her with heartbreaking sadness in his eyes. "Yes, but have you *thought* about your decision? Chance is a half-blood. How will you feel when he ages before your eyes, and you still look like this? How will you deal with the world thinking he's your grandfather or casting aspersions on him for robbing the cradle? How are you going to handle his funeral? I'm not trying to hurt you, *bonita*, but Gregor's protective side has merit. Also, I hate to state the obvious, but he works for your father. You don't expect that to get awkward?"

None of those things occurred to her. The thought of Chance dying made her chest tight, but she didn't have time to indulge the train of thought. "Assuming we all survive this, I promise I'll seriously think about what you're saying. We can't leave the others waiting. Come on, let's go." She hooked her arm through his, which made his mouth crack in a grin. She forced a weak smile through the dark storm cloud he pulled over her. Damn inconvenient logic.

"You're gonna make the man jealous." An impish grin curled his lips as Chance turned around halfway to the door. Even from this distance, in the dim light, she saw his back stiffen, but a quick smile melted all the tension from his body.

When they reached Chance, he fell in step beside her and claimed her free hand. "Nothing like an armed escort to make you feel special, right?"

Alvarez laughed before she could say anything. "Actually, it looks like she's our prisoner, *compadre*." His warm, rich laugh echoed with undercurrents of his beautiful accent. She loved it when Alvarez and his wife went off in Spanish. No matter how angry, the language rolled off their tongues like living poetry, differing entirely from the choppy Spanish she commonly overheard.

"Well, I somehow get the feeling that is *exactly* what Gregor wants." Chance meant the comment to be funny, but halfway through his sentence, the humor disappeared.

"What my father wants and what happens will most likely be two different things. Can we hurry and get inside?" A shiver crept down her spine as her eyes kept surveying the packed lot.

Spencer could easily follow them from the police station. It all depended on how desperate he was. Sure, both she and her father were targets, but would he risk making a move with Chance, Alvarez, and Cohen on alert, in the middle of a very public hotel? She had no guarantees.

The trio picked up the pace and rushed into the lobby, which seemed as disconcerting as the exterior. Modern, blocky architecture created a unique vaulted ceiling. In stark contrast, red and gold oriental rugs covered the marble floor, complete with matching neoclassical furniture. A baby grand piano perched in the center completed the bizarre mix of modern and old-world antique.

Alvarez led them to the glass elevators where they found Cohen casually leaning. "Already secretly plotting without me?"

After a pointed glare, Lilith silently stepped onto the elevator, waiting for the rest to follow. No amount of mind-numbing John Tesh Muzak could cut through the seething tension. The levels of testosterone and hostility in the cramped space could poison Hulk Hogan.

Moments later, they filed into Gregor's room, with Cohen bringing up the rear. Apart from the sloping ceiling leading to a huge balcony, it looked like any other hotel room featuring espresso prefab furniture, creamy tan walls, matching bedspreads, and pictures with the same vivid pops of red and gold from the lobby.

Gregor stood in sharp disparity to the manufactured comfort like an ominous cloud, darkening further as his eyes fell on the detective. Every trace of the loving man she'd known as her father disappeared. His rage overpowered the twinge of concern briefly shown as he glanced at her. Even with Cohen's help, she looked like a World War III victim, but evidently, he decided she'd live long enough to address other matters.

His eyes hardened on Cohen, every wrinkle in his skin leaping out of hiding and creasing his face. "Who exactly are you?" The surprisingly stern and commanding tone made her unconsciously step a little closer to Chance. Drinking in the warmth of him at her back somehow helped to calm her nerves. She never thought her father would scare her. Guess there was a first time for everything.

To his credit, Cohen didn't flinch. He leaned against the wall with a casual grace overflowing with confidence, unlike the good-hearted detective she'd first met. "I'm an interested party. I've tracked down Duncan over a few years because he has something I need. Since I have a vested interest in finding him alive, I arranged things with Lilith."

Gregor strode across the room with purpose, like a storm rolling through. Lilith, Chance, and Alvarez all backed up a step, but the detective stood his ground. "I don't believe any of that dribble answered my question." The nonchalant expression on Cohen's face faltered for a second giving her a bit of smug satisfaction.

To her utter surprise, Chance stepped around her and cleared his throat. "Gregor." Her father swung around, those piercing sky gray eyes fixing on him, making his chest rise and fall a little faster. "He's not human, and he's not a vampire. You have no reason to trust him, but he risked exposing his nature to save your daughter's life."

Something flashed across Gregor's face, too fast to identify. He decided not to waste energy on fancy words. "Explain."

Chance's eyes flickered to hers for just a moment, one not missed by her father. Perfect. "Spencer ran her off the road, beat her senseless and—"

"Spencer?" Gregor cut him off in complete shock. "He did this?" Now he truly studied her injuries with calculated eyes full of disbelief.

She nodded solemnly, wishing in her heart of hearts she could deny the truth. Her cousin was a monster beyond help. "We can discuss it later. You wanted the story about Cohen." She signaled Chance to continue.

"Lilith barely escaped. He found her and brought her to the police station. At first, she was coherent, but things changed fast." His eyes darted to Cohen, who closed his eyes with a weary sigh. He knew what Chance would say next, even though they agreed *not* to reveal the truth. Gregor would never trust a stranger without a reason, and since Cohen refused to explain, Chance had no choice but to supply him details.

"She had multiple concussions and internal bleeding. She began speaking nonsense, became pale, and I could hardly keep her awake. In a matter of seconds, the swelling in her brain was going to kill her, Gregor. It's not a figure of speech when I say she was at death's door." She had no idea how bad it was, how close she came to dying. The revelation brought her to tears, and she wasn't the only one. Gregor's gruff exterior faltered, red tinging his eyes as they fell on her.

"Cohen...he fed her his blood, and somehow it saved her life. Clearly, there is a healing property to it, and he took a bold risk revealing that fact. If what he said is true, his own family would kill him for what he did."

Her father stood a little taller, reining in his emotions, and turned back to the detective. "That all true?" Cohen nodded cautiously. "If what you did was so dangerous, why take the risk?" His eyes narrowed, studying him.

"If Duncan dies, she is the only hope I have of finding the object I'm seeking. That would be a reason enough, but beyond that..." Cohen took in a deep breath, his eyes darting around the room nervously. He hesitated a moment longer on Chance than anyone else. What the hell? "Your daughter is incredibly courageous. I read the report. It's a miracle she lived through the crash, but to fight off an attacker and claw her way to safety as she did is something remarkable. She deserved to live, sir."

Her eyes widened in shock as her father considered his words. Whether he succumbed to his soft spot for her, or because he saw the truth on the man's face, he nodded in satisfaction. "Fine, stay. If you give me one reason to doubt your sincerity, you'll be begging me to kill you, understand?" The cold, menacing tone took her by surprise again. This new view of her father twisted her insides.

Chance stepped back to stand beside her, his fingers brushing against her hand. The simple touch shot up her nerves in vibrant colors, filling her with warmth and strength—a unique sensation. Perhaps almost dying made everything more potent? Or, more likely, she required a one-on-one talk with Cohen. She didn't remember taking his blood, and no one mentioned it before. Perhaps the weird sensations stemmed from *him* somehow. But that conversation would have to wait.

"You need to tell me what's going on, Dad." She steeled herself, ready to weather his wrath, but when he turned toward her, it wasn't anger in his face but shame. "I know you want us to leave, but we can't. Your nephew isn't just helping this monster. He idolizes him. They won't stop, and he knows everything about us. We can't run. We have to end this, and you need to start talking."

Gregor sank onto the corner of a bed and nodded in resolution. "You all might want to take a seat. It's a rather long story."

Alvarez and Cohen claimed the two chairs near the balcony doors while Lilith and Chance sat on the opposite bed, keeping a little distance. They were both in for an earful later, but she saw no need to aggravate the situation.

Her father spent a long time staring at his open hands, resting against his thighs. For the first time, she saw the weight of all his years heavy on his shoulders. He looked exhausted and empty, nothing at all like the man that raised her. The sight of him so defeated broke her heart. Then, he rubbed a hand over his closely trimmed beard and finally ended the silence.

"Duncan and I used to be quite close, even after Aaron left for the Romanian countries. We established ourselves in Scotland centuries ago and lived comfortably. Taking noble names or status would draw far too much attention, so we settled into a peasant's life in a remote region. Everything has its pros and cons…"

A solemn pause brimming with foreboding tightened her chest. "I fell in love." The shadow of a smile pulled at his lips, and she saw the layers of emotions like transparent films laid out on top of one another. The deep affection gave way to tremendous pain and haunting guilt.

"Margareet was an enchanting woman, beautiful, graceful, optimistic, and compassionate, with the voice of an angel." Listening to her father speak wistfully about a woman other than her mother made her uncomfortable. Even if this woman lived lifetimes ago, the thought still made her skin itch.

"We married in a quaint ceremony and created a life on the moors where we raised two sons on our modest farm. Duncan lived with us in those days, tinkering in alchemy, resolute in solving the riddle of our kind." Imagining her father in such a simplistic life felt odd. Sure, he lived for hundreds of years, but picturing the modern man standing before her in gray slacks and a matching knit sweater farming in medieval Scotland upended her comfortable sense of reality.

Gregor's stormy eyes stared out sightlessly, lost in his memories. "The happiest day of Margareet's life was the day she gave birth to Mary." He glanced up at the ceiling, tears welling up as he rubbed his face. The depth of his heartache, his agony caused her eyes to water. She hadn't seen her father cry since her mother's funeral. Somehow, this loss seemed just as fresh, like days passed, not over six hundred years. After clearing the lump from his throat, he continued.

"Our entire world revolved around Mary, a force of nature, beautiful, compassionate, and giving, exactly like her mother." Mournful eyes settled on Lilith, and his loving smile briefly brightened the gloom. "You remind me so much of her. Stubborn to a fault." Everyone in the room disappeared into the background as if only the two of them existed. Simply a daughter and her father sharing a moment. She stared into his sorrowful eyes, and all the memories of the horrible days following her mother's death flooded to her mind. She wanted nothing more than to ease his torment as she did back then, but she couldn't—not this time.

"I remember the spring after Mary's seventh birthday. A poor lamb was born missing a leg. Without any hesitation, she scooped the babe up and named it Trinity. Nothing my wife or I said mattered. Mary set her heart on raising the unfortunate creature."

A soft painful laugh escaped as he shook his head. "That lamb hobbled around, following her everywhere. She fed her, combed her, and even brought her into the house at night whenever the weather turned cold, which was quite often in Scotland. Margareet warmed to the idea before me and started singing about Mary and her little lamb… Funny how some things survive the centuries. Eventually, people expanded on the song in the Americas, adding bits about schools and teachers." A distant smile crossed his face, but he waved it away.

"Two years later, feral dogs attacked the flock. They often plagued the area, and we lost a lot of sheep. Mary found Trinity and carried her all the way home while it bleated in terrible pain. I wanted to end its suffering and tried to explain, but she wouldn't have it. Mary bandaged her, fed her milk, cradled her, and sang to her.

"When nothing helped, she came to me and admitted I was right. Trinity was hurting and needed to be free. This nine-year-old girl told *me* not to be sad and that *she* should give Trinity peace. I couldn't let her, of course. I said I would gladly walk her lamb to heaven if she would comfort her mother. My little girl, bold, fearless, and so full of loving compassion."

Gregor paused, wiping at his red eyes, and Lilith moved to sit next to him, placing her hand on his. He squeezed it for a moment, but he wouldn't face her. Instead, he took a deep breath and pushed on with his story.

"Every fall, we went into town to sell our goods and buy supplies for the coming winter. Usually, my wife and I went alone while Duncan stayed with the children. However, when Mary turned twelve, she begged to come along. Her relentless campaign wore us down over the summer months, and we allowed her to go with us that fall. She scoured the markets with her mother, marveling over all the people, animals, and delightful little baubles, while I stayed with our goods.

"Then, my wife returned alone, panicking. In the hustle and bustle, she lost sight of Mary. We searched all through the night but found no trace of her." Gregor drew in a painful breath, closing his eyes, and she suddenly knew what came next. Duncan's notes confirmed the story didn't have a happy ending. She briefly squeezed her father's hand but had to pull away. Seeing her father so distraught was heartbreaking enough without *feeling* his pain vibrate over her skin.

"The next day, a huge commotion broke out at the tavern. I told Margareet to stay put while I investigated the cause. When I reached the building, the whispering crowd filled in the blanks. Someone murdered a poor girl in one of the rooms. Snide comments about some nobleman's son circulated, but no one dared to speak a name. I pushed my way to the front and ran inside. Upstairs, I found her… my Mary." His voice broke as he collapsed into tears, sobbing as they all watched helplessly.

"Dad, you don't need to keep going…" She wanted her words to be true. She wanted to let him stop.

"Yes. I do. You deserve the truth." When he finally composed himself, his jaw set in an angry line. "The bastard raped my twelve-year-old daughter, brutalized her. Her precious face almost unrecognizable from the beating. The spring green dress Margareet stitched for her lay torn and bloody. He strangled the life out of her when he finished and tossed her aside like garbage. My Mary, the light of my life, now only a used-up corpse on the floor…"

Despite the weird sensations she experienced, Lilith hugged her father's shoulders as he choked on his tears. This time when his agony seared over her, she recognized the emotion, but it didn't rack her body or twist her insides. On some level, the experience felt energizing, exhilarating, the guilt of which made bile rise in her throat.

She pulled her arm back, breathing a little too fast, embarrassed, and repulsed by what happened every time she touched someone. She caught Cohen's eyes on her, his quizzical expression snapping her from the private moment of self-loathing. Then, she remembered the room full of people.

No one dared to speak a single word. The deeply personal nature of Gregor's story made everyone else feel like intruders. No one wanted to see their father, or boss, or elder cry like someone wrenched the soul from his body. After a few struggling breaths, Gregor finally recovered and sat a little straighter. He needed to tell his story as much as they needed to hear it.

"The barkeep informed me that Sir Ashcroft Orrick's son, Clyde, rented the room for a piece of silver and was the last one to leave. He knew telling me might cost his life, but he had a daughter Mary's age. He explained this wasn't the first time a horrific death in his tavern linked to Clyde Orrick. I pleaded my case to every nobleman I found, but none of them would concede. The Orrick family possessed a revered and intimidating status, and I was no more than a peasant. To accuse someone of noble birth, you had to be in the same caste or higher, even with indisputable proof. A hundred peasants could watch a lord slaughter an infant, and unless the victim held high social standing, nothing would happen. Even then, holding someone responsible meant risking the exposure of secrets or even war. No neutral parties existed to settle disputes, only underhanded politics, using commoners, like my family, as pawns in their game. We had no value." Gregor's eyes searched them all, begging for their empathy. "You have to understand that social justice did not exist at the time."

Silent foreboding suffocated the room as everyone braced themselves, Gregor included. By the time he spoke again, her skin itched with dreadful anticipation.

"Margareet and I took Mary's broken body back to be burned on the moors. My beautiful wife barely spoke. The life vanished from her eyes, leaving behind a hollow shell. I had to find justice for what happened to my family, which meant exacting it myself. He couldn't continue defiling and slaughtering the innocent, and I couldn't let my daughter's death be meaningless. We needed to abolish the evil forever. And so, my brother and I began planning. Clyde Orrick, nobleman's son or no, would die for what he did, for what he desecrated and took away from us.

"Days later, Duncan announced his intention to move into town. A temporary measure to further his research. A ruse, of course, but no one suspected ulterior motives. He had nothing to tie him down and would often disappear for weeks.

"My boys took over the farm while I cared for Margareet. Mirren was twenty at the time, and his brother only two years younger. Finlay took his sister's death to heart, more so than his brother, since she helped him tend the gardens. However, Mirren spent most of his time with the flock, sleeping in a small hut, only stopping in to restock every few weeks.

"Duncan returned home at the end of each month and dragged me to his shack. He spent his time in the city tracking Clyde Orrick's movements, his habits. After a few months, patterns appeared. Every Sunday, Clyde would visit the same place and never alone. Typically, he'd pay for whores, but another altercation occurred two weeks after Mary's death. He attacked a young chambermaid, only fourteen years old. The man beat her unconscious on the bustling road in front of the tavern and dragged her inside. She didn't live through the night. No one did anything! Not even the lord who owned her. She was a slave, and therefore as expendable as a common dog."

Gregor pulled away from Lilith and clenched his fists in a surge of anger. His red-rimmed eyes hardened, the muscles tightening into furious lines. "They all witnessed him brutalize this defenseless young woman and did nothing! They went about their business like weak little sheep." His chest rose and fell rapidly as his mouth bit down, clenching tight. "If the lords and ladies listened and sought proper recompense, all this death could have been avoided."

After taking a calming breath and letting his outrage ebb a bit, he continued. "Six months after Mary's death, my brother and I both went to town, waiting for Clyde's next visit. When I laid eyes on the creature, something deep inside me turned black as night. An overwhelming hatred ate at my soul.

"I studied every detail of the ugly sot. He was short, maybe five foot, greasy black hair tied hastily up behind him. The gods did not grace him with good looks. A hideous hook nose stuck out from his squat little face like a beak, and his weak chin almost disappeared in his ragged, sharp-toothed grin. Blemishes covered his oily skin, and his thin weathered lips bore scabs. His beady eyes never stopped moving, casting about for his next victim. No amount of posh clothing or finery could disguise his vicious vulgarity.

"We stayed hidden until the depraved monster retreated to his usual room. The owner, our coconspirator, ushered us up the stairs and unlocked his door. Upon bursting into the room, we found him hunched over a serving wench, defiling her battered body with his burly hands clenched around her neck."

His head hung low while his teeth gritted in a snarl of contempt. Disgust vibrated over his entire body, and he wasn't the only one. She glanced at Chance to see his fists curled in the comforter, his knuckles white. Alvarez paled with a greenish hue. The only one who appeared unaffected was the calm and collected detective.

"It all happened so fast. I knocked the man unconscious with a chamber pot sitting by the door. Then, Duncan grabbed the girl, getting her out of the room while she gasped for breath. In seconds, I found myself alone with the monster responsible for brutalizing my daughter, stealing her bright light from the world." Gregor kept peering at his hands as shame edged into his anger. "We planned to simply slit his throat, one less demon roaming the earth. But staring down at this evil pig, a clean death was *not* punishment enough. I couldn't allow him to die with more grace than he afforded my sweet Mary.

"I tied him to the bed with scraps of his clothing. Then, I woke him with my blade slicing down his sternum in a shallow cut. Once I had his full attention, I recited his vulgar sins, including my daughter's murder, and the pig *laughed*!" Gregor lifted his eyes to Lilith's, begging her to understand what came next.

"He cackled like a hyena about raping and killing *my little girl*!" His eyes fell again, the anger altogether giving way to shame. "When I cut his tongue out, he nearly choked on the blood, so I turned his head. I didn't want him to die yet. His dwindling manhood still hung from his pants, a disgusting lump of shriveled flesh. In the midst of removing it, Duncan returned. He screamed for me to stop, to stick to the plan. However, the monster's pain became intoxicating, a dark wine sating the demon clawing my insides…as long as I didn't stop. The creature deserved no less."

His hollow voice betrayed what lay beneath the false bravado. He kept his stare fixed on his clenched fists, refusing to meet anyone's eye. "I tossed his dismembered parts on the ground and finally slit his throat, giving into my brother's screaming pleas. He immediately tried to pull me out of the room, but I refused to leave until I heard his last gurgling breath. When he lay still, blood pooling, sightless eyes clouding over, I allowed him to drag me down the stairs.

"After riding straight through the night, I collapsed into my wife's loving embrace and cried until morning. She was my savior, the only thing able to bring me back to the light after sinking into the darkest depths. Duncan, on the other hand, was not quite as forgiving, which drove a wedge between us."

She sat frozen, torn in two. Her morality warred against her sense of justice. Thinking her father *capable* of such a violent atrocity made her stomach churn. However, could she genuinely blame him?

In a heated discussion, someone inevitably stated the need to castrate pedophiles, but would they do it if given a chance? Probably not. Very few people possessed the ability to commit such a drastic and violent act. Gregor's ability to recognize his crimes as zealous and radical *had* to mean something. She couldn't face the possibility that her father lacked any remorse for crossing the line into torturous territory.

"So, Ashcroft vowed revenge for his son. That's what he's coming after?" Her voice sounded jarringly modern after listening to the increasing thickness of his English accent for so long.

He glanced at her with solemn eyes and hesitated. "Not quite. This is only the beginning of the story." He didn't want to continue. His face said as much. Whatever came next would be worse, and he wouldn't only be a victim. He stood and paced toward the balcony, turning away and distancing himself as he continued.

"For a long time, I believed I deserved to die for what I'd done. At that moment, I became a monster like Clyde, and…" His shuddering breath fogged the glass doors. "I enjoyed every second of his torment, but Margareet held me together. Months went by, and life returned to some semblance of normal.

"With spring came new life. Duncan met a sweet woman while traveling and took her as his wife. He moved home and put his research aside. My beautiful wife was with child again, glowing with an infectious light. I finally felt whole once more, as if the entire dark period remained some distantly remembered nightmare.

"Late that spring, our wives sent my brother and me into town for supplies. We burned through most of our staples during the rough winter, and she needed fabric and needles to finish clothes for the baby. So, we kissed them goodbye and bundled off with heavy hearts. Neither of us had returned since Clyde's murder. Inside the city walls, our darkest demons lurked, eager to burn through our happiness, but that wasn't all that lie in wait.

"A band of guards detained us as we attempted to leave. When they asked for our names, a sense of doom settled over our shoulders. Duncan surrendered at once, his face a mixture of acceptance and relief. I struggled with foolish desperation, however. I still had a family to fight for, but I was no match for a half dozen men.

"They escorted us to the tavern, straight up to the room where I took Clyde's life. The vivid memories of screams, blood, and vindication crippled me as they locked us in. Escape seemed impossible with armed guards at the door and on the street below. Sitting in that room, reliving my darkest moments, made me believe I deserved no mercy. So, we waited, accepting our unfortunate fate.

"Halfway through the night, the door opened, and a woman, escorted by two men, entered. Contemptuous, bitter hatred seeped from every pore as she introduced herself—Senga Orrick, Clyde's mother. She ignored Duncan, focusing her hawklike eyes on me as if aware that *I* took her son's life. I explained Mary's death to justify my actions, but she held no sympathy for a peasant's plight. *They are little less than pigs*, she said, *and Clyde had every right to do what he wanted with them*." He stared out the window as his whole body stiffened, a huff of humid breath fogging the glass again.

Chance moved away from the balcony to sit beside Lilith. Giving Gregor plenty of room seemed smart until he twined his fingers through hers. Not the best time to officially announce things. A tendril of sadness filled the void as she pulled away. Insistently, he reached for her hand again and gripped it—a declaration of solidarity and support. Without the strength or the desire to argue, she gave in.

"I braced for the killing blow, ready to accept my destiny, but she turned on her heel and left. The satisfied grin contorting her face still haunts my dreams. The guards locked the door, and I heard their heavy footsteps following her down the stairs. For one foolish moment, we believed she took pity on us.

"Then, we smelled the smoke. She intended to bum the entire tavern down with us inside. We managed to break down the door and pick our way through the inferno. We found the innkeeper, his wife, and children—throats slit, flames already licking the corpses. I wanted to pull them out, pay them respect, but the flames were too much. So, we left them and snuck out the back, but our horses were gone, claimed by Senga and her men. With no other choice, we ran through the chaotic streets and set out on foot before they realized we escaped."

He turned away from the window, about to speak, when his eyes caught sight of Chance and Lilith's clasped hands. Something flashed in his eyes, quick as lightning, but when his stare landed on Chance, the anger melted into fatigue. He no longer had the strength to attack anyone but his ghosts. After releasing a weary sigh, he continued.

"The stories of Mary and Clyde are only the catalyst to the true tragedies..."

Chapter 16

Gregor returned to the dark glass of the balcony doors, turning his back on the room again. A sense of doom settled over the space like a thick fog suffocating them in his morose guilt.

"The fire became visible from miles away, and we sprinted like demons across the moors." He paused, pinching the bridge of his nose to stop the tears welling in his eyes. As the realization dawned, her heart sank deeper into despair.

When he began again, he forced the ragged words past his quivering lips. "What we saw…the buildings ablaze, Ashcroft Orrick atop his horse, people lying motionless on the ground… Our world ended as we came to a halt, just out of sight."

Gregor choked and drew in a steadying breath, still trying to keep the worst of his tears at bay. "Duncan's new wife lay dead, her throat crudely slit. My sons…died of multiple wounds inflicted while defending the women. I couldn't turn away from their lifeless eyes, the flames reflecting on the cloudy surface. Then I saw her. My dear, sweet Margareet…" He lost his control, crouched down, and pressed his forehead against the glass as heaving sobs shook his shoulders.

She wanted to take all the agony away, but she couldn't fight the demons of his past. Even if she could, these horrible memories held the key to survival. No matter how poignant her guilt became or how much emotional trauma he revealed, she needed him to continue.

"Dad," she prompted, hating how one word could make her feel cruel and heartless.

His back stiffened as he slowly composed himself and continued. "After he ran through Margareet with his sword, killing my unborn child, she suffered the same fate as Duncan's bride. The sight of her blood soaking into the dirt destroyed everything good in my soul. As much as I wanted to cradle my wife's body and weep, running to them would only result in our deaths. So, we hid, watching our farm burn as Ashcroft continued to slice at the bodies of our loved ones with maniacal glee. Hours passed before Orrick quenched his thirst for destruction and left."

When he paused again, she found herself wondering if anyone besides her uncle knew this story. No. Deep in her bones, she knew he never revealed his tale of anguish because doing so would make it all real. She wanted to say something, but any words of comfort seemed ridiculously inadequate in the wake of such loss, like handing a burn victim a Hello Kitty Band-Aid.

Surprisingly, Cohen spoke up to fill the awkward silence. "You suffered a tragic blow and lived. I recognize your courage." A tone of camaraderie shone curiously in his voice—a feeling not shared by her father.

His back stiffened, and her nervous eyes darted between them. The seconds stretched out uncomfortably until Gregor turned to face the room, his red-rimmed eyes hardened to enraged slits. He stalked toward Cohen, who appeared unaffected by the welling wrath approaching him. In fact, his indulgent expression of boredom showed he expected this exact response. Why?

"Courage is not what sustained me. I wish it were, but blind rage consumed my very being. Because of what I am, I never sought answers in religion, but after that night, the Devil owns every stitch of my soul and Duncan's. Nothing remained. One selfish family stripped everything away. They deserved the bloody retribution coming for them, and we functioned as the Devil's tools to deliver divine punishment." The deep conviction in his voice revealed his desperation to view his actions as justified, even if it meant condemning himself to wander hell.

"We purged the world of evil…" For a moment, he found Lilith's eyes and hesitated. The reluctance to confess to her lay bare as his sky gray eyes lowered to the floor.

"We meticulously slaughtered every member of their bloodline. His remaining sons, cousins, nephews, nieces, aunts, uncles, and finally, his wicked wife." Gregor drew in a breath and backed away from Cohen. "We worked cleanly, humanely, and gave them all proper burial rights. Still, men, women, children, each of them died, until only Ashcroft remained."

Lilith tightened her hand around Chance's, floored by her father's casual confession of genocide. Glassy eyes studied every familiar line, attempting to blot out the image of him murdering children, but bile burned up her throat regardless. The blood of innocents stained his hands. Even scarier, some part of her agreed with Ashcroft's punishment. A small, minuscule sliver, but enough for her cheeks to burn with shame.

"Once Senga died, Duncan regained his conscience. He begged me to let the bloodlust go, but I couldn't stop. The nefarious beast still lived, and as long as he drew breath, my dark thirst would never be sated. Begrudgingly, my brother continued to help me, but we grew further apart with each passing day. He took to writing, pouring his soul and all its dark corners onto countless pages of parchment. As for me, the dead bodies of my family haunted every moment, waking or asleep."

His eyes flashed up to Cohen, the strength of his condemnation pinning the man in place. "What you mistake for courage is the deepest, darkest level of hatred. Something you've never witnessed, have you?"

Cohen sat perfectly still under Gregor's piercing glare. An accomplishment Lilith admired. "No." That one word rang through the oppressive silence, and she wondered if anyone else knew it was a lie.

Gregor began to turn around in grim satisfaction, but the detective continued. "Although, I do see the result of it in my work. In movies, crowds cheer for people like you, the wronged taking retribution. Those audiences do not realize the suffering never ends. Killing all those people didn't bring back your family. Instead, you traded places with the despicable man who robbed you of them, and now you will never be free."

Gregor spun on his heel, his chilling gray eyes cold as ice, and wrapped his fingers around Cohen's throat. The chair rocked back with his momentum as he snarled inches from the man's face. "Easy to spout philosophy when you aren't staring at the mutilated corpses of your daughter, your sons, your wife!" Venom dripped from his last word, but Cohen remained calm, keeping his body still. "I purged the world of their wickedness!"

"But you didn't, did you? You created something much worse." Nervous adrenaline reverberated through her body as she spoke, but the bizarre blood sample suddenly clicked into her head. The scientifically impossible markers, unlike anything seen before.

Her father released the detective slowly, the animosity melting as he turned toward her. Surprise mingled with regret and pride, creating an odd expression as he crossed the room and knelt before her. He grasped her hands as his tear-soaked eyes searched her face.

"I didn't know, Lily. You *must* believe me." Unfortunately, the desperate plea also signaled an admission of guilt. Her tenuous strength holding back the flood of emotional devastation broke, and tears flowed down her cheeks.

"For centuries, I carried this, a hollow shell of a man until I met your mother." He swallowed the lump in his throat and pressed a kiss to the back of her hand. "Please, Lily. I'm not a monster. I succumbed temporarily to my rage and heartache, but that's not *who I am*. When Rosaline gave birth to you, my soul sprang to beautiful life again. I thought my life would be an eternity of loneliness and exile, atoning for my sins. With you, I believed a higher power forgave me and bestowed upon me a new life." With steely determination, she held his gaze, wanting to forgive him, accept him, and take his pain away. However, the image of him butchering children wouldn't leave her head, and she still wanted answers. "I need you to tell me very carefully what happened to Ashcroft, all of it. Everything else can wait." This time her cheeks didn't burn when she prompted him.

Gregor nodded with a despondent expression, swallowing his tears as he let his hand slip from hers. "The torment I visited upon him was inhumane. Over several days, I hurt him in every way conceivable until his pulse grew weak and thready. I didn't want to stop, but my sense of purpose would die with him. I needed him to continue suffering." The inconsolable guilt in his voice resonated through the air, but her mind kept screaming the same sentence over and over, *My dad, my* father, *tortured Ashcroft for days and left him a mangled corpse, like Miriah.*

He remained hunched on the floor, pinned to the spot by the weight of his contrition. "Duncan tried to make me see reason, arguing and shoving me away from the embodiment of my sins. Blinded by rage, I struck back and nearly killed him, my *own* brother.

"For years, my entire existence consisted of hunting this man and his family. That mission tangled and twined with my identity, becoming my only reason to live. When faced with the terrifying conclusion, unable to view a future without it, I panicked. So, I… tried to turn Ashcroft to make his torment last forever."

Lilith's guts lurched violently as a cold sweat crept over her skin. After jumping past Chance, she sprinted toward the bathroom. A few minutes of dry heaving over the toilet reminded her there was nothing in her stomach to throw up. Finally, she collapsed against the wall, her skin hot and clammy, struggling to breathe, tears pouring down her cheeks. Her universe turned upside down and inside out. How could the same kind and loving father she adored be capable of such sadistic and heinous acts?

A tenuous knock echoed before the door creaked open. She glanced up long enough to recognize Chance but closed her eyes to kick-start her brain.

She still needed answers, but her sentimental side refused to hear them. If she didn't disconnect, didn't see this as merely another case, they'd all die.

Without a single word, his hand smoothed over her hair, and she drew a palpable strength from the simple touch. Then, her eyes flashed open with a troubling thought. Since Cohen's office, every time she came into direct contact with him, she felt his emotions as if they belonged to her. Not in a metaphorical sense, but like touching an emotional battery.

"How are you feeling?" She searched his face, which held all the markers of fatigue, and already had her answer.

"I think I'm supposed to ask you that." His charismatic smile dimmed.

"I'm serious, Chance."

This time he frowned and crouched down beside her. "I'm dead tired. Why?"

She surged to her feet, almost knocking him over. "I need Cohen."

"Uh, okay. You want to tell me what's going on?"

She glanced down into those warm hazel eyes and sighed. "Something's wrong, and I think he can tell me what. I want to speak to him in private, but can you do me a favor?"

He hopped up, sliding his hands around her waist. She felt the tension, the desire, lurking below the surface, and instinctually knew she could reach in and absorb that energy at will. His lips brushed against hers, a faint touch that burned down her spine. "Of course." The whispered words tickled along her skin like butterfly wings.

She pushed away from him, panting, certain something was wrong. Sure, he made her weak-kneed and doe-eyed before, but this...was different. "I... I can't. Not now." Fear sent her heart racing like a caged rabbit.

Judging by his expression, her words equaled a slap to the face. "Sorry, I didn't mean... You're upset. I get that. You have a lot to process, but... I thought taking your mind off things would help."

"Chance, don't. You didn't do anything wrong. I don't want to hurt you, so, please, get Cohen. I need to know what the hell he did to me."

Those words finally caught his attention, and he moved to take her hand. She stepped back as fast as possible, frantically avoiding his fingers as if one touch might kill her...or him. She had to understand the danger before she could justify risking his life.

"And keep an eye on Gregor for me. I'm sure he would welcome a break from...storytelling. Once I speak to Cohen, I'm getting an extremely overdue shower. I'm not finished with Dad, but I can't face him. Not yet."

Tears burned her eyes as this new horrific image of her father kept repeating in her brain.

Chance nodded and simply walked out as she slid down the wall, pulling her knees close and wrapping her arms around them.

She would give anything to return to New York, to her routine when things made sense.

Seconds later, Detective Cohen peeked his head into the room. "Chance said you wanted to talk?"

Her face shot up with a sharp glare. "Get your ass in here and shut the door." She hissed the words between clenched teeth.

With a pleasantly confused expression, he obeyed before perching on the sink. "I'm sorry. I wasn't trying to pick a fight with your dad—"

"What the fuck did you do to me?"

Traces of defensive pride quickly bloomed into a detached frown. "That isn't awfully specific? Explain."

"I am suddenly tuning in to other's emotions and can draw on them like a battery. I *definitely* did *not* possess this skill before taking your blood, so again, what the fuck did you do to me?"

The odd frown vanished, replaced by…amusement, humor, awe? She sure as hell didn't find it was funny. "Huh…only a rare side effect I never thought to mention."

"Which is?"

"Well, you see, my people feed on energies. Doing so affords us our long lives. Now, we have different tastes, of course, but any strong emotion works best. When have you noticed it?"

"Anytime Chance touches me, and when my dad held my hand…" She shook her head defiantly. "No. This isn't possible. Supernatural crap doesn't *actually* happen."

"So, says the vampire…" He trained his weighted stare on her, a smug grin curving his lips. "This isn't science fiction or *supernatural crap*, as you so eloquently put it. Energy is energy. It's never destroyed, only transformed. A person's emotional essence alters reality all the time. For example, a contagious laugh, sharing a person's sadness, feeling drained around someone who monopolizes your time and attention. We simply possess the ability to harness them and use them to a *biological* advantage."

She waved her hand while rubbing the bridge of her nose. "Stop. I don't want a lesson on metaphysics. Is it permanent?"

"Hmm. Probably not." He shrugged nonchalantly and leaned back against the mirror. "Then again, it could be. This is not something I've tried before."

"What? Fed blood to a stranger?"

"To a vampire. You may like to pretend you're human, but you aren't." The hairs on the back of her neck bristled. "I do not..." Then, she stopped, recognizing his attempt to get a rise out of her. "Doesn't matter. Okay, I'm a test bunny." She pressed her forehead against her knees for a moment, thinking. "Is it dangerous?"

"For you? No, the opposite. Drawing from others is exceptionally helpful for healing and focusing. Now, as for the people you take from, yes. It can be just as dangerous as a vampire feeding too much from one victim."

"Well, how much is too much? Damn it... This is the last thing I need."

"Oh, I'm sorry. You'd rather I let you die?" He shoved off the countertop, anger pulling at every muscle. "I'll keep that tidbit in mind next time. It's not a figure of speech. I am not exaggerating when I say you were seconds away from joining the rest of Gregor's family. I did what I considered necessary, the only way to keep you alive. I doubt your fiancé would give me such a tough time about your inconvenient side effects."

"I get it, but hell. You could have warned me or something."

"I didn't exactly have time to read you the disclaimer. Besides, as I said before, this is a scarce side effect that I heard about in myths and rumors. And for the record, warning you ahead of time wouldn't change anything. Your only options were side effects or death. Be careful, and you'll be fine." He stalked out of the bathroom without another word.

Awesome. With deft precision, she managed to piss off three of the four people in the next room. First, Alvarez, then Chance, now Cohen. She should scream obscenities at her dad and make it a perfect score.

Unfortunately, freaking out on Cohen prevented her from asking a whole slew of questions. How long were their long lives, and what else could he do? What allowed him to influence his partner so easily? How did he know about her family and vampires? Hopefully, she didn't waste her only opportunity.

Once the shower ran steaming hot, she stripped out of her torn-up bloody rags and dived in. Everyone could wait until she finished. The thought of another minute with blood-caked hair and clothes sticking to her skin became unbearable. More importantly, she couldn't face any of them right now, especially her father.

The heavenly quiet of the shower left her finally resembling a person again. The water not only washed away the carnage and mud but also all the noise in her head. For the first time since the lab, she disconnected her emotions and thought clearly.

After wrapping herself up in a fluffy robe, she took a deep breath and squared off with the mirror. To her astonishment, the bruises looked like week-old shadows. Even the one across her torso, the worst of the bunch, displayed diffused purples and yellows.

"Okay. No more delays. Time to get down to brass tacks."

When the bathroom door swung open, the voices stopped short, leaving a burgeoning silence. So much for slipping casually into the conversation. Gregor stood by the balcony doors, and Chance sat on the far bed, both staring at her with expressions exuding a variety of things from pity to shame. More concerning, she saw no sign of Alvarez or Cohen.

"Where are the others?"

Chance spoke up, drawing her attention away from her father. "They left to pick up our rental car and suitcases from Miriah's apartment."

"But Spencer is probably watching the place, waiting for us to return!" Her frazzled brain ached, unable to deal with one more complication.

"Exactly. That's why we can't go. He won't recognize Alvarez, and I'm sure he's aware of Cohen's involvement in his sister's murder investigation. He'll assume they are collecting evidence and impounding the car, which makes perfect sense. So, relax."

With a relieved sigh, she nodded and slid onto a vacant bed, rubbing a towel through her damp curls. Neither of them seemed to be very talkative, so she took the initiative.

"Dad, I found a blood sample in Duncan's treasure trove of secrets. The DNA makeup is unique in ways never seen before. I'm betting it belongs to Ashcroft. I'm certain Duncan knew he was alive. So, how long have you known?"

Gregor regained his composure in her absence and managed to pull on his familiar business facade. "I thought he died. No one ever survived the change, so I rightfully thought I killed him. Even Duncan thought so. Hell, we buried him. We didn't suspect anything abnormal until Rosaline's murder."

"Mom?" She stopped moving the towel as her hands clutched the terry cloth. "How does Mom's mugging figure into this?"

"Distant family members dropped off over the years. They all appeared unremarkable and never raised suspicion. When your mother died, too many similarities existed."

She shook her head vehemently. "No!" His apologetic eyes betrayed his secret, and she didn't want to hear what came next, not about her mom.

"The cuts, her pose, everything matched Margareet's corpse."

She bent over, covering her face, fighting to breathe through her tightening throat. He knew. He *knew* her mother's death wasn't random in his bones but let her believe the party line. It was another lie adding to the cesspool enveloping her, crushing the air from her lungs, tainting every aspect of her life.

Gregor pushed on with a desperate compulsion to explain. "Even then, I didn't believe Ashcroft could be responsible. It had to be some cruel trick of fate, a sickening coincidence, which is why I never told you. Duncan, however, began researching the family tree because we both had reasons to be afraid. Spencer left for Scotland alone, Miriah recently married Malachi, and you headed off to college on the other side of the country."

Get it together. This isn't helping. She repeated the mantra in her head, finally swallowing the lump of emotional garbage stuck in her throat to focus on the problem. "Assuming Ashcroft is the real villain in this story, why not simply go after you and Duncan? Why the cloak-and-dagger routine?"

"Because he doesn't want us dead, not yet. When we killed his son centuries ago, he didn't kill us. He made us suffer the way he suffered."

"But they tried to burn you alive."

"Not Ashcroft, his wife. When we captured her…" He paused, wringing his hands, not eager to dive back into his pit of demons. "She claimed sole responsibility for the attempt on our lives, proudly proclaiming she acted against her husband's wishes because she wanted us dead. Once he left with his men for the moors, she took the remaining guards and rendezvoused with her spies in the city."

"Semantics." Her chest heaved with a frustrated sigh. "So, after… Mom's death, what did Duncan uncover?"

"Nothing at first. A litany of relatives died over the years. Most of them in car accidents, muggings, but nothing stood out except the victims were related to us."

"So, he thought Ashcroft might be picking people off, staying under the radar?"

He nodded but quickly continued. "Yes, but I couldn't see the connection, or maybe I didn't want to. All the deaths seemed so normal and innocuous. I accused him of grasping at straws to fit some insane conspiracy theory, but he kept digging."

"Then, a few years ago, a young reporter on his payroll showed up with a weird blood sample. He claimed it originated from a small-town physician treating a car accident victim. The doctor pulled the unconscious man from the car, and everywhere the sun touched his skin, he broke out in horrible sores, like an extreme case of actinic prurigo. He didn't have the equipment to test it properly, so he confided in the reporter, who worked with him on complicated cases requiring more resources.

"Duncan sent Miriah to deliver the news because he believed, as you do, that it belongs to Ashcroft. Preliminary tests yielded bizarre results, but he couldn't study the sample in Goditha without someone finding out, so he hid it."

"So, if Ashcroft knew someone took his blood, why wait until now to act?"

"I don't think he did. He was probably unconscious at the time."

"No. Spencer said Duncan went into hyper-research mode a few years ago when someone murdered a reporter."

"The timeline adds up, but he never mentioned the murder to me."

"Well, if Ashcroft wasn't aware of the blood specimen, why kill the guy?"

"You're assuming the man's death has a connection to any of this. Do you even know *how* he died?" Chance chimed in with a heavy dose of reality.

"No." Lilith frowned at him, considering his point until she shook her head, resolute. "But if the case sent Duncan into a downward spiral threatening his sanity, I think it's safe to explore the possibility."

Gregor paced the room, his face drawn, deep in thought. "You're right. We need to think through every angle. If he knew, why wait?"

"Or why *now*? The elders began to discuss going public about six months ago, right?"

Gregor shot a cautious glare at Chance as if only now remembering his presence in the room. Although he trusted him with his life, this went beyond the bodyguard job description. Thanks to her big mouth and lack of a social filter, he no longer had the luxury of denial, so he reluctantly dipped his head in admittance.

"Outside of the elders, who else knew?"

"Well, you, Miriah, Malachi, Aaron's son Michael, and Spencer." As soon as the last name rolled off his lips, the entire room went deadly silent.

"That's why." The absolute certainty reverberated through her core. "You have rules, the need to keep things secret until you arrange the right scenario to come forward to the public. If you succeeded, you'd be untouchable, protected by popular opinion, and killing you would only make you a martyr. Christ, this explains the placement of Miriah's body. He wins both ways. Involve the police or, worse, the Feds, and he either forces you further into the shadows or exposes you in a horrifically negative way. Humanity may even consider him a hero for butchering us."

"Oh, god." Gregor went white as a sheet and slumped back against the glass door.

"Wait." Something occurred to her as she remembered Spencer's nasty words. "Spencer isn't aware of Ashcroft's motivations, not all of them. He said we weren't supposed to find Miriah in her office. If Ashcroft is keeping him in the dark, then he's nothing more than a pawn."

"I'm not surprised. This may be the twenty-first century, but I doubt he considers him anything more than a useful dog. He won't share any *real* power with him."

The front door opened with a bang, making everyone jump. Alvarez and Cohen's jovial conversation died as soon as they scanned the room and took in their somber faces.

"What did we miss?" Alvarez fixed Gregor with a pointed stare as he dropped his cargo and returned to his chair.

"Ashcroft's possible motives. We believe he's launching an anti-publicity campaign against us." Chance neatly condensed their convoluted discussion.

Then, something else occurred to her. "Dad, when I called, you reacted when I said Miriah's hair was damp. What's the significance?" The observation earned a pointed glance from Cohen. She didn't look forward to their next conversation, but with so much at stake, she didn't have time to tiptoe anymore. They needed all the cards on the table.

"Washing the hair of women after they die is an ancient burial tradition in the Highlands. They believed a woman's power existed in her long locks, and cleansing them would give the soul strength to move on to the next life. Duncan and I performed the rite for every female victim in the Orrick family. Our purpose wasn't to punish them in their next life because of their relatives' trespasses in this one. In Miriah's case, the ritual is a calling card, claiming responsibility, not a way of honoring the dead. I'm assuming since the belief didn't extend to men that Malachi's hair was untouched?"

"Ashcroft didn't kill Malachi." Both Gregor and Cohen glanced up, wide-eyed, with their brows deeply furrowed, but Cohen spoke up first.

"Wait. Let me see if I understand. You examined *my* crime scene, and someone murdered the victim's husband, but not the same person?"

"Yes, I discovered Miriah's body, but I couldn't exactly call it in without becoming a suspect. I assure you. I scrutinized every aspect of the body without leaving a trace, a special skill I use daily in my line of work. And yes, the police found her husband's body in New York City." She turned her attention to Gregor before Cohen could formulate a reply.

"Although the wounds appeared similar in style and position, the lacerations showed crude inexperience and an emotional drive absent in Miriah's body. I believe Ashcroft instructed Spencer to impersonate his MO and link the killings to New York City, displaying how vulnerable we are, even at home."

"Tell us everything." Cohen settled in with his arms firmly crossed over his chest.

By the time Lilith and Chance relayed everything they knew, it was one in the morning. The detective apologetically bowed out, heading back to the station to let his brain digest the details and ensure Whitmore didn't call the Feds. Alvarez, exhausted and confused, retreated to his room, leaving her alone with Gregor and Chance, neither of which she felt comfortable around at the moment.

Her father's call down to reserve the adjoining room only delayed the inevitable awkward silence. The stifling air pressed cloyingly against her skin, making the ten minutes until the bellhop arrived feel like an eternity. Chance eagerly grabbed the key and headed next door without a word. A cumbersome weight tugged on her heart as she stared after him, so profoundly wrapped in her thoughts that she jumped at the sound of Gregor's voice.

"He's pretty upset. Why?" She turned to face him as his eyebrow crooked in a remarkably familiar position, one foreshadowing a condescending lesson.

"Dad, I don't want to have this conversation."

"I couldn't care less. I sent him to protect you. I did *not* send him here to romance you or vice versa."

Her jaw set in an angry line reminiscent of teenage defiance, but with a crisp edge of clarity. "I'm aware of the full story, so drop it! What is your problem with him? He's trustworthy, intensely loyal, and fearless. How many times has he saved your life?"

"I trust him to do his job. That trust doesn't extend to my daughter's heart."

"What the…" She stopped and held up a hand. "No. I don't want to hear your inane protective father babble after the crap you've pulled. I'm a grown woman, and I can make decisions without your help."

A flicker of shame shone in his eyes, quickly snuffed out by an impassive mask. "As long as you're prepared to live with the consequences."

"What? Like you do?" The drawn, agonized expression didn't vanish this time, and she almost wished she could take it back. Things would never be the same between them. Harsh reality burned away her wide-eyed adoration, and she mourned the loss as if he died. In a way, he had, or at least the man she thought he was.

"I love you more than anything, which is why this can't happen. Don't you understand? Even if things are perfect, they cannot last because he's a half-blood. He'll only live another ninety years or so if his career choice doesn't kill him first. Are you honestly ready to deal with those practical implications?"

"Damn it. You sound like Alvarez. It doesn't matter."

Gregor stepped closer with sincere concern pulling at the light wrinkles of his face. "Lily. He will grow old and die before you stop getting carded for alcohol." His face fell as old memories haunted him. "Putting someone you love in the ground is unbearable. You deserve more."

Although she understood the sentiment, her father championing the moral high road sounded fake and hollow in the light of his atrocities. "What you are honestly saying is time with Chance isn't worth the pain of losing him. Would you take back your time with Margareet…or Mom?" Gregor's mouth opened and closed, wanting to protest but unable to.

"I thought so. The simple fact is no one knows how long another person will live. Miriah and Malachi are a perfect example. Their strong bloodlines didn't do them any favors."

"That's different..."

"Stop! This is the least of our concerns." She gritted her teeth and stared her father right in the eye. "I dated plenty of humans, and you never once gave this ridiculous lecture. So, do not stand here spouting philosophical high points with two killers hunting us."

With no further desire to trade verbal blows, she stepped into the adjoining room and closed the door on her downtrodden father. Then, she leaned against the hollow wood, closing her eyes to focus and quiet her riotous mind.

"You want to tell me what's going on?" Chance's voice loomed intrusively from the far bed. From one argument to another. If only she had a room of her own to avoid this conversation for the foreseeable future. Defending a theoretical relationship without any time to sort through her feelings on the subject left her exhausted and off-balance, but how could she explain without offending him?

She opened her eyes to find him stretched across the bed, half undressed. His shirt lay in a lump on the floor next to his shoes and socks. His jeans still clung to his hips, revealing the top of his mysterious tattoo. At first glance, he appeared relaxed, but she noticed the tension keying up every well-defined muscle.

She pulled her robe tight as butterflies danced annoyingly in her stomach. "I don't want to hurt you." She didn't dare move because every fiber wanted to trace her fingertips over his tan skin. She felt drawn to him, exactly as he said in Cohen's office. The most upsetting part was not knowing if the compulsion spawned from her genuine emotions or Cohen's blood.

He pushed up on one elbow and stared at her. "Why would you? I don't understand. Did Gregor finally change your mind?"

"No. Of course not. When I took blood from Cohen, it did something to me. I don't know if the side effects are temporary or permanent, but touching me isn't safe." Tears threatened to spill from her red-rimmed eyes again. "The last thing I ever want to do is cause you harm."

Chance patted the bed. "Come here, Lily. I'm fully capable of defending myself."

She shook her head. "Not against this. I can sense your energy, your emotions, and I can use them. If I take too much…"

"That's why you asked if I was okay earlier?" She silently nodded. "And that's why you didn't want me to kiss you?" When she nodded again, he startled her by laughing hysterically—not the expected or appropriate reaction.

"It's not funny. This is serious. I could kill you."

Chance slowly stood, rising to his full six-foot-three height. She could only gape at his finely tuned perfection. Every single muscle coiled as he stalked around the bed. Each step closer made her heart beat a little faster. Then, he stopped inches away, his head stooping to her eye level. The heady pressure of desire functioned as a magnetic field between the two of them, sparkling and crackling over her skin like magic.

"You won't hurt me." His hand moved forward, and she began to shy away, but the door at her back and the beds on either side gave her nowhere to go. Tentative fingertips glided across her shoulder and up the curve of her neck before pulling her closer. His sensuous lips crushed against hers with an explosion of passion so vibrant, her knees went weak. Immediately sensing her instability, he slid an arm around her waist, drawing her tight against him as his tongue flicked along her bottom lip.

"See? I'm fine and definitely not dead." He flashed a Cheshire-cat grin and kissed her again.

Not only did she lack the strength to fight him, but she also lacked the desire to. Shoving away all her anxiety, she wrapped her arms around him and returned the kiss with a lusty hunger. His energy and yearning burned through each cell, making her want more. When he growled against her lips, vibrations rumbled across every nerve sparking an array of fireworks.

Just as the delicate dance of seduction lulled her passion into a slow smolder, he moved forward, pinning her to the door. The sudden surge took things to a new level until he broke the kiss, leaning his forehead against hers while panting for breath. His body kept her pressed to the door as if paused mid action. Every fiber trembled as she struggled to catch her breath, swept up in the moment.

"Lily." His voice came out shaky and raw, exuding an intimate tone that stirred her blood. Her lips traveled featherlight up his neck, earning a groan in response. His panted breaths tickled her shoulder as she lightly grazed her teeth against his skin. He tasted so warm, so deliciously intoxicating.

"Lily." He forced the word out and reluctantly pulled his head back, hazel eyes a deeper green than she remembered. Their chests heaved in time with every pant, breathless in the passionate bubble. "I… If we… God, Lily." He leaned his forehead against hers again, eyes closed, gathering his strength. Then, he released a deep sigh, the hot air washing over her skin, making her body sing.

"If you keep… I won't be able to stop." His voice trembled with intimate humor.

"You started it." The words dripped from her mouth like warm honey, and she felt his heart pound faster in response.

"I did…but…" He huffed with a soft growl as her hands continued to glide over his skin, memorizing every line. "I want to Lily… God, you have no idea how much…"

Her lips nudged against his in a brief caress. "But." Suddenly, a sense of power and control lit her insides in a purely intoxicating thrill. Everything felt so vivid. The warm softness of his skin, his heady scent, the tension pulling their bodies closer, the rough sound of his voice, his hand clenched in her hair.

"But…your father is just on…"

His attempt to shatter the private moment didn't deter her. A burning need urged her to keep control. So, she interrupted him by wrapping her long legs around his waist as her mouth found his again. The thin film of reluctance fell away as his body moved with hers.

Then, he recovered and mustered all his strength to pull away once more. The panting breaths came out rough and jagged. "And…" His eyes slowly opened, holding her gaze in a burning stare. "I wanted this for so long, but I need you to be sure of what you want. This is a bridge we can't uncross."

Her palms slid up his neck, resting on his cheeks as she gazed into his hazel eyes. "Please stop questioning what I want, and you were right at the station. That kiss changed everything. We've already crossed the bridge."

"I don't want you to think…"

"What?" She leaned her head against the door with an aggravated sigh. The magical moment began slipping away, making her irritable. "Do you really think I'm impressionable enough to fall for any man showing me attention without a single thought?"

"No! No, that's not what I meant…"

Her eyebrow quirked inquisitively. "Then what *did* you mean?"

He opened his mouth to say something, closed it, and tried again. "If this isn't real… If I'm only a distraction… I can't handle that."

When he spoke the words out loud, a clear answer bubbled to the surface. "Chance, you are *not* an escape. You're a wonderful surprise. I already agreed to a date. Now, shut the hell up and kiss me already." Her smile chased all the panic from his expression.

"Yes, ma'am." He trailed light kisses up her neck to her jawline and finally reached her lips. The tender building pressure brought the heat of the moment right back but sweeter and less primal.

Then, her cell phone chirped annoyingly bright. Always something. They paused, staring at each other, both trying to decide if she truly needed to answer. In the end, he pulled away, though his smile betrayed his reluctance.

She fished the phone from her pocket and jammed the screen. *"Yes?"* The tone of her voice clearly stated *This better be damn important.*

Chapter 17

"Ms. Adams." Richard Coffee's deep voice rumbled hesitantly over her phone's speaker. "I'm sorry to disturb you, but you asked me to inform you when Dr. Nichols arrived."

"He's there?" Chance peered at her in confused interest.

"Yes, ma'am. He's jumpier than usual. Said he saw someone out front, but I haven't seen anything on the cameras."

"Do not let him leave. We're on our way." Lilith's heart pounded violently in her chest as she hung up.

"Something's wrong." He plucked the words right from her brain as he stared from his perch on the bed.

"We need to leave. Now." She swung open the door to her father's room and stormed in, determined to avoid another messy discussion. Gregor whipped around as relief washed over his face.

"I was hoping you'd come back to…" The sentence died away as she snatched their suitcases and turned back toward her room. He quickly closed the distance and grabbed her shoulder. "Lily?"

She whirled around impatiently. She needed time to process everything, and he seemed bound and determined not to let her have it. "I can't talk. I got a call from Goditha. Chance and I are heading there now."

He released her shoulder and rubbed his close-cropped beard thoughtfully. "All right. Let's go."

She heaved a deep sigh and readjusted the luggage in her hands. "You aren't going. You are staying here." Before he could formulate a response, she tossed the bags through the door and continued. "I don't want to hear any arguments." However, her steely stare didn't deter him.

"This is *my* mess." The honest and straightforward admission drew his wrinkles into a mask of resolution. "I am cleaning it up." Despite everything, she instinctually wanted to obey, but her daddy issues had to take a back seat.

"Except, Spencer revealed part of their plan while beating me nearly to death. They *want* you here, and now you are. Please, stay in the hotel where you're relatively safe." Then, something else occurred to her. "Alvarez is still next door, right?"

"No. He went down to the police station. He believed his presence would make things easier with Cohen's partner."

"Whitmore is not exactly a tolerable man, so I doubt he'll appreciate Felipe being there. Cohen is more than capable of handling him on his own. I would tell you to call him, but that might make his partner more suspicious." She lost herself in thought for a few moments, trying to figure out what to do.

"I don't want you here alone, but I can't go to the lab by myself." Thinking about how her last encounter ended sent a shiver up her spine.

"I'll be fine, and I give you my word, I won't step one foot outside."

"Whatever they have planned involves Duncan, you, and me in the same room. The longer we keep that from happening, the better. I wouldn't go at all, but this is important. I think the doctor helping with the blood sample is in trouble."

"I promise." A smile tugged at the corner of his mouth in an almost condescending way.

"What?" she snapped the question with an irritated frown.

"I don't believe Ashcroft accounted for you in his equation. For one thing, they probably assume you're dead, which might push them to move faster, make mistakes."

"Well, we better hope so because they have the upper hand. He's old, but in the basement of Duncan's house, he moved impossibly fast. With all the aberrations in his blood, he may have more tricks up his sleeve. We have no idea how he's changed." She rubbed her arms, trying to shake the hopeless sensation raising goose bumps on her flesh.

Everyone kept complimenting her, calling her brilliant and brave, but none of those words reflected the truth. Lost, helpless, fumbling in the dark. Those descriptors better matched the gloom lingering in her bones.

"We'll be back as quick as possible. Do *not* leave the room, even if Alvarez gets back before us."

Gregor nodded in silent obedience, thoughts already pulling his attention inward. Perhaps the alone time would allow him to deal with the conflicting emotions tearing him apart.

Lilith hesitantly patted her father's shoulder, still uncertain of her opinions on his newly revealed past. "We'll figure a way through this."

"Before you go…" She paused in the doorway, dread pulling at every nerve.

"This thing between you and Chance…" Her mind whirled, astounded by the unexpected change of subject. "All those years ago, I threatened Chance to protect you *both*."

"Stop. I cannot believe you are still—"

"Please." The steely confidence returned to his voice, issuing a command rather than a request. "This is important. My problem isn't simply him being a half-blood. He has an unbelievably deep well of emotions, which makes him vulnerable. When it comes to you, he can't think clearly, can't do his job."

Gregor ran a frustrated hand through his hair, reminiscent of Chance and his nervous tic. "I thought I did the right thing sending him here with you. I had no doubt he'd give his life if the situation required. I didn't count on him spilling his secrets after holding on to them so tightly for so long. I suppose I underestimated him."

"First of all, capitalizing on his emotions was manipulative and inexcusable. Secondly, the tell-all was my fault. I kept pushing." Her body language clearly signaled impatience, but he insistently refuted her simple answer.

"No. You are infuriatingly stubborn, daughter, but if he didn't want to tell you, he wouldn't. I'm sure anger made it easier, but you didn't push anything out of him. That man's mind is a steel trap. You don't know Chance as well as I do."

She sighed and patted his arm indulgently. "Sure, I understand, but can we save the heart-to-heart for an appropriate time? Sorry, but I need to go."

The pain of the evening shone in his face as he retreated to the balcony once more. She stared at his back for a few agonizing moments, wishing she could find a way to make things better for them both. Even if that particular puzzle had a solution, she had no time to find it. When she finally closed the door, the click echoed with a finality that chilled her to the bone.

She turned and watched each muscle tense and relax beneath his tanned skin as Chance pawed through his suitcase. "Put a shirt on already." The humorous tone fell flat, taking on a hollow quality as she tossed her luggage on the bed.

His eyebrows arched impossibly high as he glanced up, playing along with her failed attempt at levity. "Uh. Sorry? I'm looking for one."

While trying to keep a straight face, she snatched a random T-shirt, jeans, and sneakers from her suitcase. "Well, hurry up. It's distracting."

The quip pulled a teasing grin to his lips that brightened her mood. Before he could spot the blush creeping over her cheeks, she ducked into the bathroom.

Minutes later, she emerged, calm and collected. Chance sat on his bed, rental keys in hand, fully dressed, and peered up at her with a Cheshire-cat grin. "AC/DC?"

She tilted her head in confusion until he motioned at her shirt. She glanced down at the big black letters. "Is that a problem?" She stared him down, daring him to make a smart-ass comment, and pulled her auburn curls into a ponytail.

He quirked one brow as his eyes traveled up and down with unmistakable desire. Subtle. "Absolutely not. Although I'm more of a Led Zeppelin, Tom Petty, Pink Floyd kinda man."

"Cute *and* has good taste in music. Well, before we start sharing our desert island lists, we should get going."

"Yes, ma'am." He squared his shoulders and crossed the room to hand her something.

"A gun?" She stared down at the 9-millimeter in his outstretched hand.

"I want you to protect yourself. The NYPD requires you to log hours with a handgun, right?"

"Yes, but I don't have my conceal-and-carry permit on me."

"Paperwork is the least of our concerns. At this point, I just want you safe. Besides, I'm betting our new *friend* on the police force will help if we run into trouble."

Minutes later, they climbed into their rental car and sped toward the outskirts of town. Hopefully, Coffee managed to keep the doctor contained. With Richard standing at least two feet taller than the anorexic doctor, what could go wrong?

After arriving, they sat in the car for a few minutes, scanning the vacant lot. Nothing stood out and screamed, "*We're the bad guys.*" By Coffee's comments on the phone, she knew they had plenty of external cameras, but if a threat proved genuine, he'd simply lock down the building instead of leaving his post. Too bad real-life villains didn't use uniform black SUVs like in the movies.

At least five minutes passed with no mysterious shadows or random gunfire, but Chance still appeared unconvinced of their safety. He sat perfectly still, calculating every possibility, which left her mind free to roam.

The confusion of reconciling her father's opposite sides persisted, elbowing its way to the forefront again. On the one hand, the adoring father she grew up with flew hundreds of miles to come to her rescue. On the other, a revenge-drunk monster methodically killed an entire family line before creating an abomination through vigorous torture. How could they be the same person?

"It doesn't make him a monster." She shot a sharp glare at Chance. His unnerving skill of plucking thoughts from her head kept catching her off guard.

"How…"

"You're quiet, sullen, and your brain is working overtime. It's fair to assume you're thinking about Gregor." He turned toward her with his face eerily lit by the instrument panel. "You heard the story." His jaw clenched, and his eyes hardened. "What they did to his daughter."

"That might justify Clyde's death and Ashcroft's, perhaps even rationalize killing his wife, but the extent… He eradicated the man's entire extended family. Cousins, nieces, nephews…children, Chance. How am I still supposed to see him the same way, knowing *all* this?" Tears welled in her eyes, and she wiped at them as her mind struggled to focus.

"This happened over six hundred years ago, Lily. He isn't a serial killer taking you to dinner one night and torturing someone the next. He lost everything, and he went a little nuts."

"A little nuts?" She quirked an eyebrow at him, crossing her arms over her chest, and leaned back in the seat. "So, you don't think his actions were extreme?"

"Of course, I do." He frowned, appearing offended by her insinuation. "Taking a life is always an extreme measure. Killing an *innocent* is simply insane. I'm saying his past doesn't need to change who your father is to *you*. He loves you without question. He's always protected you, even when you didn't realize it. Whatever he was, he's a good man now to you."

Logically speaking, he was right, but she still couldn't pretend everything was normal. She knew things, and no matter what logic she used, his past changed everything. "I know, I know. I just can't. Not now."

"Give yourself time. I'm only asking you not to make a snap judgment and write him off. He's already beat himself up over six centuries. Remember, you have a father, one who cares about you. Not everyone is so lucky."

"Were you close to your parents before…?" She couldn't bring herself to finish the question, but the expression on his face surprised her. The small trace of sadness became overwhelmed by every telltale sign of fear, anger, resentment, and guilt. She knew the answer before he said a single word.

"No, we weren't…close." The awkward silence stretched on as he stared defiantly out the window. She argued internally over asking more or keeping her mouth shut. Before she reached a decision, he made one for her.

"I don't see any movement. We should move inside. Don't take an evening stroll. Run to the door and get us in fast." He pulled his gun from the holster, double-checked the clip and safety, then held her gaze with a businesslike stare. Sharing time ended as if an iron door slammed down. She suddenly remembered her father's words: *The man's mind is a steel trap.*

"Ready?"

With a nervous huff, she nodded.

Once they abandoned the safety of the car, her heart pounded, adrenaline pumping through her veins. Every sense went into hyper-drive. The subtle chill vibrated each tiny hair, her vision sharpened, the crickets reached a fevered pitch, and a million scents infiltrated the night air, which miraculously all made sense. Somehow, she doubted fear alone accounted for the change.

Chance reached the door and pressed his back to the wall while nodding at the panel across from him. Then, he focused his attention on the lot, careful eyes scanning back and forth. She flattened herself against the opposite wall and jabbed her thumb at the call button.

She waited for the crackle of the speaker and the booming voice of Richard Coffee, but neither happened. A growing seed of fear blossomed in her chest as she punched the buzzer again—silence. She glanced over at Chance with desperation as he met her eyes. The unspoken words were far too familiar for her liking. *Something was very wrong.*

As he returned his focus to the lot behind them, a tiny sliver of light caught her eye. The heavy door hung slightly open, making the blood roar in her ears like thunder. Richard would never be so careless.

"Chance." The breathy whisper barely made a sound, but he still inched backward. She pointed to the door, trembling. As his jaw tightened, he motioned for her to move behind him, and she obeyed without hesitation.

He crept forward while cocking the gun and gripped the door handle with his free hand. Every muscle in his back tensed beneath the thin fabric as fear and anger rolled off him in palpable waves. For a moment, he stayed frozen. Slowly, he glanced back, eyes searching her face as an internal war raged behind them. The raw emotions hovered over his skin like wavering air over hot concrete.

The seemingly infinite moment of eye-to-eye soul-searching finally ended, and he eased the door open, slipping silently inside. She wasted no time following him. While clicking off the safety on her 9-millimeter, she moved into the overly bright hallway.

No ominous signs jumped out at them. No lights flickered, no bloodstains covered the walls, no ceiling tiles hung down. Everything appeared normal, all the way down to the security station, which sat empty. Coffee's chair sitting vacant felt scarier than all the horror movie effects in the world.

Chance protected his back by gliding against the wall with his gun aimed ahead. All her training kicked in, and she mirrored his movements on the opposite wall, except she kept the gun by her side, loose and ready. If she held hers up, she'd be a shaking mess by the time they got to the desk. Chance trained himself to aim a gun for prolonged periods. She didn't. Movies never commented on how much strength and muscle memory were required to hold up a weapon for longer than a minute or two.

When they reached the intersecting halls, he motioned her to stay put. With a steady breath, he whipped around the left corner, eyes surveying the area as he slid behind Coffee's station. He studied the right hall for a few moments before turning his attention to the multiple rows of monitors.

Her nerves started to rattle, unaccustomed to constant surges of adrenaline. Usually, her job only required cold, hard logic. Police cleared the crime scenes before she went in. Then, she examined the dead body, the surrounding area and left. Lots of people wanted to glamorize her career and make it worthy of Hollywood. However, the truth disappointed them as it usually did.

Her nights were soothingly meticulous and a little tedious. She never chased down suspects and rarely had to interview them.

Alvarez and Gregor's security team managed those fun tidbits, especially when hunting down a rogue vamp.

After switching the gun to her left hand, she rubbed the nervous sweat off her palm. Chance continued to scour the screens, and she wanted to see what was going on. Besides, standing behind the desk seemed safer. A quick peek down both halls verified they were still empty—nothing but silence. The doors were all closed, with no signs of disturbance. Where was everyone? Better yet, where the hell was Coffee?

With her heart pounding in her throat, she sprinted around the security station, nearly colliding with Chance. He shot her an irritated glare, which melted into amusement. "See anything?" She stared down the corridor of doors, expecting one to pop open at any second.

"Easy, Kojak. The monitors are cycling. Hold on. I see a small group of scientists sitting in a break room. Wait..." He leaned in closer, peering at the center screen. "They aren't alone. Plain clothes. I can't see much else from this angle."

"What about the labs?" She turned, eyes scanning the opposite hall as her pulse quickened.

"All empty. Wait. There are two people in one of the labs. Do you think you'd be able to tell which one?"

She tore her eyes away from the ominous corridors to peer down at the screen. "It's not Cold Storage. No enormous walk-in freezer." Frustration burned as she scoured the visible equipment for some sort of clue. Then, the camera panned left.

"There!" She pointed at the faint image of a two on the wall. "Sector 2, Blood Analysis, which makes sense if he's after the specimen. I'm betting that's Dr. Nichols in the lab coat, and the other must be Ashcroft. He wouldn't trust his minion with this kind of errand. No sign of Coffee?"

"No, and they have cameras everywhere, even the hall closet."

Something sparked in her brain with sudden clarity. "Cold Storage."

"There's a camera in every room, Lily. I told you..."

"Not the lab. The actual freezer. I'm fairly certain he'd fit, and I doubt there's a camera inside."

"True. Prepping electronics to endure in a constant temp of thirty-two degrees Fahrenheit would be more aggravation than its worth. Okay, so why hide him? If they expected us, they'd spring a trap, not let us stand here chitchatting?"

"I don't think they're hiding him. If they managed to knock him out…for the life of me, I have no idea how, but the freezer consists of solid metal walls and a hefty door with a locking clasp, which would hold him when he wakes up. You're right. We wouldn't be standing here if this was a trap."

Once the words left her mouth, ringing in the silence, the weight of their meaning sank in. Richard Coffee, the linebacker over seven feet tall, a mountain of intelligent, skilled muscle, trained for this exact situation, was out of the game. Spencer, a lanky man with the muscle mass of an anorexic preteen, and a six-hundred-year-old vampire, somehow took him out. In no universe would that make sense.

Perhaps he noticed the tremors running through her or the far-off expression of growing doom, but suddenly he stood in front of her, rubbing her arms. After a few moments, she managed to focus on his warm eyes, and when she did, everything else fell away. Somehow, being under his spell scared her more than the dynamic duo with the ability to neutralize Richard Coffee.

"Lily, pull yourself together. We need to move fast before we lose the element of surprise. I guarantee they heard the buzzer, but obviously, they don't think it's important enough to investigate." His piercing stare coaxed all her remaining courage from its hiding places. "I'm going to sneak down the left hall, slip into this room." He pointed to the lab with an adjoining door to Sector 2. "Then, I'll catch this monster by surprise. He's the real threat. We can deal with Spencer later. Okay?"

"He shouldn't be a threat at all." The barely audible collection of tones somehow seemed gravely important. "He's almost as old as Gregor. He shouldn't be as fast or as strong as us. If he took down Coffee, how are we supposed to—?"

"No more second-guessing. We have a real shot here, and we need to take it." A notable pause followed as if he meant to continue explaining his plan but stopped for some reason.

Suspicion loosened fear's stifling grip on her nerves as her eyes narrowed. "What are you not saying?"

He rubbed a nervous hand through his hair as his jaw clenched tighter. "I only see one way to ensure I catch him off guard, but..."

Distrust gave way to genuine confusion. "What?"

He stared down at his hands, which still rested on her arms. "I'm sorry. You aren't going to like this any more than I do, but it's the only way."

"I cannot believe I am doing this." Lilith double-checked her gun, wasting precious minutes while she waited for her hands to stop shaking. She stared at the door to Blood Analysis, glanced down the empty hall, and took in a deep breath. "I swear, if I die, I'm gonna haunt his ass."

After a deep breath, she braced herself and shoved through the door like a woman on a mission. "Dr. Nichols! You need to follow me. I don't think the building is safe." Speaking the truth made the acting easier. She skidded to a halt when he turned. The very face from her nightmare stood at his side. A precious second of recognition flashed across her face, which she desperately hoped he didn't see. "Sorry. I didn't realize you had company, but we need to go." She forced herself to walk forward, despite her entire body telling her to turn tail and run.

Ashcroft stood an inch or two taller than her with a pale complexion marred by hundreds of crisscrossing scars, each one a testament to her father's atrocities. The dark eyes sunken deep within his skull drew her in like bottomless pits, causing the brutal scenes from her nightmares to flash through her mind. Gregor writhed and burned, Ashcroft's nails sunk into her flesh, and blood poured from Chance's slit throat. A wave of nausea hit her as the man's thin lips curled into a gruesome smile.

"Well, well, well." The deep voice trickled from this mouth like poisoned honey. One talon-like hand fastened possessively around the doctor's arm, who stood there petrified, white as a sheet. "The delicate little Lily lives."

Every instinct screamed for her to bolt from the room, but something in his voice and smug grin brought out her inner fighter. About damn time. "Are you planning to write poetry? I'm not sure that fits the current trends. You should try something more modern. Add references to guns and hos or something."

His head tilted to the side on his thin, spindly neck as dark amusement lit his eyes in a gut-wrenching way.

"You know who I am." His nostrils flared as if scenting the air. "I can smell the fear, the terror." He took one slow stride forward as she fought to keep her newfound bravado. "You know what I did to Miriah, every little delicious, intoxicating slice..." The words slithered past his lips, followed by his tongue. The hungry gesture forced the bile to rise, burning her chest.

"Still..." The dark pits in his skull narrowed as he took another step. She stood paralyzed. The serpentine grace of his movements terrified her, making her unable to look away for even a moment. "You waltz in here with the smart mouth of a person far above your station. Did your villainous father not teach you manners? How unsurprising."

Hard searing hatred burned through the fear, and she whipped her gun up, quickly aiming squarely between his eyes. "Better. He taught me marksmanship." With a satisfied smile, she pulled the trigger. At point-blank range, she couldn't miss.

In a blur of motion, too fast to understand, something changed. She blinked, fighting the sudden dizziness, and when she opened her eyes, Dr. Nichols hung like a puppet, suspended in midair. Blood welled from his shoulder, thanks to the bullet meant for Ashcroft's head. Gradually, the monster lowered the man to his feet when the pain finally registered. As the doctor began to howl, Ashcroft's face split into a toothy grin.

"Now you've gone and injured the good doctor. For shame!"

Sheer panic unfolded in her chest as she stared, transfixed by the impossibility. How could he move fast enough to stop a bullet fired from less than ten feet away?

Sluggishly, she began to back up, arms shaking while she kept the gun trained on Ashcroft. Was this another night terror? This couldn't be real!

He shoved his human shield to the ground, and for each of her shaky steps backward, he took one forward. A malicious grin pulled gruesomely at his thin lips, displaying ragged rows of sharp yellowing teeth. "Leaving so soon? Quite rude, especially after I went through so much trouble to arrange this."

Tremors of cold fear clenched her muscles, and she fired the rest of her clip instinctually. None of them hit their target as blurs of color and motion darted around the room, leaving her dizzy and confused. Not a single vampire outside Hollywood could move that fast. Not possible. It defied every law of physics. While her mind whirled, the empty clicks of her spent clip echoed ominously through the deathly silent lab. Then, her back bumped the wall—nowhere left to run.

Her brain skidded into a continual loop, stumbling over one word repeatedly. *Die.* First, he'd shove his razor-sharp nails through her skin, and then she'd *die*. Next, Chance would burst through the door, and then he'd *die*. Finally, he'd find Gregor and Alvarez, and then they'd *die*.

While her mind spun out, Ashcroft stepped closer, looming mere inches from her, his head tilting as he took in her scent. The sight of him so close, the monster responsible for butchering her cousin, her mother, Gregor's whole family, caused her entire body to shake.

"You…smell different from last time." He hovered closer, dark bottomless eyes searching her for a hint. "Why do you smell different?" Outrage flooded his face, breaking the calm facade as if personally offended by the difference. Spotting the tiny chink in his armor drew out her rebellious spirit. She couldn't give up, not now, not when so many people depended on her.

"Fuck you!" Mustering every ounce of strength, she kicked at his shin and slammed the barrel of her empty gun into his face. To her astonishment, he stumbled back, shocked, long fingers flying up to cover his nose as he doubled over. New life surged through her with the small victory. She reared back to strike him again, but this time when the gun came down, he caught her arm. The sharp nails clutched her wrist, poised to slice her veins open if she struggled.

"Such a filthy mouth." He snarled the words as blood trickled down his top lip. "I should expect no less. You are nothing but the prodigy of whores and murderers." His free hand smacked her cheek so hard, she sunk to her knees from the white-hot pain. Before she could focus her vision, he shoved her to the ground and stormed back to Dr. Nichols, pulling the unconscious man to his feet.

"I don't want our time to end so quickly. I waited centuries for another opportunity to take a child from Gregor." The hatred, the righteous indignity, the homicidal joy, the desire to inflict emotional torment all lay heavy in the air like a thick British fog rolling over her. When her skin began to tingle, she welcomed the energizing sensation, even though he meant the words to demoralize her. At last, a positive side effect.

"First, I will have a little *fun* with the good doctor." She didn't dare crack one eye open. Not only because she had no desire to see what he called *fun*, but also to avoid drawing his attention. Damn it. Where was Chance?

"Delicate Lily. I know you are awake. The fear rolling off you in waves reveals the truth. Tell me. If you know who I am and knew I was here, why would you ever come alone? Did you not consider me a threat after Duncan's house?" His throaty laughter roared across the room and burrowed into her bones, promising every sadistic atrocity imaginable.

Before she could form a coherent thought, a gunshot split the air sharply, followed by an eerie splattering sound. The echo reverberated with an increasing pitch as she covered her ringing ears.

When she finally opened her eyes, Ashcroft lay in a heap near Dr. Nichols, with Chance standing over him, gun still at the ready.

"Oops. Guess she wasn't alone." He stepped past the body and jogged over as she stared at the trail of red mist and chunks of brain matter covering the linoleum. Was it all over? Six hundred years of feuding, butchering, murder, betrayal all smeared across a laboratory floor in BFE Tennessee.

"Lily!" He lightly shook her arms, but she had to blink several times before she could tear her eyes away from the carnage. A complex mixture of worry and conflicting emotions once again flooded his face, an all-too-familiar sight. He studiously looked her over, tilting her chin one way and then the other with calculating eyes.

"Why do people keep hitting me in the damn head?"

The rough edge melted as his lips stretched into a smile. "You okay, sweetheart?"

She quirked one eyebrow and frowned at him. "Do I have brain damage, or did you call me *sweetheart*?"

"Well, I have to check somehow. Asking how many fingers I'm holding up seems so overdone."

"Do it again, and you'll be the one with brain damage, got it?" After a quick grin, she gingerly rubbed her hand over her tender cheek. Any more shots to the face, and she'd feel like a punching bag in Gold's Gym outside Madison Square Garden.

"Aye, aye, *mon capitan*."

"You know I don't speak French, right?"

While he grinned down at her, a movement caught the corner of her eye. Damn, she almost forgot about Nichols, and he had a bullet wound, thanks to her. She shoved Chance aside, expecting to see the man struggling with an injured shoulder. Then, everything tilted into the world of complete impossibility.

Chapter 18

Lilith's jaw dropped, her brain trying in vain to make sense of the grotesque spectacle transpiring before her eyes. No. Impossible. It wasn't real. It couldn't be.

She watched in absolute horror, transfixed, as Ashcroft's hand clawed the floor, pulling his limp body closer to the unconscious doctor. Black eyes glistened with a cloudy glaze as his brains trailed behind the shattered skull, clinging together by stringy blood vessels and mangled tissue. The sick wet sound of bloody flesh dragging across the linoleum made her stomach convulse violently.

Chance turned in slow motion, reluctantly following her line of sight. He jumped back, screaming a litany of obscenities her mind couldn't understand. Everything dissolved into a muted background as she gaped, riveted by the unimaginable monstrosity in front of her. She couldn't tear her eyes away, couldn't breathe, couldn't even hear her heartbeat.

One long talon-like nail slid down the center of Nichols's shirt, and the revolting noise of flesh and cloth tearing preceded the blood-curdling screams. The man's back arched, his body convulsing as the nail cut straight to his navel. Blood blossomed across his white lab coat, quickly saturating the cloth.

Ashcroft's mouth opened in a delirious sigh, making her skin crawl. Then the death glaze cleared from his deep-set eyes as they rolled into his skull. When the gravity of his actions finally struck her, she flinched and scooted away, putting her back to the wall. The torture had a purpose, not to fulfill his gluttonous appetite for torment, but to heal him.

His talon continued rending and tearing while the man kept screaming, and she sat powerlessly captivated by the macabre beauty. How could he possibly use blood and torture to regenerate tissue?

Someone shook her, called her name, but she ignored them. The screams rattled in her brain, but their invigorating effect turned her stomach more than the cries themselves.

As blood began to pool on the cold floor, Ashcroft's tongue snaked out, lapping the sticky substance with a horrible moan of pleasure. She marveled while the edges of his skull began knitting new bone. Not only was the regeneration too fast, but nothing she knew of could create complex tissue. How was he doing it? A result of being turned? But how could vampire and human DNA fuse to cause such an anomaly?

She found herself scooting closer, caught up in the enigma, suddenly desperate to understand the answers. The screams didn't hurt her ears anymore. They sang in her blood, like an eerie siren's call, drawing her toward the ghastly dance before her.

Suddenly, a sharp pain flared across her cheek, snapping the gruesome spell. After blinking a few times, she finally recognized Chance looming before her. The emotions playing across his face surprised her. The worry and fear she understood, but disgust mingled with them as he gawked at her. She didn't know what felt worse, his expression or the slap.

"We *need* to go. Now!" In mere seconds, his usual business expression slammed into place like an iron gate, cold and impartial. After snatching her gun and shoving it in his holster, he grabbed her arms and hauled her up. "Hurry!" Then, he unceremoniously shoved her toward the door.

She stumbled into the hall, and she crashed into a warm, fleshy body. She turned and stared right into Spencer's grinning face. Her eyes widened as she tried to back away, but Spencer moved faster. He snatched her wrists and pulled her toward him.

"Now, now. Where are you going?" The grin splitting his gaunt face made her stomach lurch all over again. Somewhere in the back of her mind, she knew Chance stood on the other side of the door. Hell, she heard his gun firing but still felt alone. Not only alone but also isolated with the monster who helped slaughter his family and nearly killed her hours ago. "I'm guessin' you're not dumb enough to show up by yourself. Let's find someplace more…private so that we can talk." Nothing in his tone indicated a desire for rational conversation.

Her heart thumped wildly against her ribs like a scared rabbit in a cage, but her muscles froze up in dread. *Come on, Lilith. Get it together! You got away from this prick once. You can do it again!* The inner pep talk slowly kicked her brain into gear as he forced her toward an adjacent door. Then, clarity settled over her shoulders like a calming blanket. She knew where to hurt him.

A slow smile crept over her lips, and his cocky grin faltered. "What are you smiling at, bitch? I'm going to cut the smirk right off your damn face!"

"Let me know how that works out for you." She slammed her head forward, landing a cracking blow to his already broken nose. He howled in agony, hands racing to cover his face as the blood rushed down. The second he took his hands off her, she sprinted full speed down the corridor.

His footsteps echoed fast on her heels. Either he recovered quicker than before, or his rage outweighed the pain. He wasn't out of the fight.

She thought over her options as she accelerated into a desperate all-out run. If she reached the security desk, she might find a weapon. If not, she'd have to square off with him, which didn't work out well last time. Unfortunately, Chance had the keys, so heading outside made outrunning him her only option. Not wise with him hot on her heels and gaining fast. Where the hell was Chance?

With no more time to debate, she swerved to the last inside door, slamming it closed behind her. No interior locks. Damn. Of course, why bother with a colossal giant for a security guard? After quickly taking in her surroundings, she wedged her body between the door and a sturdy shelving unit as her pulse raced. Her body weight wouldn't keep him out for long. She needed an answer, a weapon, a way out, anything.

Her mind scrambled as he slammed his fists against the wood. “Yeah, run and hide, bitch. You’re only delaying the inevitable!” Then, he shoved hard, and she lurched forward but kept her foot braced against the shelves. If she could hold on until Chance caught up. Her blood pounded so loud in her ears, it became impossible to differentiate from Spencer’s fists hammering on the door.

Talking wouldn’t magically shake sense into him, but it might stall him. “You are a fucking idiot.” Okay, not the calmest opening ever. “Ashcroft is taking advantage of you. He plans to expose us to the world. We’ll all be hunted down, even you. He told you what you wanted to hear to get close to the family!”

“Liar!” The snarled word snapped seconds before he crashed into the door so hard, she flew forward, slamming her shoulder into the shelving. She spun around just in time to see him come careening through the door. His beady bloodshot eyes narrowed on her with a deep well of hatred and disgust. She scrambled backward, eyes scanning the room for weapons, anything to give her an advantage.

“You’re a lying bitch. He is the *only* one who gives a shit about me. He made me strong, showed me his secrets. All he wants is your family dead for what Gregor’s done. Your *father* is the true abomination! Pretending to be a champion for our race after committing genocide! Now, you want to finish his work and butcher us both because we dared to stand up for ourselves.”

She hopped to her feet and continued to back away, keeping the lab table between them. “You’re delusional, a loyal peasant dog, and nothing more. You aren’t his blood. You belong to the enemy. When he has what he wants, he’ll slice you up like your sister and relish every second.”

“Lilith!” Chance’s voice boomed down the hall, and her pulse slowed a touch. Her eyes snapped up to the open doorway instinctually, and Spencer took advantage of her momentary distraction by lunging over the table.

After ducking his sweeping arm, she darted for the corridor with everything she had. Before she escaped the room, a gunshot pierced the air, and searing pain ripped through her shoulder as she stumbled sideways. The adrenaline kept her moving, but she felt blood running down her arm. She hadn't seen the gun earlier, but thankfully, he wasn't a great shot. Still, to make herself the smallest possible target, she dove for the hallway floor.

Footsteps stomped closer as she clawed her way back to her feet. With a knot of fear lodged in her throat, she ran for the cover of Coffee's desk, but he was too fast. A few feet from her goal, he tackled her from behind, sending her bloody shoulder into the cold unforgiving floor with bone-rattling force. Before she could catch her breath, he turned her over. Then, he slammed a fist into her gut, knocking the remaining wind out of her. Finding the strength to fight him off seemed impossible while hysterically gasping.

"I'm tired of this fucking game. You are too much trouble. He'll understand." Spencer jammed the gun under her chin, his face contorted in hatred, barely resembling anything humanoid. Her eyes watered as the hard metal pinched her skin, still warm from the earlier shot. Where the hell was Chance?

"You think he's using me?" He shoved the gun upward, bruising the muscles below her jaw and digging against bone. Tears cascaded down her cheeks with the excruciating pain, forced to face her mortality. No headbutt would save her this time. She had mere seconds left until he pulled the trigger. Then, she would simply end.

"He already taught me his power. I can taste the terror on you like dark candy." A smug grin crooked his vicious mouth as he closed his eyes, savoring the moment. When he opened them again, a deadly determination lit them, and she knew this was it. Time was up.

She squeezed her eyes shut, awaiting the inevitable and praying it didn't hurt too much. In those precious seconds, she thought about all the things she wanted to tell Chance and her father.

A shot cracked through the air, but the blinding pain never came. Something hot and wet splattered her face, which shocked a scream out of her. When she opened her eyes, nothing made sense.

Spencer's bloodshot eyes glanced down at his bloody chest and then found hers with an expression of astonishment. Somehow, he finally resembled the boy she'd once known, the one who cared about his family. He toppled to the side with a thud, blood quickly pooling on the linoleum. In a frenzied panic, she shoved his legs off her and scrambled backward until her back met the wall. Chance stormed up to loom over him, but she stared at her cousin, frozen in total disbelief.

Finally, her eyes traveled up to Chance, who stood over him. Savage contempt contorted his handsome face as he trained the gun on the back of Spencer's head. A cold, calm detachment settled over his features once he lined up the shot, and without a second's hesitation, he pulled the trigger. Blood splashed violently across the gleaming floor. A fine red mist reached her jeans as her cousin's mouth fell open in a final gasp, the life draining from his eyes.

She drew her knees in, hugging them close as she gawked at the brain and skull fragments littering the ground. Blood poured onto the floor in pulsating spurts that eventually became a steady stream. The fast-growing pool nearly touched her sneakers, and she quickly scrambled away as if it was poisonous.

"Lilith!" Chance's voice jolted her mind back to reality. She swung her head up, eyes refusing to focus at first. This was almost her blood flooding the hallway. She blinked through her hazy thoughts to peer at Chance as if seeing him for the first time. He stooped down and grabbed her arm, hauling her up again. "We need to get out of here *now*! I put four clips in Ashcroft, but the fucker won't die! He's still slicing up that man and healing like some sideshow freak. Gregor's not telling us everything."

When she didn't move, he squared off with her. "Are you okay?" The stiff impatience in his voice pulled a frown to her lips. A mixture of emotions infected his touch, but she found herself too overwhelmed to sort through them.

"Lilith. We *have* to go. Now." He sprinted toward the door with her in tow, which left her struggling to stay upright.

Seconds later, they burst out of the building and raced through the lot. As soon as the crisp night air hit her skin, her brain crawled out of its panicked fog. All the answers to her questions about the blood specimen died with Dr. Nichols. How could she kill something that refused to die? What the hell did Gregor create? She felt like a teen stuck in a 1980s horror movie, stalked by some unkillable man in a hockey mask. Sadly, this was real life and death, not special effects.

With Spencer dead, she should be happy they solved at least one of their problems, but part of her mourned the loss. Yes, he became a vicious monster, but his pathetic need for approval begged for sympathy. His desperation led him to conspire with a sadistic serial killer and help butcher his family. How did no one see it coming? How did she not see it? If someone had, perhaps Miriah, Malachi, and Spencer would still be alive.

As they ran for the car, she stole a glance at Chance, trying to sort through conflicting thoughts. Spencer deserved to die, but the cold, unemotional look in his eyes as he pulled the trigger scared her.

Once they crammed into the rental, Chance slammed the car in reverse and peeled out of the lot. Thankfully, the industrial park sat in the middle of nowhere with no witnesses to describe their vehicle pulling away. Even though her heart still pounded, her logical mind took over, running through all the evidence left behind. No way could a small-town detective cover this up. However, Goditha was a family-owned private lab, and Gregor held the controlling interest, which gave them some measure of oversight and discretion.

In a hurry to stay on top, she dialed Cohen's number. No answer. "It's Lilith. There's a scene at Goditha Labs which is still *extremely* hostile. Keep everyone clear. I don't want a bunch of cops dying unnecessarily. We need to talk." She hung up and gripped the dash as Chance swung the vehicle around a corner.

After they reached a safe distance, he finally broke the silence. "What the fuck was that, Lily?"

His jaw clenched, brown eyes narrowed, nostrils flared, knuckles turned white from his death grip on the steering wheel. To her surprise, he wasn't scared. He was pissed off.

"I…don't know. Nothing can heal…"

Without warning, he swerved through traffic, interrupting her as she braced herself again. Her chest tightened as memories of her earlier crash flooded her mind. Then, he slammed on the breaks, bringing them to a screeching halt in a downtown parking space.

"Damn it, Chance!" She leaned forward, putting her head between her knees as she tried to breathe. "Are you trying to kill me? Seriously? Perhaps it escaped your fucking memory, but I barely survived my last car crash!"

For a moment, he sat still, staring out the windshield. Tension sang through the air, twisting her stomach in knots.

"Yes, I realize. I held you in my arms while you nearly died. And I'm not talking about Ashcroft." When he turned in his seat, all his anger came with him, weighing on her like a lead noose. A deep blush crept across her cheeks because, on some level, she wanted his fury, craved it like some depraved animal.

"What the hell is going on with you? You see Ashcroft's wrecked body torturing that man, and your reaction is to move *closer*? Panting like a hungry dog?"

She flinched, not because he shocked her, but because he voiced her inner thoughts, forcing her to confront them. She wanted to crawl under a rock and hide. Nothing made sense anymore, and talking about her chaotic feelings terrified her. Anger worked better.

"You want to pass judgment? Executing Spencer sure didn't bother you in the slightest. Another tally on your kill sheet."

He blinked, stunned by the hateful response. Then, the outrage and exasperation set in. "Are you fucking kidding me? That man, family or no, engineered the murder of his sister, kidnapped his father, and placed him on a silver platter. He butchered his brother-in-law and nearly beat you to death! Hell, if I didn't act, you'd have a bullet through your brain! What the fuck did you want me to do? Distract him with a song and dance routine? Do not sit there and tell me you feel sorry for him!" He slammed his hands against the wheel to channel his rage.

Despite the knowledge that he'd never hurt her, she still cowered against the door. Everything he said rang true. With a bone-weary huff, he hunched over the steering wheel, fighting with himself. The sight drained every stitch of her defensive rage, leaving her vulnerable and embarrassed. She scrambled for something to say but came up empty. Her only escape was to bail out of the car and run off like some temperamental teenager. Not a real solution.

"Lilith. Talk to me." His gruff voice passed through clenched teeth in harsh, clipped tones. Tears welled in her eyes, trying to breathe around all the words lodged in her throat.

Finally, he raised his head and turned to her. When he spoke again, gentle concern filled his words. "I'm worried about you. Since Cohen fed you, you've been…different. When I pushed you out of the room with Ashcroft, you had a nasty bruise covering one side of your face. And now…" His eyes flickered with a mixture of desire and fear, making her heart sink.

She hastily flipped down the visor mirror and gaped in surprise. Not only did the bruise disappear, but her skin looked flawless. A perfect complexion that would make a supermodel envious. Her eyes shone brighter, and her lips appeared plumper as if she spent all day in a spa. How?

Frantically, she pulled at her shirt to see the deep seat belt mark gone entirely. With rising panic, she yanked the shoulder of her t-shirt down to gawk at the fresh bullet wound, now merely a pink scar in her skin. What the fuck?

Cohen claimed any strong emotion would do, but this felt different. "I tried to tell you earlier, and you laughed. Cohen feeds on energy to stay alive and help him heal. I can sense emotions like something tangible and use them, but I don't know a lot. We didn't have much time to talk earlier."

Fear crept back into his hazel eyes. She couldn't stand him, of all people, looking at her like that, so she gazed through the windshield as tears slipped down her cheeks. "Stop staring at me. I'm not Ashcroft! Just fucking drive." Did he think she wanted any of this, to feel like an alien in her own body?

"Cherie." The lilting tones of his Cajun accent rolled intimately off his tongue, but she ignored it. When his fingers brushed over her arm and slid down to take her hand, she shoved him away.

"Don't touch me! I wouldn't want to *hurt you*." Although her spiteful tone surprised her, none of it fazed him this time.

He pulled her in close as she feebly tried to bat him away. "Lily." He calmly pinned her against his chest while she gave up and dissolved into tears. "Shh. You aren't Ashcroft. You scared the crap out of me, and when I saw Spencer with his gun under your chin…" His eyes fell for a moment as he searched for the right words. "I had to ensure he never touched you again."

When she relaxed into his arms, he cupped her face and tilted it toward him. The fear lingered but outweighed by compassionate determination and desire. "I simply need the information to deal with this. I won't let anything happen to you."

Her voice fell into quiet sadness. "Something already has. Cohen saved my life, but he changed me. Ashcroft even said I smelled different. What if this isn't temporary?" With effort, she swallowed the hot lump of tears in her throat. "I want to go back to my normal life, investigating stupid crime scenes. A world without Ashcroft or Cohen."

He nestled his chin in her hair with a wistful sigh. "Doesn't work that way, *cherie*. The monster is still out there, and we need to pull together, find our balance. You have to be strong because I need you."

The tears stopped, and she pulled away, nodding. Funny. Chance, the voice of reason. Not something she ever expected to hear.

"Now, stop your crap before I smack some sense into you." The amused tone and roguish grin coaxed a smile out of her. That was the Chance she knew.

"Hey. I'm thinking out loud here, but could Ashcroft be healing the same way you are?"

The sudden subject change kicked her logical brain into high gear, giving her the cold clarity she needed. All her emotional baggage slid down into the dark. One day, she'd have to deal with the contents of that bottomless pit, but not tonight.

"If we go off his story, Cohen is the only one of his kind here, and no one has attacked him. Plus, healing a bruise or a small bullet hole is one thing, but brain matter and bone to replace half of his head? I don't understand how it's even conceivable."

"Well, it looked pretty damn possible from where I stood. Assuming the side effects are permanent, he could have fed at any time, right? What if they build up over time with multiple feedings?"

"Those aren't questions I can answer. I still don't know how he survived Gregor turning him. Duncan always said it was theoretically possible, but no one's ever seen it happen. We should talk to Cohen. Maybe he can tell us more."

Chance quickly kissed her before settling back into his seat. "Off to the precinct." She simply shook her head in sheer amazement as he pulled back onto the road. With the universe going to hell, the quirk in his smile made everything seem inconsequential. Okay, not *inconsequential*, but at least less terrifying.

The churning growl of his stomach interrupted her thoughts. "Uh, can we swing by a Drive-Thru joint on the way?" His eyes narrowed in sudden thought, studying her. "Aren't you ravenous?"

She stared off through the windshield and couldn't recall when she'd last eaten. Croissants and coffee? Why wasn't she even vaguely hungry? The damn blood. She wanted to be furious with Cohen, but he was right earlier.

He saved her from death, and now she had to deal with the consequences. There was always a price.

When she met his gaze again, she couldn't bear to see the fear in his eyes, so she lied. "I'm starving for a huge burger. Adrenaline can only sustain a person for so long."

The slight suspicion in his eyes quickly vanished. "Well, let's check out what twenty-four-hour places are near the precinct. We can eat and grill Cohen at the same time. Should be fun, comparatively speaking."

Half an hour later, they jogged into the police station with an armful of greasy burgers.

"We need to speak with Detective Cohen urgently." Chance ushered her past the speechless desk clerk. Every eye in the bullpen stared at her as they headed for Cohen's office. She frowned in confusion until she looked down at her clothes. So much for a low profile.

Chance didn't bother knocking, instead opting to burst through the door like he owned the place. Cohen looked up in surprise, which quickly melted into concern when he spotted Lilith. Whitmore surged to his feet and stalked right up to Chance, trying to make every inch of his stocky five-foot-seven frame count. It wasn't enough.

"What the fuck do you think you're doing?"

"Whitmore." Cohen's voice boomed with callous authority. "Give us a minute."

The aging detective turned to his partner with an exasperated expression. "You don't owe these two anything. They can't barge in here—"

"A minute!" Cohen cut him off with clipped words and a weighted glare. While the two stared each other down, Chance and Lilith didn't dare move a muscle. Then, with a final snarl at Chance, Whitmore stormed out of the office, slamming the door behind him.

"Sorry. He's starting to crack." His gray eyes lingered on the closed door with a twinge of sadness.

"Have you worked together long?" She assumed Cohen would keep his distance since his partner was human, and he…was not. Her first assumption probably said more about her than Cohen.

"Since I came here. A few months. The man isn't a bad cop, but patience and open-mindedness are not his virtues." With a nonchalant grace, he stood and strolled around the desk. After carefully inspecting her, he finally rested his crisp eyes on Chance. "I got the message, by the way. I'm assuming things aren't going well?"

"Understatement." She watched as anger rolled off Chance, followed by a bristled frown from Cohen. Before she drowned in testosterone, she slid into an empty chair and broke the tension.

"Where's Alvarez?"

"He left about forty minutes ago. He and my partner are like oil and water. I sent him back to the hotel since he did more harm than good. I'm sure you didn't come down here for Alvarez…or to probe the depth of my relationship with Whitmore. So, what do you need from me? Something to do with the blood you're soaked in, I assume." The sharp tone clearly stated his annoyance.

She ignored his smart-mouthed comments and cut right to the heart of the matter. "We simply need some straight answers, and we'll be out of your hair."

Cohen appeared genuinely confused and a touch offended as he sat on the edge of his desk. "You say that like I haven't been honest. I told you everything you need to know. If you insist on rehashing our conversation, I'll need to clear things with Whitmore first. We don't want to provoke him further. He was discussing what he found on Phipps Bend when you burst through the door. I keep a sweat suit in the bottom drawer of the file cabinet. I suggest you change out of those bloody clothes. Keeping Goditha a secret won't be easy, and you're in a building full of cops who typically want to know why a woman is covered in blood."

He leveled a significant glare at her, curtly nodded, and slipped out of the room.

"Have I mentioned how much I don't like him?" Chance dropped into the chair beside her, snatched a burger from the bag, and tore into it.

"I think you've made your opinion quite clear on several occasions."

"I know the man saved your life, and believe me, I'm grateful, but if he hadn't kept me in the interrogation tank, your life wouldn't have been in danger in the first place."

"Hindsight is twenty-twenty."

"No. I'm saying if Cohen knew Duncan disappeared, he would have seen the connection when he discovered Miriah's body. It clearly shows a pattern of violence against the family. So, what does he do? He ensures you're isolated, making *him* your only lifeline. What better way to get you in his debt?"

"You're paranoid. He's balancing power with Whitmore, who didn't want to let you go. Therefore, you stayed in the tank. Not everything is a conspiracy." She started strong, but as she thought through her conversation with Cohen in the station, her conviction wavered.

"I don't trust him." That said, he turned his attention back to his burger.

With a head full of chaotic thoughts, she pushed out of the chair.

"I thought you were hungry?"

"Yeah, but I can't take another minute covered in blood. The least I can do is change my clothes." After striding across the room, she pulled open the bottom drawer of the file cabinet. Inside lay a dark blue tracksuit emblazoned with KPD. Thankfully, Cohen was a lean man and only a little taller. She tossed the suit on the desk and started to pull off her ruined AC/DC T-shirt when she caught a glimpse of Chance. He paused in mid bite to openly stare at her.

When she cleared her throat, he finished taking his bite, chewed, and quickly swallowed. "What?"

She spread her palms out as if the answer should be obvious. She wanted to be mad, but his roguish charm made it impossible. "Do you mind?"

"Of course not." He nodded for her to continue and took another bite.

She flashed a tight, sarcastic smile. "Cute." After motioning for him to turn around, she ended with a parting shot of her middle finger.

With an amused grin, he held up his hands in surrender. "Okay, okay."

Reluctantly, he turned his chair while she stripped off another set of blood-soaked clothes, her mind wandering.

She didn't feel comfortable depending on people, but she couldn't imagine enduring the last few days without Chance. However, he also threw her off-balance. Thinking back to her father's words, she knew he was right. Chance couldn't do his job with her serving as a distraction, affecting his judgment too much. With a glance at Chance's back, she realized he wasn't the only one. How could she keep a clear head around the man glued to her side?

As she wrangled her messy auburn curls into a ponytail, he turned back around. "Now, you need some handcuffs and a night-stick." One eyebrow arched in a leering grin.

"Keep your bizarro fantasies to yourself." Her internal frustration came through in her voice as she tossed her bloody clothes in the trash can.

"And here I thought you wanted to know about my *bizarro* fantasies." Although he meant his wounded expression to be humorous, she caught sight of the tightness around his eyes.

"Can we be serious for a minute?" Usually, she loved the banter, even more now with actual substance behind it, but she felt unsure about everything around her. She rubbed her cheeks and paced, so distracted by her thoughts that she didn't notice him until his hands rested on her shoulders.

She glanced up, expecting another injured expression, but too worn out to babysit the emotions of her bodyguard. Why couldn't he be the strong one and just hold her while she unraveled?

To her surprise, a calm strength softened his chiseled face as he pulled her against him and wrapped his arms around her. He said nothing. He simply hugged her close and rested his chin on her head. A perfect moment so still and comfortable, she lost track of how much time passed.

When he finally spoke, the sound startled her.

"Come sit down. Eat some food. You can't keep running on fumes, *cherie*."

She nodded gratefully and let him lead her to a chair. After she sank into the seat, he placed a burger in her hands and sat down next to her. Somehow, she managed to get the food down, even under his vigilant supervision, and felt better.

While they waited in silence, he slid his fingers through hers, thumb rubbing her skin in soft, soothing circles. A distant smile graced her lips as she leaned her head against his shoulder and let her mind go blank. She ignored the intrusive thoughts of murderous revenge plots, fathers slaughtering family lines, and unstoppable psycho killers. She even released her anxiety about feeding off emotions like a suckerfish. With a deep cleansing breath, she decided to soak in the warm moment for as long as it lasted.

Chapter 19

A door opened and closed, startling Lilith out of her sleep. She must have drifted off against Chance's shoulder. She silently observed Cohen cross the room in weary strides and plop down on the corner of his desk. A lot of weight rested on his shoulders, indicating things didn't go well with Whitmore. After rubbing his face with a tired sigh, he glanced over at the two of them cuddled up on the couch.

"Well, ain't you two cute." The sickly sweet Southern twang sounded unnatural after hearing his European accent. The humorous remark held a strong undercurrent of sarcasm, and she wasn't the only one irritated by it.

Tension raced down Chance's arm, and she squeezed his hand a little tighter to distract him while she spoke. "Things settled with your partner?" The detective cocked his head to the side and narrowed his eyes. "Tell me something. I realize lying is par for the course with being...nonhuman, but you two aren't engaged, are you?"

She gaped at the personal question mostly because it came out of left field. "What?"

With a satisfied smirk, he shifted his weight to a more relaxed position. "Well, you aren't wearing a ring, and you two are a *volcano* of unsatisfied sexual tension, so I'm assuming you lied about the engagement."

Chance gripped the arm of the chair and forced his voice through gritted teeth. "Can we focus on something that might keep us all from dying? What happens in our personal lives is none of your fucking concern."

Cohen held up his hands in a show of surrender but showed no sign of intimidation. "Curiosity. No need to get all bent out of shape.

She's an intelligent, gorgeous woman. I don't blame you for wishing the lie were true."

With that, Chance surged to his feet, a ball of tightly wound rage. "Don't." She whispered the word and tugged on his hand. Reluctantly, he sat back down, eyes still burning holes in Cohen's head.

Then, she turned her attention to the demon in the room. "Are you seriously picking a fight right now?"

He shrugged and made a feeble attempt to appear modestly ashamed. "I suppose we have more pressing matters."

She narrowed her eyes as Chance's theory ran through her head again. The man's antagonistic behavior made it easier to believe. "You *suppose*?" If you want a prayer of getting my help with your little family quest, you better start playing ball with us."

His smooth brow furrowed as he frowned. "My apologies." Calm gray eyes slid from her to Chance, the hostility leaking from his face. "I shouldn't be picking fights with my tentative allies." A subtle hint of amusement lingered, which made no sense to her, but saying something would only set Chance off again, so she let it go.

"Things going that well, huh?"

This time, every emotion slipped away, leaving behind a blank mask. "No," he snapped, ignoring her sarcasm. "We'll discuss the details later. Ask your questions."

"Can you tell us more about your race and abilities?"

He crossed his arms with a stern glare that marred his boyish looks and made him appear ten years older. "I took an enormous risk telling you anything. I put my life on the line to save yours, Ms. Adams. I don't see how any further disclosure about my *race* is relevant or necessary."

His European voice rang with all the warmth of a corporate press release as he reverted to a last-name basis. *Wait. Do I know his first name? Does it matter? Cohen probably isn't his real name anyway.* She shook off the internal rambling and focused on what mattered.

"I understand the risks, but this information won't go beyond us. I want to understand what's happening to me besides being the emotional lint trap for everyone who touches me. Also, we have some theories on the case, and if we're right, your people would want to know."

The last bit piqued his interest, head tilting to one side inquisitively. "I'm listening."

"How do you feed on emotions? How do you heal? What else you can do?"

"Lilith," he huffed and sat down on his desk in disappointment. "I told you earlier. Emotions are simply energy. Thousands of songs and poems refer to the *electricity* between two people, saying they're *attracted like magnets*. Those things are real and a purer source than what humans gain from food. In people who receive our blood, the ability is a rare side effect, but in most cases, it passes with time."

"You said you never donated to a vampire before, but have others?"

His elusive gray eyes tightened with suspicion. "We don't voluntarily socialize with vampires. I'm not here to form some coalition of nonhuman species."

This time, Chance squeezed her hand to distract her. "I'm not playing games. I'm trying to prevent this asshole from slicing my remaining family into julienne fries. I want straight answers, or our cooperative partnership comes to an end here and now."

Cohen appeared humbled by her threat as he shifted uncomfortably on the desk. His light blue eyes stared at the linoleum floor, formulating his thoughts. *Wait. Blue? Weren't they…?* Before she could finish her thought, he spoke up.

"I'm sorry." He released a slow breath. "The things you're asking… You do not appreciate how serious they take their secrecy. They possess unlimited resources. You do not realize what you are asking me to do. Between what I said already and feeding you my blood…"

A profoundly haunting shadow passed behind his eyes. So far, Cohen proved to be an excellent actor, but this held layers, revealing a pattern of fear accumulated over the years, perhaps decades. Her throat tightened slightly in response, but she still needed answers, so she backtracked to something simple.

"I promise the questions are important, not simply to appease my curiosity. Do you think the side effects happened *because* I'm a vampire?"

"Possibly. Only one or two humans ever showed the symptoms...but I can't be sure they were completely human."

"How does your healing work?"

"Can we skip to the part that concerns me?"

"I *am* talking about you. How does *your* healing work?"

He hung his head in thought for a moment before speaking. "What *specifically* do you *need*, and why are you asking?"

Chance spoke up first, bored with the tiresome back-and-forth. "We ran into Ashcroft tonight, and he performed one hell of a magic trick."

Cohen appeared genuinely confused. "How does—"

"This pertain to you?" She interrupted him impatiently. "Chance blew away half his skull, and he still crawled to a lab tech, sliced him, and let us watch his bone and brain reform."

"He what?" Cohen's jaw hit the proverbial floor. "The bone *actually* grew back? Entire missing chunks at a visible rate?"

"Not exaggerating. The ability to slice a fingernail down the guy's body with half his primary motor cortex missing is beyond me, much less the rest of it. Your race is the only one I'm aware of that heals faster than ours. So, I need you to tell me what is possible and what isn't."

"Whoa." Cohen quickly put his hands up. "We heal fast, but rebuilding missing tissue on that scale is *way* beyond us. Impossible."

"Well, he made it look damn easy. We both witnessed it." Chance leaned forward, daring him to call them liars, chomping at the bit for an excuse to knock him out cold. "What I don't understand is the scars. If he can rebuild tissue like that, why would he be covered in them?"

She glanced over at Chance with a puzzled expression. "An excellent question. He certainly wasn't filling in the gaps with scar tissue at the lab. Perhaps he's perfected the ability over time?" She turned back to Cohen, desperate to find some answers. "What about feeding?"

"I explained all this."

"Yes, and now I need a better explanation. What happens to the people you feed on?"

"Earlier, Chance tried to comfort you, and you drew on his strength, which weakened him. You appear exceptionally healthy now, he doesn't look any worse for wear, and he isn't dead, so I'm assuming you discovered a"—he glanced at her six-foot-three bodyguard and rephrased his statement before speaking—"better way."

"I wouldn't say better. Spencer died in front of me. The various emotions don't have the same potency, do they?"

"True." Another internal battle played out as he decided what to tell her. "Not all things are equal, either in mode or efficiency. We take strength from a comforting loved one to their detriment. On the other hand, a few things cause energy creation, a give-and-take, an equilibrium. The most successful one is sex..."

Cohen glanced at Chance with a contented smile, waiting for him to take the bait. He bristled, but thankfully, didn't rise to the occasion. After a disappointed sigh, he continued.

"The majority of my race creates ways to obtain what they need without causing harm. Ironically, seduction is the very reason people call us monsters from some imaginary hell."

"Wait...feeding off sex? Like some kind of succubus?"

"Well, for me, incubus, since I have man bits." Despite the death glare from Chance, he flashed her an amused smile. "Several subspecies feed this way, but incubus, succubus, demon are old terms coined hundreds of years ago by overly religious, sexually repressed fools. We aren't the spawn of Satan, assuming such a thing exists. Back in olden times, people commonly blamed the objects of their attraction, freeing themselves of any responsibility."

She stared at him in confusion, lost by his sudden rant. "I'm sorry. What?"

"For example, when a married man is caught drooling over a vivacious young woman, the fault lies on her for the clothes she wears or the perfume she uses. He labels her as a seducing demon to minimize his guilt. They displaced the blame to keep their virtue. I'd like to say humans evolved since those days, but...," he huffed with an irritated expression.

"Okay, obviously some pent-up issues there. Can we back up, though? Explain about this seduction thing."

He quirked an eyebrow in a gesture of astonishment that felt fake. "I think your dad should be the one explaining the birds and the bees. I assumed you already knew those sorts of details." This time, he didn't spare a single glance for her bodyguard. Either he didn't see him as a threat or trusted her to keep in check. For once, she didn't want to be Chance's anchor to the rational testosterone-free world.

Her eyes narrowed to angry slits. "Cut the crap, Cohen."

"Fine. Sexual tension, affection, sex...they build energy between two people. Ideally, they give and take in perfect balance. We feed, and they suffer no effects, short- or long-term." An immense sense of relief washed over her. So, he didn't turn her into some black widow, soul-sucking demon.

"Are there people who survive on other emotions, pain, for instance?"

"Of course. Psychos exist in any species, including yours. Some attend funerals or support groups for sorrow and grief, while others inflict pain to drink it in. The well-adjusted ones who crave pain accomplish their goals by taking part in BDSM, privately or professionally. Rogues, the ones who desire only true torment, don't last long. The families strongly *discourage* buying into the moral concepts of pop culture." When Cohen realized she had no idea what he meant, he elaborated. "Evil is stronger than good."

"Uh, I think popular culture believes the opposite."

"Oh, really?" He crossed his arms again and leaned back on his desk with a smug grin. Playing devil's advocate seemed to be his favorite game.

How fitting. "I believe turning to dark alternatives to gain greater power is a predominant theme. Blood magic allows more than *white* spells. The Dark Side holds more power than the Force. Vampires drinking humans dry gain more than those surviving on rats. Have you tried that, by the way?"

"Rats don't work, only human blood. The concept stems from the same Hollywood bullshit that makes us sparkle in the sun like fairy princesses."

"Hmm. Anyway. The holier-than-thou message revolves around the high price of dark power. The *good* guys only win out of pure luck, greater numbers, or by the consequences that villains bring upon themselves. Idealism is not a weapon."

"Fascinating point of view, but can we drop the philosophy lecture and return to facts, please?"

"Duly noted." Most likely, the contrite smile stretching his lips stemmed from embarrassment over his impassioned rambling. Chance shifted in his chair, still a volcano of animosity waiting to explode. Cohen didn't appear intimidated by him in the least, but she was sure he wouldn't like the result if he pushed too far.

"What about slowly torturing a victim, keeping them alive for hours or days of traumatizing pain? Would that overcharge the *batteries*?"

Cohen frowned in obvious distaste but took a moment to ponder her question. "We can feed as long as emotions are there to fuel us. Pain is a generator, like sex, but the body can only take so much before it dies. In theory, if they kept the victim alive, the supply would be…endless. Rogues and Moral Followers consider pain the most powerful source, not that it's scientifically proven, mind you. The higher-ups often end up sanctioning their execution because ritual murder is a hell of a lot harder to hide than copulation. Sex addicts litter the world, but people don't line up for true torture. However, the *batteries*, as you called them, can only charge to a certain point. There is no way to *overcharge* them."

"Does taking a life cause anything special?"

This time, his expression went beyond distaste. He seemed deeply offended by her question.

"Besides the intense sensations involved before the death? No. What about you?" Although he snapped the rhetorical question out of irritation, she answered anyway.

"No effect, negative or positive. We aren't supernatural. Blood is blood. All we need is healthy human hemoglobin."

"Interesting." The calm scientific reply caught him off guard, and his thoughts wandered again.

"Is the energy before death more intense than others?"

Cohen bristled and shifted uncomfortably, rubbing his too-small chin before answering. "Perhaps, but no one could survive on that alone. You know better than anyone how a trail of bodies compromises everything."

"Would it increase the other abilities, like speed? Allow you to…let's say, dodge a bullet?"

His eyebrows skyrocketed. "No, I don't see how. To use your analogy, if you charge a C battery with enough juice to power a car, it wouldn't magically change form to allow the extra current. It'd either stop accepting the charge or explode."

"What about the side effects? Would multiple feedings build over time?"

Once again, he paused in thought. "To some extent, but still… Even if you factored in the extreme feeding methods, draining a hundred of my kind wouldn't allow him to do any of those things. Besides, we may be more secretive to the public, but we are close-knit. We keep tabs on each other. One breach of our defenses means extermination. Believe me. We would notice if someone drained an entire family line." As soon as the last sentence left his mouth, a sense of dread settled over his shoulders, recognition passing behind his shifty eyes. Something she failed to pick up on.

With a deep sigh of frustration, she shrugged into her chair. "I still don't understand how he survived the change in the first place. During Duncan's experiments, fever killed the subjects before any major transformations occurred. No one has ever lived."

"Do you know, for a fact, he was human to start?"

It was a simple question, but one she never considered. "No, but now that I think about it, Dr. Nichols said the original DNA strand appeared to be absorbing the vampire markers from the second strand…"

"I don't know much about DNA, but it sounds to me that to undergo a radical evolutionary change, he would have to be a fast-healing race *before* the attack. I don't know why the concept didn't occur to me sooner. Not all the old families are recorded in our histories due to dissension in the ranks. Some refused to join the council entirely. However, reflecting on Gregor's story, Clyde sounds like a Rogue. What if Ashcroft and his family were like me?"

While her mouth slowly fell open, her mind scrambled to comprehend the full magnitude of his question. Several times, she began to say something and stopped, unable to form a single word.

"Look, Clyde *regularly* tortured and killed young women as if on a schedule. Gregor said so himself. Typically, these aggressive acts are compulsive crimes of opportunity, but not his. His timing was methodical, though his choice of victims seemed opportunistic. However, once he captured his prey, he lost control like a glutton at a buffet. He got what he needed and tossed them away like empty wrappers."

"Oh my god..." In a blazing moment of clarity, she covered her mouth to contain her nausea. "Spencer said he shared his secret. If he gave him a bit of his blood, showed him his methods...which explains why Malachi's wounds resembled Miriah's so much, why Spencer said he *felt* my fear, how he was suddenly stronger and faster. Ashcroft was *never* human. Gregor just never knew."

Cohen released a long, painful sigh as if trying to breathe past a knot of terror in his chest. "If we are right, we *have* to kill him before anyone else finds out. If we don't, the council will execute anyone with possible knowledge of this. They won't stop with us. Everyone at the lab, the cops, Alvarez's family...anyone with any connection, no matter how small." His eyes rested on her with all the weight and importance he could muster. "We can't survive exposure. If one human found out about the properties of our blood... We need to finish this fast and quiet, or we will all be dead."

"Well, then we need to find a way to ensure he dies." With that glib comment, Chance finally rejoined the conversation. "I blew half his head off, filled him with four clips, and the bastard didn't die. How are we supposed to kill him?"

"I can help there. We need to isolate him from any possible *food sources* and burn him to ash. But we are running out of time."

"He won't kill Duncan until he has everything and everyone he wants, and for now, things are under wraps—"

"Not what I meant. Whitmore dug up a bunch of info on Phipps Bend, the property you mentioned. Spencer bought it through a dozen or more dummy corporations. The interesting point is someone put major muscle on the county to sell. I doubt Ashcroft has any other allies, and Spencer, from what you say, was a loner. So, who pushed the sale through?"

"A great question I wish I had the answer to." More puzzle pieces that didn't fit. Awesome.

"Well, my partner is all worked up, and I can only coerce him so much…"

"Wait. Coerce?"

Cohen sighed in defeat and nodded. "At this point, how can it get worse? Yes. We affect some people, motivate them to respond a certain way. Not mind control, but it helps." After a brief pause, expecting more questions, he continued.

"Still…he thinks this case is bigger than us, and he's right. I suppressed all calls about Goditha, but it's only a matter of time. As it is, he's only willing to wait twenty-four hours before calling in the Feds. We have to wrap this up quietly and completely before then, or all hell breaks loose. If he discovers the scene at Goditha, we may have less time."

As if right on cue, Cohen's phone lit up like a Christmas tree. He held up a stern finger to Lilith and pressed the answer symbol.

As the mystery person on the other end spoke, the color drained from his face. When he hung up, he couldn't look her in the eye. "We have a bigger problem if such a thing is possible at this point."

Her skin threatened to crawl right off her body. Whatever news he had, she *knew* she wouldn't like it, and she already had a hell of a lot to choose from in the *not liking it* department.

"There's a fire. Whitmore and Humphrey are at the scene." After swallowing a lump in his throat, he finally met her eyes with an expression full of apologies. "The Riverfront Marriott. I think Ashcroft made his move."

Chapter 20

The parking lot overflowed with a dissonance of sirens, screams, and alarms, deafening even through the car windows. Complete pandemonium surrounded the concrete hotel with a sea of people running toward the emergency vehicles. Thick smoke like an eerie fog reflected the red and blue lights. Five fire trucks lined the front with their ladders extended, dumping gallons of water onto the roaring flames.

Lilith stared in utter shock as an explosion erupted, raining glass on the screeching crowd below. *What if Gregor and Alvarez didn't make it out?* She couldn't help but imagine her nightmare coming true. Her father in flames, screaming and writhing. She didn't recognize her death grip on the door handle until her fingers began to ache.

Cohen inched the car toward the scene but couldn't get far. She watched in horror while an entire line of ambulances struggled with the overflow as firefighters continued to pull people out of the inferno.

"I'm sure they got out, Lily." Chance's quiet and unsteady voice sounded less than reassuring. She wanted to lash out for saying something so ridiculous but stopped. She realized he spoke the words to convince himself more than her. After all, Gregor was the closest thing he had to a father.

When she glanced back at him, tears stinging her eyes, he wore the same horrified, heartbroken expression. His eyes left the window with soul-crushing guilt weighing on his shoulders. Every time he fell short, unable to protect someone, the failure wounded him to the core.

She opened her mouth to say something comforting, to tell him this wasn't his fault, but they rocked to a stop, and suddenly, finding her father and her partner became her only goal.

"Okay. The first thing we need to do is find..." Cohen was mid sentence when she tore open the door and ran. Chance and Cohen's shouts died out in the tumultuous clamoring crowd.

Barreling into the chaos stole her breath, like plunging head-first into a tank of ice water. The sensations of despair, pain, loss, fear, anger, and desperation all permeated the air in a suffocatingly thick cloud. They vibrated painfully over every inch of her body, bringing scorching tears to her eyes. The pressure, tight against her skin, threatened implosion, forcing her to struggle for each panting breath.

Everywhere she turned, people cried and choked behind oxygen masks while injured victims searched aimlessly for their kids, wives, husbands, siblings. One little girl clutched a singed teddy bear, sobbing amid the churning crowd, tears leaving trails through the soot covering her face. As Lilith shoved past EMTs and trauma nurses, she grabbed one and pointed out the lost girl with the teddy bear. She belonged to somebody out here, but Lilith needed to find her own family.

She frantically ran by every ambulance, searching for any sign of Gregor or Alvarez. Suddenly, someone grabbed her from behind, and she spun, ready to attack, but came face-to-face with a strange woman, covered in ash.

"Please, has anyone found my son?" She clutched Lilith's arm like it was a rock in a surging tide. Her touch burned like hot pokers, searing the mark of her pain into Lilith's body. She wanted to yank her arm away, but the woman's bloodshot eyes searched hers with heartbreaking desperation.

Then Lilith finally realized the police tracksuit made her look like an off-duty cop here to help with the catastrophic scene.

"I'm sorry I haven't heard anything." The woman still wouldn't let go. She kept clinging to her, staring at her with those pleading eyes. On the verge of panic, trying to pry the woman off, she heard a familiar Southern accent.

"Ma'am, we will help you as soon as we can." Cohen appeared and gently pried her loose. "We'll find your son. Give your information to the cop over there." His eyes met hers with a significant weight, which Lilith thought might be genuine.

The woman nodded while wiping at her soot-covered cheeks and shuffled off in the direction he indicated, disappearing into the chaos. Cohen watched her leave, but once she was out of earshot, he rounded on Lilith.

"Are you insane??"

"I *need* to find them!" She spat the words at him and started back toward the crowd.

He snatched her wrist and yanked her backward. "Getting yourself killed will not help anyone! You go charging around here alone, and that's exactly what will happen!"

"Let go!" Without warning, she spun and swung, nailing him right in the jaw. While the shock rattled him, she ripped her wrist away and tried to run.

"Damn it!" He seized her arm with a fierce grip, pulling her back around again. This time, he held both her wrists to prevent another punch. "Stop! I'm on your side, remember? We must stick together. Ashcroft might be in this crowd."

She tried to tear free again, her panic bubbling to a frenzy that tightened her lungs. "I know! I have to find them before he does!"

"And then what?" His scream startled some fight out of her. "Assuming they are here, and you find them, what happens when Ashcroft finds you? What are you going to do to him in a crowd like this, a roving buffet? All you'll accomplish is becoming another hostage or worse."

Her eyes lit up with tears as she glanced into his hazel eyes, but she couldn't concentrate. Everything swirled around her like a hurricane of shattered glass, preventing her from making sense of anything else. She simply swayed with the ebb and flow while struggling to breathe.

"Lilith!" Once her unfocused eyes met him again, he continued. "The call came in twenty minutes ago. Judging by the injuries, the fire alarm never sounded. It's an old hotel. Without much warning, they may not have made it out, and if they did and Ashcroft hasn't found them yet, he will. There's nothing we can do to stop him, not here. We need to isolate him somewhere."

"But I can't leave." He was right, but how could she give up and allow a monster to take her family? "If there is any chance I can find them first and get them out of here, I have to take it!"

After searching her eyes for a tense moment, he reluctantly released her hands. "We will talk to the cops and EMTs here, have them escort us around if possible. It won't be an easy accomplishment in this mess, but I'll make it happen." A slight upturn of his lips told her he had zero confidence in his words, but he had every intention of helping her anyway. "Have you seen Whitmore or Humphrey while running around?"

She shook her head, still trying to catch her breath with the chaos swirling around her as Chance caught up to them.

"What the hell, Lily? Are you trying to get yourself killed?"

After spotting the sorrowful expression on her face, Cohen stepped forward, rubbing his jaw. "Your woman has one hell of a right hook."

The comment defused the situation, actually pulling a smirk out of Chance. "About time someone took a shot at you." The momentary distraction ended as he stepped close, cutting Cohen out of the conversation.

"You cannot pull a stunt like that again." His hazel eyes flecked with green pleaded and begged. "I'm barely holding on here. I need you to stay with me. Let me do one damn thing right with my life. Please."

She hung her head like a scolded child, strongly regretting her decision to barrel into the tumultuous crowd alone. "I'm sorry for being impetuous, but please stop blaming yourself, Chance. You aren't responsible for the entire world."

"You're right. I'm not. My sworn duty only applies to you and your father." His hands slid up her shoulders to cup her face, making her heart race, even in the middle of a disaster zone. Everything else faded into the background. The raging storm died down, giving her one blissful moment of quiet in the eye of an emotional hurricane. "Please, *cherie.* Let me do my job."

"I hate to interrupt you two lovebirds, but we are at the scene of a major hotel fire." Cohen's voice snapped with irritation. When Chance moved to reply, she caught a glimpse of the detective's blatant scowl, and his arms crossed angrily over his chest.

"What I *was* saying when Ms. Adams shot out of the car like a mental patient..." Once he held their undivided attention, he continued. "If we find Whitmore and Humphrey, they'll know more about what's going on here and who's in charge of the scene. Let's split up. You and Chance stick together and search the perimeter, and I'll go behind the police barricade and look."

The weighted stare he pinned them with grew stern. "Do *not* go looking for Gregor and Alvarez through the center of this mess. Stay on the fringes where you have room to escape. If you see Ashcroft, run. This is *not* the place to confront him. Do you understand?"

"And how is it okay for you to run off alone and not me?"

"So glad you asked." The overly sweet smile stretching his lips dripped with sarcasm. "Unlike you, Ashcroft isn't after me. I'm only a meddlesome detective, not a target." The barely restrained anger in his voice didn't match his expression. Fear saturated his eyes, and the downturned corners of his mouth showed sadness. An odd mix she didn't understand.

He noticed her staring at him a little too intently and ran his fingers through his short blond hair. "Stay safe, text me if you find something, and I'll do likewise." After issuing his hurried instructions, he turned and disappeared into the pandemonium.

"You heard him, *cherie.*" When Chance grabbed her hand, she instantly felt stronger and better equipped to quell the overwhelming emotions from hundreds of terrified people. He quickly flinched and withdrew his hand. The storm didn't engulf her this time. Her breaths came easier. She could focus, push back the tide, keep her head above water. She smiled in relief until she saw Chance's face.

He appeared pale and disorientated, unsteady on his feet. "What was that?"

A tiny ball of dread knotted her stomach. "What was what?"

Frowning, he gazed down at his hand as if he'd never seen it before. "I don't know. I grabbed your hand, and then I got dizzy and light-headed." She flashed back to their conversation with Cohen, and the dread bloomed into real fear. Scared he'd see her guilt, she averted her eyes to scan the area. She had to get a grip, or she'd end up hurting someone. "I don't know. Are you okay? Do you need to sit for a minute?"

He shook his head, trying to shake the cobwebs. "No. I'm good. Let's move." She whispered a prayer of thanks for avoiding another lengthy discussion.

Despite Cohen's strict instructions, she desperately hoped they'd spot her father. Logically, she understood his reasoning, but if Gregor was out there, maybe they could sneak him away. If she didn't try, it meant a life of regret and self-loathing.

They spent the next hour pushing their way through clustered groups around the perimeter, avoiding the thick throngs in the center. Most of the ambulances pulled out, replaced by another dozen cop cars to contain the chaos. Although firefighters continued to battle the inferno, they stopped pulling people out of the building. Anyone left inside was beyond help. Cops organized the uninjured, herding them toward buses lining the end of the lot, which waited to transfer them to new accommodations. While the torrential sensations of anarchy and despair lessened, her panic grew to an inevitable climax, which finally erupted.

"Where the fuck are they?" They found no trace of the detectives, her father, or Alvarez in the sea of nameless faces, and she could no longer contain the anxious energy clawing at her skin.

"You *need* to calm down." His voice held a stern warning as he scanned the surrounding people.

"No, I don't! I have every right to freak out. They aren't out here, and they aren't answering their phones. They either burned up in that damn monstrosity of a hotel, or they've fallen into Ashcroft's hands. I can't take this!" She spun around, fixing Chance with a pointed stare. "Why are you so fucking calm? Don't you care?"

"You know I do, but freaking out won't save them! If they're dead, all we can do is not join them!"

He caught her wrist before her open hand could connect with his face. "How can you say that?" Fiercely determined, she unsuccessfully struck out with her other hand, hot angry tears stinging her eyes.

"Because it's the truth! Stop, Lilith." He held her arms effortlessly while she struggled, patiently waiting for her to run out of steam. When she finally fell against him, sobbing, he scooped her up and carried her away from the chaos to an alley one block over.

When he found a quiet spot free from prying eyes and ears, he set her on her feet. After wiping her eyes, she glanced up into his handsome face, set in stern lines.

"You're losing it, Lily. You can't flip out like that in public!" Something more profound lingered beneath the surface, just out of reach.

"Stop…"

"No." The surface broke, revealing a burning rage as he hovered closer. "You have *no right* to tell me I don't care! I'm not a soulless monster just because I choose not to lose my shit in front of hundreds of humans!" When Chance punched the brick with a guttural growl, she flinched like a terrified bird, a learned response from her college years. The sudden memory only fueled her animosity.

"Feel better?" Somewhere in the back of her mind, she knew she wasn't mad at him. The real targets were her past, current circumstances, and an uncertain future, but like in Duncan's basement, she couldn't stop. The fury took over, forcing her to watch with no control over her actions. "Go on. Break your hand, and see if that helps! I'm sure Ashcroft won't attack if you're injured."

The hostility in her voice cut deep, and his eyes snapped down to hers with a smoldering glare. "*Stop* pushing me, Lilith! You aren't going to take everything out on me just because I'm fucking convenient! I'm not your fucking punching bag!"

The intensity of the moment quickened her pulse as she panted for breath. He was right, but the part of her in control didn't believe he deserved an apology. Their eyes locked in a turbulent showdown, the seconds stretching into minutes. A swell of righteous indignation rose in her chest until her hand rose to slap him.

As if expected, he caught her wrist and pinned it above her head. He leaned closer and forced his words past clenched teeth. "*Stop* trying to hit me, Lilith. It won't make you feel any better."

Without any warning, his eyes suddenly fell, glancing at her full lips. Instantly, intense desire tore its way through her body, overwhelming her anger and assuming control. She couldn't tell how much came from him and how much belonged to her. She didn't care.

With wanton abandon, she closed the distance, her lips colliding with his. The heated kiss froze time, neither of them moving or even breathing. Her mind started to balk, terrified she made a colossal mistake, certain he'd pull away at any second and storm off.

Then, he dropped her wrist. One hand slid up her neck while the other circled her waist, both tugging her closer while burning the lingering doubts from her mind. The floodgates opened, releasing a torrent of repressed emotions, and the sensuous kiss deepened as she sank her hands into his hair, fingers tightening.

He displayed no hesitation this time, only raw, inescapable need as he pressed her back to the brick. The purely feral moment of power brought a low growl trembling across her lips, making her quiver.

Without warning, his strong hands surged down her body and hauled her up, pulling her legs around him. The weight of him pinning her to the wall didn't bring a sense of helplessness, quite the opposite. Vivacious passion hummed deep within, even before his teeth grazed against the tender flesh of her neck. She had control. She had power.

Although her soft moans were the ones filling the air, she was the catalyst. Her responses determined what happened next. She drove his desire, drew it out of him, and pulled it toward her. Having so much sway over another person was a frightening realization but also exhilarating, like nothing she experienced before. She clutched his shoulders as if clinging to him was the last sane thing left in the world.

Leaning his forehead against hers, he broke the kiss and panted for breath. For one terrifying moment, she thought he might put on the brakes once again. All her lusty bravado began to falter as she studied him, the seconds stretching into eternity. His eyes closed as if steeling himself, bracing to reject her *again* with inconvenient logic or romantic rhetoric.

"I need you, Lily." The quality of his voice made her tremble as she prayed his words weren't a figment of her imagination. When his salacious eyes opened, her breath caught in her throat.

The weight from a decade of hopes, desires, fantasies all came crashing down on her. All the insecurities and indecisiveness vanished in the haze. They burned with profound confidence like she'd never seen before. No questions, no second guesses. He knew what he wanted, which made her heart race as a glow started in her belly and quickly consumed her.

"I need you too, Chan—"

Before she could finish her sentence, the moment exploded into a deep, enthusiastic kiss, his tongue gliding across hers. A wave of carnality crashed over them, and the undertow swept her away, caught in the very current she created. As he caressed her hips, fingers tugging at fabric, her deep need disrupted any remaining internal thoughts.

In a flash of carnal necessity breaking all pretenses of control, their hands impatiently stripped away all clothing, both desperate to remove anything preventing their skin from touching. His warm hands slid up her stomach and under her lace bra, the last remnant of cloth between them. He hesitated, teasing the tender skin before ripping her bra away with an animalistic hunger that made her tremble.

Then, the world blurred into intense moments with groping hands, grazing teeth, thrusting bodies, and passionate moans against the rough brick. Breathlessly, she dug her nails into his back, holding on as visceral waves of pleasure racked her body. His growls rumbled over her flesh, hands gripping her hips with bruising strength. One last vigorous thrust left them clinging to each other, glistening with sweat, hearts pounding in rhythm while they gasped for air.

Chance leaned his forehead against hers, eyes closed, hot breath rushing over her lips. She tried to stop quivering, but her skin tingled and crackled with energy, making her feel vibrantly alive like never before. Distantly, she wondered how much had to do with the demon blood, but she quickly dismissed the unwelcome fear, content to bask in the glow they created.

Neither of them spoke. Even if she proved capable of forming words, she didn't wish to break the magic. She wanted to stave off the inevitable awkward moment for as long as possible. The vulnerable insecurity, wondering if it was a mistake, and if not, did they feel the same way? Sex changed everything. A tiny bubble of panic tightened her chest. What if this was it? Goal achieved.

As if reading her mind, his hand slid up her neck, fingers delving into her auburn curls, and he kissed her tenderly. After brushing the matted hair from her face, he stared into her eyes with a slow, mischievous grin. Everything felt so natural, which eased her panic. She nuzzled his neck with a breathy kiss and relaxed into his arms, feeling safer than ever before.

"Not that this is my favorite suggestion, but"—the sound of his voice almost startled her in the wake of the comfortable silence—"we may want to put our clothes back on."

Reality came crashing in. They stood entwined, stark naked in a dark alley with cops and fire trucks passing by at regular intervals. Under any other circumstances, she'd be mortified. However, since the past few days resulted in Chance pinning her to a wall, she couldn't help but laugh. He frowned for an instant before grinning like a Cheshire cat.

"As I said, not my favorite suggestion."

"And what would be your *favorite suggestion*?" She quirked an eyebrow with a slow impish smile. Before he said anything, she pressed a feather-soft kiss to his lips. A languid growl escaped his throat, hands tightening around her, and the heated rush flushed her body again.

Lilith's phone ringing broke the blissful moment like a shower of ice water. "Shit. Cohen." She glanced up at Chance, and his smile faltered.

With an almost inaudible sigh, he kissed her softly before putting her down. Thankfully, he didn't let go of her until her legs stopped shaking.

"You should answer. Maybe he found something." The steady and even tone of his voice held an indifference that sent her mind racing, running through all the possible reasons behind it. She pushed them all aside. She couldn't drive herself crazy, not now, not with so much on the line.

After shimmying back into her clothes, she dug out her phone to see a dozen text messages and a missed call, all from Cohen. Crap. She reluctantly dialed the number as Chance grabbed his jeans.

While impatiently waiting for Cohen to pick up, Chance turned around, and then she saw it. Just below his navel sat a beautiful white lily with a curling scroll bearing her name. He slowly followed her gaze down to the tattoo. When his eyes met hers again, the fragile confidence they contained laid all her unraveling doubts to rest, and she beamed with an infectious luminosity that brought a tear to her eye.

Cohen's voice suddenly blared in her ear, startling her, and she nearly dropped her cell. "Where *the hell* are you two?"

His furious tone was equivalent to a cold shower, and she rubbed contritely at her blushing cheek. "Did you find something?"

"I've been trying to reach you for half an hour! What the hell is going on? Are you two in danger?"

Chance tugged on his shirt, his hazel eyes watching her with leisurely desire. Suddenly, she wanted to hole up with him in a hotel room for a week. Damn, he was distracting. "Uh…no. We're okay. We came up empty." She squeezed her eyes closed in a frantic attempt to focus. "We'll meet you at the car and figure out what to do next." She almost hung up, but he kept talking.

"Well, move your asses. Whitmore called. He posted men at Phipps Bend, and they radioed in some suspicious activity about forty minutes ago. My partner is heading there with Humphrey.

We could have all gone together, but *someone* was too damn busy to answer their phone."

The chastising comment sobered her up instantly. "Sorry. We'll be right there." She hung up before he had the opportunity to say anything else.

"Whitmore and Humphrey are heading to Phipps Bend. We need to meet Cohen so we can catch up." She leaned back against the wall with a heavy sigh.

Part of her felt guilty for not staying focused on the case, but she completely broke down in the crowd. Chance cured her panic attacks and stopped her from running toward literal fires. No, more than that. She exuded robust power, refined control. For the first time since she arrived at the abandoned Italian joint in New York City to rendezvous with her father, everything seemed clear.

When her eyes fell on Chance, she noticed the nervous tension writhing under his skin. "Into the lion's den."

He nodded firmly with a sense of resolve, but fear still lingered plainly on his face. It wasn't a fear of death, but of not being enough to protect her. He stared at the pavement and tentatively took her hand, fingers slipping between hers. Slowly, he raised his eyes. He needed to say something but couldn't bring himself to speak the words out loud. After a final sigh, he bit the bullet.

"You realize, if Cohen didn't find Gregor or Alvarez, it means Ashcroft has them."

She didn't want to face that particular truth. "They might have escaped..."

Chance cradled her face and stooped to stare her straight in the eye. "Lily, Ashcroft went through a lot of trouble to set the fire. We both know the man's capabilities. He wouldn't let them burn up and lose his opportunity for revenge."

"Why are we talking about this?" She breathed a little faster, losing some of the calm clarity he gave her.

"We both should be prepared. They may be in rough shape."

"Come on. We need to meet Cohen. We can run through all the worst-case scenarios on the way. Although... I had my heart set on a game of *I spy*." Lately, her short temper earned her a hurt expression from him, but this time he simply kissed her lips before tugging her back toward the scene.

"The place is at least an hour and a half away. I'm sure we'll have time for both." His mischievous grin stole her breath as flashes of his delicious mouth and everything else circulated through her mind. For a moment, she enjoyed the internal playback, ignoring the commotion ahead. Not only the raging inferno but also their plan to rush into the home turf of a supremely sadistic man, a monster gradually assassinating her family over the past six hundred years. One who appeared impossible to stop.

Chapter 21

Cohen didn't speak a single word when they reached the car, and the uneasy silence continued for most of the drive. His typically calm composure vanished. He stared at the road with his jaw clenched, arms locked, and hands gripping the wheel while his lead foot attacked the gas pedal. Either he cared about his partner more than he let on, or something else nagged at his mind.

At least he had the foresight to put a flashing siren on the roof of his car. She could just picture their ludicrous explanation for rocketing down the interstate at five in the morning.

I'm sorry, Officer, but we are rushing off to an abandoned nuclear plant. If we don't leave now, a six-hundred-year-old monster will slice up my dad and a bunch of other people. The same guy set fire to an entire hotel earlier this morning and butchered a scientist in a secret lab after we blew half his head off. What kind of monster? Oh, he's a vampire-incubus hybrid. They'd all end up in white padded cells.

Chance gallantly volunteered to ride shotgun, allowing her the relative safety of the back seat. The air hung thick with an uncomfortable tension, like sitting in a car with her dad after he caught her sneaking out. Then again, perhaps she read too much into things. One powerful emotion superseded all the other subtle nuances in the car—fear.

She hated silence because the absence of distractions left her mind free to roam in a million directions. She thought of Alvarez and Gloria, thriving in a happy marriage for hundreds of years when most humans couldn't manage a decade.

The thought of facing Gloria, telling her that the man she loved for centuries, her husband, father of her beautiful daughters, would never come home. If anything happened to him, she would never forgive herself, and neither would his wife.

Lilith leaned forward, elbows on her knees, and rubbed her face. The convoluted web of tangents infiltrating her brain wouldn't help her ensure Ashcroft stayed dead.

Besides, her partner wasn't the only life she found herself responsible for saving. Gregor, Duncan, Chance, Cohen, Whitmore, *and* Humphrey. She chuckled to herself, marveling at the ridiculous notion of *her* protecting four cops, a professional bodyguard, and her father from one old man. Any other day, she'd collapse in laughter, but today, the internal laugh rang with hysterical desperation.

Her mind snapped to the present when Cohen clicked off the siren as they hit the exit ramp.

"We're meeting them a half mile from the structure they identified." The overly assertive tone made sense. The other cops had at least a forty-five-minute head start on them thanks to an accident backing up I-40E. Hopefully, they waited in the car and didn't rush inside, trying to be heroes.

"How is this—" Cohen cut the corner as if chasing a terrorist with a dirty bomb. With her heart in her throat, she latched on to the back of Chance's seat to keep from flying across the vehicle before continuing. "Going to play out?"

"What are you talking about, Adams?" The Southern accent returned chock-full of animosity.

"First off, I'm not a damn cop, so don't call me by my last name. Secondly, how are we going to handle Whitmore and Humphrey? They're humans, oblivious to the real danger. They're lambs for the slaughter."

"Don't you think I *know* that?" He slammed his hands against the steering wheel, and in the corner of her eye, she saw Chance tense. The detective raked a shaky hand through his short blond hair and sighed.

"I've contemplated the problem the entire drive. Whitmore called in the FBI, and they'll be here in about twelve hours. He won't walk away. I don't see any choice but to bring him with us and pray for the best. We should split into two groups to minimize exposure.

Whitmore will stay with me. I can influence him, especially without you two around. He's not fond of either of you. Humphrey appeared mostly neutral, so I'll send him with you."

Chance finally spoke up now that the conversation steered away from dramatics and into the more comfortable realm of tactical decision-making. "Both of them going with you makes more sense. You can keep an eye on them, use your persuasion, and Lily and I will be free to maneuver."

"You *obviously* do not remember meeting Whitmore." Cohen's laugh exuded a little too much sarcasm and awkwardness to break the oppressive tension. "My partner will *not* let you go anywhere without a police escort, Mr. Deveraux. They are not enemies. They can be our allies."

Something in his voice revealed far more emotional turmoil than expected. Perhaps the ghosts from his past magnified the strength of his reaction. The curious side of her wanted to ask, but this wasn't the time to go digging.

"And what do we say when one of them takes a shot at Ashcroft, and the monster dodges or heals?" Chance voiced a valid point. Everything about the situation screamed disaster.

"Besides, didn't *you* say we needed to take care of this *quietly*? I have a..." Chance faltered for a second, and she wondered what he was about to say. "I plan on returning to New York. With the FBI involved, our narrow window of opportunity is shrinking. I will *not* survive Ashcroft only to be taken out by a pack of secret emotion suckers, no offense."

"We don't have a choice now. Whitmore is with me. Humphrey is with the two of you. Period."

"What if we knocked them out?" She meant her voice to sound confident but failed.

"Are you fucking serious?" Cohen coughed on his breath as the car screeched to a halt at a stoplight. "This isn't some stupid buddy-cop flick. We can't assault two human police officers because they might be inconvenient."

"Don't patronize me. I'm aware it isn't as simple as a tap on the back of the head, but it would solve the problem of seeing something unexplainable. Chance is right. I don't want to survive this only to be assassinated because we didn't take proper precautions."

"And what do I tell them when they wake up? It would only confirm we have something to hide. He will dig and dig until he either ends up dead or we do."

"But if they see something we can't explain, they'll dig anyway." She released an exasperated sigh and sunk into the seat. They were all screwed. Even if they survived, the atrocities at Goditha hitting the spotlight would send things spiraling out of control. Gregor's plan to go public centered on the labs and their contribution to society. A way to buy favor with humans.

If the slaughter at the Knoxville lab surfaced, then Ashcroft would win regardless. Unceremoniously shoving them into the limelight with the devastating circumstances he contrived would result in catastrophe. They could only hope he merely prevented them from leaving the shadows and didn't push them further underground.

Cohen's voice dragged her out of her spiraling thoughts. "You may not want to hear this, but we might need their help. We can concentrate on damage control *after* we walk out alive."

Chance sighed heavily from the front seat. "I hate to admit it, Lily, but he's right. The two of us couldn't take him. No offense, but I don't think Cohen is going to make much of a difference." He craned around to capture her gaze. "Plus, the madman has hostages, ones we care about, which might make us hesitate."

She sank backward, trying to avoid his eyes while he pinned her with a weighted stare. "Fine." They outnumbered her, but bringing two human cops into this mess still screamed utter disaster to her. This time she pulled the resulting silence around her like a blanket.

She stared out the window as they approached the Phipps Bend property. According to Cohen, the state halted construction back in 1981. Now it loomed in the dark, a cluster of buildings beaten by the elements for the past thirty years. The massive reactor base, a delicate ring of intersecting lines, sat barren and skeletal in the overgrown field.

Beyond lay a dozen or so complexes scattered over a thousand acres, which melted into a vast forest. If Whitmore hadn't posted men to watch for unusual activity, they'd have no idea where to start.

Cohen pulled up behind a black sedan parked outside a gate surrounding an eerie collection of unfinished buildings. She gaped openly at the cylindrical monolith of stained concrete dominating the structure.

Whitmore hauled himself out of the driver's side, wiping powdered sugar off his tie. His jowls moved, chewing something, probably the food of champions among cops. Amazingly, the husky detective still managed to scowl simultaneously. He stalked up to their vehicle as Humphrey made his appearance. With no way to delay the inevitable, she took a deep breath and stepped out into the dark.

The night wind howled and whipped around her. An instant chill soaked into her bones, a feeling she found hard to shake. As if sensing her discomfort, Chance draped an arm around her shoulders, shielding her from the cold as they joined the others.

Whitmore kept as much distance as possible between himself and Chance. His obvious distaste extended to her as he glared with a menacing frown. Then again, considering he was a short, grumpy, aging detective with a spare tire around his waist, scowling might simply be his modus operandi.

As they stood in the cold, something occurred to her, and she scanned the area but didn't see any other cars. "Where are the men you stationed here?"

Whitmore's face screamed *Go to hell and die*, but he still answered in an impatient huff, "I sent them back to their station." Then, he rounded on Cohen. "You finally gonna tell me what in the hell is going on?" His clenched hands landed on his well-padded hips as he continued to vent. "You send me on one more goddamn goose chase without explaining anything, and I swear to Christ—"

Cohen headed everyone off at the pass. "No time for details. We have a highly dangerous suspect with three possible hostages inside." He popped the trunk and rummaged while talking. "Time is essential. Our perp has held one of the victims for at least three days. He is probably delirious and injured, so approach with caution." Cohen slapped a 9-millimeter and two clips into Lilith's hands before looking up at Chance.

"I have one, but if you're offering…" For a brief second, they shared a conspiratorial grin, a temporary bond over testosterone and firepower.

"More can't hurt." The detective passed him a shotgun complete with ammo.

"Wait. You're giving *him* a gun? You said *one* suspect! We don't need his help."

"An *extremely dangerous* one. I want to err on the side of caution. More than we need is better than not enough."

Whitmore gazed out at the weather-stained buildings towering over them in the darkness with surprisingly shrewd eyes. Perhaps a real sleuth existed beyond the prejudice and small-minded country-hick attitude. In any other circumstance, she'd find the concept inspiring, but she needed him to be a dumb country cop. A smart human heading into Ashcroft's den terrified her.

"Is he heavily armed? I didn't bring the vests."

"No. The perp is quick, strong, sneaky, deadly, and still a threat without a weapon. He might be on PCP or something. No hesitations once we're inside. If you see a crazy-eyed man with crisscross scars on his face, shoot and keep shooting until you're out of bullets."

"Shit, fucking drug addicts." Whitmore shuffled back to his sedan and pulled out his standard cop-issued shotgun.

She leveled an incredulous stare at Cohen, who simply shrugged. Comparing Ashcroft to an out-of-control druggie with an ax to grind was like comparing a betta fish to a great white shark. At least he tried to prepare them with a plausible explanation, even if it was woefully inadequate. What else could he do? Tell them the truth?

"Okay." Cohen stuffed a .38 Special in his side holster and grabbed another shotgun before closing the trunk. "Whitmore, you're coming with me. Humphrey, you're going with these two."

"Wait one damn second. We are not—"

Cohen cut his partner off with a steely glare that would intimidate anyone. "No discussion. The building he's in is huge, and we need to act fast and use the element of surprise. Plus, stomping in like a team of Clydesdales is a bad idea. Let's move out."

He headed straight for the gate, leaving everyone behind. Whitmore jogged to catch up. Not a pretty sight. However, Humphrey decided to walk several paces behind her and Chance like a prison guard while tension pulled at every muscle in Chance's body.

Lilith slid her fingers through his, not only to show support but also because she was scared out of her mind. Yes, being escorted like two death row inmates felt immensely uncomfortable, but what waited for them in the looming block of concrete went beyond terrifying. Her mind flooded with images of Ashcroft. His cruel pointed face hovered over her, smelled her, grinned with his crooked teeth. The sight of his splattered brains trailing behind him as he sliced through the doctor's skin seared into her head.

Chance squeezed her hand and leaned in close enough for his breath to tickle over her ear, derailing her morbid thoughts. "If we can withstand the officer staring holes in our back, I think we'll be fine." She stole a glance over her shoulder to see Humphrey's death stare firmly in place. She mustered a half smile and squeezed his hand a little harder.

Once they passed through the gates, Cohen signaled to them and disappeared with Whitmore down a dark alley to search for secondary entry points. Thankfully, Chance spoke cop sign language and steered her toward the front doors.

Ashcroft expected them. The ostentatious fire forced them in an inescapable direction. Either they left their loved ones to die or walked into a trap. With all his research and reconnaissance, Ashcroft knew running away wasn't a choice for them. Setting the blaze seemed risky to the untrained eye, but he knew the outcome, the inevitable result—checkmate.

Chance took point, motioning for them to stay back. After pumping the shotgun, he propped it against the fleshy crook of his shoulder and crept toward the ominous double doors of a one-story building.

Their only advantage cut both ways. Without a single window, the enemy couldn't see them approach. However, it also meant they had no choice but to go in blind.

Of course, she didn't expect Ashcroft to pounce on them as soon as they arrived. He didn't need to. He could sit back and let them come to him, another sign of his narcissistic ego.

The man wanted acknowledgment for his deeds. Although Gregor's plan to go public served as a catalyst, she suspected he harbored a deep desire to display his handiwork. The staged muggings and car accidents didn't satisfy his thirst or instill the terror he sought.

Ashcroft loved satisfying his monstrous appetite. He craved the violence, the hunt, the fear, perhaps even more than his demand for justice.

Behind her, Humphrey clicked off the safety on his handgun, reminding everyone to do likewise. Once again, she kept the gun loose at her side until she had a reason to aim. If they survived the night, she intended to log more hours at the shooting range. Part of her hoped it wouldn't be necessary, but her life kept evolving in new and violent ways.

Chance put his back to the wall beside the dilapidated structure's double doors. Lilith and Humphrey followed his lead. The scent of wet mildew filled her nostrils as the damp cold of the concrete seeped through her police sweat suit, a dank chill crawling up her spine.

An eerie quietness surrounded the place, similar to a graveyard or a haunted house. The sinister silence crept into her bones, making every hair stand on end. The half-finished structure couldn't be soundproof, which meant Ashcroft decided not to play with his new toys yet.

Her optimistic relief only lasted a second. If he didn't need to carve up his guests, he must have fully recovered. The uproar at the hotel probably supplied more than enough sustenance.

She shook the thoughts from her head and focused on her breathing. Driving herself into a panic only helped the enemy. *Just breathe. In and out.*

They stayed crouched with their backs to the wall for what seemed like an eternity. Either Chance was allowing Cohen and

Whitmore time to get into position, or he was focusing on his breathing too.

Eventually, he grabbed the door handle and ever so slowly tried the latch. Unlocked. Why would an omnipotent demon bother with a dead bolt? Besides, how many people would break into a place like this apart from teenage Satan worshippers and ghost hunters?

When Chance eased the door open, the low groan of metal on metal hummed through the air. Not silent, but better than the rust-induced banshee scream she expected.

He nodded to Humphrey, who did the same with a unified purpose. Huh. So, if you gave two enemies guns, dumped them in a mutually threatening position, and stuck a girl between them, they'd work together? Hell, they could make playdates to bake chocolate chip cookies if that got her home safe.

While her thoughts rambled, Chance slipped inside, and she hurried after him with Humphrey hot on her heels.

The door slowly shut behind them with a quiet little click that echoed eerily. Complete darkness enveloped them, and she froze, petrified. Her chest tightened as her eyes scurried everywhere, trying to find some pinpoint of light. She panted each strained breath, head spinning in dizzying circles like a disoriented diver. She tried to move, but her body refused to listen as if her legs turned to stone.

Something brushed her back, and she jumped, barely keeping a scream from leaving her throat. She choked on the thick, stale air while her entire body vibrated with the urge to run but still refused to take a step. She couldn't breathe. She needed oxygen, fresh air. She reached in the direction of the door when a muted flashlight kicked on.

"Lily." Chance's rushed whisper exuded empathetic authority. "Stay close." Her vision flicked to the side, catching the highlights of Humphrey's scowling face hovering beside her.

As her eyes began to adjust, she finally reined in her panic. If only she possessed the superpowered night vision of Hollywood vampires. Of course, the all-black leather outfit and impractically high heels which turned them into instant kick-ass ninjas would be helpful too.

With a deep breath, she snuck up next to Chance and leaned in close, whispering. "Sorry. I… This place…" Terror distorted her voice as her eyes roamed the dark frantically, certain the boogeyman would slice them up at any second.

His smile displayed so many micro-expressions, she couldn't pick them all out. Fear, compassion, and desire stood out the most.

"Here. Take the flashlight. I need to keep my hands free. Walk one step ahead of me, hug the wall, and don't point the light any higher than hip level. Don't swing it around wildly. Move in slow, steady arcs, back and forth." His soothing voice wrapped around her like a soft blanket.

As impossible as it seemed, she suddenly knew she loved him. He stood before her, saying the perfect thing in an ideal way. Not only did he understand how to ground her and calm her fraying nerves, but also, he never hesitated to do so.

The epiphany brought tears to her eyes, so she quickly stared down at the light in her shaking hands. She tightened her grip and squeezed her eyes closed, trying to pull the tattered ends of her mind together in some semblance of control.

With one last exhale, she met his hypnotic stare as his hand caressed her shoulder, sending ripples of warmth through her body.

"You don't have to do this. You can go back to the car. We can handle this." Desperation shone clearly in his eyes, willing her to take the out. Not for chauvinistic reasons but because he desired nothing more than keeping the person he loved safe.

Despite every instinct, she couldn't leave for the same reason. Focusing on her mission to keep the man she loved alive brought calming clarity.

"We don't have time for a pep talk. While we're standing here with our thumbs up our asses, the detectives are in the open without backup." Although Humphrey had a valid point, the irate words rubbed her the wrong way. Fortunately, anger helped her focus, which was precisely what she needed.

Chance threw a menacing look at the officer, silently telling him to *shut the fuck up*. Before he could say anything, she spoke up confidently.

"I can't. I need to find Dad and Felipe." She faltered for a minute, nerves rattling for an entirely different reason. "And I can't leave you." She caressed his cheek with a small smile. "I need to know you're okay. I'm all right, just scared."

Saying the words out loud strengthened her resolve. *I'm okay. I can do this.* After standing a little straighter, she held the light steady with one hand and gripped her gun with the other.

"Let's go." A conflicted expression of pride and fear lit his face before she pushed her way in front of him.

The newfound bravado slowly dwindled as she hugged the wall, her heart pounding. Sickly off-color paint peeled from the rotting drywall, making a rough texture against her back. The light moved over ancient yellowed linoleum littered with dirt and chunks of crumbled drop ceiling.

The air felt colder inside the building, like a looming cloud of ice tightening her chest with the scent of death and decay. The entire hallway seemed surreal, like walking through a video game or a horror movie, but unfortunately, something real lurked in the dark, waiting for them.

Each time they encountered a doorway, Chance swung out, shotgun at the ready, while she angled the light around the corner and held her breath. When nothing happened, they collectively released a sigh of relief before pushing forward to the next vacant office. Several rooms contained rusting desks bolted to the floor and moth-eaten chairs, random clumps of thirty-year-old furniture as abandoned as the building itself.

Further down the hall stood a solid metal door covered in rust and curling paint, the end of the visible road. When the continuous arcing motion brought the light back down, it glinted against something on the floor. She inched forward a little faster, following the glimmer, and stooped down. Her fingers brushed over dead leaves and debris until they touched something smooth and metallic. She quickly snatched the object, angling the light to identify it, and her eyes widened in shock.

A name badge. Her thumb rubbed over the engraved letters as if it would magically change the inscription. *Humphrey.* Wait. That meant…

A shot pierced the ominous silence behind her, and she instinctually jumped back against the wall. Blood roared in her ears as she whipped her 9-millemeter around with the flashlight. Chance's chiseled face appeared genuinely confused. Was she hearing things? Terrified, panicked, yes, but delusional?

As his eyes slowly looked down with the same confounded expression, the seconds stretched out in slow motion. She followed his line of sight and frowned, unable to make sense of the wet spot on his black T-shirt. Was the ceiling leaking? It wasn't raining outside.

Then, his shotgun clattered to the floor, a sound she somehow knew would haunt her for the rest of her life. The spell of denial snapped as he grabbed at his chest, eyes meeting hers with shock and utter despair.

"No, no, no, no, no!" Her voice trembled as all the oxygen left her lungs. She scurried over as Chance sank to his knees and fell forward on all fours, coughing. Blood splattered across the floor, a gut-wrenching noise that shattered her heart. *This can't be happening!*

When she reached him, she cradled his face in her hands, trying to see past the flood of tears in her eyes. "No, god, Chance. Please! You have to stay with me!" Blood trailed down his lips as he tried to focus on her. He began saying something but gurgled and coughed, more blood bubbling from his mouth. Tears rolled down her cheeks as she dropped everything in a frantic attempt to help him lie down.

The wet spot bubbled and sank with each labored breath—a punctured lung. If she didn't stop the bleeding, he'd drown in his blood. God, there was so much, so much blood.

Her hands scrambled to put pressure over the sucking wound in his chest, but the blood seeped through her fingers at an alarming rate. *No! Not like this!*

The click of a gun cocking rang through her bones. She froze and looked up at Officer Humphrey, aiming his pistol as her heart went into overdrive, pounding furiously in her chest.

"He said he was an unnecessary threat. He serves no purpose. You, on the other hand, he wants alive." His voice held no trace of his usual Southern drawl. It was calm, emotionless, dead inside.

Chapter 22

Lilith scrambled for the gun, but it slipped through her blood-drenched fingers. As she reached again, Humphrey snatched her by the hair, pulling back hard enough to make her scream. Chance's eyes widened, but when he tried to move, violent coughs racked his body as more blood gurgled from his mouth.

Desperately, she reached up and clawed at the man's hand while her feet slipped and skidded in blood, Chance's blood. Her nails dug bloody furrows into his arm, but to no avail. Without a hiss of pain, he flung her against the wall and shoved his pistol against her head.

"Stop resisting. I don't want to hurt you, but I will." The cold detachment in his voice made him a million times more dangerous than Spencer. No buttons to press, no way to goad him into making mistakes. The hopelessness of her situation sent rage and desperation searing up her spine.

"What the fuck are you doing?" Blinded by tears, she slapped his gun away and flung out her fists, landing a shot to his thigh that made him stumble backward. She immediately propelled herself off the wall, charged past Humphrey, and skidded across the floor toward Chance.

Her fingers brushed over her gun, but before she could grip it, Humphrey grabbed her by the hair, yanked her up, and slammed her into the wall again. While her bones rattled, his arm pressed against her throat, making her choke as he pinned her in place.

"He's going to die! Please let me help him!" she pleaded in utter desperation, willing him to take pity. Although she wanted to empty every single clip into him for what he did, she was physically powerless in her current position.

"Ashcroft wanted him out of the way." He jerked his arm forward, and she gasped as her vision blurred. "Now settle the fuck down."

"He's out of the way. He doesn't need to die! Please, let me stop the bleeding." Her voice croaked out through her compressed windpipe.

"You won't care for long. He's expecting you." Panic seared through her body, not because of what Ashcroft would do to her, but because she couldn't let Chance die, not without her giving him a shot at survival.

With blazing clarity, she remembered the parking lot, when she took Chance's hand for strength, and he became dizzy. Cohen stated that drawing too much of a person's energy would cause serious harm.

With determined focus, she wrapped her fingers around Humphrey's arm, closed her eyes, and concentrated. Religious types might have called it prayer, but in her mind, she screamed her distraught plea to the universe. A surge shot up her arm, lighting up every nerve ending. She watched as his scowl faltered, turning into a confused expression.

The weakness in his eyes fueled her fire. Anger and hatred consumed everything else. She wanted him to suffer. Her nails bit into his skin as she concentrated on ripping away every stitch of energy he owned.

His color faded to a sickly pallor, the pressure on her throat lessened, and when he stumbled, she utilized the wall to push off and knock him to the ground. As he fell, she pinched her nails harder, drawing blood before letting go.

She immediately jumped on his chest, pinning him, and hammered her fist into his face. The first shot knocked him out cold, but she kept punching. She dissolved into seething fury and tears, releasing all her pent-up resentment, screaming with every connecting hit. Her knuckles burned, but the abrasions healed as soon as they occurred. For once, she exuded strength beyond the ability to survive. She overcame her enemy. No one would make her their punching bag again.

A gurgled scream from behind stopped her midmotion. "Lily!" Chance's voice cut through the red haze. When she glanced down at Humphrey's face, a mass of bloody bruises, she recoiled, horrified. Her hand fell limp at her side as she thought about Miriah's face after enduring Spencer's handiwork.

What am I doing? Chance...he's the reason I fought to get away from Humphrey.

With a sickening sensation in her stomach, she hurried away from the unconscious officer. When she reached Chance, his eyes rolled aimlessly, unable to focus, and the gurgling cough became more violent. By screaming, he only made his situation worse. God, he was so pale.

Blood barely trickled out of the bullet hole. He lost too much blood while she beat Humphrey senseless, and now, he was going to die. Her throat tightened with tears, and she pulled him closer as she sobbed. *No. Not like this. Not now.* She *needed* him to live.

Then a thought occurred to her from either a moment of clarity or sheer desperation. Cohen's blood saved her life at the last possible second. Perhaps enough of those healing agents remained in her bloodstream to help Chance. An unfamiliar pang seared the roof of her mouth as her fangs clicked down as soon as she thought about them. Without any hesitation, she bit deep into her wrist to ensure the gash didn't close right away. Then, she held the wound over his mouth and shook him.

"Drink, Chance. Please, please, please. I need you. You can't die on me. Please!" His unfocused eyes closed, but the muscles in his throat moved.

"That's it. Drink." She smoothed her hand through his auburn flecked hair in soothing strokes as tears trickled down her cheeks. This *had* to work.

When he started coughing, a sign of possible aspiration, she pulled him into her lap, allowing gravity to help the fluid go down the right tube.

After several minutes, the sucking sensation stopped, and she tore the gash open again. She had no idea how much he needed, but she'd donate every drop if that's what it took.

This time, when she pressed the wound to his mouth, his lips closed around it, which she took as an encouraging sign.

With her free hand, she pulled his shirt up to see the bullet hole. His typically tan skin looked incredibly pale between the patches of smeared blood. The puffy angry exit wound in the upper right side no longer bled. Hopefully, a sign the wound started healing and not an indication of severe blood loss.

As soon as the thought crossed her mind, his lips stopped moving. *No!* Sudden panic stole her breath as she studied his face. Eyes closed. Mouth open but unmoving.

"Chance?" The tenuous word hung in the air while her lungs burned as if about to implode. "Chance, stay with me!"

She shook him, but his eyes didn't open, and he wasn't moving. *"Chance!"* She erupted in tears again and shook him harder. "You can't leave. I love you. I need you here. I can't lose you. Not now. Not like this." She buried her face against his neck, dissolving into gut-wrenching sobs. Why couldn't she just wake up from this nightmare?

A tickle of warmth touched her hair. *A breath?* She froze for an instant, paralyzed, afraid to believe but fiercely wanting to. Again. She slid her trembling hand onto his torso, shut her eyelids, and waited. A faint heartbeat vibrated beneath her hand as his chest expanded with shallow breaths. A spark of hope lit her from inside. He was alive!

She stayed perfectly still as if moving would disrupt the delicate equilibrium. She simply counted each glorious beat of his heart. She sobbed with joy and whispered a silent thank-you to whatever corner of the universe listened to her plea.

For a long time, she stayed hunched over with her palm on his chest, silently counting breaths and heartbeats as they grew stronger. Although he was still unconscious, knowing life flowed in his veins eased her panicked mind.

In those crucial moments, she didn't think about the creepy hallway lit only by a flashlight pointing at the wall or Humphrey's unconscious, possibly dead, body lying a few feet away. Not even her concerns about Gregor, Alvarez, or Ashcroft infiltrated her thoughts.

Her entire universe consisted of *one, two, three, breathe, one, two, three, breathe.*

"Lily?" His weakened voice hovered in the air so faint that she almost thought she imagined it. *"Cherie..."* This time, she knew it was real.

She quickly pulled back as pure joy lit every inch. His voice was the sweetest sound she could ever remember hearing.

When she peered down at his face, the joy faded a touch. His color improved but still appeared starkly pale with dark circles beneath his hazel eyes, which roamed wildly in confusion.

"Chance? I... I was so scared I lost you." All her emotions clogged in her throat as she wiped at her cheeks and tried to breathe.

"You can't get...rid of me that easy." His soft lips stretched into a tenuous grin. She half laughed, half cried, and bent down to kiss his fragile grin.

He squeezed his eyes shut for a second, his chiseled face drawn in pain, and released a small breath. "I hurt like a son of a bitch...but I think I'll...live." He still struggled with his breathing, the left side rising higher than the right, indicating his lung remained collapsed. "Can you help...me sit up?"

With a determined nod, she wiped the rest of the tears from her face. Gently, she slipped out from under him, lowering him carefully to the floor. Once she hooked her arms around him and locked her wrists, she slowly worked up and back until he rested against the wall. The winces of pain continued, but his color kept improving, and his eyes could finally focus.

She crouched in front of him, studying his slightly stubbled face, memorizing every line. She came so close to never seeing him again. The very thought made her chest tight. Her hand slid through his chestnut brown hair before tenderly cupping his cheek. With a soft sigh, he closed his eyes and leaned into her palm. She nearly lost him. He almost died. The thought kept repeating in her brain in an endless terrifying loop.

"I'm still mixed up. What happened?"

"Humphrey...he shot you."

"Humphrey?" Chance frowned, perplexed. "Why?"

"Ashcroft got to him. I found his name badge on the ground, and then I heard the shot. When I turned around, he stood behind you with a smoking gun. He said Ashcroft wanted you out of the way. You weren't...useful." She hated saying the words even if they didn't belong to her.

"Where is he?"

A cornucopia of fear, anger, guilt, and resentment washed over her, and she glanced down the hall at the man she brutalized and then left lying on the floor.

Chance followed her eyes in confusion. "Is he..."

"Dead? I don't know."

"Well, do me a favor...check him. If he's unconscious, we need to find a way to secure him."

The heavy guilt pressing on her shoulders kept her from meeting his eyes. She focused on his chest and simply nodded. After Spencer, she was quick to lecture him, confident she could never be capable of such violence. However, when her moment came, she acted like an insane animal, unleashing all her pent-up emotions on a man's face. She suddenly understood how her father could lose control.

While lost in her dismal thoughts, Chance crooked a finger under her chin and tilted her head up, gently forcing her to look him in the eye. Although tiny lines of pain lingered on his face, his lips curled into an encouraging smile.

"I'm going to be okay. Whatever you did is working." When his words didn't melt her hesitation, he glanced down the hall, and everything clicked into place. His palm caressed her cheek as he studied her haunted olive eyes. "You did what you had to."

She squeezed her eyes shut and pulled away. "No. I lost control."

"Lily." His hand slipped around the back of her neck and brought her closer. "*Look* at me." Reluctantly, she opened her eyes to witness his face set in stern determination. "Don't overanalyze yourself based on one situation with overwhelming circumstances. You are okay. I'm going to live. Now let's make sure everyone else gets to as well, Gregor, Alvarez, and Duncan, especially. Okay?"

As always, he was right. She couldn't dissolve into a puddle of self-hatred. Chance wasn't the only person counting on her. "Okay."

"Now, go check for a pulse."

She nodded obediently and crawled to Humphrey. Standing and walking seemed wrong for some reason. She couldn't tell if the hits broke anything between the swelling and the bruising covering his face. The puffy skin made it difficult to be sure. Blood trickled from the corner of his mouth and his nostrils. Fresh guilt washed over her until she remembered the bastard almost killed Chance. He shot him in the back like a coward.

Hesitantly, she pressed her fingers to the carotid artery while keeping her eyes on his face, waiting for any sign of consciousness. A feeble pulsation met her fingertips, and a sigh of relief rushed past her lips, comforted by the fact that she *didn't* pummel a man to death with her bare hands.

Staring down at his mangled face, she wondered how Ashcroft swayed him. And more importantly, why? Why enlist the help of humans? Was this part of his sick game? If his pawn failed to eliminate the threat, then he'd force his enemies to kill a human cop. There didn't appear to be a downside for him.

She glanced over her shoulder to see Chance leaning his head against the wall, eyes closed. A moment of panic sent her heart racing until his face tightened in pain, and he opened his eyes again.

"He alive?"

She nodded absently, a million thoughts still racing through her head. "Do you remember how Cohen said he coerced his partner into doing certain things? He said it was minimal, but…"

He lifted his head and peered at her thoughtfully. "You think Ashcroft might have some type of mind control on top of everything else?" This time when he paled, she couldn't blame it on blood loss.

"Well, Cohen doesn't seem to have super speed or insane healing. If those skills are enhanced, perhaps his ability to coerce people is in hyperdrive too. The name badge I found indicated Humphrey entered the building before we arrived. If I'm right, Ashcroft turned him into cannon fodder."

She moved next to him with a sudden desire to be close, to feel his warmth, and let it chase the cold from her bones.

"Whitmore wouldn't let him go in alone. You need to call Cohen. He's in danger."

Damn. She didn't think that far ahead. She quickly fished her cell out and dialed the detective's number. The call went straight to voice mail. An all-too-familiar fear crawled up her spine, making her stomach flip-flop.

"This whole thing is fucked. If Whitmore got Cohen, then I'm the only one left. How the hell am *I* supposed to take down Ashcroft *alone*?"

When faced with a fact he was trying not to think about, dismay flashed in his eyes. "Leave, Lily. Ashcroft has everything he wants. Take the car, drive to the airport, and board the first plane out of here."

She craned her neck to stare at him in disbelief. "No. I'm not leaving you here. Not you, not Gregor, not Alvarez, not Cohen, and not Duncan. I'll find a way." She leaned her head against the wall and closed her eyes. "If I can surprise him—"

He moved and lightly gripped her face, turning her toward him, their faces inches apart. The motion had to be excruciating, but he gritted his teeth and held on with tears stinging his eyes. "This one time, please, listen. He will tear you to pieces, and I can't do anything to stop him. *Please*, don't be brave and stubborn, *just* this one time."

A single tear trickled down her cheek as she stared into his green-flecked eyes. In the past few days, he became part of her life, one worth fighting for with every last breath.

"I can't. I can't abandon you. Please, don't ask me to again. Would you run if the roles were reversed? No. I know you wouldn't. You'd fight until nothing remained. You mean too much to me. I need to set you up someplace safe before I go find Gregor and the others, though."

Although his jaw clenched in frustration, he didn't argue. He couldn't change her mind, and he knew it.

"Help me into one of the offices, and leave the shotgun with me, but you better promise to find me in one piece." He grabbed her hand, pleading with every fiber of his being for her to listen.

"If you find them and can't save them, get out alive. The last thing Gregor wants is for you to die trying to rescue him. If you discover the mission is impossible, you come back up here, grab me, and we'll run. We can take care of Ashcroft another day. I know you don't want to hear this, *cherie*, but you knew going in your dad may not survive. Getting yourself killed isn't an honor. It's a waste. Do you understand?"

Once again, he was right. His gift for voicing painful truths frustrated her, but he forced her to face the ugly things she wanted to avoid. While attempting to imagine a world without her father or her partner, she nodded bleakly.

"I need you to promise me and say the words." He gripped her hand a little tighter, his other still cupping her face while his stare pinned her in place insistently. "Promise me, Lily."

Before she could speak, she swallowed the lump of emotions stuck in her throat. "I promise." Relief washed over him, loosening the tension in his body. "Now, let's move you someplace safer. We're both sitting ducks out here."

It took three attempts before she got him on his feet. They quickly discovered keeping his right arm at his side, stabilized the bullet wound. So, he leaned heavily against her with his left arm draped across her shoulders. Shock and blood loss left him weak, but thankfully, he could support most of his weight.

Flashlight in hand, they staggered to the first door and slipped inside. Gingerly, she maneuvered him into the corner behind the door and helped him to the floor. Besides a few coughs, he didn't make much noise, and the wound didn't reopen, but the short trip left him exhausted and out of breath.

Once in place, she studied his heavy breathing and saw both sides of his chest expand equally—a bright spot of hope.

"I'll be right back. I'm going to move Humphrey and grab the shotgun."

"Be careful, Lily. He might wake up."

With a nod, she raced into the hall, leaving her apprehension behind. Humphrey lay still, exactly how she left him. After putting the flashlight in the crook of her neck and grabbing his wrists, she waited, watching for any sign of consciousness. When nothing happened, she started dragging him.

He turned out to be much heavier than he appeared. Perhaps the beer gut hid a full keg. Her muscles began to burn with each tug as time stretched into an eternity.

Finally, she managed to yank his body into a vacant office. She frantically searched the room for a way to lock him or restrain him but came up empty. Then, her eyes fell on the hulking desk dominating the space. More specifically, the hex bolts anchoring it to the floor.

She snatched the handcuffs from Humphrey's belt, slapped one side on his wrist and the other to the desk leg. Even if he woke up, he wasn't going anywhere now. After hurrying out and closing the door, she scooped up the shotgun and raced back to Chance.

She crouched down in front of him as he leaned against the wall again, eyes closed. Her fingers ran gently through his hair as she sighed wistfully. "We're gonna make it home." A soft smile pulled at the corners of his mouth. "After all, you owe me a date."

His smile widened as his eyes opened to meet hers. "Yes, *cherie*, I do. Speaking of which, was it a blood-loss-induced delusion, or did you say you loved me?"

Her cheeks burned brilliant crimson with embarrassment, which made denial a futile endeavor. "Yeah, um…well, I thought you were—"

"Dying?" An amused grin curled his lips as her panic set in.

"Yes, but please don't freak out. I know using those three little words so early is—"

He pressed a finger to her lips, stopping her short as his eyes met her gaze with a substantial weight. "It only took thirteen years and a bullet to the chest for you to catch up." He brushed an auburn curl from her face with his left hand. "Come back to me alive. I can't let the love of my life die on me before our first date."

Whether he meant it jokingly or not, her whole body blushed. She leaned in, and the kiss they shared exuded such intimate tenderness that it brought tears to both their eyes. "Stay safe."

"Text me when you find them. I'll feel better knowing where you are. Okay?"

"I will." With a deep breath, she pushed the shotgun into his hands, rushed out of the room, and closed the door. Then, she snatched her pistol from the floor, wiping the blood off to get a secure grip, and squared her shoulders—no time left for scared little rabbits. Kill or be killed.

She trained the light down the hall, focusing on the metal door at the end. Since all the others led to empty offices, the rusting hulk ahead, looming in the dark like the gate to hell, remained her only option. Each step closer tested her resolve, but she refused to back down.

Once she reached her target, she put her back to the wall, eased the heavy door open, and braced herself for a high-pitched screech that never came.

Thank the elusive higher power for small wonders. However, a larger miracle would be helpful. Smiting Ashcroft, for instance, would be an excellent place to start. The internal banter calmed her nerves as she stepped into a square room with doors on all sides.

Of course. More choices. With a frustrated huff, she carefully studied each one, looking for a clue, some indication of which way to go. When the thin light from the xenon bulb traveled over the door to her right, something caught her eye—a dark smudge on the handle. She crept closer, fixated on the spot. Blood. Not the most positive sign.

The ominous door led to a descending flight of stairs dimly lit by emergency floodlights. Odd they worked in the stairwell and not the main floor. Deciding to conserve battery power and take advantage of the current illumination, she clicked off the flashlight and sent Chance her location in a quick text.

The stairs seemed to lead to a basement of some sort, which only made sense. What villain would pass up a basement-level torture chamber? All stereotypes were rooted in a grain of truth, after all.

Once she wrapped her fingers securely around the gun in a two-handed grip, she crept downward with her back hugging the wall. Blood pounded loudly in her ears, expecting someone to jump out at her, but she steeled her nerves. No matter what lay ahead, she refused to slip into panic mode. Too much rested on her shoulders, so she bravely took one step at a time as silently as possible.

The switchback stairs ended at another metal door. Lilith pressed her ear to its surface, listening...nothing. Cautiously, she eased the door open, which thankfully stayed silent.

It seemed to be a utility tunnel with dozens of pipes lining the walls of rough cinder block. To her surprise, the stale air grew warmer, either emanating from the pipes or produced by a furnace or something similar.

Once she turned the corner and slowly shut the door, she glanced down the hall. A warm light glowed from the end. For a moment, she froze, vividly reminded of her nightmare, crawling through a tunnel to find a monster holding her father hostage. Silently, she prayed the correlations ended there. On the plus side, she wasn't naked this time.

As she inched closer, sounds began to emerge over the mechanical din—muffled voices, movement, whimpers of pain. The lack of screams brought her some small measure of comfort. Then again, if Ashcroft decided not to play with his toys, it meant he was waiting for her. He wanted her father to watch his ghastly handiwork, tormenting him as he did Duncan. She swallowed hard around the lump of fear stuck in her throat before pressing on.

The glow grew brighter as she moved, flickering in random patterns, which indicated an open flame. The old lanterns from her nightmare flashed through her mind. Between the increasing heat and the growing sense of doom, her palms became slick with sweat.

She paused, wiping her hands on the borrowed tracksuit while she focused on each breath. Rehashing her nightmare was pointless because it wasn't real. *Focus on the positive. Chance is safe, relatively speaking.*

After a deep calming inhale, she continued to creep down the hall. Her ears pricked at every sound, trying to decipher them and picture the scene. Voices circulated in the air, still incomprehensible but growing more distinct with each step.

As she approached the corner, shadows danced along the wall, cast by the bright light ahead. One figure paced around two hunched shapes, swaying back and forth like shock victims. She wouldn't be surprised if the simile turned out to be true.

Among the figures stood a deep shadow stretching from floor to ceiling. Probably a structural support or pillar of some kind. She studied the shadows' movements with her back flat to the wall and the gun pointed up, but they only told her so much. Eventually, she had to muster the courage to glance around the corner, but if he saw her, it would all be over in milliseconds.

A deep, steady breath traveled past her lips before she peeked her head into the room. Olive eyes scanned every inch as fast as possible, and then she snapped back to review everything she observed. A technique she learned about in college for hostage situations and hostile crime scenes.

Duncan sat huddled in the left corner with his knees against his chest. His red delirious eyes stared at his toes as if seeing them for the first time. Between Gregor's statements and Duncan's own writing, the man's grip on reality was tenuous *before* witnessing days of his daughter's torment. On top of everything else, the sickly pallor of his skin indicated Ashcroft was refusing to let him feed.

Very little doubt existed in her mind. Nothing sane remained, only a dangerous lunatic with no hope of reversing the damage. She shoved the painful thought from her mind and returned to her mental map.

Alvarez rested a few feet from Duncan. No blood, no signs of injuries. He simply hung his head in defeat. A cylindrical column did indeed dominate the center of the room with someone strapped to it. She couldn't be sure since the concrete blocked her view, but she assumed it was her father.

Ashcroft hovered over a tray of instruments on the right side of the room, drumming his fingers in glee. The expression reminded her of a demented child deciding which crayon to use first.

Then, the shadow on the wall moved again, snapping her out of the mental picture. A figure, which had to be Ashcroft, paced the floor in anxious circles. He waited six hundred years for everything to align, but he needed one last thing—*her*.

"My, my, my. We have a guest." When the monster spoke, dread seized her heart, and her stomach churned. She was so careful. How could he know she was here? Although, since the man possessed the ability to dodge a bullet, what made her think she could sneak up on him? *Damn*.

Chills ran down her spine as she peeked around the corner again. Ashcroft stood over Alvarez while facing the opposite side of the room. In one swift motion, he bent down and snatched her partner by the hair, pulling a sharp squeak of pain from him. A solitary tear slid down her cheek, but she didn't utter a sound, didn't move, didn't even breathe.

"Come out, or I'll slice through the Spaniard's windpipe and sever his spine." A deadly cold tone infiltrated his voice as a long knife glinted against Alvarez's throat.

If she revealed herself now, they'd all die. Sacrificing herself wouldn't save him. Surrendering meant embracing unimaginable pain at the hands of a madman until he tossed their used carcasses on the floor as his son did with Mary six centuries ago. Still, she couldn't watch him die. *Fuck*. He knew every weakness to exploit. He held all the cards, and he intended to play every one of them.

Chapter 23

The sound of shuffling footsteps distracted Lilith from her internal battle. They appeared to emanate from the opposite side, beyond the pipes and spigots. They echoed with a hollow quality, indicating another tunnel or hallway lay on the other side of the room.

She immediately thought of Chance, but with his injuries, she doubted he could hobble around yet. Besides, if he did follow her, he wouldn't go all the way around the building to do so.

Cohen's short blond hair and almost handsome face emerged from the darkness. A massive welt surrounded his right eye, slowly turning into a hideous bruise covering half his face. He limped along, favoring his left leg while cradling his right wrist. The lack of visible blood meant they weren't bullet wounds. If the damage resulted from a fistfight, then the other guy had huge fists…

Before she finished her thought, Ashcroft's shrill voice boomed with childlike joy. "Ah! My fellow demon!" In an instinctual desire to make herself as invisible as possible, she crouched against the corner and watched.

Ashcroft dropped Alvarez like a sack of potatoes and stepped over him, outstretching his arms as if greeting an old friend. For a moment, she studied her partner, but he didn't move, and his eyes were closed. Hopefully, he was unconscious and not dead.

"My, my, you look a bit rough." Ashcroft's thin head tilted to one side, while a finger curled over his pointed chin. The abomination stood and studied Cohen like a socialite contemplating modern art. "No matter. You'll heal very soon. Now, where is your partner, little demon?"

The squat aging detective strode into view, keeping his shotgun trained on Cohen while rubbing the back of his neck. A jumble of confusion, anger, and pain lingered in his face.

"Fuckin' prick hit me in the back of the head, but I could have handled him on my own. You didn't have to send your damn ape." His face wrinkled in disgust as he shoved the barrel into Cohen's back, making him stumble forward. Cohen whimpered in agony as his leg folded, sending him down hard on the concrete floor.

"Your bigotry will be your downfall. You ignore the value in a tool simply because of its color." Ashcroft sighed heavily at the tedious predictability of the detective's comments.

"Yeah. Okay." Whitmore rolled his eyes and shouldered his gun. "Whatever you say. My partner is here, as you requested. The bitch forensic investigator and her fiancé bodyguard are here, too, but Cohen insisted we all split up. They went with Humphrey..."

Ashcroft's head snapped up, and his words lost all their tedious grandeur. "They are to be wed?" The shrill tone jumped a few octaves into maniacal glee. For some reason, their *engagement* seemed vitally important to him, but why?

Whitmore blinked, perplexed by the sudden and excessive reaction. "You mean, married? Uh, yeah. That's what they said."

Before the madman could respond. "Ashcroft's ape" marched out of the shadows, and her heart sank even further. The odds were already against her, but this? How could things get any worse?

Security Officer Richard Coffee loomed over the rest of them, stooping to fit through the doorway. Rays of light from the scattered lanterns glinted off his ebony skin like warm moonlight on a black lake. Apparently, Ashcroft decided to upgrade when replacing Spencer. Cohen's injuries suddenly made sense. One massive fist supplies the beating, not an entire gang of flunkies.

"Ah. Sir Richard Coffee. Perfect timing. Go upstairs and search the building. I want Lilith and her beloved brought to me now. He is no longer a useless threat. In fact, he will be quite...valuable, as it turns out." His frenzied elation set her teeth on edge as the panic set in again, sending her heart racing. Her hands tightened around the gun while she tried to decide on a course of action.

The dark mountain of a man nodded, turned, and stalked back down the corridor behind him.

Shit. He is going to find Chance! Indecisiveness froze her muscles as logic and emotion went to war in her head.

Her first instinct was to run upstairs and stop him, but Coffee wouldn't kill him because Ashcroft wanted him alive. Besides, how exactly could she stop the giant?

Okay, think! A quick text would allow Chance to prepare or hide, but from her vantage point in the deep shadows, the light from her screen would stand out like a beacon. No. Either Chance would disable Coffee, or he'd join them in the basement of horrors.

"You're sending the steroid-infused monkey to do more dirty work? Whatever. You can order your jigaboo around how you damn well please. Just give me what you promised, and I'll go." Whitmore rubbed at the back of his neck again, moving his head side to side and wincing with the strain.

One second, Ashcroft stood in the center of the room, and the next, he hovered over the balding detective. "You think I would give you anything? You're nothing but an ignorant, insignificant little bug that's outlasted his usefulness."

After a disorienting blur of motion, Whitmore's knees hit the ground. When Ashcroft stepped aside, she witnessed blood pouring down the detective's shirt and tie. He clutched his neck, eyes widening in shock as he frantically tried to breathe. The choking, gurgling gasps echoed eerily around the room.

Cohen struggled to his feet, reaching for his partner. The man was an extreme bigot and an asshole, but he didn't deserve to die. However, Cohen's futile attempt to help only earned him a swift kick that sent him sliding to the floor.

"Don't be greedy. You'll eat soon enough, but I don't want you healing just yet." Ashcroft lorded over him like a teacher lecturing a troublesome student. "Your injuries aren't life-threatening, and I don't think you share my vision…yet." He bent down and studied him, the ghastly face crisscrossed with scars mere inches from Cohen.

"You still want to help them? You mourn the idiotic human, and you choose monsters who wish to drain you dry over your own kind? Is your entire family this foolishly sentimental, or only you?"

Every muscle in Cohen's body tensed with an old hatred that had nothing to do with the current circumstances. Ashcroft struck a nerve.

Cohen flung his uninjured hand at the demon's grisly smile with every ounce of strength, but Ashcroft caught his wrist in midair.

"Petulant child. You don't fully appreciate your gifts. You will learn. I've waited a long time to meet another of my kind. When I finish these bloodsuckers, I'll use what's left to reveal your *true* potential. Then you will understand how insignificant all of this is."

"What? Why?" The detective turned ghostly white with the realization that Ashcroft wanted him here for a reason. He intended to turn him, make him into the same type of abomination, mold him into a dedicated student. That mortified reaction relieved her. All the supernatural abilities Ashcroft gained would tempt most people.

When Ashcroft Orrick stood up straight, she finally noticed his clothing. Medical scrubs. His talon-like fingernails, scarred face, and deep black eyes distracted her. Odd. The sinister grace of his movements didn't match the stiff green scrubs that hung loosely off his bony frame.

Grabbing them from Goditha made sense. Not only did he desperately need a costume change after their run-in at the lab, but also, his new threads helped him blend into the crowd at the hotel fire. Hell, she might have seen him from a distance and dismissed him as a medical worker.

"I owe you a favor, and this is how I choose to repay you."

Cohen scooted back against the wall, still cradling his wrist. The movement drew Duncan's attention, and he eyed him with an eerie hunger. The chains kept the detective out of reach, but that didn't stop Duncan from scooting as close as possible, drool dripping from his thin, chapped lips. Cohen glanced at the delirious vampire and returned his focus to the real monster in the room with an expression of pure disgust.

"I haven't done you any damn favors. You're delusional!"

Ashcroft's laugh exuded as much villainy as his gaunt face. "My dear boy, but you *have*!" His profile revealed a nefarious smile, crooked teeth glinting in the lamplight. If he turned his back on her completely, she could sneak up and untie Gregor. Her father was only a few feet from her, at least thirty from where Ashcroft currently stood. With the possibility of his peripheral vision detecting her, she didn't dare try it yet. She needed him distracted.

"My minion lacked the finesse I required of him. He nearly killed my most coveted toy. I know you saved her. I smelled you in her blood. Of course…" His eyes narrowed, and his mouth closed in a firm line. "You didn't fully comprehend the consequences of such an action, but you are young, and it couldn't be helped, I'm sure."

"What consequences?" Her father's voice startled her, and Ashcroft had a similar reaction. As he started to turn, she quickly pulled back behind the corner to avoid his direct line of sight. Although, if he came much closer, he'd hear her heart beating like a damn drum.

"Answer me, you monster!"

"And why should I tell you?" Ashcroft spat the words with such venom she could taste it, like bile lingering on the back of her tongue.

"You consider yourself a noble vindicator, but you're a filthy gutter rat who slaughtered my family, defenseless women, and children. You dare call me a monster? After you tortured me for days? Carving names into my flesh, destroying my face all in the name of supposed justice! Then, when your malicious fun came close to an end, you tried to make me like you to continue mutilating me!"

"You aren't innocent! You slaughtered my family like livestock."

"Do not *speak*! I want you to have your tongue when I cut the eyes from your daughter's skull, but I will rip it out by the root if you speak again!" His words reached a fevered pitch that boomed through the room and down the corridor.

Lilith pulled her knees to her chest with fresh tears as Miriah's face, the product of Ashcroft's handiwork, flashed through her mind. Squeezing her eyes shut didn't help. The disfigured face bobbed back and forth, the sliced ribbons of her ears flopping with a wet slapping sound. Bile rose in her throat, and she struggled to keep her delicate stomach from giving away her position.

Silence settled over the room, and she tried to stay quiet. Logic and her promise told her to sprint upstairs, grab Chance, and run, but her heart yelled something else entirely. Still, all the bravery and courage in the world meant nothing if she didn't think up a plan fast. Leaning her head back against the wall, she attempted to recreate the room in her head. There had to be something she could use.

Twelve barrels sat on the left side, and he positioned the lanterns along the opposite wall near a massive furnace. If the barrels contained something flammable…everyone would die. A great self-destruct plan, but overkill for a distraction. *Fuck.*

Her hands gripped the gun tighter in frustration as her legs started to quiver from staying crouched too long. If she didn't stretch, she wouldn't be able to take advantage when an opportunity arose. Slowly, she straightened, standing tall as pins and needles crept through her legs, but she ignored them. Instead, she focused all her energy on listening for movement.

"His actions don't make *you* any less of a monster." Alvarez's familiar voice made her smile, and she peeked past the corner enough to see.

Ashcroft turned his back on Gregor and hovered over her partner. "Hold your tongue, Spanish mongrel. You know nothing. You blindly defend your master." The monster was losing his cool composure, unwilling to allow anyone to portray her father as a victim.

If Alvarez could hold his attention long enough, she could free Gregor. Of course, goading the psycho could also get her partner killed.

Ashcroft turned away, and for a brief second, Alvarez stared right at her in an intense moment of understanding. He planned to give her the distraction she needed.

"You're nothing but a bitter man losing his sanity. You use the death of your family as an excuse to exercise your sick fantasies. That doesn't make you righteous, just psychotic." The nearly unrecognizable voice lacked a single inflection of her partner's usual Spanish accent. The flat, bored tone reminded her of a psychologist doling out a predictable and uninspired diagnosis.

When Ashcroft turned his back on her again, she took a moment to inspect the room in greater detail. A roughed-up "Flammable" sticker stood out on the side of a barrel, confirming her assumption. Was that Ashcroft's endgame? Torture and kill them, then burn down any trace—no contradictory evidence to demolish whatever story he chose to tell the FBI.

"Psychotic?" Ashcroft stepped forward, moving further away from her and closer to Alvarez. *Now or never.*

With a determined grimace, she stooped down and inched around the corner.

"The fiend you call master instigated this madness and is guilty of the same crimes. Yet, you slander *my* name?"

She ignored the rest of the conversation as her world narrowed to Ashcroft's back, studying every shift in his posture. The tension of each controlled footstep made her body tremble. As she pushed through the paralyzing fear, she kept her breaths even and shallow, making her way closer to Gregor.

A movement to the left caught her attention, and her eyes flickered over to the source. Cohen spotted her and held her gaze with significant weight while straightening his injured wrist. He was healing. Now that she looked closer, the welts and bruises covering his face appeared lighter. With a quick nod and a finger pressed to her lips, she swung her eyes back to the real threat.

Alvarez and Ashcroft still argued back and forth, but she didn't care about the words if the monster kept his back turned. When she finally reached her destination, she glanced at the room one last time before she examined the ropes binding Gregor. The knots didn't appear complicated, fortunate since she didn't have a knife.

After tucking the gun into her pocket, she bent down and got to work. She stopped several times, clenching her fists to control the shaking. Thankfully, Ashcroft's anger distracted him from sensing the fear rolling off her in waves or the blood roaring in her ears. At any second, he could turn around, and the column wouldn't completely hide her.

A thrill of excitement warmed her stomach when the first knot came free, and she slowly lowered it to the ground before moving on to the next. She glanced up in time to watch him backhand Alvarez. The slap rocked his head to the side, a warning shot. She had no doubt the villain could knock a man's head clean off his shoulders. For now, he seemed content to loom over him, running his bony hand over Alvarez's balding head, crowing with malicious glee.

The second knot came free in her hands. Once she set down the rope, she tackled the one at his waist. An edge of panic began to taint her excitement. Soon, Ashcroft would grow bored. If he saw her, she'd be subject to his mercy, and he had none. *Focus. No worst-case scenarios. Focus.*

As Alvarez began screaming, his words reverting to Spanish, she peered up, but nothing changed. She still had time.

Another knot fell apart in her hands, freeing Gregor's waist and wrists. *Only two more to go.* Rising hope mingled with the mounting panic. Little by little, she stood, pins and needles shooting down her legs again. They weren't accustomed to the abuse. *I need to work out more.*

Lilith put all her energy into attacking the restraint across his chest. *Come on, come on, come on.* Her sweaty hands kept sliding around the rigid rope. The frustration and trepidation causing her body to shake only made things worse. *Only two more knots. Come on. Get it together.*

When she finally untied the knot, she nearly laughed in pure joy. *Only one more.* She lowered it to the pile at Gregor's feet and grabbed the last obstacle with fierce determination. *One more. Just one more.*

"You're an utter disgrace to our kind!" Cohen's voice sounded hysterical, which surprised her. Why draw attention to himself? "Plenty of acceptable ways exist to get what you need. Instead, you leave a path of misery and destruction in your wake. Your son was a sadistic psychopath, and so are you!"

She glanced up while she worked. Ashcroft stood in the same position, blocking Alvarez from view, but he stared down Cohen, which put her in his periphery. *Damn.* She froze, hoping the column hid her enough to avoid detection. She silently observed, holding her breath, as Ashcroft turned and stepped toward Cohen. Then, her world fell away.

She bit her lip, drawing blood, to keep the scream from leaving her throat. Through the tears flooding her eyes, she witnessed blood pouring down the front of her partner's shirt, his balding head slumped at an unnatural angle. Time slowed as he collapsed, his face colliding with the cold concrete.

Her heart stopped still in her chest as she stared into the lifeless eyes of her mentor. The one who trained her, the one she worked beside for nearly ten years, her best friend. Gloria would never see her husband again, never kiss him goodbye. The girls would never hug their father again or hear his hearty laugh. They would never forgive her.

The remaining pieces of her world shattered as she pressed her forehead to the cold cement. It was all her fault. If she listened to her father, if she flew home when he asked, Felipe would still be alive and well in New York City.

"A pathetic argument. Humans are capable of surviving on plants, yet they choose to slaughter animals for food. I am no different. Can you honestly tell me you never tasted something darker, my dear detective? It's delicious. The screams, the quivering muscles, the way the pale skin blushes around the blade as it slices in, that virgin drop of blood that blossoms… It's intoxicating."

In the beginning, he sounded like a schoolteacher lecturing an idealistic student, but his tone quickly dissolved into a serial-killer version of dirty talk. The sinister sigh of desire made her stomach churn. A desperate need to get out of the room overcame her. She needed to get away from the soulless abomination who slaughtered her partner. *Get it together.*

She couldn't let Felipe's sacrifice be meaningless. If she broke down in tears, wallowing in her grief, and got caught, game over.

"Did you resort to torture because seduction wasn't a viable option? I mean, even barmaids and peasants have standards." The snide comment brought a smile to her face, which quickly faded. Ashcroft's growing bubble of anger gathered strength like an electrical storm. It was vast and ominous, making the air taste sour. She had to move fast.

One more knot. She hid as much as possible and zealously attacked the final restraint.

"You know nothing of true power!" The barely discernible words closely resembled the snarling roar of a beast. *Focus. One more knot.*

"Do you think flirting with some imbecile girl can compare to the power gained by careful, controlled torment?" The fevered timbre of his voice began to fade. His slight frame straightened, and when he spoke again, his depraved composure returned.

"You never truly know a person and delve into their deepest energies until they are at the mercy of your knife! The unfortunate gift the vampire bestowed on me only made it sweeter. Blood saturated in fear, pain, terror, and hatred is far more potent. Imagine not only drawing on their energy but draining every drop of their physical life force, devouring their very soul." The wistful words reminded her of a young man describing the love of his life. Although his rhetoric sickened her, what if it was true?

Could that explain his speed, strength, and healing, abilities so drastically advanced than those in either species? If he literally drank every bit of blood and emotion from his victims, perhaps he was eating their souls, if such a thing existed. He didn't torture people purely because he enjoyed it. He did so with clear, calm purpose, as insane and atrocious as that purpose may be.

"You're an abomination." Cohen's soft, breathy tone held no confidence. As if he was trying to convince himself, not Ashcroft. *God, no.*

With him as an ally, they had a small chance of survival, but if he switched sides, the path of disaster wouldn't end in this room. She had no illusions about Ashcroft shedding his monster skin and retiring from his sordid, bloody life once they died. He would continue killing, and with Cohen at his side, the entire world would cower to their vicious reign of terror.

As her mind reeled with horrific possibilities, the rope slid through her fingers. Several seconds passed before she realized her father was free. When it hit home, her entire body sang with jumbled nerves, and she lowered the last rope to the ground.

Ashcroft stood in front of Cohen, his back to the room, intent on swaying him. Her father took advantage of the distraction, glancing over his shoulder and meeting her eyes. After jerking her head toward the corner, she watched the soul eater while Gregor inched toward freedom.

Once he reached the hallway, she released a silent breath of relief and finally got a good look at his face. Under the dirt and sweat, he didn't appear injured. At least she kept *him* alive and in one piece so far. Perhaps Alvarez would still be alive if she moved faster or had a useful weapon like her UV flashlight. Ashcroft didn't seem too fond of it in Duncan's basement.

Gregor glanced out at the room, stepped back, and frantically motioned to her. When she double-checked, Ashcroft continued to use his silver tongue on Cohen, who still seemed to be resisting.

She wondered if the mind control only worked on humans or if he simply refused to use it, depending on persuasion to win his case. In the end, the result mattered more than the method.

One delicate step after another, she backed away but kept her eyes on the demons. When she finally reached the corridor, she glanced back, looking for Gregor, but he was gone. Anger bubbled inside her veins. Did she save him only to have him abandon her? The whole point was to gain an ally who could help her save the others. Instead, the coward ran.

Now she was alone again. One woman with a pistol and a flashlight versus a soul-eating uber vampire-demon. With an overwhelming sense of futility, she leaned her head against the wall, closed her eyes, and silently breathed the word *fuck* repeatedly. *I promised Chance.*

A hand touched her shoulder, and she just barely stifled the yelp of surprise in her throat. Gregor shook his head and mouthed the words "Trust me" before pointing down the hall. The two of them crept down the long corridor and swung open the door to the stairs. Once inside, he collapsed with his face in his hands.

"I am so sorry, Lily." The tears in his voice made her eyes water. If only she could go back in time and see her father through rose-colored glasses. Things would never be the same.

Moments ago, she wrote him off as a coward. Even if they survived this mess, the wide-eyed blind trust was gone forever. She would always question his motives, wonder what he was hiding. The person she used to be died the moment Gregor shattered her reality with the ghosts of his past. She mourned that loss as much as she mourned Ashcroft's victims.

With a reluctant sigh, she crouched down, ignoring the screaming pains in her legs, and put a hand on his knee.

"Dad, I know. I know you didn't think any of this would happen, but it has. You can't fall apart right now. People depend on us. We need to end this here and now. If we run, you know that he will track us down again, and he can influence an entire army on the way. You know what he did to Whitmore and Humphrey."

"And Coffee," Gregor added.

She grabbed his hand and waited for him to meet her eyes. "We have to finish this. The odds suck, but it's our only chance."

"Wait." Gregor's eyes widened as if something only now occurred to him. "Where is Chance? Why isn't he with you?"

When she hesitated, he jumped to the logical conclusion. "Humphrey killed him?"

"No. I mean, almost. I managed to save him, but he's injured. I set him up in an office with a shotgun, but you heard Ashcroft. Coffee will find him. It's only a matter of time. We need to end this before that happens. I can't let him die, Dad." The mere possibility brought fresh tears to her eyes.

"Lilith." He sat up straighter, a determined set to his jaw. "Go. Find Chance and run. I'll try to rescue Cohen. This is *my* fight, not yours." It wasn't a hollow gesture to appear noble. Every single word rang true. No matter what sins he committed, he was still her father. He was willing to lay down his life to keep her safe because he loved her more than anything, even himself. That had to count for something.

The last thing she wanted to do was walk through that door again. She could take Gregor's offer, grab Chance, and leave. But then what? Live in the same dark self-loathing as her father until the monster found them and sliced them up anyway?

"Bullshit! This is as much my fight as it is yours. Because of Ashcroft, I've almost died three times, a cop shot Chance in the chest, and my partner is dead. He slit his throat without a care in the world. He needs to pay, and I want to be there when he does. This is *our* fight now."

Instead of arguing, he simply nodded. "I never wanted any of this." The agonized sigh, coupled with his demolished expression, told her the monster already won. She could see the shame, regret, and soul-crushing guilt suffocating his tormented soul.

"I know." She threw her arms around him and hugged him tightly, savoring the moment. "Dad." She pulled back and locked eyes with him. She needed to see the truth. "What about Duncan? Can he be saved?"

"He's my brother, and we've survived so much together." The downcast eyes, the subtle sigh, the tear rolling down his cheek all revealed the sad reality before he spoke.

"He's been slipping away for a while now. I knew it, but what could I do? And now…no recognition exists in his face, even for me. Seeing his daughter tortured and his son side with an abomination for approval stole his remaining shreds of humanity. He needs help but *not* to survive."

In her gut, she knew he was right. The past few days' events reduced her uncle to a ravenous animal devoid of any real cognizance. She angrily wiped the tears from her cheeks, realizing she'd cried more in one day than her entire life. So much hurt, so much pain, so much loss, and it wasn't over.

"Do you have any ideas on how we get out of this alive?"

An odd chuckle of despair escaped his lips as he combed a hand through his gray-flecked hair. "Not a single one."

Her tired legs groaned as she stood up and paced the tiny area. "I have my pistol, but that won't stop him…" A thought occurred to her, and although it made her stomach churn, she needed a logical approach.

After a deep breath to steel herself, she continued, "He's eliminated most of his *food* sources. He can't obtain what he needs from a dead body. If I catch him by surprise, away from Cohen and Duncan, and land a headshot...the barrels of flammable material could burn him, and without a source of energy, he won't survive."

A small spark of optimism lit up his sky gray eyes. "We better hurry. I'm surprised he hasn't realized I'm gone. He must be determined to sway Cohen to his cause."

"Yeah, well, let's hope he doesn't succeed." If he did, going back into the lion's den would be pointless.

They both nodded with a singular purpose. Time to take the monster down or go out fighting. She pulled the gun from her pocket, switched the safety off, and gripped the door handle. She never considered herself religious, but she needed all the help she could get, so she closed her eyes and sent another prayer into the universe. *Please, let this work.*

Sadly, the higher powers were fresh out of miracles. Before she could turn the handle, the door swung open, yanking her forward, bringing her face-to-face with Ashcroft's beady eyes.

"Coming to see me?" His thin lips stretched into a malicious grin, displaying all his crooked, rotting teeth. The overpowering scent of death enveloped him like a demonic shield.

Even with bile rising from her stomach, she managed to scream, "Dad! Run!"

The dry, leathery skin of his taloned hand closed around her throat, and he leaned closer, taking in a deep breath, smelling her. A sick groan of pleasure itched across her cheek, leaving a feeling of corruption in its wake.

"He can run. You are what I want. You are such a lovely little thing. I'll enjoy drinking you dry"—his narrow eyes took in every curve of her body with a slow, languid gaze of desire that she could never unsee—"once I finish playing with you, that is."

Chapter 24

Lilith's scream turned to a strangled croak as Ashcroft's grip tightened around her throat. With no other option, she squeezed the trigger and felt the gun recoil against his abdomen. The muffled shot produced a second of shock in his eyes, but they quickly hardened. Before she could squeeze off another round, he tore the gun away and threw it to the floor like a parent getting rid of an inappropriate toy.

"No!" Gregor's voice boomed behind her, and she closed her eyes, wishing he listened. If Gregor and Chance got away, it would make her death less tragic. But her father decided not to leave, and now she would die for nothing.

"This is between us. Enough innocents died at *both* our hands. Take me and let it be enough." His voice trembled under the weight of six hundred years' worth of blood, persecution, and self-condemnation.

In a blur of motion that left her dizzy, Ashcroft spun her around, using her as a human shield. His long nails dug into her skin, accompanied by the wet sting of blood welling up around them. She struggled to swallow her panic past his crushing grip and stayed perfectly still. One false move…

Ashcroft's laughter crackled through the air like a burgeoning thunderhead, ready to rain down misery. "Are you giving me an order, peasant? If I ripped out the throat of every single person who has ever set eyes on you, it would not be enough! Do not beg mercy of me, coward. *You* sent her here!"

His acrid breath washed over her skin as he leaned closer. "I should thank you for my present." The sinister desire in his voice brought a new wave of nausea. The thought of ending up like Miriah made her entire body shudder.

"I didn't know." He wasn't speaking to Ashcroft. Gregor stared into her eyes with tears streaming down his cheeks, his heart shattering, and she couldn't do anything to help him or herself. She was helpless. Or was she?

An odd calm settled over her shoulders as she focused everything on drawing his power away as she did with Humphrey. Tapping into his deep well of twisted energy made her feel dirty, contaminated. She wanted to stop, but this was her only shot, so she gritted her teeth and concentrated with all her might.

"Oh, you knew. Perhaps you didn't want to admit my existence, but you knew when I slit the throat of your pretty little wife in Central Park. These are the consequences of your actions…" His venomous voice trailed off.

The sharp growl in her ear made her lose the metaphorical grip on his vitality. "Creative little insect, aren't you? Not even Cohen's blood will save you." His slithering voice dripped with murderous exhilaration before he returned his attention to her father.

"I'll be back for you." His voice held a distinct promise, foreshadowing the grim things to come.

Everything blurred into a whirlwind of movement, leaving her dizzy and disorientated. When it stopped, she doubled over in dry heaves, bile burning up the back of her throat yet again. Despite squeezing her eyes shut, the room still spun. Staying upright took all her focus. As she finally caught her breath, Ashcroft snatched her neck again and slammed her into something hard and unforgiving with enough force to make her bones rattle. Fiery torment ran up her spine and exploded at the back of her head.

After losing consciousness for a few moments, her eyes fluttered open to see the torture room, but from a new perspective. The view from the concrete pillar caused despair to sink in. Instead of increasing her odds, she merely swapped places with her father, and now she'd die. No, not die, at least not yet.

The torture would stretch out for hours, maybe even days like Miriah. When he finished, she'd be a pile of mangled flesh unrecognizable as human or vampire. He let Whitmore and Alvarez off easy. She wouldn't be as lucky. Endless pain and darkness awaited her as Ashcroft meticulously stripped away every shred of her physical identity.

She didn't bother putting up a fight when he grabbed her arms. What was the point? He was stronger, faster, and she had no weapons.

She stared down at Alvarez's pooling blood as Ashcroft tugged her hands up to a pair of manacles hanging above her. Finality rang through her bones with the metallic click as they locked. The pipe they looped around sat lower than the ten-foot ceiling, but the length of the chain forced her to stand on tiptoe.

"I have eagerly anticipated this moment." The sheer glee in his voice fractured her heart into painful shards. Bony fingers caressed her cheek, his black beady eyes studying every line. "Almost a pity. You are quite a remarkable specimen. Even more so after drinking the demon's blood, and the subtle changes it caused."

She couldn't bring herself to care about his words. None of it mattered. Game over. Ashcroft won. Gregor wouldn't leave now, and even if Coffee didn't capture Chance, he wouldn't walk away. Alvarez and Whitmore lay dead in front of her, Humphrey would die from his wounds, and Cohen... Her eyes glanced past the monster but couldn't see the detective. Where the hell was he?

"I have a suggestion." The sound of Cohen's voice right beside Ashcroft startled her. A rare glimmer of hope flashed in her mind. If he could help her...

"The effects on her are rare, incredibly so. We should study the changes thoroughly. Once we can safely and consistently replicate them, you can do what you please with her."

Her jaw dropped in utter shock. "Are you kidding? You're on his side now?"

"Survival instinct." Cohen's shoulders shrugged in a carefree manner, which only made her chest tighten more. "That's why my species isn't on the brink of extinction like yours. If I strengthen my foothold in the world, then it doesn't matter who my allies are. Besides, you failed to hold up your side of our bargain, and my family will come after me now. They won't stop until I'm dead *unless* I bring them something of equal value. I should have seen it earlier. You aren't an ally. You're a charity case." The callous cold in his eyes ignited a fire in her belly.

She spat at him while her face snarled in anger. "You spineless coward! Tell yourself whatever lies help you sleep at night. I hope he turns on you and slits your throat just like he did to your bigot partner!"

Calmly, Cohen wiped the spit from his face and stared down at his hand for a long moment. Then, his crisp blue eyes glanced up with a hardness she never expected. It was like the mask slipped, revealing the horrific reality beneath for the first time. *This can't be happening!*

First, Spencer and now Cohen. Was he under Ashcroft's control? Or was Chance right not to trust him from the very beginning? While her mind rambled, Cohen reeled back and slapped her across the face.

Ashcroft silently studied him during the entire exchange with skeptical eyes. Now, he grinned like a kid with a new toy.

"Your suggestion is intriguing, boy. I'm glad you came to your senses. Morality is a human concept, and we are above such petty things. However, the child must suffer the sins of the father. I cannot break a holy covenant. If it were anyone else…"

Whether the result of Cohen's betrayal or his brutal slap, she suddenly didn't care what they did. She simply wanted to hurt them both. Like her moment with Humphrey in the hall, blind rage took over everything else.

"Oh, the little kitten is angry. Can you feel that?" Cohen's lips stretched into a lazy grin as he closed his eyes. He leaned his head back and drank her rage like a fine wine.

"Fuck you!" She threw him a disgusted sneer before turning on Ashcroft.

"You are a hypocritical lowlife. In the same breath, you claim you're above morals and then spout Bible scripture? You're simply a convoluted asshole who happens to have power. Who are you avenging? Your piece-of-shit son who liked to rape little girls? Your back-stabbing wife who covered up his dirty secrets? Sorry, the martyr card isn't working for you."

"They were my *family*! He had no right!" Ashcroft screamed the words in her face, his acidic breath coating her skin. Earlier, the concept of death terrified her, but its inevitability brought clarity. Her only play was to piss him off enough to kill her quickly.

She leaned forward, straining against her manacles to come as close as possible to his scarred face. The monster flinched with a millisecond of surprise, unaccustomed to people moving *closer*.

"And neither did you! You're both like toddlers arguing over a stupid toy. You wanna kill me, fine, but don't spout philosophical bullshit about your *noble* cause, you pretentious piece of shit."

Ashcroft whirled toward the instrument tray, but not at hyper speed. Perhaps it required concentration. Cohen lightly grabbed his wrist before he touched the scalpel.

"Wait. She's simply trying to goad you into killing her quickly. Don't let a mere *vampire* cheat you out of your life's work."

"Oh yes, give the demonic abomination a pep talk. I'd hate to think of a world where a supernatural serial killer doesn't have a life coach to help him hone his craft." Her already abused muscles started to spasm as she tried to stretch her legs. Standing on tiptoe was torture in its own right.

"No. I must teach the little bitch respect, but I won't kill her. I'll simply cut her tongue out…slowly." When his face contorted into pure malice, it became even more horrifying. The network of scars around his beady eyes resembled something from the pit of hell. Although she tried to latch on to her calm demeanor, the epinephrine flooding her body made her heart race, her skin flush, her breaths faster.

"No. If she can't talk, it will hinder the research…"

"I'll never cooperate with you. Whether or not I have a tongue." Her confident wrath wavered as Ashcroft approached her with his scalpel gripped tight. As much as she wanted to stare daggers at Cohen, she couldn't take her eyes off the monster looming closer, light glinting off his blade.

Her pulse grew dangerously fast. All her false bravado dissipated, and the room began to spin as she teetered on the verge of passing out. That would be a mercy if only a temporary one.

Cohen stepped between them, giving her a brief reprieve, and suddenly, she could breathe again. Was his cooperation just a ploy, trying to catch Ashcroft off guard?

"Wait. I understand you want her to suffer, but I want her alive…"

The monster's beady eyes narrowed. "Your soft underbelly is beginning to show, Detective." The blade changed positions as he stepped toward Cohen, who held his hands up in surrender.

"To study. I only earned her trust so I could test my theory. I knew she would never survive long enough to help me find the book without my blood. Why do you think I locked up the bodyguard? I needed her injured, and your minion did a perfect job." Chance was right. Cohen freely admitted to everything he suspected, but Ashcroft still appeared hesitant.

"There is a way we can both get what we want."

"You are wearing on my patience, demon. What is your solution?" Eagerness hummed over his skin, making his long bony fingers flex around the blade.

"No offense, but you are too emotional. She will keep pushing you, and you'll get carried away. She is too valuable. Let me be the one." Cohen reached slowly for the scalpel, as Ashcroft stood still as if considering the offer. Not that it mattered to her. They both wanted to inflict pain. They merely held different philosophies on how to accomplish their goal. The end result remained the same—torture.

"I can stay impartial and work under your direction, a buffer to prevent overzealous measures. You satisfy your revenge, and I still have a specimen to study. Partners?"

She simply couldn't wrap her head around Cohen's offer. Swapping sides was one thing, but offering to slice her up, to function as his tool? Her hopes of him merely acting as a distraction faded into nonexistence. This wasn't some hollow promise he could deny later. Cohen volunteered to torture her, right here and now. How many people had to betray her before she learned to stop giving people the benefit of the doubt?

"You are right to some extent. I can still enjoy the peasant's torment even if I'm not the one inflicting it..." The grin tugging at Cohen's lips made her skin crawl.

"However..." With that one word, the blossoming grin faltered. "You will only do so until you satisfy the questions of your loyalty, and I regain my calm. I will oversee you. Every single move, every breath. Any indication of insincerity and I will string you up next to her, slice the lids from your eyes, and force you to watch every lurid thing I do to her." Her nausea returned as she squeezed her eyes shut and focused on her aching muscles.

The detective calmly nodded, accepting his terms without a second thought.

"Retrieve the bucket of tubing and the two embalming needles on the instrument tray. I will prepare the blood supplies."

A sudden breeze swept over her skin, and when she opened her eyes, only Cohen remained in front of her, facing away. One last shot to reason with him. She leaned as far as the manacles allowed and urgently whispered, "What the fuck are you doing? No one is coming to save us, so buying time is pointless. Stop stringing this out."

Without a single word, he walked away.

Her eyes roamed the room in shock, tears burning her eyes. Whitmore's stocky body lay lifeless on the floor with Alvarez only a few feet away. Their darkening blood spread out to form one massive congealing pool, which tainted the air with the scent of copper. Duncan strained against his chains in a furious attempt to move closer. His red-rimmed eyes widened as blue-tinged lips snarled in a feral growl.

Feeding wouldn't help him. The anoxic brain damage destroying the higher functions was permanent. She doubted even Cohen's blood could restore him. Her father was right. All her uncle needed was a merciful death, an end to his suffering, and he wasn't the only one.

The basement would claim her cognizant existence one way or another. Even if she survived the torture awaiting her, she'd be as insane as Duncan, a starving, traumatized animal in a human-shaped shell.

Ashcroft reappeared with several blood bags and an IV stand, confirming her suspicions about the puncture wounds in the crook of Miriah's elbows. He gave her transfusions to keep her alive. The growing bubble of panicked despair only grew when Cohen returned with the bucket.

"Attach a needle to the tubing and place the receptacle under her left side." He dutifully followed Ashcroft's direction like a mindless drone. Could he be under Ashcroft's spell? If so, it didn't explain the idea of keeping her as a science project or his confession. No. She couldn't chalk up his actions to mind control. *Stop making excuses. He is the enemy.*

With a surge of uncontrollable anger, Lilith kicked out when Cohen bent over to position the bucket. Her foot connected with the side of his face, knocking him to the ground, but her smug satisfaction didn't last long. The lack of support put all her weight on her wrists, the manacles biting into the skin and straining her shoulder joints. With a grunt of pain, she scrambled to get back on her tiptoes to relieve the tension.

The horrifically scarred face suddenly appeared before her again, coupled with the cold pressure of a scalpel against her throat. "Demon, secure her legs." The snarl wrinkled every scarred line of his face into a hideous mask of hatred. Then, he turned those lifeless eyes on her, and she found herself staring into an empty black abyss. "Kick again..."

Something inside snapped. "Or what? You'll kill me? Go ahead. Spare me from staring at your fucked-up face and enduring tyrannical speeches so you can hear the sound of your own voice."

She kicked hard, and the pop of his knee dislocating came seconds before the screeching howl. He stumbled backward as she struggled to regain her balance again.

"I have the prisoner, sir." Coffee's deep, booming voice knocked the wind out of her small victory. Ashcroft stood and popped the joint back into place with a hiss. His cruel eyes bored into her with demented delight as his thin lips gradually curved into a sardonic smile.

"Oh, I won't kill you, my dear. However, if you don't wish to witness your betrothed die a prolonged, agonizing death, you will not struggle again."

Lilith stared past Ashcroft at Richard Coffee with his massive hand grasping Chance's entire shoulder. Her heart split into a million sensations.

Not only was he alive and walking, but he looked healthy. He ditched his shirt, and all that remained of the gaping hole in his chest was a pinkish-red blotch.

On the other hand, his presence in the den of horrors meant her actions had consequences—a weak spot for them to exploit. The engagement was a cover, but the deep feelings weren't fictitious, and both Cohen and Ashcroft knew it the second she laid eyes on him.

When Chance caught sight of her, strung from the pipes overhead, he tried to move toward her. Richard's heavy hand tightened, and Chance collapsed to his knees, crestfallen. "I'm so sorry, Lily." Tears choked his voice as desperation infiltrated his beautiful hazel eyes. At least she could take comfort in seeing his face one last time. If only she could shield him from witnessing her torment.

Lilith didn't utter a word or twitch a muscle as the detective wrapped her ankles with rope. She stared at Chance, focusing everything on him. She memorized every line and wished that she had the power to wipe the pain from his eyes.

"What are you doing, Cohen? Are you helping him? I swear to god, I'll choke the life out of you with my bare hands, you fucking *bon-ayen capon*!"

"We don't need his tongue if you're itching to cut something." Somehow the flat, emotionless tone in Cohen's voice fit him, ringing with more honesty than he'd displayed so far.

"No!" When she screamed the word, Ashcroft tilted his scarred face, considering her for a long moment.

"Let him keep it for now. He may be of use." The curling sneer did little to relieve her. The supposed mercy would come at a cost, one both she and Chance would pay.

Ashcroft's hooked nose sniffed the air, and his grin widened, revealing jagged teeth. "Oh yes, there is the sweet bouquet." He slithered closer, and her heart tripped again. He leaned into her neck, his wiry hair scratching her cheek. For one terrifying moment, she thought he might bite her. So stereotypical. He didn't even have fangs, or did he?

He simply hovered, his gaunt body inches from her. The revolting scent filled her nostrils, making her want to vomit. "Your fear for that man is intoxicating." His words slithered into her ear and down her spine, the cold infecting every inch of her body. "Shall we see if his feelings are true as well?"

Before she could comprehend the question, Ashcroft grasped the zipper of her tracksuit and tore it down. His nails made quick work of the sleeves, and he tossed the torn fabric to the ground in an overdramatic gesture. Despite the warmth from the furnace, her skin became instantly cold and clammy.

The madman's thin frame blocked her view, but she heard the screams and commotion as Chance struggled. She closed her eyes, every muscle in her body trembling with fear. Chance couldn't do anything to save her, no matter how much he wanted to. Even if he miraculously got past the mountainous man, he would never take out the monster and his new helper.

They would force him to sit and watch them torture the woman he loved, knowing he couldn't stop them, and she couldn't save him from that grim fate. Silent tears slipped down her cheeks as bony fingers slid over her bare shoulder and up her arm.

The caress wasn't sensual, but a touch of ownership, admiring the blank canvas, picturing the masterpiece he intended to create. The sharp stab in her arm surprised her, but she bit back the whimper for Chance's sake. When she peered up, Ashcroft checked the IV line filling with blood, now firmly implanted in her medial cephalic vein.

The second puncture caught her by surprise, and this time a whimper escaped. She watched while Cohen repositioned the needle in her left arm, trying to find the vein. When blood finally flashed in the tubing, he ran his fingers down the line to the bucket.

"I don't think you will get much from this angle. If I lowered this arm..."

"No! Stupid boy. The idea is not to bleed her dry. As her pulse quickens and the blood pumps harder, it will provide what I need without killing her quickly. I know what I'm doing."

While he lectured, he wheeled the instrument tray closer and studied each tool, trying to decide which one his accomplice should use first.

"The scalpel. Shallow cuts. Deeper ones will overload or destroy the pain receptors." The brusque tone revealed his reluctance to hand over the reins.

Then, the mounting frustration broke as he turned, heading straight for Richard Coffee and Chance. *No!* Her heart hammered against her chest like a wild animal stuck in a cage, accentuated by the increased stream of her blood echoing in the bucket. She knew he didn't intend to sit next to them and merely drink in the emotions.

Chance met her gaze with a silent but tearful apology, pouring thirteen years of devotion into one expression. Uncontrollable sobs overtook her with the realization that she wasn't the only one slated for physical torture tonight.

Cohen appeared in her peripheral vision, light glinting off the blade, but she couldn't take her eyes off Chance as Ashcroft closed in on him. The monster could cross the room in the blink of an eye, but he enjoyed drawing things out to prolong their suffering.

The sharp sting of the blade slicing across her chest came seconds before a shot rang through the basement like a crack of thunder. Ashcroft stumbled. The muzzle flare from the second shot gave away the shooter. Gregor's determined face emerged from the shadows as he moved closer to the furnace, hugging the far wall with a shotgun in his hands. Part of her wanted to scream in joy, but she knew how ineffective guns were against this monster. Her father was purposely signing his own death warrant.

"You are a miserable waste of skin!" Her father's lips curled into a snarl of hatred as he reloaded and squeezed the trigger again. "You took *everything* from me!"

The blur of motion made her heart sink, and suddenly he held Gregor suspended in the air, Ashcroft's bony fingers clutching his throat. "You think your little gun will hurt me? I am the embodiment of divine vengeance! God placed me upon this path to cleanse the world of your existence and everything you've touched for the crimes you visited on me!"

Gregor kicked and gasped for breath as he struggled against Ashcroft's iron grip, a futile effort.

"You will watch as we strip the flesh from your daughter. I will take everything I can from her and her betrothed until only empty husks remain. You will join your brother at my feet as unthinking and insane as a rabid dog until you starve!"

Lilith's eyes fluttered shut, losing consciousness for what seemed like seconds. Then, shrill screams and shots rang in her ears, making her head throb. Her glazed eyes scanned the room, trying to pinpoint the source. Why did she feel so weird?

A wave of dizziness washed over her as she glanced at the bucket. Blood flowed at a fast pace, regardless of her arm's position above her head. Ashcroft was right. Increased heart rate, elevated blood pressure, all the result of profound fear. The high bloodcurdling screams continued, and it took a moment to be sure she wasn't the source.

With a sudden thought, her eyes darted to the IV transfusion. She shouldn't feel this weird if they were giving her blood. A pattern of small bullet holes peppered the almost empty bag. Awesome. If they all survived, Gregor needed to put in time at the shooting range.

"Stay awake." Someone whispered in her ear, and her mind swam through the possibilities. It wasn't Chance or Gregor or Ashcroft. She whipped her head around as the room spun and stared straight into Cohen's almost handsome face.

"Fuck you. I'm not your science experiment! What did he do to my father? Gregor?" She fought against the manacles, straining and pushing. Trickles of blood followed the sharp sting as the metal cut into her wrists. With grim determination, she fought to look over his shoulder, but he wouldn't move.

"Please! Stop! I need to get this!" Cohen reached for her arms, but she wasn't about to let him touch her again. The screams intensified into ear-splitting shrieks, fueling her fire.

She gripped the chains for support and, in one swift motion, lifted her bound legs off the ground and kicked out. The traitor fell hard on his ass, but her moment of triumph was short-lived.

Due to her lack of upper body strength, her muscles gave out, leaving her dangling by her wrists yet again. The metal cuffs tore into her flesh, and she screamed in agony as blood slid down her arms in thicker lines. She flailed in a blind panic, feet slipping on the wet floor with the same deafening shrieks echoing in the background.

Again, she teetered on the edge of consciousness while someone lifted her, taking the weight off her wrists. She sucked in a deep breath as the sharp pain ebbed away. Through her tears, she saw Chance's face hover over her before her eyes closed.

"Lily!" He firmly patted her face, trying to wake her up. "Lily, *l'amour de ma vie, mon cherie*. Wake up!" Panic trembled through him, hazel eyes flooded with tears, but she didn't understand. Her drowsy eyes kept searching for the source of the deathly screeching.

Cohen suddenly appeared over his shoulder. "No! Behind you!" She screamed and fought against Chance's warm arms, but he only tightened his hold.

"Stop! You need to stay still!"

"No! Don't you fucking touch him! I swear to god, I'll slit your damn throat myself if you even—"

Chance turned, but when he saw Cohen, he didn't have the reaction she expected. He seemed relieved. "Hurry the fuck up."

The detective reached for the manacles again, but this time she didn't struggle, lost in her muddled thoughts. Why would Chance help him? Why could she suddenly taste his guilt on the back of her tongue like burnt oil? Her foggy brain didn't want to work. How much blood did she lose? What the hell was happening?

Nothing made sense anymore. Tears coursed down her cheeks as she wept uncontrollably. Cohen betrayed his family, sure, but the thought of Chance doing the same thing to Gregor? To her? She couldn't even begin to comprehend the concept.

A hand caressed her cheek, wiping the tears away, and a warmth glowed where it touched her skin. The sensation sunk into her blood, relaxing every muscle. When she finally looked into the hazel eyes flecked with green before her, all the panic melted away along with her doubts.

"Lily, please. Listen to me." Although Chance's voice had a calming effect, it still held tones of fear and urgency. "Stop struggling so Cohen can unlock the restraints. He won't hurt you. I would never let him."

The basement, the screams, everything faded away in a sea of hazel as she stared into his hypnotic eyes. Cohen gripped her arm, trying to fit a key into the lock, but she was too distracted to care. Chance's lips met hers in an overwhelmingly intimate kiss before he rested his forehead against hers.

A sudden sting at her elbow broke the spell. Cohen threw the needle and tubing to the floor in frustration and reached for her other arm. This time she braced herself, which minimized the pain. In a panic, he glanced over his shoulder and then grappled with the manacles again. Seconds later, the metallic clink signaled her freedom as her wrists fell limply to her sides. Chance caught her weight and scooped her up, cradling her in his arms.

"Come on. There isn't much time. We need to get the hell out of here." Cohen's rattled voice set off the alarms in her head again as he tossed a bag of blood into her lap. "You'll need this. Let's move!"

"My father!" The screaming still ricocheted around the room, burrowing into her head. *Damn it, where is he?*

Chance swung around, and her eyes finally took in the gruesome scene playing out behind them. Ashcroft stood pinned to the furnace by Richard's massive body, screeching as his skin burned against the hot metal. Coffee's face didn't show his usual businesslike expression of calm authority. Instead, it contorted in anguish though she couldn't detect the source of his agony.

Gregor stood to the side, thankfully alive. A colossal weight immediately lifted from her heart. He snapped the monster's arm, holding on to it for dear life. If he held it at that angle, Ashcroft might not heal or at least not as fast, especially with half of his body seared to the scorching furnace.

Now that she was safe with Chance, Cohen surged forward, grabbed hold of Ashcroft's arm, and shoved with all his momentum. The bone snapped like a dry twig, piercing the skin as blood spurted wildly. The shrill shrieks became deafening inhuman howls as his face contorted in torment.

A dark satisfaction settled over her, momentarily darkening her soul. He deserved every ounce of pain and so much more. For Gregor's family, her mother, Miriah, Malachi, Spencer, Alvarez.

Another wave of dizziness made her head spin, and she tore open the bag of blood and quickly drained the contents. She needed every advantage if she wanted to live. The warmth rapidly spread through her belly, clearing the light-headed sensation.

"Gregor! We have to move! We're out of time!" She followed Chance's line of sight. Several lanterns lay shattered on the concrete, their ignited oil pools closing in on the flammable barrels. "This place is gonna go up in flames any second!"

Her father hesitated, and she knew precisely why. If they let go now, Ashcroft would be out the door before any of them. Hell, he might decide to cut his losses and lock the door.

"Burn! Burn!" The sudden shouts caught her attention. Duncan pulled and strained against his chains while his red-rimmed eyes lit with manic glee. The bones of his wrists lay exposed with the skin and muscle torn away by the chains. His feet slid in his own dark blood as he flailed around in some macabre dance. Seeing her once brilliant uncle reduced to a golem-like creature was heartbreaking.

"He's too far gone, Lily." Chance glanced down at her with regret and a sense of failure. "If there was any way…"

"I know. We can't fix what Ashcroft broke in him, and you're right. We need to move before this place becomes an inferno. I'm okay. You can put me down. We'll both move faster if I run on my own."

Reluctantly, Chance placed her on her feet but kept an arm around her, thankfully. Her muscles groaned and seized as soon as she tried to use them, and he deftly supported her weight, keeping her upright.

"Chance, I can't let him go! He has to die, no matter the cost!" Her father's voice emerged strained and sorrowful as he continued to fight against Ashcroft's arm. Even with the bone snapped, his nails clawed at Gregor's hand, leaving bloody furrows.

"Get her out of here, Chance! Now!"

As she struggled to escape his grip in a desire to haul her dad away, Coffee's booming voice filled the room. "All of you get out of here. I'll hold him long enough for the fires to consume us. I won't make it out anyway."

She didn't notice before, but blood covered the basement floor at his feet. A flickering flame moved closer, less than a foot from the barrels, and caught the moist glint of something hanging from the enormous man's stomach. After a few moments, her brain finally deciphered the image. Ashcroft was clawing his way through the security officer's massive body. A wave of nausea smacked her as she realized that the dangling loops were intestines shining in the firelight.

"Go! Now!" Unshakable resolve resonated in his booming voice. Anything she could do to save him would end up killing them all.

He threw back his gargantuan head in a feral roar, and she caught a glimpse of fangs before he struck. Ashcroft went utterly still as Coffee gnawed viciously at his neck. Then piercing screams exploded with a vociferous force as the monster thrashed and fought in sheer desperation.

Chance and Lilith sprinted for the furnace, grabbed both Gregor and Cohen, and raced down the corridor. Her muscles burned like molten lava, but she refused to give in. She pushed through the agony because she had no choice.

Bloody shrieks and booming roars chased them down the hall as the light behind them grew brighter. Any second, the flames would ignite the barrels, and the whole place would go up. She pushed her body harder and hit the stairway door first. After ripping it open, she tore up the stairs, with Chance, Gregor, and Cohen hot on her heels.

She reached the first landing and raced around the corner, but hit the next step, smashing her shin on the concrete. The sudden pain brought tears as she wailed, grabbing at the bloody gash. Without skipping a beat, Chance scooped her up as if she were a paper doll and kept climbing upward. She wrapped her arms around his neck and held on tight, hoping they escaped the hellish building before it became their tomb.

Cohen reached the door first this time and held it open, waiting for everyone to pass before following them. She still didn't trust him, but questioning his motives could wait until they were all safe.

Her heart raced a million miles an hour as they crashed through the rusting door and into the familiar hallway. They were *so* close.

The floor rumbled violently, throwing them all off-balance. Her father glanced off the wall, and Chance briefly stumbled with her added weight. Cohen took a little longer to recover, but he stayed on his feet.

Weak light illuminated the edges of the double doors ahead—sunlight.

"Cohen! Get your keys ready. As soon as you hit the exit, head straight for your car and pop the trunk." Once he nodded in reply, she glanced back at her father. If it was still early or overcast, he might survive long enough to reach the car. What choice did they have?

Staying inside was not an option. The intermittent vibrations meant the barrels were starting to ignite. He could duck into one of the other structures, but they had no guarantee it would be any safer. She didn't know what kind of chemicals were down there. If Ashcroft counted on his super speed to escape his grand finale, the explosion might take down the whole damn complex.

They almost reached the exit when the entire building shook, raining loose ceiling tiles on them. They all choked on the thick dust falling from above, burning their lungs, but kept running. As they collided with the double doors, the hiss of flames grew to an ear-splitting roar, and she whispered prayers. *Please, don't let us escape that madness to die now!*

Once they emerged into the early morning light, Cohen broke off in a sprint, taking the most direct route to his car. Gregor chased after him, his skin already turning bright pink.

Carrying her weight slowed Chance down, and the horrifying sound of the fire reached a fevered pitch. With apprehension, she glanced back over his shoulder. As the double doors started to swing shut, a blinding burst of light erupted at the end of the hall. "Take cover! Now!"

Chance swerved and ran as fast as he could while Lilith hung on for dear life. She squeezed her eyes shut, praying again. He ducked behind the next structure and sprinted down the alley, counting on the walls to provide a buffer from flying debris.

An enormous explosion of pressure boomed around them. The ground shook. Concrete blocks shifted and began to fall. Then, the real force of the blast hit, knocking them both hard to the ground. Everything went dark, and the last thing she remembered was Chance curled over her like a protective blanket.

Chapter 25

A high-pitched tone pierced Lilith's ears, drowning out everything else. Someone screamed what might have been words, but she couldn't understand the muffled voice. Every struggling breath hurt as a tremendous weight pressed down on her. Was she buried beneath a ton of bricks?

She blinked several times before successfully opening her eyes. Cohen hovered over her, shouting as he tugged at something. Once her eyes focused, she realized Chance lay limp on top of her with his eyes closed. Pure panic gripped her until she forced herself to concentrate. The steady rise and fall of his chest indicated he was unconscious but alive.

Her eyes flashed back to Cohen as the memory of his betrayal roared to the forefront of her mind. The slice along her collarbone suddenly burned like napalm, reminding her of its existence. Yes. He helped them escape, but only *after* the tables turned. Until then, he functioned as a willing, even eager participant in Ashcroft's sick games. She certainly didn't forget his idea to study her like a lab rat. He kept barking orders, but the ringing in her ears still made his words impossible to decipher.

Cohen finally rolled Chance off her. When he stooped down to check his pulse, she scrambled to her knees and clocked him in the jaw. He stumbled backward and landed on his ass with a shocked expression.

"Don't fucking touch him!" The bra didn't provide much protection from the blast, and every movement made the abrasions covering her torso scream in protest.

"Damn it! I'm trying to help!" He jumped back to his feet and grabbed her shoulders while she attempted unsuccessfully to evade his grip. His hazel eyes caught hers, and the weight in them momentarily suppressed her internal rebellion. In the far corner of her mind, she wondered how the color change was possible.

"Listen to me! I was *never* on Ashcroft's side. Please, let me help you both, and then I'll explain. I promise. We need to leave before the cops show up." He tugged his shirt over his head and tossed it to her. "Put that on."

She stared down at his blue button-up as her foggy mind tried to catch up. Mixed into the soot and dirt were specks of blood. *Her* blood. Why would she trust him, and why did she already feel like she should? Then, her shrewd eyes glanced up at him.

"Did you just *influence* me?" She shot up to her feet, every nerve in her body singing with tension.

With a heavy sigh, his head slumped down. "We do *not* have time for this! Put it on. I need your help with Chance. We can discuss it later." When she didn't move or say anything, he stood and grasped her shoulders again, waiting for her shell-shocked eyes to meet his gaze. "No tricks." His eyes glowed with the same crisp blue she remembered seeing the first time she met him.

"Your eyes…" She stumbled over the thought, unable to form the question.

"I'll explain. I'll tell you everything…*in the car*!" The demanding tone dissolved into a desperate plea. "I never desired to hurt you." His calm stillness made her indecisive. Was he being honest or simply saying what he needed to?

Then, her logical brain finally kicked in, and she realized Cohen's motivation didn't matter. She had no other option. He had the keys, Gregor was in his trunk, and she couldn't move Chance by herself. Gut feelings or not, she needed his help. Reluctantly, she nodded and pulled on the shirt. Her battered skin welcomed any protection from the biting breeze.

Together, they dragged Chance past the remaining buildings. The explosion did a lot of damage, and they carefully picked their way through chunks of cement and debris. Somewhere in the back of her mind, it finally registered. Ashcroft was dead, and he would never hurt her family again. It was all over.

Once they hauled Chance into the back seat, she double-checked his pulse and breathing, both strong and steady.

"Get in!" Cohen yelled from the driver's seat, already starting the car.

Hesitantly, she pulled back and hopped into the passenger's seat. As soon as her door closed, he threw the car in gear and peeled out of the parking lot. He sped away from the ominous site as if their lives depended on it, which wasn't far from the truth. With no believable explanation for their presence, they'd face lots of possible jail time if they didn't get to the interstate before the cavalry showed up.

When they hit the on-ramp, an enormous weight lifted from her shoulders. They survived. Against the absolute impossible odds, they won. Her brain couldn't fully comprehend it, perhaps because of the price they paid. Coffee and Alvarez both sacrificed themselves to let them escape.

Tears trickled down her cheek as she thought about her partner. The way his balding head slumped at an unnatural angle, his shirt soaking with blood. She couldn't even retrieve his body before the explosion. At best, she'd be bringing him home in charred pieces for his family to bury. While wiping away her tears, she tried to think about something else, anything else.

"Were you and Alvarez close?" Cohen's voice sounded soft and tender, even soothing, which somehow pissed her off.

"Of course! He was my partner for ten years. I drank coffee with his wife every Sunday and shared dinner with his family twice a week or more. What kind of question is that?" His eyes widened as if her shrill tone surprised him.

"What? You think because you helped us after the odds changed that we're best pals who chat about our damn feelings. Fuck you, Cohen."

His arms tightened with tension as he gripped the steering wheel. A million conflicting emotions flashed across his face in rapid succession, most of them indiscernible. Beneath his undershirt, every lean muscle tensed in anger. Why did he look like a kicked puppy ready to bite her? Better yet, why should she give a damn?

"My name is Andrew, not that you care, and I told you before, I was never on Ashcroft's side."

"Uh-huh, sure. If you say so." Sarcasm dripped from every syllable as his face reddened. After a tired sigh, she shook off her contemptuous attitude enough to hear him out. What else could she do while trapped in a car with him? "You said you'd explain, so talk."

The tension eased as he took in a deep breath. "He didn't sway me. I would never hurt you." His eyes flickered over to her with a raw pain that made her skin itch.

"Bullshit. What do you call this?" She yanked on the shirt, displaying the slowly healing slice along her collarbone. "A stall tactic? Besides, I gave you opportunities to signal me. Nothing!"

"I needed the fear and anger to be real. We sense emotions, Lilith. If I tipped you off, he would have instantly known." Cohen's jaw clenched again.

"Believe me. I wanted to tell you, but I couldn't risk it. So, I utilized my extensive experience of walling off emotions. A trick I use to survive my family. I had to keep him from killing you, or the plan would be worthless." "What? To study me like a stupid lab rat?"

"Hold on a second. This isn't a conspiracy. Let me explain."

Lilith clamped down on her temper as anger rolled over her skin like oil on water. She needed him to tell his story while she studied every muscle in his face with careful precision.

"While I explored the south corridor with Whitmore, he began acting strange. I know...*knew* him well, and the subtle differences in his behavior didn't make sense. Normally, he'd spend most of his time bitching about you and Chance, but he didn't bring you up again after we split up, not once."

"So, your proof of innocence consists of a few minutes where Whitmore wasn't a total dick? Wow. Compelling."

He decided to ignore the snide comment and continued his story. "Coffee showed up as Whitmore made his move. A shot rang out somewhere, and I overpowered Whitmore during the distraction." He paused to glance over at her, and every micro-expression on his face appeared genuine. "Do you know who fired the shot?"

"Humphrey." As the memory of those horrible moments replayed in her mind, she paled. Chance stumbling to his knees, coughing up blood, dying. She couldn't help but glance back at him as if some part of her wanted to ensure he was still there and alive.

Cohen's eyes briefly left the road again, as concern began to blossom in his face. "What happened?"

With a tremendous effort, she swallowed the sudden lump in her throat before speaking. "He shot Chance in the back and barely missed his heart." She struggled with the words, clearing her throat as tears threatened to spill. After a steadying breath, she continued.

"I knocked Humphrey out and tried to help Chance, but he was dying." The flashback dominated her attention, and she glanced down at the ragged pink scar on her wrist. "I panicked. He lost so much blood, and he couldn't breathe. The bullet collapsed his lung. So, I did the only thing I could. I gave him my blood, hoping whatever healed me would do the same for him. Obviously, it worked."

"What? You fed him your blood?" Cohen blanched, completely panic-stricken.

She bristled at his reaction and crossed her arms over her chest. "You did the same for me. I couldn't let him die. I would give him every drop if that's what it took. He is an innocent, dragged into this mess by my father and me so, skip the judgmental bullshit."

After visibly reining in his anger, he nodded, deep in thought. Thankfully, he didn't push the issue, but she still wanted to sock him in the jaw again. Questioning her decision to save Chance didn't decrease the desire. Of course, since he was an emotional sponge, he knew better than to press his luck.

"So, you made your move on Whitmore..." She gruffly prompted him to return to his story.

"Yeah. I hit Whitmore on the head with my flashlight, and he went down like a pile of bricks. As I grabbed his gun, Coffee appeared. I nearly shot him, but he held up his hands in surrender. Then, he pulled me into a room and explained everything."

Her brow furrowed in confusion. "Wait. He just surrendered and told you everything? Wasn't he under Ashcroft's control?"

"No, actually. Our influence doesn't work on his kind. Obviously, Ashcroft didn't recognize his species—"

"Stop. His species? What the hell… I saw his fangs. I watched him bite Ashcroft—"

"Yeah, because vampires own the monopoly on fangs…" He laughed sarcastically, but when she didn't join in, he peered over at her in surprise. "Huh." He shrugged with a nonchalant expression. "A conversation for another time. Can I finish? I'd rather focus on moving past the phase where you want to stab me in the throat for being a traitor. After that, we can have a heart-to-heart on supernatural species."

The frustration kept mounting, and she rubbed at her temples to relieve the pressure. "Yeah, sure."

"Thanks." His eyes flashed forward in time to swerve around a white Celica driving below the speed limit in the fast lane.

"When our bad guys hit the lab, Ashcroft knocked Coffee out before he had a chance to stand up. They locked him in the cold storage freezer, and I assume that's when you and Chance arrived. After your encounter, Ashcroft returned alone and tried to persuade him to join his cause with promises of power. He knew if he didn't play the part of a dutiful minion, the monster would kill him. So, he followed orders, waiting for an opportunity to present itself."

"So, he told you all this while Whitmore was unconscious?"

"Yeah. We decided there were too many variables to go in guns blazing. We still didn't know your location, and I figured if he compromised Whitmore, he probably did the same to Humphrey. So, we played along. Coffee threw a punch to illustrate a struggle, and then, he woke up my partner."

"*A* punch? As in one? Hell, the black eye covered half your damn face."

Subconsciously, he rubbed at his cheek. "No, kidding. I barely stayed conscious."

Despite their tenuous alliance, she found some smug satisfaction in that fact.

"Well, considering Coffee could break the Hulk in half, it's not that surprising." Chance's voice from the back seat sounded like sweet music to her ears.

She glanced over her shoulder to see his face looming between them, and a deep blush inexplicably crept over her cheeks.

"So nice of you to join us." Cohen's attempt at a light and friendly tone failed. He sounded irritable, impatient, and…disappointed?

"Did you know about this *plan*?" The blush quickly faded as she fixed Chance with a skeptical frown, but he didn't blink at the question.

"Yes. Coffee filled me in when he found me upstairs. I nearly shot him when he busted through the door, not that a shotgun blast would have done much damage." With an aggravated sigh, she pushed past her burning questions about Coffee's lineage to focus on what mattered.

"But you tried to attack Cohen in the basement."

"I had to act the part, *cher*. Besides, it didn't take much acting. Yes, Cohen and Coffee were on our side, but that didn't necessarily mean any of us would survive. It was pure luck that we got an opportunity before he really…hurt you." He stumbled over the words while swallowing hard. The expression on his face clearly stated there was more to it.

"I felt what Ashcroft wanted to do to you." His skin paled, and he looked sightlessly through the windshield. "I almost *saw* his plan, and…" Chance rubbed at his face and cleared his throat again. "Anyway, it was bad."

"A side effect of the blood?" Her voice trembled as she tried not to envision a fate worse than Miriah's.

"I never experienced anything like it before."

As she mulled over the implications, another thought occurred to her. "Wait. What about your confession? You told Ashcroft that you threw Chance in holding on purpose to isolate me. You wanted an opportunity to give me your blood and study the results."

"What?" Chance growled ferally from the back seat, and she suddenly remembered he wasn't present for the bulk of Cohen's alleged performance.

"Whoa. Hold on. None of it was true! Ashcroft started getting suspicious. So, I spun a story to earn his trust." When neither of them appeared convinced, he continued, "Whitmore insisted on holding you as I said before! How could I possibly know Spencer would attack her or that my blood would do anything other than heal her?"

"And how do I know you aren't just covering your ass so that we trust you?"

"You don't." Cohen flexed his fingers around the wheel, settling into his usual calm indifference. "But we're alive, and he's dead."

"Do you really think he's dead?" Goose bumps spread up her arms, and she rubbed at them absently as terrifying possibilities circled her thoughts. If he somehow survived, they'd never get another chance like that to bring him down.

The uncomfortable silence that settled over the car didn't improve things. Finally, Cohen spoke up. "Between Coffee and the furnace, he wasn't healing fast enough, even by clawing through the massive body pinning him. I don't see how he could survive the explosion on top of that. However, there are other problems about to rain down on us."

Confusion clouded her expression as she struggled to think past the cycle of death between Ashcroft and her father. Why wasn't her brain working? Trauma, blood loss, concussion, any of them were reasonable causes, despite draining one little bag of blood in the basement.

Cohen sighed in irritation. "Whitmore called the FBI..." He shook his head when he finally saw the realization dawning on her face. With his eyes back on the road and his fingers gripping the steering wheel, he continued, "The DNA from the bodies will complicate things. Even without the anomalies in Duncan, Ashcroft, Coffee, and Alvarez, Humphrey and Whitmore will lead them to me, which will lead to you. I have no idea how to keep the three of you out of this. I have an entire station full of witnesses connecting us."

His concern didn't involve a desire to make their lives easier. Their involvement brought him too much attention, and she strongly doubted his family would appreciate the limelight.

"Fuck." His hands slammed against the wheel, making Lilith jump in her seat. "I'll get you to your rental car. Drive straight to the airport and take the first flight to New York. I'll figure out the rest." He had zero confidence in his last statement and with good reason. An overwhelming amount of evidence tied them to everything, most of which directly tied them to Cohen.

"No." Chance spoke up before she could. "A hefty amount of my blood is in that building, as well as Lilith's. If we run, we'll appear guilty, and it won't look good for you either. We need a solid explanation. One plausible to humans that omits the supernatural elements. If they firmly see us as victims and not suspects, things will go much easier."

"Well, I'm not roughing you up if that's what you're asking." Cohen's strained laugh revealed how stressed and distracted he was.

"Look. You have proof and witnesses that I was a victim. The entire station saw me roughed up on more than one occasion, and with Chance in holding, he's cleared for at least part of this."

When Cohen glanced at her, the expression wasn't friendly. "A cut, lacerations from the manacles, a few bruises, and week-old scars? I don't think it's enough to convey the severity of your attacks or explain the gravity of the situation."

"Leave that to me." The smile she flashed appeared confident, but her brain was grasping at straws. *Come on, think.*

"The FBI will only stay involved as long as they think there is an active threat. Leak the attack on Goditha, a private lab doing genetic research. We have paperwork prepared for emergencies that corroborate the socially accepted projects and will connect Duncan and Miriah. A cop in the forensics lab, Jenkins, is on our payroll. Have him confirm DNA from Goditha, Phipps Bend, and Miriah's office. Hell, you can even include the hotel fire. We can prove we stayed there."

Then, Chance chimed in, providing the perfect ending to her story, "A terrorist group warring against genetic experiments. They focused on destroying her family's work by attacking the lab, destroying samples, kidnapping scientists, and murdering anyone who got in their way by extreme means to deepen the threat level. Jenkins can prove they are all related and that the perpetrators are dead. Threat eliminated. The FBI will be satisfied and go home. You may even get a promotion out of the deal." Although Cohen's face brightened, his mouth still pinched into a skeptical line. "And what about you two?"

Lilith glanced back at Chance, still impressed with his quick cover story, and couldn't help but smile. "We will play the part of victims, stay until Miriah's body is released, and then fly back to New York so we can bury her and Malachi in the family plot. Just normal grieving relatives who survived thanks to a very heroic detective."

Cohen nodded and relaxed for a minute. Then, something else occurred to him. "And what about your father?"

Chance cut her off before she could say anything. "He must be kept out of this. His aversion to sunlight is too inconvenient. You're the only one who knows he's here."

The detective still appeared skeptical. "Contrary to pop culture, most FBI agents don't want to investigate *every* angle. If we hand them a virtually closed case, they'll work the preliminaries and bow out. The truth is they hate butting into a local investigation when they can avoid it. I have firsthand experience."

Cohen glanced over at her as if truly seeing her for the first time and busted out laughing.

A combination of defensive pride and confusion left her frowning. "What's so funny?"

"Six hundred years of assassinating your family, plotting, eluding law enforcement, bypassing security measures, torture, and mayhem, and that superhuman monster is outsmarted by *you*. If his endgame was to ruin your family's public image irrevocably, his biggest mistake was underestimating you. I'm sure he never saw losing as a possibility. Yet, here you are, explaining everything away, and handing the FBI a neat little package topped with a bow."

Embarrassment flooded her cheeks, and she turned away to stare out of the car window. "He underestimated everyone. My part was all luck, not some master plan. I'm not some superhero in black latex."

"Well, we can all dream." She caught Cohen's grin seconds before the animosity in the back seat reached a fevered pitch. Cohen must have felt it, too, since his grin dissolved into a grimace. Being subtle was challenging in a car full of empaths.

"Since we're all confined in here, how about you explain this shit a little more." Chance's growling voice was about as friendly as the holes he stared into the man's head.

"What shit?"

"Your blood and how it works, how your hair and eyes change color. That shit." Huh. With all the hits to the head she sustained, she figured the fluctuations were hallucinations. Obviously not if Chance noticed them too.

"Or we can discuss getting Gregor out of the city during the day." He caught Chance's eyes in the rearview mirror with a firmly commanding expression. As much as she wanted to know how the changes worked, Cohen was right. They had more significant concerns than a few parlor tricks.

With a drawn-out huff, Chance finally caved. "The airport should be our objective. I'll call Timothy and fill him in. The jet will draw too much attention, so he needs a commercial flight. The fire destroyed his fake passport and ID, but if we keep him out of the investigation, using his real name shouldn't be an issue." He leaned back in the seat and fished out his cell phone to start making calls.

"Right." Her brain went into overdrive, trying to figure out the best solution. "It has to be an evening or red-eye flight. We'll stop somewhere close to the airport. Any hotel will do. Cohen can go in and get a room since you're shirtless, and I'm a little too memorable in a button-up men's shirt and police track pants. We'll move him in as fast as possible, and, Chance, you can fill Timothy in on his location. After that, we need to stop at Target or Walmart."

Cohen glanced over in bewilderment. "What the hell for?"

"For three reasons. All our stuff burned up in the hotel fire. We need clothes, makeup, and first aid supplies."

"Umm. None of us require first aid. I mean, the incision is already closing, and I don't think FBI interviews require makeovers." Cohen glanced at her as if she sprouted a second head.

"You said my injuries weren't extensive enough, and neither are yours. If we want them to see us as true victims, we need to amp up the sympathy factor. Never thought I'd put my artistic talents to work this way, but then again, I never thought I'd be covering the trail of a six-hundred-year-old serial killer either."

A contagious rush of excitement filled the car as a ray of hope broke through the storm clouds. The feeling was fleeting for her because deep in her gut, she knew everything in her life was changing in painful ways. Dark things awaited her in New York, even if she managed to keep them out of the FBI's claws.

Chapter 26

Lilith stepped outside the police station into the weak evening sunlight. With the FBI agents satisfied by their terrorist cover story, they were finally free. Chance left to grab the rental car from the impound lot while Gregor sat in a hotel, waiting for his flight back home. The corpses recovered from the crumbling building confirmed Ashcroft's ultimate demise. No loose ends remained, so why did she feel so uneasy? Was it merely the cost of winning?

The weight of every death lay heavy on her shoulders. Miriah, Malachi, Duncan, Coffee, Humphrey, Whitmore, Alvarez, Dr. Nichols, even Spencer comprised a lengthy list of casualties. One made even longer if she included the thirty-eight people who perished in the hotel fire and all of Ashcroft's previous victims.

Of all of them, her partner's death affected her the most. Tears burned her eyes every time she thought of returning to New York with his unrecognizable body. For ten years, he played an integral role in her daily life. On a noticeably short list of friends, he lived in the number one spot. She never truly realized how important and irreplaceable he was until it was too late.

Not only did he back her up at crime scenes and wrestle in suspects, but also, he kept her focused, mentored her, made her part of his family. She'd miss his Spanish-flecked voice chirping from her Bluetooth with his Don Juan bravado. She'd even miss the awkward blind dates masquerading as cozy dinners, which she'd happily sit through every night if it meant getting him back.

A siren blared close by, pulling her attention away from her morose thoughts. The sound echoed around the buildings, making it impossible to pinpoint. She glanced up and down the vacant street, only spotting autumn leaves blowing in the light wind. Odd.

The other day, when Cohen released her, she stood in this same spot with the sidewalks full of people. She dug in her pocket for her cell to check the time but found nothing.

What the hell? Where is my phone? She must have lost it somewhere along the way. *Fantastic.* Another errand to run when she got home. The thought set her teeth on edge. There weren't many things she hated more than standing in a never-ending line to sell her soul for another two years to a random jackass with gel-spiked hair.

The siren grew louder, but still no glimmer of flashing lights. Her brow furrowed in confusion as she strolled past the station. Then, she noticed the huge chains wrapped around every shop door. Who used chains to lock a glass door?

The clouds blackened along with her mood, making the sunlight increasingly faint. The darkness closed in, suffocating her. Something felt wrong. A sudden crack of thunder boomed overhead, heralding the fast-approaching storm. Then, lightning split the sky, bleaching the whole street in blinding light. That may explain the stores. Perhaps the news channels ordered people to lock down, hide in their homes, and wait it out. Funny, why wouldn't the cops mention it?

She stepped into the middle of the empty street. While staring up at the heavy clouds, a drop landed on her cheek, but when she wiped it away, the consistency seemed unexpected, thicker, stickier. She glanced down at her palm to see a red smear. *What?*

Then, the skies ripped open, flooding the streets in red rain. The overwhelming scent of blood made her nauseous as she ran for cover. A bare bulb provided the only light in the gloomy alley as the ominous clouds blocked out the sun.

Her heart sped up, beating furiously against her ribs. What was happening? Was this another trippy side effect? When she peeked out from her hiding spot, the image of blood rushing down the road, gurgling in the storm drains seemed so surreal. How? This was an ordinary street in Knoxville, Tennessee, not a haunted hotel in the Colorado Rockies.

The sick scratch of metal on metal echoed sharply, and she whirled around to face the end of the alley. That sound, she heard it before…in New York City. The knot in her gut grew as she peered up at the light bulb above a familiar chipped and faded green door. The Italian place where she met Gregor, the spot of Malachi's final moments.

This couldn't be a side effect, could it? No, she had to be dreaming. Not only were hallucinations something entirely new, but also, the other abilities appeared to be dwindling since the catastrophe in the basement. Absently, she rubbed at the slow-healing incision along her collarbone.

"Wake up," she screamed to herself. "Wake up now!" The metal shriek sounded again, grating up her spine. To hell with it! If this was a dream, then nothing could hurt her, and she already experienced enough fear for three lifetimes. After surviving Ashcroft, she wasn't about to let a simple nightmare terrify her.

With defiant purpose, she stalked toward the screeching sound, determined to face her inner demons, and bent down to peek behind the dumpster. Despite her newfound bravado, her nerves frayed at the ends, but it didn't stop her.

Suddenly, hands grabbed her from behind, and she spun around, screaming. Her fist flew out instinctually, striking Chance in the jaw.

"Damn, woman. Cohen wasn't kidding about your right hook." He rubbed gingerly at the side of his face with a proud smile curling his lips.

"Oh, shit." She stepped forward, full of apologies. "I'm so sorry! Are you okay? I didn't mean to—"

"I'll live. I think you bruised my ego more than my face. What are you doing down here?" A slight tone of irritation infiltrated his voice amid the amusement and concern.

"I ran into the alley to get out of the rain, and I thought I heard something down here…"

"Do you always investigate creepy sounds? Personally, I head in the opposite direction, but to each their own." His enigmatic grin warmed her down to her toes, chasing away the gloom.

Unfortunately, the moment didn't last. He paused, his smile turning into a deep frown, which slowly revived her fear. "Wait. What rain?"

Chance appeared genuinely confused, and he certainly wasn't covered in blood. His chestnut hair was bone-dry. She peered down, expecting to see blood smeared across her palm—nothing.

Weak sunlight from the lightly overcast sky flooded the mundane alley. No blood, no green door, just the sound of the bustling street behind her. What was happening?

"I thought..." The words trailed off. She didn't need him locking her up in a padded cell. "Never mind." Her half-hearted chuckle didn't exactly inspire confidence. "I need to sleep. Did you get the car?" When her eyes opened, her heart stopped dead in her chest.

She stared right into Ashcroft's black beady eyes, bottomless pits of despair and anguish. Her whole body screamed for her to run, but she couldn't move, paralyzed with devastating terror.

"Aww, there it is...fear mingled with defeat." His eyes rolled in his head as he breathed in deep. "Yours is most exquisite." Thin lips stretched into a gruesome smile drenched in blood with the scent of death on his breath. Her heart threatened to beat right out of her chest as her eyes hesitantly followed the trail of blood to his feet.

Chance lay crumpled on the asphalt, blood pouring from a gaping wound in his neck, the flesh torn and ragged. Tears sprung to her eyes as she squeezed them shut. *Please let this be some trippy-ass vision or a nightmare or anything that* isn't *real.*

But when she opened her eyes again, nothing changed. Ashcroft still stood in front of her, hovering over Chance's lifeless body. Her world narrowed to that one view, Chance...dead. The monster lost all his power over her because he took away her last reason to fight.

Ashcroft clamped his steely hand around her throat and dragged her closer, but she couldn't take her eyes off the man she loved.

"Oh, don't give up so easy, my dear. It's not any fun if you meekly resign yourself to your fate." His vile breath curled over her skin as he leaned in. "I wouldn't want you to die too quickly. Not like your partner. Alvarez was his name?"

While the memory brought fresh tears, she still refused to meet his eyes. With a guttural snarl, Ashcroft threw her down, and her bones rattled against the hard concrete...floor?

She crawled up to her knees and scanned the area with a growing sense of doom. Pipes hung from the ceiling, barrels lined the wall, and a boiler sat in the corner. The Phipps Bend basement? *I must be dreaming.* Her mind rebelled against the obvious possibility that she never left.

"Damn it, Lilith. Wake the fuck up!" she screamed vehemently, but when she looked up, Ashcroft stood behind Alvarez, who knelt on the cold concrete, bound in chains. Beside him lay Miriah's mutilated corpse clinging to Malachi's in some macabre embrace.

Duncan's lifeless eyes stared out on the other side. He gnawed his chained arms to the bone, and bits of his flesh hung from his gaping mouth. Coffee lay, sprawled out before the trio, his enormous torso reduced to a hollowed-out husk with glistening intestines dangling to the floor.

As she struggled to get to her hands and knees, she choked on the bile rising in her throat from witnessing the abhorrent scene.

"You will never be free of them or me!" His lanky arm gestured toward the grotesque row of corpses, all the people she failed. "I want you to see this." His laugh made her skin crawl as her stomach continued to lurch violently. The monster's bony hand slid under her partner's chin. Felipe broke out in a cold sweat, eyes flickering around wildly.

At first, she didn't understand why he stayed so silent, why he didn't scream and plead. Then, she saw the rough stitches through his lips. The nefarious demon sewed his mouth shut.

"You didn't get to watch last time. I want you to witness every last second of his life."

"No!" The screech ricocheted through the cavernous space. She tried to scramble closer, but the chain around her ankle kept her out of reach. Furious tears poured down her cheeks as her fists pounded against the concrete. "No! You're dead! This whole place is gone!" Her horrified shrieks continued until her throat felt raw.

The madman's sinister cackle grew louder as the straight razor pressed against Alvarez's neck. The stitches pulled at Felipe's lips, hindering his attempts to scream. He focused on her as he wept, helpless and hopeless. She howled and scratched like a wild animal, desperate to save him. Dream or not, she needed him to survive this time.

"You let them all die. Was it worth it?" Ashcroft's words seared into her skin like a hideous tattoo, a physical representation of her guilt. It was her fault. She *let* them die.

The scalpel slid into his skin, blood instantly welling up around the blade. "To think, this man..." The monster bent to whisper the words near his ear, but the beady black eyes stayed on her, sparkling with amusement. "This man will never kiss his beloved wife good night, never embrace his children, and never meet his new grandchildren. And for what? So, you could free your murderous father?"

A high maniacal shriek of laughter filled the air as the blade carved a path through Felipe's throat at an excruciatingly slow pace, prolonging the suffering. Lilith's heart shattered as she wailed, choking and coughing on her tears. Alvarez simply stared at her expectantly while she crumbled under the weight of her failure.

As her nails clawed uselessly at the concrete, her partner screamed, and the stitches tore through his skin, leaving his mouth a mass of torn flesh. With one last nefarious howl of laughter, Ashcroft whipped the blade through his throat, and hot blood spurted across her face, blinding her.

"No!" She woke up screeching as she fought her way out of the bed and scrambled into a corner. Goose bumps covered her cold, clammy skin, and her whole body shook fiercely. Her shell-shocked eyes scanned the room and found little comfort in the plush carpet and red drapes. Although she huddled in the bedroom of her New York apartment seven hundred miles from the location of her nightmare, she didn't feel safe.

Yes, Ashcroft was dead, Chance was alive, and her father was tucked away in a hotel room, secretly working with Cohen in Tennessee. Still, she struggled with each breath as she pulled her knees close and wrapped her arms around them.

All the bloody memories burned into her mind, branding her. Every time she closed her eyes, all she saw were the litany of corpses left behind. She stayed there, curled in the corner, cold and alone, tears streaming down her face, her entire body trembling. She could shirk responsibility for Miriah and Malachi, but the others rested firmly on her shoulders. If she did things differently, they might be alive. Ashcroft held the knife, but her actions set the stage.

Lilith stepped out of the cab and stared up at the full moon hanging ominously over the graveyard. The crisp autumn chill cut through her long black dress and matching coat. Halloween wasn't for a few days, but she already felt haunted. She stared out over the eerie gravestones with tears in her eyes. *Felipe is dead.* Three days after the night terror, she still couldn't shake the expression on his face.

The canopy surrounded by floodlights seemed wrong, intrusive. Abrasive light in a place meant for private grieving as if insisting she publicly participate instead of hiding in the shadows. A growing crowd of people milled around the site, talking in hushed tones, clasping hands, embracing, sharing their condolences.

Although the effects from Cohen's blood seemed to diminish each passing day, the hailstorm of emotions still shimmered over her skin, making her uneasy.

Lilith jumped in surprise as Chance slid his fingers through hers. With a sigh of relief, she closed her eyes and tried to get a handle on things. After a few quiet moments, her heart slowed to a normal pace once again.

"I wasn't sure you'd show up, but you're gonna be okay." The warmth of his breath trickled through her ice-cold body as he whispered against her ear. Her grip on his hand tightened, but he never complained. He simply stood beside her, patiently, like a reassuring beacon of goodness.

They returned to New York several days ago, but she couldn't call the city home anymore. Everything changed. Unable to fathom training a newbie, she decided to take leave from work until after the funeral. No, it was more than that. She didn't trust her instincts, which made her a dangerous partner. Staring out at the gathering crowd, she wished things happened differently for the millionth time.

"She still won't answer the phone or call me back. I shouldn't be here."

The loss of Gloria, her closest friend, cut deep. One more painful thing on a pile of excruciating experiences. All the death, betrayal, horrifying family secrets. Somehow, she found herself in an alternate reality where Chance stood alone as her only connection, keeping her anchored to the real world. If someone told her a week ago he would be her confidant over her partner, her best friend, or her father, she would have cackled hysterically. Now the surreal concept defined her new reality.

After shoving her chaotic thoughts aside, she turned toward him, finally taking in the view. He abandoned his usual T-shirt and jeans, opting for a more appropriate and sophisticated look. The black slacks with matching shirt and tie suited him. Under other circumstances, she would have appreciated it a lot more.

"Lily, she's mourning her husband. This is not your fault. None of it is. If she holds you responsible, it's because she needs an outlet for her anger and sorrow. You need to remember where the blame belongs, on Ashcroft's smoking corpse and nowhere else."

Lilith nodded absently and stared down at her hand, resting in his. Logically, he was right, but it did little to ease the weight on her heart. If she didn't hang up on her father or lie to Alvarez. If she warned him or moved faster in the basement. But in the moment, she didn't do any of those things, and he suffered the consequences.

The Ashcroft in her nightmare might not be real, but his words never left her. She let them all die and could only bring back a charred, unrecognizable corpse. Dental records and DNA represented the only closure she could provide Gloria and her children. That and a litany of meaningless apologies.

"I still shouldn't be here." Her skin flushed with heat, her vision swimming. He squared off with her, grasping her shoulders and waiting for her eyes to meet his.

"You deserve to be here." His voice held the same ironclad determination often used by her father. "He was your partner and a dear friend. You need to grieve him properly, *mon cherie*."

"And if Gloria disagrees? What are you going to do, shoulder check the widow?" The futile attempt to formulate a smile only made her feel hollow.

As if sensing the chill infiltrating her bones, he hugged her close and evaded the question.

"Have you heard from Gregor?" Right from one painful subject to another. "Is he planning to be here?"

"I have no idea. Timothy is supposed to pick him up at the airport. He decided to stay and anonymously help Cohen clear things up. All I know is that the investigation is over, and Cohen is receiving a commendation."

In truth, her father called a dozen times, but she still wasn't ready to talk to him. She suspected his absence involved avoiding the turmoil of coming home more than helping with the FBI.

Until recently, Gregor was more than just her adoring father. He was her best friend, a crucial focal point of her life, someone she trusted unflinchingly. Now life presented her a new, terrifying image of her father as a mass murderer capable of slaughtering women and children. He tortured Ashcroft for days, breaking the mind of an already monstrous creature. No matter his reasons, the acts seemed unforgivable.

Even if she dismissed his distant past, he still lied about her mother's death, kept secrets, threatened Chance into submission, and sent them to Tennessee unprepared. That wasn't the father she knew. He was a stranger, and she had no idea how the interloper fit into her life and if they could share any semblance of a father-daughter relationship again.

Since returning to New York, her hatred for Ashcroft only intensified. The monster stripped everything away from her, left her adrift with no oar to steer. Suddenly, Chance squeezed her hand once again, pulling her out of the dark depths of self-pity. Perhaps her life wasn't entirely without direction.

She peered up at him quizzically as a thought occurred to her. "You head his security team. Haven't you spoken to him?"

He flashed a tight smile, which appeared painful, and slowly began ushering her toward the grave site. "We're not phone buddies who chitchat and swap gossip, *cher*. Tim called and told me to take a week off. Either Gregor decided I earned vacation time, or he's still pissed at me for telling you about...everything."

At last, a subject change she could handle. "Speaking of which, you still owe me a date, and for the record, this doesn't count." She managed to pull off an upbeat tone and genuinely smiled this time.

"Oh, I didn't assume it would." The teasing grin warmed her soul and made her chuckle. He interlaced his fingers with hers again as the grin melted into a more somber expression. "Even under normal circumstances, something like this wouldn't be easy..."

"Now that might win the *Understatement of the Year* award." Although she intended her comment to be light, she failed miserably. Normal circumstances no longer existed. Enduring this with the lingering aftereffects of Cohen's blood would be a real challenge. The fact that Chance suffered from the same side effects in all their full-strength glory made her appreciate his insistence to accompany her even more.

His fingers squeezed around hers, bringing her back to reality once again. "Yeah, well... I thought I could cook you dinner at my place afterward. No pressure, just peace and quiet away from everyone else." Before she had an opportunity to respond, he nervously changed the subject.

"So, how is a night service arranged? Doesn't it raise eyebrows in the police department? I mean, this isn't exactly normal, especially for an officer who fell in the line of duty."

Unable to tell if she was the source of his anxiety or the swirling emotions of the crowd, she found solace in the logical question. As they grew closer, the sobs became audible. Even without over-amped empathic abilities, grief hung thick in the air, palpable and suffocating. She needed the distraction.

"True. The task is never easy or painless, but stipulations in your will certainly help. People tend to write them off as eccentricities. In Felipe's case, he requested an evening mass to be followed immediately by his burial. When you cite religious reasons, people become too concerned with offending the family to object. I suppose that's one plus side to the age of political correctness."

"Not that I'm an expert on Catholicism, but isn't that reserved for Christmas Eve?"

They skipped the Catholic Mass not because she didn't respect their religious beliefs, but because Gloria limited it to immediate family. Over half of their descendants flew in for the service, a considerable number. Explaining over fifty children and hundreds of grandchildren to a roomful of humans would be difficult. So, in her efficient fashion, she designated the burial to friends and coworkers, keeping them separate from family, one Lilith no longer belonged to, apparently.

"True, but they made sizeable donations for thirty years. Money greases all kinds of wheels in a Catholic church. Hell, for the right amount, you can buy your ancestor's way out of purgatory."

"Reminds me of a bumper sticker I saw once. *If money is the root of all evil, why does the church want so much of it?* Never seemed right to me."

Quietly, she chuckled under her breath. "You and me both, you shouldn't try to make me laugh, though. Some people might find it inappropriate." She tempered her chastising tone with a wink, earning a brief smile from her escort.

Then, he stopped in his tracks as if hitting a brick wall, and the sensation of grief tingled along her body. "So..." He glanced over with a nervous expression. "How are you feeling...since Tennessee?"

There was no need to elaborate. Although she still sensed emotion, it no longer possessed her, consumed her. The healing ability also dwindled to a slight advantage, and thankfully, she didn't come across any new surprises.

"I'm more interested in how *you* are feeling."

After staring at her expectantly for a few minutes, he realized she had no intention of answering his questions until he answered hers. With an aggravated huff, he finally caved.

"I'm emotional flypaper. It's distracting and more than a little unnerving, but I'm managing. Besides that, I am stronger and healthier than ever." Not only could she hear the strain in his voice, but also, tension strummed over his skin in slight tremors. Her eyes watered, overwhelmed with appreciation. No matter how challenging it was, he stood steadfast by her side because she needed him.

A comfortable silence settled over them as she laid her head against his shoulder. If only she could lose herself in the warmth of his solace without the nagging feeling that horrible consequences awaited them for escaping. A gut reaction that an overpaid psychiatrist would label survivor's guilt.

"Breathe, *mon cherie*." His low rumbling voice infused her dark thoughts with affectionate light, making the future seem less ominous.

With a tear-filled expression of gratitude, she gazed up at him. "What does that mean, by the way? I never took French."

For a moment, he seemed content to simply smile down at her with a brilliant glow as if trying to convince himself that she was real. "It means *my sweetheart*."

A luminous smile lit her face as she pressed a tender kiss to his lips and whispered, "I love you too."

She started to pull back, but he wrapped his arms around her, still trembling. Slow, deep breaths tickled along her neck, moist with tears, as they stood enveloped in a bubble of warmth, fending off the darkness surrounding them.

Then, she realized their seemingly private moment was too public. Dozens of eyes openly stared, most of them brimming with camaraderie, the shared grief for a coworker. However, more than a few studied Chance curiously, and several made their distaste for the show of affection quite visible.

Sensing her apprehension, he let her go and took her hand. "Are you ready?"

"No, but I'll never be ready." After placing an encouraging kiss on the back of her hand, the crowd parted for them. As Alvarez's partner, the cops considered her as significant as the widow. Unfortunately, she had the overwhelming feeling that Gloria didn't share that opinion.

Chapter 27

Lilith drew in a deep breath, bracing herself as she followed Chance through the multitude of mourners. Her iron grip on his hand served as an anchor, preventing her from going adrift in a sea of grief. She didn't need supernatural powers to feel the pity and sorrow reflected in their eyes. Dread began twisting her stomach into knots with every step. Finally, the emotional wind tunnel became unbearable, and she dropped her eyes to the ground.

Then, a silent stillness suddenly spread through the crowd as if they were collectively holding their breath. Shaking with fear, terrified of what she might see, Lilith slowly met the eyes of Felipe Alvarez's grieving widow, Gloria.

An onslaught of memories instantly flooded her mind—chatting each Sunday over coffee, dozens of dinners, birthday parties, the girls' confirmation ceremonies, serving as best *man* when renewing their vows three years ago. All of those cherished memories disintegrated. No trace of them remained in Gloria's enraged eyes. She stood alone in a long black dress with a matching veil covering her tear-streaked face. A regal air infused her posture with confident righteousness, something lost in the modern world.

Under the significant weight of her stare, she wanted nothing more than to slink away. After everything she endured, her best friend terrified her more than any of it. The sentiment said a lot about how much she valued the few emotional connections she had left. In the end, she owed Gloria, Alvarez, and their family more than a coward's retreat.

"Gloria, words can't express how sorry I am…" She managed to keep the tremble out of her voice but didn't know how to finish the sentence. Everything that came to mind seemed extremely underwhelming, like informing a stage 4 cancer patient that Neosporin works wonders.

For a terrible moment, Gloria didn't move a single muscle, didn't even blink. Lilith held her breath, desperately clinging to the tiny glimmer of hope that Gloria would hug her and cry, sharing their grief. However, the optimistic thought faded with every passing second of silence.

With shaky fingers, Gloria lifted her veil. The once openly friendly face twisted into a mask of agony, mascara running in streaks down her face. The palpable pain resonating from Felipe's widow left her light-headed and heartbroken.

As much as she wanted to comfort her friend, she somehow knew touching Gloria would be a mistake. Any remaining hope withered away in the awkward silence. The staring contest finally captivated people's attention, and soon, every eye rested on them. Her deep-rooted desire to run and hide became overwhelming. She hated the spotlight on an average day, but under these circumstances, she squirmed, begging for the tension to break.

"You!" The solitary word held so much venom that Lilith felt physically sick. Gloria's lips curled into a snarl as her Spanish accent grew thicker. "You have no right!"

She flinched at the poisonous words, mostly because they echoed her internal thoughts. How could she defend herself? "I never…" The explanation died in her throat, unable to come up with anything significant to change her own mind, much less Gloria's.

The widow's face twisted in sadness, her deep brown eyes blinking back tears. "We trusted you. Felipe trusted you. You were part of *mi familia*." She clutched a handkerchief to her chest as the tears choked off her words. For a moment, she swayed, and one of the officers moved quickly to keep her steady on her feet. Then, she wiped at her face, smearing the mascara across her cheeks, and continued, "Felipe called me. He told me why he was there." Her rage resurfaced, erupting through her overwhelming misery. "You refused to listen to your father. You condemned my Felipe to die because you chose not to come home, behaving like a spoiled child!"

Gloria straightened, standing tall, and shook off the officer supporting her. She squared her jaw and slapped Lilith across the face with righteous indignity, but the physical pain paled in comparison to the emotional whiplash.

Before Lilith could say or do anything, Chance pulled her behind him. "I understand how you feel. You've suffered a loss greater than anyone here could imagine. Now, Lilith may be willing to let you punish her for Detective Alvarez's death, but it is not her burden to bear. You will *not* make her into a convenient scapegoat for your fury." His voice held a perfect blend of calm restraint and forcefulness, and for a moment, Gloria didn't know how to react.

"Chance, don't—" When she attempted to move past him, he kept her firmly in place, ignoring her protest.

Gloria's eyes hardened on Chance with laser focus. "I do not know you. Do not pretend to—"

Chance quickly cut her off. "With all due respect, you have *no* idea what happened in Tennessee. I was there when Felipe died, and I have worked with him for years as the head of Gregor's security team. I was also present the multiple times Lilith was seconds from death. She could have run away at any time. She could have left us all to die and saved herself, but no. She came back *every* time, every single time, and fought with everything she had because she refused to leave *anyone* behind!"

Gloria's eyes flickered from Chance to Lilith for a second, as doubt and concern crept into her face. Then it vanished like smoke, and only anger remained.

"Chance…" Lilith grabbed his arm, but he glanced back at her, firmly telling her to let him do this.

His speech made her out to be some kind of hero, but she wasn't a noble knight on a white horse. She simply tried to survive, and although the altruistic spotlight made her uncomfortable, arguing with Chance seemed pointless. With a resigned sigh, she leaned against his back, ignoring her tumultuous emotions.

Then, he turned back to Gloria to finish what he had to say. "You have no right to blame this on her." He edged closer, which surprised her, and lowered his voice to a growling whisper.

"If she followed Gregor's orders and came home when he told her to, the terrorist who killed your husband would have followed to finish his work. He wouldn't have stopped with Gregor, Lilith, or even me. Felipe would still be dead, and you and your daughters would have joined him. Felipe knew this. He sacrificed himself to ensure we could end it and keep you and your family safe. It's a miracle that any of us survived. Mourn your husband, but be grateful and honor his sacrifice. Don't tarnish his memory by treating his partner like she's a pariah for being alive."

Surprise, confusion, and a grain of fear polluted Gloria's regal face, but Chance didn't allow her any time to recover. He simply turned, grasped Lilith's hand, and marched her up to the open grave site.

"Chance…" Before another word left her mouth, he handed her a rose and softly kissed her cheek.

"You've earned the right to tell him goodbye. This is about you and Felipe, no one else."

She smiled up at him with tears of immense gratitude. "Thank you." Her eyes drifted to the bloodred flower in her hands. She pressed a kiss against the plush petals, infusing it with every ounce of love and regret she had left. With a deep, steadying breath, she released the flower into the grave, watching the darkness swallow it up.

When she finally turned around, he wrapped his arm around her shoulders and escorted her past the crowd. Gloria caught her eyes, and for a moment, she softened, but the expression faded as she pulled her veil down over her tear-streaked face. The rest of the mourners stared in profound confusion as Chance led Lilith straight to the car.

As they walked, her thoughts wandered again. Felipe's widow wasn't the only one affected by the brutal truth Chance laid at her feet. He was right. If she left when her father ordered her to, Ashcroft would have followed them to New York and destroyed anything and everything they loved. She still felt a sense of responsibility, but some of the weight lifted from her weary shoulders.

The first time Lilith stepped into Chance's apartment, the decor and design completely shocked her. She expected a sleek woman-snaring pad with mood lighting and all the gadgets to accommodate his voracious love life. Now, the view only emphasized how much she misjudged him. After meeting the real person behind the smoke and mirrors, the place perfectly reflected his self-image. He spent years hiding everything beautiful and unique about himself beneath layers of societal expectations. He camouflaged himself as much as the dilapidated exterior of his building hid the gem inside.

She stood inside his sanctuary, admiring the warm wooden floors and the haunting artwork with tears in her eyes. She'd been so blind, wasted so much time viewing him as a fixture instead of a person.

Chance tossed his black suit jacket on the back of a chair and rolled up his sleeves. "So, what kind of food do you like? I know you and Gregor usually meet at Italian places, but I didn't know if that was your preference or his."

Overcome, she suddenly choked on her tears as she watched him move about the elegant kitchen, grabbing pots and pans before strolling to the fridge. *Why am I losing it now?*

Perhaps the funeral's emotional turmoil finally caught up with her, or was it the realization that this version of Chance truly existed? He loved her. The meaningless sexcapades, the cavalier attitude, the smart-ass banter, he utilized them all to hide that one simple fact for *thirteen years*. Somehow, being in his apartment made everything vividly real.

When she didn't respond, he turned around with concern pulling at every muscle. "Lily?" When he saw her standing near the elevator, crying, a tear slid down his cheek as he strolled toward her. Strong arms enveloped her like a warm blanket of security, and she released a soft sigh of contentment. He hugged her tighter in response, his face nuzzling into her hair.

"Everything will be okay, *mon cherie*. Give her time." Lost in his soft and soothing voice, she clung to him until the tears finally stopped. Without speaking another word, his hands rubbed her back in slow circles as they clung to each other. Each muscle gradually relaxed. She didn't realize how much energy she expended bracing herself for the funeral. Now that the ordeal was over, her soul ached from the effort.

"You're right." Although her voice strained under the weight of her tears, it somehow remained steady. With a massive sigh of relief, she let everything go and pulled back, wiping her tear-soaked cheeks. "I'll be okay, eventually." She forced a tiny yet grateful smile while he watched her with guarded caution.

As much as she craved the comfort he provided, the expression on his face reminded her of the consequences of putting her needs first. He deserved more than that.

The balancing act of a relationship wasn't in her skill set *before* the layers of trauma she recently accumulated. During her moment of realization, he reached out to brush his fingers over her shoulder, and she stepped back. A small action, but a flicker of rejection still crossed his face as he swallowed the sudden lump in his throat.

"I should go home." She felt lost, overwhelmed, and worn the hell out. The funeral maxed out her ability to process complex thoughts and emotions. Still, she owed him a lot, especially a truthful explanation.

"With the funeral and everything, I'm exhausted." She stepped closer and twined her fingers through his. "Nothing has changed, Chance. I still want…this." While struggling to find the right word, she realized they never defined things, but that wasn't the point.

"I feel like a live wire stripped of all its protective layers. I'm frayed. Can we have dinner another night?"

Disappointment lingered in his eyes, but he nodded softly. "I didn't mean to push, *cherie*. Do you want me to take you home?"

With a faint smile, she leaned up on tiptoe and gave him a feather-soft kiss. "You aren't pushing. I need to sleep and decompress, and I don't want our first date to consist of you making me feel better." She held his gaze as her palm caressed his cheek. "You deserve more than that. I'll call a cab." Suddenly, his arm slid around her waist and pulled her against him as his lips crashed against hers. A wave of passion that belonged solely to her tingled over her skin, leaving her breathless. The sudden surge of heat told her the alley was not a fluke, and it wasn't the result of Cohen's blood either.

When he stepped back, a roguish grin lit his face. "A small reminder of what is waiting for you, and thank you, Lily." Even his charismatic wink made her muscles tremble. All of a sudden, she didn't feel quite so tired. "Unless, of course, it changed your mind about leaving."

After a deep, cleansing breath, she moved back. "Nice diversion tactic, tease, but I want to be clearheaded for a rare event like a man cooking me dinner. I wouldn't be great company tonight."

The twinkle in his hazel eyes made her feel unbelievably relieved. "In that case, how about we share a drink until your cab arrives?" She cracked a smile and nodded before perching on a barstool at his kitchen island. Downplaying the formality and importance of the evening alleviated the pressure immediately, allowing her to breathe easy.

After two tall glasses of wine and a game of *I Never*, she rode the freight elevator down with thoughts of Chance skinny-dipping. A million different times, she wanted to call and cancel the taxi, but the evening's events still weighed heavily on her mind. It left her off-balance and powerless around him, and she needed to reclaim her sense of self before trying to wade into emotionally deep waters. Not just for her sake, but his as well.

Halfway down, her cell phone chirped, knocking her out of her thoughts. She fished it out of her pocket and glanced at the number before answering.

"Hey, Timothy. Did everything go okay at the airport?"

"Well, no one frisked me, but we have a big problem."

She growled in irritation. With her nerves already worn thin, the last thing she needed was Timothy shredding what little patience she had left. "Yeah, I figured that when you called. What's going on?"

"I'm here at the gate. I watched everyone get off the plane, and Gregor isn't here."

Somewhere deep in her brain, warning bells went off, but her sheer mental exhaustion stifled them. "Did you call him?"

"Of course!" He didn't bother hiding his aggravation. "It went straight to voice mail. I tried to call Detective Cohen since he sent me the flight info, but he didn't answer either."

Her phone beeped in her ear once, then twice. "Hold on. I'm getting another call." As the elevator lurched to a stop at the bottom floor, she glanced at the familiar number flashing across the screen. "That's Cohen on the other line. I'll call you back."

Before he could respond, she switched over to the incoming call. "I assume you're calling about why my father isn't stepping off a plane in New York City? Is he playing hooky again?" she chuckled as she leaned down to grab the strap to the gate. This made the fourth time her father missed his flight.

"Lilith?" The whisper-soft voice made her pause. Coupled with all the static, she couldn't be sure it was him speaking.

"Cohen? Speak up. I can barely hear you."

"I can't, and there's no time…" More muffled noise cut him off.

Fear sizzled down every nerve as her hands began to shake. "What is going on?"

"Lilith, listen to me very fucking carefully. They got to your father…"

"What?" She shot upright. "Who? Who has him? You aren't making sense."

"I don't have time to explain. Please, listen. They know about you and Chance. You *have* to run!"

"Who, the FBI? Run where?" Her stomach twisted in knots as dread tightened around her chest like a boa constrictor.

"Goddamn it, Lilith. Just run, *now*!" The line went dead as she heard shattering glass above.

"Fuck!" She needed to grab Chance and figure out what the hell was going on. She mashed the second-floor button, and the elevator jerked into a painfully slow crawl upward. She tapped her foot impatiently as a thousand scenarios ran through her brain. *Come on, come on, come on!*

She wished she had her gun. As soon as the doors opened, she'd be walking in blind with no defense and no weapons.

To make herself a smaller target, she crouched into a corner. Not the best cover, but it was all she had. Her mind kept going over and over the call. What did Cohen mean *They got to your father*, and who were *they*? Ashcroft was dead, and so were all his flunkies. Cohen said the FBI closed the case, so what was going on?

The elevator ground to a halt and gunshots rang out. She flattened herself against the wall as the doors opened and carefully peeked out. Three black ropes dangled through the shattered window like something out of a cheesy action movie. Chance fought off two guys in what appeared to be tactical SWAT gear. *What the hell?*

The first henchman slashed at him, but not fast enough. Chance easily dodged the blade and slammed his open palm into the man's elbow. With catlike reflexes, he stooped down to avoid a blow from the second man and shot up, shoving his arm into the man's chest with a crack.

For a moment, she crouched, mesmerized by his fluid movements. With all the insanity in Tennessee, she never saw him in proper action. Someone always pointed a gun in her face or beat her senseless. Then, reality crashed over her. This wasn't a performance piece. He was fighting for his life. *Come on, Lilith. Get it together.*

Then, she caught sight of a third man coming up behind Chance with a tactical knife while he slammed henchman number two into the ground. Her heart skipped a beat as everything slid into slow motion. Blood pounded in her ears, and she screamed at the top of her lungs, "Behind you!"

For a split second, Chance glanced up at her with terror and shock in his eyes. Time froze as she suddenly realized her warning was more distracting than helpful. Fortunately, Chance stepped deftly aside, shooting his fist into the man's ribs with pounding force. A sigh of relief escaped her lips, and she clung to the elevator's gate.

Chance whipped his head around to stare at her again. The pain and emotional agony in his eyes tore at her. "Run! Get out of here!"

While her finger hovered over the elevator button, she heard him grunt as one of the thugs caught him with a blow to the kidney. She couldn't leave him like this. They didn't survive all the crap in Tennessee for him to die now. The memory of holding him in her arms as blood poured out of his chest flashed through her mind. She could never live with herself if she pressed that button and lost him forever. Weapon or not, she *had* to do something.

Then, a SWAT guy barreled straight for her, taking the choice out of her hands. The gate was still down, providing a barrier, but it wouldn't help Chance. With fire in her belly, she slammed the gate up. A split second of surprise lit the man's face, but he didn't falter. He kept on running, and a plan formed in her head. She could use his momentum against him, sidestep, and slam him into the back of the elevator.

Before he reached her, Chance tackled the runner to the ground with bone-rattling force. "Goddamn it, Lily. Get the fuck out of here! Now!" The man used Chance's distraction to knock him off-balance, and they wrestled, trading vicious blows. Meanwhile, the guy with the bum elbow picked up number three's knife and stalked up to the wrestling match.

"Oh, fuck you all." Her tolerance for the endless parade of crap reached a breaking point. With a snarl of determination, she dug in her heels and sprinted for the henchman with the blade. As she got close, she lowered her shoulder and lunged for his abdomen. The man rocketed back, and she fell on top of him, tangled up in her floor-length dress. While the mystery guy struggled to catch his breath, the knife clattered to the floor.

She stumbled over him a few times, trying to get to her feet. Damn heels. Every time she got into a fistfight, she happened to wear the most inappropriate footwear. She should start wearing sneakers exclusively.

The man feebly grasped at her legs but only managed to trip her. She glanced up to see a pistol lying a few feet away, and victory flooded her jangled nerves. She lunged for the gun, curling her fingers over the handle.

Suddenly, a combat boot stomped ferociously on her hand, sending a sharp pain roaring up her arm. With a scream, she tried to pull back, but the man kept her pinned. She scrambled to get her legs underneath her so she could throw him off-balance, but a blinding kick to the face sent her crashing to the ground. Lights flashed before her eyes as the pain in her hand gave way to a roaring headache.

Lilith blinked several times, attempting to clear her blurry vision. One of the anonymous henchmen stood over her, pistol in hand. She peered up at his face with terror pounding through her body, but what she saw surprised her.

When Spencer held her at gunpoint, sick satisfaction and maniacal glee covered his face. This man's expression displayed a calm as smooth as polished stone. He showed no signs of murderous rage. He merely studied each reaction with his gun aimed, like a cop waiting for a suspect to make a move or surrender.

Two gunshots rang out, and she squeezed her eyes shut, waiting for the pain to start. When it didn't, she gazed up as the gun fell, and he crumpled to the floor with two shots to the chest. Without hesitation, she snatched the pistol and jumped to her feet, fighting off the wave of nausea stemming from her aching face.

She spun on her heel in time to see Chance drop the guy's arm, which held the smoking gun, and cleanly snap his neck. The scene felt surreal, like she suddenly stepped into a badass action movie. As he threw the body to the floor, their eyes met for a moment with purpose and determination.

Her eyes scanned the apartment until she saw the last henchman sprawled on the ground with his neck at an impossible angle. That was it. It was over.

Even through the buzz of adrenaline flooding her system, she felt the pressure as her cheek and nose began to swell. The room spun for a moment, indicating she might have yet another concussion. Great. At this rate, she'd develop CTE faster than the Jets' quarterback. Chance grabbed her arms before her mind registered his movement. "Are you all right?" He gingerly angled her face up, examining the puffy skin, but something in his expression bothered her.

She pulled away, annoyed. "Yeah, I'm fine."

Chance huffed irritably and snatched her arm, leading her away from the shattered window. "Why the hell didn't you get out of here? Why did you come back?" His face contorted into a tangled mess of anger, guilt, and irritation—a lovely combination.

For a second, she merely stared at him in disbelief. Then, she shook her head, thinking the answer was obvious. "Are you fucking kidding me? Why do you think?" As she let the question sink in, something else caught her attention.

"What's that sound?" A hollow droning filled the background, muffled but familiar.

"That's just the…" His face instantly changed as his color drained away. "The elevator! How many shots do you have left?!"

She checked the clip while he did the same. "I'm full. Guess he never got the opportunity to use it." A sly smile pulled at her lips until she glanced over at his stern frown.

"I've got eleven. Okay, take cover behind the island. I'll use the kitchen corner. As soon as the doors open, line up a shot, and take it."

After kicking off her heels, she crouched and put her back to the cabinet. With slow, deep breaths, she continually adjusted her grip on the gun, eyes closing with a silent prayer. It was getting closer now, almost to the top.

Then, the freight elevator stopped, and she opened her eyes to see two men in similar SWAT gear already standing in front of her. Before she aimed, they hauled her to her feet. She screamed and fought against them, but resistance seemed futile.

As Chance turned to train his weapon on them, a high-pitched screech filled the air, slicing through her brain like a hot knife through butter. She doubled over, reeling, and struggled to cover her ears. The men flanking her seemed unaffected. Beyond the migraine haze, she spotted yellow earplugs. They came prepared. Whatever made the hideous shriek was clearly on their guest list.

She released a scream as the sound intensified, which instantly drowned in the deafening roar. As she fought off wave after wave of crippling nausea, she watched Chance drop his gun. No pain twisted his handsome face—quite the opposite. Every line smoothed into an expression of pure bliss. His eyes glazed over as he stood motionless. Even without the banshee screams, she couldn't comprehend his reaction.

The gate flung open, and the screech receded to a dull buzz. Lilith sagged heavily between the two men, trying not to vomit from the intense pain splitting her skull. Somewhere in the back of her brain, she felt a tiny twinge of attraction, which definitely didn't belong to her. Finally, the roaring headache receded enough for her to scan the area, searching for the source.

A tall curvy woman sauntered out of the elevator clad in a skin-tight lavender dress as platinum blonde tendrils bounced over her shoulders. Her full lips parted in an odd expression reminiscent of a Marilyn Monroe movie.

Then Lilith realized the noise, once deafening and now merely an irritation, came from the bombshell. The woman's lips barely moved, but she was definitely…singing? Lilith glanced at her two guards but only found the expected traces of natural attraction. They weren't the source of the intensity tickling over her skin.

Then, her eyes drifted reluctantly to Chance, and her heart stopped dead in her chest. Completely mesmerized, he staggered toward the woman as her lips curled into a grin. Then, a note ripped through the air sending both Lilith and Chance to their knees, but for vastly different reasons. While blood trickled from her ears, he gazed up at the blonde with complete adoration.

The sudden pain in her chest felt like her heart shattered, and her panicked breaths sped up. She would endure a lifetime of banshee screams to unsee the expression on his face at that moment.

The woman set her ice-blue eyes on Chance as her nefarious shriek subsided again. While she sauntered up to him, four men in uniforms came up to flank her with their weapons resting casually in their arms.

The bombshell tickled her fingers through his chestnut brown hair, lighting an instant rage in Lilith's belly. "So handsome." The woman's voice held a singsong quality that set her teeth on edge. "And such a good boy." Voluminous lips stretched into a wicked grin, and she raised her calculating eyes to Lilith, cocking her head to one side. "I don't suppose you'd let me keep him?"

Lilith exploded into a whirlwind of movement, screaming and fighting furiously against the two men holding her. "Don't touch him!" Her heart pounded ferociously as her anger chased away every trace of physical pain.

The woman's lips formed a perfect pout. "I take it that's a no. Pity." Reluctantly, she motioned to the men at her side and nodded curtly. The four men surged around Chance and dragged him into the elevator. When the henchmen securing her moved forward, full panic set in. In a last-ditch effort, she smashed her heel into one man's shin and brought her head straight up into the chin of the other. Their grip faltered, and with every ounce of strength she had left, Lilith charged the blonde bombshell. No way was this bitch taking them anywhere.

In one fluid motion, the seemingly frail woman snatched Lilith out of the air and pulled her close. The next thing she knew, a knife hovered at her throat. She wanted to break the woman's face, but the sharp blade bit into her skin, drawing a drop of blood. A sudden sense of déjà vu froze her in place as the memory of Ashcroft's cruel face infiltrated her mind.

"Who the fuck are you?"

"Who I am is not important." Her sensuous voice slithered into the air with a lilting quality that should sound beautiful but somehow seemed malicious.

"Who sent me should be your concern. I don't think they care about the handsome one. So, perhaps they'll let me play with him." Lilith swallowed the nervous knot of bile in her throat as her eyes watered.

"I wouldn't need to force him, you know. He will come to me… begging." The sky blue eyes studied her reaction, reveling in Lilith's anguish, like a serial killer twisting the knife. No. She refused to give her the satisfaction.

A murderous calm settled over Lilith's face as she stared back, defiantly. "You better hope whoever hired you kills me because if they don't, I will shoot you in your pouty face, you toxic bitch."

A peal of laughter filled the room like nails on a chalkboard. "Oh, this is going to be so much fun."

To be continued.

About the Author

Jenny Allen, the author of the Lilith Adams series, also published several poems and short stories in university journals while spending time as a reporter and photographer for the Chattanooga State College newspaper. Ms. Allen studied forensic science, compiled extensive research in world myths, and applied them into a thrilling supernatural series. Her background as a published photographer and award-winning artist helps her visualize scenes when writing, contributing to her unique style of vivid imagery.

Born on a royal airbase in Lakenheath, England, she left the UK at age 9 to travel the United States and Germany. In her sophomore year, she began writing poetry after the suicide of a close friend in San Antonio, Texas. She later graduated to short stories and narratives until, in 2002, she wrote her first novel, *Lilith in London*, which was never published but still exists as 432 handwritten pages. Over 12 years, it underwent a metamorphosis, eventually becoming her first published novel, *Blood Lily*.

Currently, Ms. Allen lives in York, Pennsylvania, with her husband, Eric Deardorff, and their two sons, Kaidan and River. When not working as a full-time RN, she is editing the second book in the series, *Rose of Jericho*, and working on the rough draft of book three, *The Lotus Tree*. She plans to continue her book series while pursuing her medical career.

"More than anything, I wanted to challenge the concept of reality and the supernatural while truly digging into the emotional grit of tragedy. I often began writing with a clear goal in mind, but the characters swayed me in different directions. I've fallen in love with the ways they've developed and grown over the first two books, and I look forward to discovering the surprises they have in store for me in the future."

CPSIA information can be obtained
at www.ICGtesting.com
Printed in the USA
JSHW021906220723
45080JS00001B/3